Offerings to the Flower Moon: The Tale of the Abrams Witch

J.E. ERICKSON

Copyright © 2022 J.E. Erickson

This is a work of fiction. Names, characters, businesses, places, events, locales, and incidents are either the products of the author's imagination or used in a fictitious manner. Any resemblance to actual persons, living or dead, or actual events is purely coincidental.

All rights reserved. This book or any portion thereof may not be reproduced or used in any manner whatsoever without the express written permission of the publisher except for the use of brief quotations in a book review.

All brand names and product names used in this book are trademarks, registered trademarks, or trade names of their respective holders. The author is not associated with any product or vendor in this book.

Soft Cover ISBN: 979-8-9869508-0-8
ISBN eBook: 979-8-9869508-1-5

Cover Design by Kristina Osborn
www.truborndesign.com

To my beautiful and wonderfully supportive wife,
and to everyone who listens to the voices in the dark.

Chapter One

Moira didn't like to keep big secrets, but she didn't mind holding onto all the tiny ones for as long as it took her to figure each one out. She was a burden on Rachel, as it was. There was no need to dig up every under-analyzed worry and unleash her every fear onto the woman who was the only family she had left. So, they stopped talking about the nightmares, and they never discussed graduate school or her plans to move away after graduation, even though the thought of leaving Rachel behind gnawed at her resolve.

Keep steady, she told herself. One thing at a time. Let her see you smile.

"Something on your mind, lovely?" Rachel, her great-grandmother, asked between stitches. "You seem pensive."

Moira stared through the weave of rainbow yarn wrapped around her fingers, past the streaky window, and out to the swampy field to where men poured fire out of red drip torches onto parched grass and black smoke spiraled upward in the lazy breeze. It was just like her nightmares. Only in those, a tall woman cloaked in wildflowers did the burning, and the fire wasn't controlled.

"Mo?"

If she didn't pick at least one worry, Rachel would suspect there was more Moira wasn't telling her and start prying. It was like she could read her thoughts, sometimes.

"You're sure it won't spread this way?"

"Positive, dear. It's just a little fire." Rachel flicked a liver-spotted wrist, and the top row of yarn skipped up and over Moira's purple-painted fingernails to become another half-double stitch. "They do it every spring. It's a slow burn, and they're very careful. See over there? They have a water truck parked near the road."

The fire was close enough that Moira still worried, despite Rachel's reassurance. Though she looked and acted like a woman in her 70s, Rachel was nearly 90. She also lived several miles out of town. Moira doubted the rural fire department could get there and pull her out of danger before the farmhouse went up like a dry matchstick.

"It didn't snow last year, Gamma Rae. It hasn't rained. Everything is so dry."

Rachel's eyelids draped dreamily over irises the same cinnamon and brown of the leafless maple towering between the shed and the garden of Lenten roses kissing the sunlight blooms of forsythias. "I hadn't noticed, honey."

It wasn't a dismissal, yet Moira still narrowed her own dark eyes. Rachel was trying to distract her. Trick her into changing the subject to one that didn't include Moira's concern about Rachel's age and safety. It had become something of a little game they played when it was just the two of them sitting quietly together, no television, phones or radios, only the honeybee buzz of the refrigerator and an oscillating fan whispering the secrets of lavender and bergamot between them.

"Meteorologists are saying we're going to have another spring and summer of below average rain."

Rachel clicked her tongue, scoffing. "They tell the future now?"

A dusting of freckles on Moira's cheeks brightened when she grinned. She readjusted herself in the wicker chair and put her elbows onto her knees, to relieve her shoulders. "Well, with computer modeling, predictive analysis, various measuring tools, and satellites that can basically measure the moisture content of clouds in the jet stream—"

"Moira Elizabeth," Rachel said with a playful growl, her youthful voice still decades behind the thin cracks at the corners of her mouth. "Stop mansplaining weather to your grandmother."

"I don't think I can mansplain, Gamma." Moira laughed.

They were quiet again.

Moira struggled to still the nervous bouncing in her heel as the memories of a column of fire drawn by a chariot of larkspurs, poppies, and forget-me-nots played in her mind.

Rachel paused. The neck of the pink needle hooked between her index finger and a twist of yarn, she winked from behind a long curtain of bunny soft, white hair. "When I was a young girl, we had some of the worst droughts in Minnesota's history. Summers with no rain. Days when the sun beat down so hard you could light a cigarette off the back of the tractor. Years so awful the soybeans turned to dust, people starved. But even in those dry years, when the grass was yellow it crunched under your feet like walking on potato chips, we still burned the pastures because we knew it was necessary. We were smart about it. We knew when it was the right time, when it was safest to send our loves out into those dry fields with torches and hoses, to put them and ourselves in danger so our farms and our legacies wouldn't starve or shrivel up and blow away. There were lean years, to be sure, but we survived them. We Clarkes are tough cookies."

Rachel pulled Moira's hands to her lips and planted a light kiss on a knuckle. "Nature will do as nature must, lovely. It's the way of it, for good or for bad. So don't think of the fire as death and destruction; this evil thing that is coming to get us, think of it as purification. The new — the strongest — roses bloom in the withered petals of the old." After giving Moira's wrist a gentle pat, she returned to her work. "It's just a little fire, baby."

Moira's bone marrow groaned as if winter never turned to spring; only Rachel's warmth ebbing into her hand kept her from freezing solid. Rachel knew exactly what to say to make her heart sore. Knew how to say she was old and dying without speaking the words. Moira hated how the older Rachel got, the more cavalier about her mortality she became.

"Just keep 911 handy. Maybe Caroline can leave the garden hose out? In case the fire gets past the tree." The hose wouldn't put out an acre-wide fire. She hoped Caroline, Rachel's live-in caregiver, had the sense to get them both out of the house before the fire got close. Moira's smile squeezed something blurry back into her eye. "Please?"

Rachel nodded once, as if it were a fair compromise. "Of course. Though I would like very much to see firefighters charging in with their trucks to save the house. Wouldn't that be something? I could be their damsel in distress. Oh! Woe is me. They have the cutest little butts in those uniforms. Just ask Carrie."

As if summoned, the front door brushed against the little chimes hanging from the ceiling, announcing Caroline with their cheery twinkling. She wore an expansive blue dress and a dress hat with golden flowers that wobbled as she dragged her shoes on the mat. "Well, Momma Rachel, it looks like the DNR boys are here to save us. Maybe we can get them to take off those itchy shirts and give us a little dance?" Her dark skin brightened when she laid eyes on Moira. Her smile was a sunbeam. "Well, well. I'm very glad to see you, Moira. Where is my brain? I thought you were coming next weekend."

Moira waved with the web of yarn between both hands. "Hi, Caroline! How was church?"

The lines on Rachel's face deepened. "Still a bunch of men prattling on about their invisible daddy issues?"

"Same shit, different day." Caroline smiled. "Should I make some lemonade and sandwiches for lunch?"

"That would be lovely, Carrie. Thank you. After you've changed out of your church clothes, of course." Rachel sat up straight with a haughty shake of her wrinkled chin. "That's another thing one shouldn't worry about. My knees were never suited for kneeling as much as the church likes. I'm too delicate for that sort of bullshit."

The freckles on Moira's nose crinkled. "Did you just say bullshit, Gamma Rae?"

"Of course, I did." She whipped another length of yarn in an arc over Moira's hands. "I much prefer the older stories to church stories. Stories of monsters, witches, heroes, and such. The sort of stories you like to study." Another strand of yarn curled over thumbs. "So, tell me about school. Do you have a cute boyfriend? One of those football players in the tight pants?"

Moira laughed hard, half-forced, and was surprised at how much the echo of her own voice sounded like Rachel's. "No. Not yet. I've hung out with some guys. But, you know, I get busy." Half a lie wouldn't hurt, she supposed.

"Perhaps it's not boys? Do you like girls? This Danielle you've told me about?"

"What? No. It's not like that."

"You said she was beautiful."

"Dani happens to be a friend who is, you know, pretty. Really pretty. The prettiest woman in Mankato."

Rachel's eyebrow wiggled with a playful twitch. "It's okay if you do. I liked girls when I was your age."

"Gamma Rae!" The notion that her grandmother might not be joking made her blink like a cartoon character. "Wait, really? Are you serious?"

Rachel cackled and gave an enigmatic shimmy of her shoulders and hips but said nothing, instead switching crochet hooks and applying delicate finishing touches to what looked like a scarf. She readjusted the neck of her salmon-colored dress, pulling it back up over her bony shoulder. "I've lived a lot of life. There's plenty you don't know about your dear old granny Rae. Just as I'm sure there's plenty you haven't told me." She winked. "Don't worry, dear. I'll keep your secret."

Moira didn't ask what secret Rachel could be referring to, but she was glad she had yet to bring Dani over to meet her.

Her shoulders and thumbs throbbed with gratitude when Rachel pulled away the coil of yarn and set it in her lap. "How've you been sleeping?" she asked. The sharp turn away from their previous conversation wasn't surprising; Rachel usually got chatty around lunchtime. Strange that she brought up the nightmares, though.

"Okay," Moira admitted. "The nightmares aren't so bad anymore." Another half-truth. If it didn't dream of her mother's face melting to the vinyl passenger seat, she watched the lifeless twitching of her father's head in the cradle of a misshapen steering wheel. She was 11 when she survived the accident. Now she was 22 and still hadn't pushed past the nightmares, though she felt valleys away from her gnawing grief. "Less about mom and dad now. I think the ones I've been having are more about stress than bad memories." When Rachel gave her a look, she added, "It's not like high school. I can handle these ones. I can still focus. I'm good."

Rachel returned to twisting and sewing the ends of the scarf into a circle. "You put too much pressure on yourself. Too much work. You should be having fun, meeting people, doing what you love, finding who you are."

"But I do love this, Gamma Rae. I love learning and college. I love old stories, too. The ones with the silly monsters and the witches; all the social constructs people are forgetting and replacing with mass media garbage. And I love the idea of teaching people who like them. I know you always pushed me to be more introspective and not let other people define who I am— "

"Damn right."

"—but there is only so much self-discovery I can do before it becomes too much of a distraction. I'll be a professor someday, Gamma. I'm going to be unearthing stories and illuminating minds. It's not like I'm going to be saving lives or risking my own. Still, it takes work. It can't all be fun."

Rachel grunted, not lifting her eyes from her work but clearly making sure Moira saw the deep scowl on her brow. "Still. You work too hard when you should be playing, living, falling in love, and breaking hearts."

She did all those things, in her own way. Sort of. "Is this because you don't want me working on my project over the summer? Abrams isn't far."

A witch lived in Abrams, Minnesota. Not a real one, but a piece of living folklore; a story that wasn't ancient or a historically revised, misogynist cautionary tale. Since the 1940s, the Abrams Witch had been blamed for everything from deaths and crop failures in the 50s and missing persons in the 80s. Moira found the subject terribly interesting. She planned her capstone project around it.

When she first told Rachel, Rachel merely humored her excitement in her own unreadable, grandmotherly way, and suggested that afterward Moira take her friend Danielle somewhere like Cancun or England. But this project was her ticket into graduate school. Her trust fund from her parents' deaths and Rachel's generosity had paid for her everything throughout college; it was time she ponied up and started taking care of herself.

"This is because I want you to be happy, safe, and sane." Rachel's face beamed with a satisfied smile; her own project complete. Rachel inched behind Moira's chair and slipped the stretchy fabric around her neck where it burned with the fragrance of flowers and lavender. Rachel flipped Moira's auburn hair through it and wiggled it up above her ears. Satisfied, she led her over to the small wall mirror with the plastic pumpkins and cauldrons she refused to switch out after last Halloween. "What do you think?"

Moira thumbed the turban-style headband with a twist between her thin eyebrows. Though it was beautiful, she didn't like how it drew out the color of her cinnamon eyes, narrow nose bridge, and angular jaw. She didn't like that it reminded her of how unnervingly like her mother she looked; the reason she never wore her hair back when she had her contacts in. "It's lovely, Gamma Rae. You didn't go through all this trouble to make this for me, did you?"

"Trouble, shmubble. I can crap out two of those things in a day for Carrie to sell at the craft fairs." Rachel stuck out her tongue and crossed her eyes until Moira laughed.

They leaned into each other for a few minutes, arms wrapped around shoulders, quietly breathing in unison. Moira tried not to think about how frail Rachel felt, how delicately her skin clung to old bones. But when she breathed in the tang of the distant smoke creeping in through the window, all she could think about was how the woman cloaked in flowers, the one burning the world in her dreams, looked just like Rachel.

"Moira?" Rachel whispered.

"Yeah, Gamma?"

"You're strong and beautiful and brave." Her eyes locked with Moira's in their reflections, and her voice deepened. "Never forget who and what you are."

Moira nodded, though she wasn't entirely sure what Rachel meant. Before she could ask anything, Caroline announced lunch was ready. With an excited and silly cackling noise, Rachel tugged against Moira.

Arm in arm, walked into the dining room for a small lunch of cucumber sandwiches, potato chips, and lemonade.

After a few post-lunch games of cribbage, which Rachel won handily, it was time for Moira to leave. Finals week started in the morning, and she still had a couple of papers to finish.

Caroline held the door as Rachel hooked her arm in Moira's offered elbow with a huff. "I'm not infirm, Mo. I can still walk to the end of the driveway."

"I know, Gamma. I just don't want the smoke to irritate your lungs."

"Bah! The only thing that's irritating is how old you think I am." Rachel gave her a playful pinch on the arm.

Moira tossed her backpack into the back of her maroon sedan and gave her great-grandmother a hug. Rachel gave her a strong squeeze and pulled away.

"You know," Rachel said, trading Moira for Caroline's arm, "A very long time ago, a few of us Clarkes traipsed around the state and settled in Abrams for a spell. There might be some of your own history there. Might even have some blood there, too."

"Really?" Moira wondered just how much of her family tree she didn't know. "You think they're still there? Cousins, maybe?"

"Maybe. It's been a long time, but you never know. We can dig through some old pictures and papers for anything we can find to help with your project next time you stop by." She reached a knobby hand for Moira, pulling her in for another hug. "Be careful, Mo. I know you like digging. Even before you could speak straight, you were asking questions and hounding your parents for books and stories.

"This Abrams Witch you're chasing after might be more than just a simple story, Mo. Stories are magic, but not all stories are good. They all come from somewhere, usually places of pain. Actual pain. The kind of pain that can infect kind people, put hate into their hearts, make them do wicked things. Don't let that confuse you, though. Find the difference between wickedness and justice." She held Moira at arm's length, then squished her cheeks between her palms. "And don't let that mean old witch scare you. If she does, tell her she'll have to answer to me."

"I'll be careful, grandma." The tickle of worry dancing around Moira's stomach quickly calmed when she breathed in her grandmother's air. "And I'll let the witch know who she's messing with."

"That's my girl." Rachel placed a soft knuckle against her chin and give it a proud twist.

Moira stepped into her apartment and plopped her backpack onto her futon before marching over to her refrigerator and pouring herself a glass of cold red wine. As she sipped, she fished the complaining phone out of her jacket pocket. It was a text from Danielle.

Yo, Slo-Mo. What kind of nightmarish shit r u Nancy Drew-ing? Check the shared inbox.

She didn't care for that nickname. It wasn't her fault everybody liked to put everything off until the last second, and then rush to get their papers done while she took her time to thumb through every book, essay, and peer-reviewed article before committing to a thesis statement. She was thorough, not slow.

She typed, *What did you find?* before logging into her laptop. Attached to the email were images of newspapers taken from old microfiche rolls dating back to the mid-1980s. Each one opened to some dark story about a missing child or teenager, a bloody farming accident, and rumors of incest and murder. There was even one about cannibalism. Her stomach shivered; the wine tasted sour.

What is this weirdo shit? She hoped it was Dani's attempt at a joke.

Her next unread email was from twelve hours earlier.

From: Hopkins, Daniel R
To: Clarke, Moira E

Subject: RE: Anthropology Project Assistance Request

Dearest Ms. Clarke,

I hope this message finds you in good health. Your email to the City Administrator regarding your request for any archival information regarding the folklore and history of our little town has found its way to my desk. As the Abrams resident historian (we are a small town, so many of our unofficial town records are fostered by humble volunteers), I would be delighted to help you find anything for which you seek.

Unfortunately, we do not have much in the way of electronic files. Much of our historical record is still in paper form. However, I would like to personally invite you to Abrams to review our extensive collection of papers, family records (where given permission by the families) and various interesting histories. It may take you some time to review them all, so room and board can be arranged by the church, if you wish.

Please respond at your earliest convenience.

Rev. Daniel R. Hopkins.

Multiple beeps from her phone clashed into a single, tinny scream. One was a text from Danielle: *Creepy haunted hillbilly shit, hot stuff. Nothing about a witch, but maybe they made it all up to explain away the creeper crap? If u go, bring pepper spray.*

Moira huffed a chuckle and put her phone down. Whatever the Witch was, she was going to find out. It would be amazing, and it would be her ticket into grad school with a full ride. No more living off her inheritance or taking Gamma Rae's money.

Another beep announced an email from the Abrams Church.

From: Abrams Evangelical Lutheran Church
To: Clarke, Moira E

Subject: Anthropology Project Assistance Request

Stay the fuck out of Abrams. Keep away. Forget this project. Stay out of Abrams or they'll kill you. Do not respond to this email or they'll find us both.

Moira blinked and read the email two more times before her brain accepted it as reality. What sort of prank was this? Would church kids do this?

A third email arrived, this one from the same email address, also unsigned. Like Dani's email, this one contained several attachments. She was reluctant to open them, but a second glass of wine awakened her curiosity.

Most of the files opened to newspaper articles about a missing girl, Celeste Martin, and a group of her frightened friends. The rest was a mess of personal documents and incomplete information regarding the Abrams Witch. The most interesting file was the hardest to read; it was nothing but a series of cloudy scans of lined paper. At least the handwriting was good. Clear cursive lettering that reminded her of the loops and flourishes her mother used to sign Christmas cards. She followed each smooth curve and bend in the letters, up and down, back, and around, until the fog in her eyes from an early morning and late wine made it difficult to pay attention to the words. Not even her obstinate nature nor her constant, studious drive to 'fight the tired' could clear the drowsiness.

Damn, she was tired. Maybe she should just put her head down for a few minutes.

Moira closed her eyes and rested her head onto a stack of books and dozed, oblivious to the thin shadows cast by the light of the waning gibbous moon peel themselves from the wall behind her peace lily. The shadows twisted into a single knobby strand and crawled soundlessly along her floor, along the metal frame of her futon and up her chair. It pulled itself onto her back, pausing only when she stirred and scratched absently at her cheek. Once she started taking long, even breaths, the shadow pushed a lock of auburn hair away from her ear and crawled inside, bringing her another nightmare.

The Circle

1

Celeste Annaliese Martin disappeared in August 1984. She was fourteen years old.

She prepared all week for that Friday. It was the night of the farm party at Matthew Miller's house. Brian Hopkins, the cute boy from another school who her older friend, Heather, introduced her to at the spring parade, would be there. And there weren't supposed to be many others, something she preferred. Crowds of strangers weren't really her vibe; she felt awkward and quiet in large groups. Keeping the number of other boys and girls small meant she could spend more time talking to Brian.

"It's more intimate that way, Celly," Heather told her, winking heavily mascaraed lashes from behind a curtain of black bangs. "A chance to be alone with someone."

Intimate. The word made her warm and sent a minty sliver of cold running along her lower back.

She would have to lie, though. Sneak away. Heather and Brian were older, juniors, and seemed to enjoy escaping from their parents. Celeste was a sophomore because she skipped second grade. Her parents were rarely home, but she wasn't happy about it the way Heather was. The reason they moved to the outer suburbs was to spend more time at home, together. However, with the continued proximity to the city came job promotions, which had them working well past dinner on most nights, left Celeste to fend for herself. That made her a latchkey kid, according to the six o'clock news. The last to leave home in the morning and the first to come home in the afternoon. She spent nearly every day without her parents, watching whatever she wanted on television and doing her homework in a cold, quiet house full of nothing. As angry and sad as it made her, she was still reluctant to lie and say she was sleeping over at Heather's house to watch movies and play games.

But it would be intimate. Brian would be there. The boy from another school. That meant she could be whoever she wanted to be. The bad girl who smoked cigarettes and drank wine coolers. Maybe the shy girl who wasn't so shy she made boys angry, but the kind who made them chase after her, to want to know her. She could be anyone but little Celly Martin for a night. Intimate.

"What's the deal, space cadet?" Heather snapped her gum. "You're staring. Are you scared that mommy and daddy are gonna get mad and ground you for the rest of the summer? Oh god!" Heather sat straight, the bangles on her wrist sliding to her hands with little clinks. "You're not on your period, are you?"

"What! Ew!" Celeste ripped up a handful of grass and threw it at Heather. "Weirdo."

Heather laughed and lit a cigarette. "Do you have any pads? I think mine's coming on. It's about time, too. I was worried for a couple of weeks."

"No. I haven't— I don't have any… with me." Celeste passed her tongue over ashen lips. Her face flushed with heat.

"What about inside? This is your house. You didn't steal it, did you?" Heather turned over onto her stomach, earrings flashing silver in the sun and the wide collar of her shirt falling off her shoulder to reveal the black bra strap beneath. "Oh, my god. Celly! You haven't gotten your period yet. You're in tenth grade, right?"

Celeste's face practically boiled. "Hush, airhead. I have so had my period."

Heather's taunting laugh made her insides shrivel. "Sure, spaz. Don't be mental. There are a lot of late bloomers." She reclined on the lawn and passed the cigarette to Celeste. "You're not missing out on anything. I should've been born a guy, so I didn't have to deal with babies and shit."

Not even the mentholated smoke masked the bitterness coating her tongue. Celeste desperately wanted to change the subject. She held her dark hair away from her face and blew out a lungful of smoke. "I want to be a mom. Someday. I could be a good mother."

"That's so cute."

Celeste hated when Heather talked down to her like a babysitter and Celeste was a child babbling some easily brushed off and imaginative tale. "Why would you even need to worry about it yet? It's not like you've gone all the way."

Heather closed her eyes and raised an eyebrow. "I don't know what it was like at your old school, but just because you haven't, virgin, doesn't mean the rest of us haven't."

Celeste gasped. It wasn't hearing that Heather wasn't a virgin; it was the way she said it that sent a shock through her ribs. How easily it slid out of her, like she had the same confidence as the older boys she smoked with in the parking lot after school. "You have? What was it like?"

Heather took the cigarette from her and smiled. "Fucking gnarly."

Celeste paced her bedroom floor, struggling to pick the right outfit. What did one wear to a farm party? She went through four combinations, throwing each rejected outfit into a pile on her pink and white comforter before settling on her black flats, pink socks, stonewashed denim skirt, a green button-up with pink vertical stripes, golden stud earrings, and a splash of her mother's expensive perfume. She did her black hair in a topknot held together with a black and silver scrunchie and let the rest spill down to her shoulders.

On her way to the door, she scooped up a light jacket for when she got chilly, turned on the living room lamp, grabbed her purse, and spared a last glance to the empty room. "I love you," she said to no one, and locked the door behind her.

Whooping and laughing, she rushed across the manicured grass to Heather's Audi. The upholstery smelled of stale smoke and hairspray. A few neighbors out watering their lawn looked their direction and shook their heads. Apparently, being in a 'nice' neighborhood meant monochromatic houses, manicured lawns, painted fences, church bells, and acting dismissive to everything and everyone that may be just a little fun.

"Ready, Freddie?" Heather clicked the radio dial. Rock music crooned out of the front speakers. She wore ripped skinny jeans the same color as her blood red lipstick and a Ratt t-shirt. Combined with her short, feathered hair, dark eyeshadow, and steel neck chains, Heather looked like she could front a punk band. "You remember your pills?" she asked.

Celeste checked her purse for her heart medication and shook the amber bottle. "You look awesome." she said, giggling at the butterflies in her stomach. "This is going to be so radical!"

With a squawk and a roar, they were off, leaving the suburbs in the rearview while singing along with Billy Squier's latest.

The drive to Abrams was long and Heather was the only one with a license—she reminded Celeste more than once—so they stopped for lunch at a burger joint at around the two-hour mark so she could rest. Heather was infinitely less snide after a cheeseburger and fries.

Celeste dipped a fry into a tiny paper cup of ketchup. "These outdoor tables are nice. They didn't have many of these downtown, and all the restaurants are fancy or stuffy cafes where everything is deep fried, or it takes forever to get to your table."

"Fast food is the future." Heather lit a cigarette with an incredulous stare at Celeste. "How are you a city girl?"

"What do you mean?"

Heather leaned into the shade of the table's umbrella. "You. A city girl. How are you one? You're so shy and… conservative. All my friends from the cities are party girls."

"Like you?"

"No. Way crazier than I am." Heather flicked an ash and blew her smoke into the wind. "You just seem so innocent. I bet your first smoke was with me." When Celeste's face flushed, Heather said, "I thought so. Listen, I'm not making fun of you. You just don't seem the city girl type. You wear dresses and you're smart. My friend Jodi is a city girl and a ditz, but a ditz who can get me pot."

"Yeah, well, I guess not everyone is a cookie cutter person."

"Hey." Heather reached over and rested her fingers on the cloth bracelet around Celeste's wrist. "It's just an observation. I like you, Celly. You take things in stride most of the time. I like that you're smart and not some mental chick trying to be the coolest girl in school."

"Because I make you look cooler?"

"Exactly!"

Heather smiled and laughed in a way that made Celeste grin. There were times she could be cold, but Heather was never cruel.

Sometimes kindness poked out from behind the black curtains. It brought with it the sort of warmth that she imagined came from an older sister or a close cousin, two things Celeste silently prayed for when she was little.

"Listen, Celly. I want you to know something about tonight." Heather's voice dropped an octave. "The boys are going to prank you. There's a plan."

Celeste's pulse throbbed and her heart started beating in its strange, off-kilter way. She thought of her pills but didn't take one. "Prank? Why? I don't want to do anything weird or be made fun of."

Heather waved her hand. "Nothing like that. They're going to try to scare you because you're the new girl and you're younger than us. It's just hazing, okay. Nothing weird." She edged closer with a conspiratorial wink. "But we're not going to let them."

Her appetite disappeared and her throat dried as thoughts of shaming and laughter and pointing broke into her mind. "I don't want to be hazed." She wanted to be mature, attractive, maybe a little mysterious, not the child of the group. She ground her teeth. "And I don't need a babysitter."

"It's not like that, Celly. We're going to make their little prank backfire. I know what to do."

"Because they told you?"

"Because they did it to me two years ago." Anger flashed past Heather's eyes, then hardened like dark glass. "You ever heard of the Abrams Witch?"

Celeste shook her head.

"It's a backwater fairy tale. Small town yokel bullshit meant to scare the pants off the kids, so they won't go too deep into the woods or fuck with the old farm widows. It's based on a real story about a woman in the 30s who was accused of being a witch and burned out in the woods outside of Abrams."

"Burned her?"

"And they teach us in History that sort shit didn't happen out here. That Salem was the first and last place in America where they killed women for dancing naked and fucking anyone but their husbands."

Celeste hushed her when an older couple nearby shot them a dark look.

"Whatever." Heather took a drag of her cigarette and waved at them, a sinister smile on her face. "Anyway, she was murdered, and the baby was taken away. Of course, the woman now haunts certain places in the town. People talk about seeing a strange woman in white walking down the road alone in the middle of the night and chasing cars off the road. When an animal dies, they blame the Abrams Witch. Deformed calf? Witch. Sometimes she just screams from inside the woods." She pounded her cigarette into the glass ashtray. "But, trust me, she's just a scary story people tell to freak out the new kids."

Celeste's cheeseburger slid down her throat. Sure, it was a made-up story, but telling herself that didn't make the eerie sensation of shadows crawling in the darkness go away. "So, what are they going to do? What do you want me to do?"

Heather took one of her fries and dipped it in the ketchup. "Are you a good actress, city girl?"

2

At some point, the highway became a dirt road. Suddenly. In one moment, the yellow lines tick-tick-ticking down the center of the pavement became the rumble and clanking of gravel under tires and rattling around the car's undercarriage.

Celeste leaned forward, massaging the stiffness out of her neck.

"Crap. Was I sleeping?"

"Like the sweetest little baby."

Celeste cursed in her head. Only children slept in cars. "Sorry," she said. "Do you want me to drive a little?"

Heather cracked the window. "Don't sweat it. I totally love driving. And it's good that you caught some Zs now. You'll be wide awake when those dweebs tell their scary story and drive you out to the crossroads with their warped bullshit." Heather flashed her a smile. "And then we can stay up drinking."

That's what they did to Heather. Made her stand in the middle of two roads with just a dying flashlight, then they jumped out from the corn to scare her. There was another girl with her, too, but it wasn't long before she sprinted out of the circle screaming and crying in terror.

Heather told her it wouldn't happen ever again. "We're not little dolls for their juvenile enjoyment or to laugh at when they make us freak out. Nah, not you. Not my fucking Celly. You're going to stand out there all glam and make them look like a bunch of assholes. When they can't scare you, they'll know they're messing with a bad ass Betty."

That made Celeste smile. She forced herself to stare at Heather's face to hide her shyness at the compliment.

Rural Minnesota was a different world entirely. Endless rows of emerald shimmering with gold draped over a landscape broken up only by pastures of droopy-headed cows and the oases of aspens and birches that served as little hideaways for big houses, huge red barns, and bullet-shaped silos. Even the sun shined differently, as if a giant paintbrush spread sparkling light across the land. Nothing like the harsh brightness of the suburbs and the dim distance of the downtown streets. On the horizon, giant pines waved, greeting them with the wind.

The car rumbled past wire fences, patches of well-manicured grass, and ditch ponds swimming with ducks. They kept the music blaring to keep out the external roar of the road. Heather complained her car would never be clean again as she downed another Tab and tossed the empty can onto the backseat floor.

After an hour, they turned away from the sun and toward a pair of silos and a barn with a slouching roof. Heather pulled into the driveway just past a mailbox which read "Miller".

The house was a large, creamy stucco stained green and brown at the foundation. Birds fluttered near its windows and around the few dangling feeders that weren't being attacked by leaping gray squirrels. Bees swarmed a multicolored garden of zinnias and dahlias while a blushing ceramic pig in overalls stood watch under the stubby, whitewashed balusters that jutted off the end of the porch like a row of evenly spaced teeth. A door with an oval of ornate glass dominated the house's face.

Celeste closed the car door, stretched, and breathed air thick with the aroma of cut grass, fresh earth, and the unappealing sharpness of animal dung. "This is wonderful!" She meant it.

Heather coughed. "It reeks." The trunk popped open with a small cloud of dust. Heather shouldered her massive mauve purse that clattered with chain links and homecoming buttons, and then carefully closed the trunk to keep the dirt from clouding up and getting in their hair. "Let's go find the nimrods and get this party started." She raised her arms and howled to the sky.

Before they reached the barn, a young man in a blue and black checkered shirt and jean shorts jogged from around the corner. His dirty blond hair spiked like Billy Idol's, and he had the most handsome smile Celeste had ever seen. "Hey ladies." A warmth filled her middle at the sound of his voice. "Come on back here. We're just setting up the fire pit."

"I come bearing gifts." Heather opened her purse and let him peer inside.

Brian reached in and pulled out a bottle of something red. "Mad Dog? Hell yeah!" He said, "I'll put this in the fridge. Matt's around back." He headed to the house, stopping when he finally noticed the other girl standing there. "Hey! Celly, right?"

Celeste was glad to be in the shade of a birch so Brian couldn't see her face flush. "Hey, Brian. Cool hair."

Heather gave her a black look from behind her bangs. All part of their game, Celeste thought.

"Thanks," he said. "You want to come in and help me carry the cooler out here?"

A smile threatened to crack her impassive facade. She gave a practiced, non-committal shrug, said, "Sure," and followed Brian into the house.

They walked behind the barn several minutes later, a dripping Coleman cooler between them, and Celeste laughing a little too loudly at Brian's poor joke. Heather sat on a vinyl lawn chair in the shade, smoking, the calf of her right leg bouncing on her left knee. Not far away was a wide ring of heavy stones. The other boy, Matthew Miller, cracked sticks over his knee and tossed them into the center of the stones. Celeste remembered him from a baseball game the previous spring, as well.

They worked around Heather to start a small fire—they were saving the bulk of the wood for sunset—set up some lawn chairs, and to fire up the charcoal grill. "You like hot dogs, Celly?" Brian waved one at her with a suggestive leer.

She answered, "Only if they're adult sized."

Matthew laughed at that. When his giggle fit passed, he tossed more crumpled newspaper to the side of the pit and slapped his hands against his bare legs. "This wood is too wet," he said to nobody. "I can't start this." He walked away.

"Heather?" Brian stroked the limp wiener with a finger. "Would you like a little something?"

Heather clicked her tongue. "Is this a party or a picnic?" Her acidity caught Celeste by surprise.

"Parties have food, Heather," Brian answered over the sizzle of wet meat on hot iron. "It's summer, the wind is cool, Matt's parents aren't here, we've got plenty of beer, and a couple of babes brought Mad Dog and rum. Lighten up."

"Yeah, Heather." Celeste made a face to show Heather she was kidding. She poured half of her drink into a plastic cup and handed it to Heather. "Here, I made this for you."

Heather snatched from her hands so fast it sloshed over the rim, and she stomped past her with a sidelong look. "Sure, Brian. I'll take some tube steak in front of the kid."

Shame heated the sides of Celeste's neck until she felt blurry, a reflection over hot tarmac. Celeste plopped into the chair Heather abandoned and stared at the ribbons of dark smoke curling up from the damp, smoldering newspaper while Brian and Heather had a hissed conversation. They knew each other but sounded like they might be more than just friends. Her mother and father argued the same way.

She fished a cigarette out of Heather's purse and tucked it behind her ear. With her drink in one hand, Celeste took little bites of her food, eating as if she didn't care what they said, or care what they argued about. She was busy thinking her own thoughts, regardless of how loudly the whispers seemed to reverberate off the old barn behind her. If any of them looked, they'd just see Celeste, aloof, enjoying herself by herself.

But the whispers were so loud, especially around the words *waiting*, *kissing*, and *inside me*. More heat surged up her neck. She was always feeling hot. Stupid and blushing and hot. *Grown-ups don't blush.* Celeste fought it down, the childishness. Packed it into a tube in the back of her mind, and squeezed it into the fire pit, willing the fire to burst into existence and burn away the last of 'baby Celly' who got cooed at by her mother, patted on the head and shoulders by her father—*You don't need to worry about things like that, sweetie. Let your future husband work it out.* The Celly who still watched Saturday morning cartoons. That wasn't her. That wouldn't be her. She was beautiful. Beautiful and smart and mature and women should want to be her.

This is where she would change; her turning point. Celly Martin would die in that crossroads tonight. There would be no more friends calling her 'kid' and keeping her in their shadow. No handsome boys who ignored her or parents who didn't listen to her when she told them she was lonesome and tired. The other ones didn't know it, but they were going to be a part of her change. Heather wouldn't boss her around and make her feel stupid. Brian would take her hand, walk her away from their group, and whisper sweet things to her. And they would watch, she would see them, she wouldn't blush, and she wouldn't giggle like a complete idiot!

The fire whooshed to life.

The dull ache in her lower abdomen that had been there since morning gave her a quick stab. A reflexive hiss escaped her throat. She winced.

Matthew rounded the corner with a chubby red gas can in his hand. He stopped whistling when he saw the flames. "Hey-o! I did it, losers. No need to thank me." He looked at the can, said, "Won't be needing this," and set it against the barn. "You okay?"

Cold peeled away the heat from Celeste's back and hips. Every thought of heat and warmth flushed into the ground. "Yeah. I just had a weird pain. Right here."

Matthew nodded until his long hair shook free from his orange trucker hat. "Gotta poop, huh? That's hot."

Her eyes rolled. She made a show of vomiting. "Gag me, stooge."

"It's our secret, kiddo." With a jab of his thumb in the house's direction, he added, "Nobody uses the one on the top floor except my mom. It's all yours. There's Lysol up there, too." His hyena laugh grated on the tender nerves in her ears, and it was all she could do to ignore him. She didn't know Matthew well. She didn't know him at all, frankly. But she was learning they would most likely not get along.

When he walked away, Celeste relaxed, sipped her drink, and watched the fire build, while quietly missing the whispers and the warmth.

3

The afternoon flew past once they poured the booze. The sky dimmed to brushed shades of red, gold, and blue, and the air perfumed itself with pollen and dew. Matthew gradually added wood to the fire until it burned high enough to chase away the shadows leaning over their shoulders. Brian brought out a boom box connected to a brown extension cord so they could listen to the new The Cars cassette. Heather pretended to laugh while Brian and Matthew told the latest dirty jokes they learned at school.

Celeste was already on her third drink and feeling like a happy piece of cotton floating above her seat. "So, are we the only ones here? Are there more people coming?"

"Yeah, party boy!" Heather gave a weak kick in Brian's direction. "Answer the lady's question."

Brian pawed at Heather's foot. "More people? It's just us. Matt's parents are out of town."

"It's their anniversary," Matt said.

"Nobody else called me back. But it's not like I invited a bunch of people."

Heather leaned forward, firelight burning in her eyes. "How many did you invite?"

Brian finished his beer before answering. "You two."

"Dude, are you serious? That's so lame!"

"What?" Brian looked injured. "I thought a smaller group would be more—"

"Intimate." Celeste's eyelids were heavy. At least the ache in her stomach was fading.

"Scary." Brian grabbed another beer out of the cooler. "I thought it would be scarier if it were a smaller group, is all."

"Scary?" The lump in Matt's throat rose and fell.

"Yeah. Scary." Brian turned down the volume on the cassette player. "Look, I haven't played it yet, and I didn't want to do it in front of a bunch of people and find out it's a joke some kid was playing on his little sister, you know?"

"Play what?" Matt asked.

"We all know about the Abrams Witch, right?"

Heather turned her head away from the fire and gave her a wink. "Everyone but Celeste."

"And we all heard on the news that when you play some records backward, you can hear messages from the devil."

A chill, like so many invisible fingers, raced along Celeste's ribcage. Scary stories were one thing—vampires, werewolves, and witches were for children—but this was another matter. The devil was real. She kept her expression even, hoping it would sober her up faster.

Heather sneered. "Shut up."

Brian nodded and unzipped a cloth bag of tapes. "You know how Dan is studying to be a pastor, right? Well, he came home a couple of weekends ago and brought this."

In the firelight, Celeste recognized the silver and black of a blank cassette. TDK-90. She'd made plenty of mixtapes in her time. "What's on it?"

"He says it's an actual recording of a spell used in the fifties to summon the Witch."

Celeste's heartbeat thickened in her ears until she felt it hammering in the back of her neck.

Heather's eyes narrowed. She smiled and said, "Bullshit."

"Yeah. What's it from? A Supremes' record?" Matt laughed.

Brian shook his head. "No. There was this band, some small-timers who tried to make a deal with the devil to get famous. I guess they were a part of this crazy cult. They made songs and put the messages on it so they could secretly spread the spell to the entire country through the radio stations."

The ache in Celeste's stomach came back. Matt looked at her with wide eyes, then he said to Brian, "Celly says you're full of crap, man." His nasal voice was shaky, almost whiny.

"Across the country? I thought you said they were small-timers." Heather walked over, knelt and, facing Celeste, dug through her purse while mouthing the word *bullshit*.

Celeste nodded. This must be part of their prank. Even knowing what it was, the fright oozing from the darkness still leeched the warmth from her bones. She edged closer to the fire.

Brian shook the cassette. "I guess the deal didn't work out. But Dan says this is the real thing."

"Why did he tape it?"

"So he could listen to it safely. I guess you need the record to get the spell to work. It's like the magic, the real magic, gets scraped off during the recording or something." He raised his hands at Heather's accusing glare. "Don't look at me! I'm not a priest or a producer or anything. As far as I know, they use magic to make records and tapes. This could all be some kind of bullshit Disney movie recording. I don't know."

Heather crossed her legs and blew out a lungful of smoke. It was Celeste who asked with genuine concern, "Did you not listen to it because you're scared that it might not be, you know, fake?"

Brian's face slackened in the fire's glow.

"Oh, Brian Hopkins," Heather squealed. "I thought you were brave, but you're just a chicken shit like every other little boy.

"Are you scared?" Celeste teased.

Heather leaned forward. "The new girl got you by the short and curlies."

"Come on. Shut up." Brian's scowl matched the sharpness of his demand.

"Look how scared you are. She's right." She howled into the air and the rows of corn. "The mighty future president of the free world is undone by a Cyndi Lauper bootleg and sweet little Celly's powers of observation."

All of them, including Brian, laughed until Brian tapped the tape against his leg. "Let's listen to it, then."

The laughter trickled away.

"I-I don't know, man." Sparks rolled upward. Matt added two additional logs to the fire. "It's all fun and games until someone needs an exorcist. Nobody wants to hear that shit."

Heather raised an indifferent eyebrow but said nothing.

"I do." Celeste moved her chair closer to Brian to show she wasn't afraid. This was all a part of the prank.

"But tell us how they summoned the Witch while it's playing." Everyone stared at Heather. "What? You wanted scary. So make it scary."

The play button clicked into place, and the hiss of the speakers mixed with the crackling of the fire in the cool summer air. All four of them clenched their jaws, forcing themselves to silence, waiting for the first sounds of the magical spell that would summon the Abrams Witch. Brian and Heather stared at one another, expectant looks on their faces. Heather shook her head when Brian gave her an uncertain shrug.

But Celeste heard, and she listened to the whispers. The gentle hisses of leaves rubbing together in a gentle forest breeze. She let them blow against her until her feet felt rooted in place, allowing her body to sway in the wind.

"Sounds bitchin', Brian."

"Just give it a sec." He turned up the volume until there was a constant monotone exhale from the speakers. "He probably started recording early."

They waited in the electronic buzz of the cassette player. Heather rested her head against her palm, bored. Matt drank straight out of his bottle. Celeste stayed standing, hypnotized by the dance of the fire and the song of the whispers calling to her from beyond the corn.

"You gonna tell us how to call the Abrams Witch?" Heather leaned into the firelight and looked at both Brian and Matthew. "How do we summon the devil?"

Matthew hid his eyes behind the brim of his hat while Brian lowered his voice an octave, as if about to tell a campfire tale. "I was told that she can be summoned from the forest, where four paths meet. A crossroads. When you find one, you stand in the center. Place a circle of candles around you—the light keeps her away from you—and stand there until she calls your name or until hers is whispered to you and you call to her. But never leave the circle. If you do, she'll rip out your stomach and swallow your soul."

Heather pretended to shiver. "Oooh. And how do you know this? Did you get it from a Ouija board?"

"God no!" Brian put up his hands. "I don't fuck with those things. Those are the real deal."

"Are you saying the Abrams Witch isn't?" Heather gave Celeste a knowing look.

"Well, I mean. Yeah. But that's not—"

"You're such a fucking dweeb."

"What! That's what I heard, dude! Gimme a break."

As the tape continued to sigh its sizzling noise, Brian and Heather's sarcastic arguing became distant and dim, muffled and inhuman noises on the outside of a glass enclosure. Celeste knew she should be scared, frightened into a dead sprint to somewhere safe, into the house or Heather's car, safely tucked under a coat amidst the trash in the back seat; anywhere far away from the feverish warmth and chill of standing still next to a fire on a chilly night. But she couldn't move. The ache felt too good. The rolling, stretching ache in her abdomen. A longing for something she didn't know she needed or could understand how her body screamed for it. A dull throbbing that wrapped around her like a belt being tightened with each heartbeat, tighter and tighter, until her small breasts felt full and heavy, and her lower half tingled with anticipation. Underneath her clothes, the skin of her legs was electric. Her blood sang, howled, as it rippled from behind her knees and up her backside, tracing the outline of her spine to the little hairs on her neck. The whispers seeped into her ears, growing louder and louder. Clearer. More distinct.

Eem. Eem oo-ut.

Her body rejected her mind's scream to run, to hide. There was only the bliss of the sounds and the wind and the fire.

Eem oo-ut. Muh-uhk. Eem oo-ut muh-uhk. Ts-ehl-eh-s. Eem oo-ut muh-uhk.

Whispers became the air, became the sound in her mind, the repetition of her name, over and over. Celeste. Celeste. Celeste.

The click of the stop button being pressed clunked like an axe into petrified wood.

It took a moment for the whispers to subside and the shadows to draw back into the night sky, and she then realized Brian and Heather were staring at her, their eyes wide and crinkled with impish grins.

"What're you doing there, hot stuff?" Heather winked at her. "The rum hitting you in the right spot?"

"If she wants to dance, let her dance." Brian's eyes were wide and dark as they tracked the outline of her body, from her legs to her chest. "You want me to put on some more music?"

Heather flicked ash in his lap. "Christ, Brian. She's fourteen."

Celeste smiled at him. "I want to see her." Her voice felt husky and weighty in her throat. "I was promised a witch."

"I mean, sure. I—I don't know. I guess we could—"

"Is there a crossroads nearby?" Celeste asked to Heather's clear astonishment.

Brian's jaw hung open. "Uh, sure. Yeah. Just down the road there's—"

"A convenient X that marks the spot?" She took a step forward. The world listed a little to the right but immediately corrected itself. "Show me."

A barely perceptible smile crossed Heather's lips. "Celly, maybe we shouldn't."

"Yeah." Matt shook his head and corrected his falling trucker's hat. "I don't think it's a good idea. We've all been drinking a little too much, and I'm kinda freaking out right now."

"You boys aren't scared, are you?"

"No way," Brian said. The dark boldness that had glistened in his eyes when he looked at Celeste softened and receded.

Matt gripped the plastic arms of his chair. "Are you kidding me? I'm terrified, man!" He sucked down his beer and seemed on the verge of tears as he wiped his mouth with the back of his hand.

Brian calmed him. "Ease up, man. It's nothing. This shit isn't real. It's not like there was anything on the tape. Shit's blank, man."

Matt quieted, but he didn't seem convinced. "There's something weird in this town, man. You don't know." His squeaks changed to slurred whispers. "You don't know. You don't see it."

Brian waved a dismissive hand at Matthew, then turned his attention to Celeste. "You think you can handle it? I bet you don't make it twenty minutes."

"I bet she can make it an hour."

Brian gave Heather a suspicious look and received a shrug in return.

"I bet I can make it longer than you think." Celeste folded her arms across her chest and raised her eyebrow the way her mother did. "Show me your scary little witch."

4

They jumped in Matthew's loud pickup and drove less than a mile to where a pair of roads divided the soybean and corn fields into quarters. Using the glow of the headlights, they scraped an expansive circle in the dirt with a jack handle and two boards rummaged out of the truck bed. Brian handed her a plastic tube flashlight when they were done.

"The batteries are new, so they shouldn't go out." He flashed it underneath his chin. "Don't get eaten by the Witch, Celly."

Celeste took the flashlight with a nod and a shivering smile, her earlier self-assurance fluttering away in the midnight chill.

Heather took off her red flannel shirt and wrapped it around Celeste. "It's a little big, but you wear it well." When Brian was far enough away, she lowered her voice and said, "We'll be back soon. Last time, they didn't give me a flashlight or talk about candles and shit, so it shouldn't be too scary. Here." She slipped several cigarettes and her lighter into Celeste's shirt pocket.

"I don't know about this, Heather," she admitted, ice trilling in her veins. "I'm having second thoughts. Maybe I'm not… you know. Maybe I shouldn't do this."

"You're a bad ass bitch, Celeste." Heather hugged her shoulders and kissed her cheek. "Don't worry. I'll howl like a wolf when we're coming. Matt's babying out, so it'll just be me and Brian, and he can't keep a straight face for more than a minute. Which isn't the only thing he can't keep for more than a minute." She looked back at him. "But don't worry. We won't be more than an hour. Okay? He'll wait long enough until he thinks you're so scared you can't take it, then we'll be out here." The corner of her mouth curled upward. "Just pretend to be scared when we get here."

Celeste nodded, thanked Heather for the shirt and cigarettes, and watched as they turned around and drove away. When the taillights of the truck disappeared over the little hill, Celeste aimed the flashlight at the ground and clicked it on, creating a circle of orange light surrounding her.

Heather and Brian returned to find Matthew pacing around the fire and chain-smoking cheap cigarettes. Every few steps, he would grind his palm against his jean shorts and readjust his cap.

"What the hell is your deal, dude?"

"I got a bad feeling, Bri. I don't feel good about this, man. Not even a little bit." He crushed the bill of his hat into a tube in his free hand. "I heard things when you were gone, man. Whispering and shit."

"Dude, it's probably just the wind. Sit down and take a breath. What's gotten into you?"

He was about to answer when Heather grabbed Matthew by the arm and spun him around. She sniffed around his shirt collar and neck.

"What the hell, Heather? You a dog or something."

"Where is it?" she asked, pushing him backward with her index finger. "How much do you have left?" To Brian, she announced, "Matt's got pot, and he didn't share. That's why he's all worked up and paranoid; he smoked too much too quick and thought he could hide it from me." Three slaps landed on Matthew's chest. "Where is it, you bogarting butthead?"

Matthew stomped his foot and started swaying. "I smoked the last half of the joint while you were taking Celly down the road." He smeared his hat over his eyes.

"Ugh. If you're going to cry, cry in the house." Heather pointed toward Matthew's house. "Go. Sleep it off, weed hog. You'll be fine in a couple of hours." When Matthew didn't immediately take off running, she urged him with a whispered, "Do you want the Witch to get you?"

That was enough to make Matthew amble back to the house, shoulders slumped like an admonished child. The screen door slammed at his back.

Brian's eyebrows arched with astonishment. "Bit harsh, don't you think?"

"He'll get over it. Besides, that gives us the chance for you to make good on your promise." Heather pressed her body against his.

"What promise?"

She hooked a finger into the front of his shorts and pulled him back toward the fire. "You said you wanted to fuck me again. Now's your chance."

Brian looked around. "Here? What about Matt?"

A hand slithered down between his underwear and hair, grabbing hold of his flesh. "Let him watch."

"But Celly—"

Heather sighed and coaxed him with a gentle squeeze. "She's basically still a child, dipshit. Celeste has a puppy crush on you." She followed Brian's weak attempts to back away. "What happened to that 'Heather, you have a woman's want and I have a man's desire' poetry class bullshit? Or are your horny little phone calls just sissy posturing?" She grinned when his breathing picked up and his body began filling her hand. "That's what I thought. Now, lie down over here and remind me why I like you."

It wasn't long before Celeste grew restless. The hour was going to take forever. The upper half of her stomach felt full and strange. She should have peed.

The beam of the flashlight diffused around her, reaching the edge of the tall corn and disappearing into the darkness along the roads. Everything was so dark. She never spent much time in the country. She wasn't used to the eeriness of the silence, its thousands of eyes watching her from the crops, appraising the stalks of her legs and the flowers of her torso. There was no moon, and the stars gave precious little light. The tiniest sounds, scratches in dry grass, seemed to call out from miles away. She desperately wished to call out to them in return, if only for a little noise. Just a little sound. Maybe a passing car or the roar of a distant jet to ease the widening hollow of disquiet her cramping stomach tightened around.

She held as still as she could. Each time she moved the flashlight, a fresh horror appeared from the darkness, only to be revealed as a field mouse scurrying across the road or a half-eaten corn cob she hadn't noticed before.

That's how they would get her, she realized. In the light. It wasn't the darkness that made her afraid; it was the light and the skittering, orange half-shadows. And there was just enough light that her eyes couldn't fully adjust to the darkness. That's where the fear lived; in the halfway world between the flashlight and the night. The realization melted the chill around her lungs into a warm puddle in her intestines. She relaxed a little.

They probably thought there was too much light. Thought they could hide in the shadows and jump out at her. No way. She was going to beat them at their own game.

She stood the flashlight up on the ground between her shoes, watching the glow burn pink through the plastic, and squeezed her eyes shut until the sparkles behind her lids dimmed and everything was blacker than black. When she opened them, she marveled at the night's beauty. Half of the world was black, bumpy, and stringy at the top. The other half was alive with glittering starlight. Behind her, the blue glow of the farm's security light arched over the hill like a false sunrise. To her left, a dim orange radiated from a nearby town. On her right, a sheet of endless night. It was beautiful, she thought. Intimate.

Celeste squeezed her eyes again and waited for the sparkles to fade so she could see just how dark the night could be. Giddy expectation bubbled in her stomach. When she opened her eyes and saw the dark outline of slender shoulders and a head haloed by long hair waving softly in the breeze, her mind struggled to accept it as reality. She blinked again. Tremors rattled in her chest.

The outline, a shadow against the night, remained. It spoke with a woman's silken voice.

"Hello, Celeste. I've been waiting for you."

5

Celeste grabbed the flashlight from between her feet and pointed it down the road.

There was nothing. Left, right, behind; nothing. Endless darkness in every direction.

"H-Heather?" She pointed the light into the corn and the soybean fields. "Brian?"

No response.

The darkness gathered around the farthest glimmer of light until the stars slowly dimmed and her night vision decreased. She remembered the circle drawn in the crossroads and reminded herself it was all a part of the prank. Everything was fine.

With a calm, steeling breath, Celeste pointed the flashlight back down, filling the circle with light.

"I thought you wanted to find me."

She whipped the flashlight to her right. Nothing.

"I thought you wanted to come home."

To her left, more darkness.

"Who's there?" she asked, unable to control the shaking in her voice or the rumbling squeezing of her chest. She coughed it away. "You guys got me good. This is really scary." Another minute of watching, waiting, and listening passed before she stood straight and held her chin up. With half-hearted bravado, she called out, "I'm gonna close my eyes again. I hope nobody jumps out of the corn to grab me."

She turned off the flashlight, shut her eyes, and counted to ten.

When she opened them, the shadow stood to her left. "Please stop doing that."

How was Heather moving so fast? How did she change her voice like that? There was no way it was Brian. What was going on?

The flashlight rattled against her stomach. She clicked the light back on, illuminating the circle once again, just in case.

"How are you doing that?"

"Doing what?" It came from behind her.

"That! How are you moving so fast? I don't know what you're doing, but it's really creepy and I don't like it."

"Then I'll stand here." It came from her left. "As long as you promise to not aim that light at me again. Otherwise, I won't be able to keep the darkness away."

"The darkness? It's nighttime, so that'll be hard." Celeste pinched her cheeks between her teeth. She was brave. She was brave.

"Look at the stars, Celeste. Doesn't the corn seem to be growing taller?"

Even though she didn't want to look away from the shape of the woman, Celeste turned her head. Almost imperceptibly, where the stars met the tops of the corn, they winked out, one by one. Deep roars rolled through the corn; silent thunder with teeth. Her insides shook, and she stumbled several steps back. "What's happening? How are you doing that? Please stop."

"I'm not doing it."

This wasn't right. Something was wrong. Things saw her, watched her from the corn. They lifted their necks high into the air and erased the stars. "Please, please stop." Celeste begged. "You guys win. I'm really scared, and I don't want to play anymore." A spot above her bladder clenched like a fist until her back was sore. "Please. Heather, can we please stop? I want to stop."

A wave of concern radiated from the ghostly shadow. "Oh, dear. I'm not Heather."

"Who are you? Are you Brian's sister? His mom?" Celeste knew neither of those to be true.

"You know who I am, Celeste. You heard me calling for you. Come to me."

Her body folded inward at her navel. "Are you the Witch?" Her voice was a desperate squeak.

"I've been called worse." The sensation of a warm smile floated from the shape. "Do you want to know my name?"

Celeste shivered. Tears budded in her eyes. "No. Please, no." She began backing away, her feet taking over when her mind spun its wheels.

"Don't leave the circle, Celeste," the voice urged. "I don't think you can outrun it."

A phlegmy growl from the darkness behind her carried the sinister promise of fangs and torn flesh.

Celeste screamed and pointed the flashlight at an empty dirt road. "What was that?"

"Did you think an open door wouldn't attract more than one hungry beast?"

Celeste stood and walked back to the center of the circle, aiming the flashlight in every direction except at the woman. The squeezing in her chest and stomach worsened. Salty tears moistened her lips.

"You know about doors. Don't you, Celeste? Always locking and unlocking. Coming home to an empty house. Yet when the house is full, there are only more locked doors; doors with voices behind them. Never happy, never satisfied. Angry voices."

"My parents aren't angry people."

"It's their quiet anger that hurts the most, isn't it? Their indifference. Knowing they're there. Knowing they know you're there waiting for them but never coming to see you unless it's to look down at you and remind you that regardless of where they are, no matter where you are or how long you've been there, you still must be and act as their little girl. Little silly baby Celly."

"Don't call me that!" Celeste screamed. Her eyes burned and her body quivered with terror. She wanted to scream more, tell the woman she was wrong and that she could go to hell. But she wasn't wrong. Celeste could go days, weeks without seeing her parents. The loneliest nights were in the summer, when she was left to watch the neighbors playing in their pool and grilling hamburgers together. When school was out, there was supposed to be more time for fun and family, not loneliness.

"And when you are with them, are they truly there? Dinners in silence. Birthdays with more of their presents than their presence. Do you know how many nights you spent behind your own door, crying yourself to sleep, hoping they heard and would come running to hold you? To kiss your hair? To tell you they loved you and that everything would be alright? That their little girl didn't have to be afraid of the dark anymore because they were there? 'Mommy and daddy got you. Hush now, little Celly.' You would have settled for anything, though. Even if they yelled and screamed at you to be quiet. Yet, they never came. Never once."

Silent, boiling tears ran down Celeste's cheeks. No matter how deep the breaths she took, or how hard she forced the air out of her lungs, she could only cry in silence. Everything the woman said was true. Celeste was always alone. Every promise her parents made to her about working less and spending more time together, they broke. There was no together even when her parents were together. They even slept in separate bedrooms.

"But I came, Celeste. I'm here."

Fingers touched her back.

"I'm here, and I need you."

Celeste fought the sudden urge to urinate as the light flickered and dimmed. A grinding in her chest screamed for her medicine, but she was too terrified to hear it.

"Please, please, please. I want to go home. I want my mom." A trickle melted down the inside of her thigh and past her knee. "I don't want to do this anymore. You win. I'm scared. Can we please just go home now?"

The scritch-scritch of approaching claws in the loose gravel announced several sets of glowing eyes and heavy, animal sniffs. But there was nothing there. Everywhere Celeste aimed the light, there was nothing but corn, soybeans, and road dust. However, wherever she pointed it, more sounds rose from those roads she left dark. There was no way to light them all. All she could do was aim the light downward, illuminating the circle around her feet. She blinked twice before she comprehended the red streak dribbling past her skirt and down her leg.

"It's okay," the woman said. "Don't be afraid. The true power of nature is in its transitions, its awakenings. We may tend the soil and water the seedling, yet we never truly see the flower for what it is until it blooms. Don't be afraid."

Celeste reached down at the tickle. When she drew her fingers back, she saw red.

Blood.

She screamed. A sudden surge of compressed agony twisted the space around her lungs until she collapsed to her knees. Pressure built in her neck and face. Her heart wheezed. Abandoning the flashlight, she patted her pockets and searched the ground for the purse she didn't bring.

She had forgotten her medication in the car. Lifesaving pills she was never supposed to be without.

The growling drew closer. Sharp, angry shadows shrouded the road to Matthew's farm with a boiling blackness.

Heather lay back, naked from the waist down except for her thin, grass-stained socks. Her warm skin cooled in the dying fire. She lit a cigarette and rolled onto her side and faced Brian. Running a finger through the sweaty reflection of flames on his chest, she purred, "That was better than expected." When he said nothing, she slapped his shoulder. "You're welcome, asshole."

"Sorry," Brian mumbled, distracted. "I just think, you know, I should've…"

"What? Pulled out? Wore a rubber?"

He shifted his weight away from her and made a noise of disgust. "Do you have to be so vulgar?"

"Yeah." She came to her knees and straightened her shoulders, proudly letting his seed slide out of her, and added, "Yeah, you probably should've. But don't worry, sweetie. It doesn't really matter, anyway."

He winced and started to dress. "Yes, it does! If my parents find out about… If something happens, I don't—I mean, you might have to—"

Heather stood and faced him. She petted his hair, twirling a little lock into a spike with his cooling sweat. "There, there, little bear. Mommy and daddy won't find about your little whore." With a twist around her finger, she yanked down.

"Ow! What the hell?" He ran a finger through the injured area. There was no sign of blood on his fingers. "It's not that. I just don't want to be stuck in this town forever. I want to go places and do things. Somewhere not Minnesota. Besides, we're seventeen. We can't be ending our lives like that before they even begin. Kids are expensive." He rubbed his scalp. "Why do you have to be such a bitch?"

"Why do *you* have to be such a bitch?"

Brian buttoned his shorts, scowling and ready to argue, but stopped short when the sounds of scratching, an animal clawing its way through a wooden box, broke the night's silence. He pulled his shirt over his head while Heather dragged her jeans back on. They both jumped up and looked around.

"What the hell is that noise?"

She shrugged and looked around. Then she spotted it and exhaled impatiently. "You left the radio on."

Brian snatched up the cassette player. "No, I didn't."

The button clicked on its own.

D-eh-d eed-ehr-loh ruhw

D-eh-d eed-ehr-loh ruhw

D-eh-d eed-ehr-loh ruhw

"Turn it off, Brian." Heather hugged her chest as the eerie sound of the stilted voices drew goosebumps from her flesh. "I don't like it."

"I-I-I'm trying. It won't…"

The button was stuck.

Ooy vyass tnak eesh

Ooy vyass tnak eesh

Ooy vyass tnak eesh

"Turn it the fuck off!"

"I can't!" Even when he popped off the back and tore out the batteries, the tape kept spinning out the sepulchral whispers. "It won't shut off." Desperation trembled on his lips. "I don't know what to do."

Heather ripped the player from his hands and pressed the stop button, over and over, cursing it when the volume knob did nothing.

Heather

She immediately dropped the radio on the ground and grasped at her stomach.

We will have your child, too

Brian rushed over, ignoring the hissing laughter. There was no blood, no apparent injury, yet Heather felt as if a knife sawed at her guts. She pointed to the fire. "Throw it in! Burn it!"

He shoved the plastic player into the fire, speakers first. A screeching blared in the smoldering wood before a loud pop sent a cloud of smoke and ash into the sky like a pair of wings taking flight.

Silence.

Brian lifted her to her feet, and they both ran into the safety of the shadows between the house and the fire pit, clutching each other. "What the hell did we do?"

"It wasn't real. It was a joke, right? Your brother gave us a joke tape for you and your creepy witch game."

"It knew your name, Heather. There's no way Dan knows about us. He wouldn't know you were here or that I'd play the tape for you and…" A shared realization chilled their flesh.

A distant scream cracked the sky.

Heather breathed, "Oh God. Celly!"

6

Dim light barely painted the far edge of the circle in an oily orange glow. The batteries were dying. Once they were gone… She didn't want to think about that. All she could do was scream herself hoarse for Heather and Brian and her parents. Her voice never got above a pained shout; they never came. They left her to lie there, heart hammering like a rubber ball in an oblong room, and crimson spotting the earth between her shivering thighs.

"Are you still here?" she asked the darkness.

"I am," the woman's dewy voice spoke softly into Celeste's ear.

Celeste sobbed. She needed her pills, needed a clear path back to the farm and away from the beastly shadows nipping at her with black fangs. Despair and sadness tightened around her bowels with each flicker of the dying light. The stars disappeared. The wind stilled. There was only the shadow woman and puffs of dust blown up from the edge of the circle by invisible hounds. "Please. I'm sick. I need my pills. Please let me just get my pills. I promise to come back. I won't tell anybody."

An herby, floral scent caught the air. The woman's voice drew closer, soft and thick with compassion. "They'll never let you past. If you step outside the circle, they rip you apart. There is no going back, sweet Celeste. Even if you could, your heart can't make it to the farm. I'm sorry."

Celeste sobbed and coughed when her chest rumbled with agony. She was going to die. "What do I do?"

"Come with me. We'll keep each other safe while we wait."

Celeste shook her head. Everything seemed slowed. Her dry and tender eyes felt heavy and numb. She wilted into the dirt, unable to keep the flashlight aimed much longer. "I don't know."

"Come with me, Celeste. I need your help."

"My help? I can't help anyone."

"You can help me. You're special."

"I'm not special."

"But you are. You are so special and so beautiful. Think of us as two flowers sharing a stem, apples on the same branch. We share roots, you and me. That's why you could hear me, and I could hear you, why you answered when I called." Growls spat dust from the darkness. The woman's voice grew serious and protective. "Now that you're no longer a bud but a growing flower, you're special to other things, too."

Celeste stared at the smears between her legs. "I don't want to be special."

Things surrounded her. On three sides were gnashing, drooling fangs. Behind her, the woman. As much as she begged for this to be a part of the prank, it wasn't. This was real. The *thudda-thud-thuddup* of her failing heart was real. "What do I do?"

"Come to me. Come to the edge of the circle. There you go. Keep the light up. Good, good. Now lean back."

Celeste hesitated. She could just make out the thick ditch of dusty earth next to her thigh. Her ribs and spine rattled as if she were freezing, yet sweat dripped down her brow. "Will you take me home? I want to go home."

"We'll go home together."

The flashlight flickered once, twice, but could only maintain a dim, glowing memory of light. Darkness plodded closer.

Celeste leaned backward into a very real, very soft, warm body. Hands smoothed her hair from forehead to crown with a soothing "Shhhh" from the woman. Warm, slender fingers with nails crusted in brown, the creases of knuckles blackened with soil, slid atop hers, thumb over thumb on the flashlight's plastic button. Celeste thought she smelled flowers.

Shadows closed in around them. Hot breaths tickled her ankles and knees. The light died with a click.

Rubber ground against rock and dirt. A pair of foggy headlights bled a lifeless yellow into the stalks of corn as Matthew's truck kicked up clouds of swirling dust, stopping just short of the crossroads.

Heather rushed out, screaming, "Celly! Celeste!" louder and louder, until her voice cracked with terror and worry. Brian joined in, his flashlight illuminating the quiet stalks at the corners of the crossroads.

Other than the discarded flashlight and a few drops of red in the dry sand, there was no sign of Celeste Martin.

Chapter Two

Moira awoke with a shattering headache and a cheekbone that felt flattened like warm clay. While it wasn't the first time she had woken up after falling asleep at her desk, it was one of the worst. And she had barely touched her second glass of wine. It was still there, half-filled next to her laptop.

She let the nightmare play back in her mind before getting out of her chair and stretching the soreness out of her back. The strange whispers from the cassette player rubbed the frozen claws along her spine.

Heather Ylva. Brian Hopkins. Matthew Miller.

She took a breath to clear her head. This nightmare wasn't as bad as others. At least she wasn't sweating, and her heart didn't try to burn its way out of her chest. The room mercifully remained still. She sensed she could function like a normal human being. The headache must've been a mixture of inhaled smoke, dehydration, and sleeping with her face plastered against wood. A shower might not clear it all up, but it certainly couldn't make matters worse.

Before getting out of the chair, she tapped her laptop awake and made sure she saved the files to her desktop. She'd have to read it again to separate the facts of the material from the remaining fog of her nightmare; it wasn't the first time her imagination had taken a few details from a tale or someone's story and ran with it. Dani joked with her about it. "You know, Mo, most people have trains of thought that stick firmly to their rails, even when they hit an obstacle. But your thoughts are more like a Roomba: mostly reliable, but sometimes they smash into a wall a little too hard and just take off in all sorts of crazy directions. That's why you're totally my super-secret lady crush."

She'd have to call Dani after she packed.

A hot shower and a cold pressed coffee with jelly toast rejuvenated her blood and replaced the headache with dull excitement. There was a real, living folk tale here in Minnesota. People somewhere still believed in the existence of a supernatural being and may still have rituals and stories and personal practices that illuminated it.

The Abrams Witch. Graduate school admission.

This was going to be a good summer.

Not long after she folded a shirt she wouldn't need for the week and put it into her suitcase, her phone buzzed. It was Dani.

"Hello?"

"Rise and shine, clementine. I love it when your voice gets all raspy and sexy in the morning." She growled. "Get it, girl!"

"Shut up." Moira couldn't help but laugh. "Good morning, lovely. How are you?"

"Just dandy. I was wondering if you wanted to lunch me after your meeting with Dr. Emily. Lunch me hard."

Shit. She forgot about the appointment with her adviser. Keeping the phone to her ear, Moira upturned her backpack and searched for her day planner. She must've left it at her grandmother's. She threw herself back into her webbed chair and checked her calendar on her university account.

Dani made a noise. "I am taking your frantic mumbling as a complete and total personal rejection of me. Since I may never get over you, I'll forward you my therapy bills as a way to passive-aggressively maintain distant but never-ending emotional contact."

"No," Moira said, a little too whiny for her liking. "I want to lunch you. I just forgot about the meeting."

"Forgot?" Dani gave a dramatic gasp. "Are you alright? Wanna day drink and talk about it? All of my finals are over before noon."

"Lucky. I'm fine, just had a weird night. I stayed up and read all that stuff you sent me, and it went to my head." She looked at her phone. "Listen Dani, I got twenty minutes to get to Zebka's office and my hair is still wet. Let me get through the meeting. Then you can take me to lunch, and I will tell you all about them. Okay?"

"It's a date. Wear red."

Moira laughed and said goodbye. Hurrying, she pulled on a pair of jeans, a tank top, and a candy red button-up shirt. Checking from her window, it was a crisp morning, but not unpleasant; she'd let the April wind dry her hair.

She poured a little water into her lily's pot. Its alabaster hood was soft and feathery under her fingertips. Rachel would be proud about how surprisingly fast it had bloomed.

The meeting didn't go as well as she'd hoped. How she imagined it going included more discussion about her project and Dr. Zebka's willingness to write her a letter of recommendation. How it went was her spending too much of their 45 minutes defending Dani.

Dr. Emily Zebka thought Moira was pulling more than her fair share of weight on the project and Dani simply glommed onto her for the easy pass. Moira assured her Dani was putting in just as much work and effort. She did her share of the more difficult research, including tracking down many people and historical events that have been difficult to locate. Most of that was true. Zebka argued the whole time, and they left the conversation at a stalemate. She wondered if what Dani told her was accurate: Zebka didn't like her.

Frustrated and distracted, Moira marched through the center of campus. After her conversation with Zebka, her thoughts burrowed into a stormy place in her brain she called 'the Dani Problem.' Once that rainbow tornado started spinning in her head, she might as well write everything off for the day.

Not that Dani was a problem, it was the opposite. She was a loyal, wonderful friend; a hardworking academic partner, and…. And there was the problem. There was always an 'and,' and it wasn't because Moira, like most writers and readers, had a penchant for lists. Lists were useful. She made them to help her figure out what the Dani problem was *not*, even though she knew exactly what it was. The Dani Problem wasn't a brick wall taller than the sky was high. Nor was it a black hole-like bend in reality she slipped past whenever she tried to touch it. The Dani Problem was a poem. A billowy, curly-haired, candy-coated song that wasn't supposed to be a riddle, but felt like one anyway because she refused to open herself to it. Maybe she couldn't.

There were days when her heart had its own gravity. Times when she wanted to pull the problem toward her, wrap herself in its Dani-shape, and breathe in its sweaty, perfume-kissed air until it was inside her and she was inside it. Until everything ached and smiled at the same time. It just was easier to not complicate things. To orbit the problem and appreciate it for what it was: something that didn't have to hurt when it inevitably fell apart. So, she'd just keep moving forward in her Moira-shape, trying to control the things she could control and letting the complicated parts of her life just happen to her.

Then again, maybe someday she'd grow up.

In the distance, the familiar rumbling of an engine pulled into her complex's parking lot. A loud blue and black muscle car pulled up beside her. The driver whistled at her, suggestively and parked nearby. Aluminum chains outlining the license plate glimmered in the sun. A stuffed unicorn squished against the rear window, and a glittery silhouette of She-Ra with her sword decorated the bumper. The car's name was *Dad's Midlife Crisis*. DMC for short.

Dani stepped out. Her glossy lips split into a smile. "Hey there, sugar bear." Shining coils of ombre hair, black at the roots and burning golden brown to the tips, bounced at the shoulders of her open-collared pink blouse. The thin gold chain with a half-moon charm Moira bought for her birthday rested under the hollow between her collarbones. A lacy, white undershirt curved just below the dark brown cleft at the top of her breasts.

Moira's middle felt like a shaken bottle of sparkling water, fizzy and full. "Hey," she said, keys digging into her first. "You, um, your hair looks gorgeous!"

"You like it?" Dani rolled her eyes and gave her head a silly, coquettish tilt.

"Yeah. It's looks really" —she reached up but pulled her hand back— "shiny."

"It's okay." Dani brought Moira's hand up and led her fingers into the silky ribbons. "You can touch. As long as you don't mind getting a little of me on you."

Moira remembered to breathe as soon as she realized she was smiling.

"Something on your mind?" Her grin steamed the hot coffee brown of her eyes. She folded her arms across her chest. "I know you didn't forget our date, because you're wearing red."

"Of course I didn't forget. How could I? You were all Zebka would talk about."

Dani's eyes narrowed. "She doesn't like me. It was bad, wasn't it? Did she accuse me of cheating or something?"

"No. She was just being… She was being a professor." Moira ran a hand through her tangled hair. "I told her you were doing just as much work as I am. She didn't ask for proof or anything."

"Too bad, because I have news for you: I have a lead on Jennifer Lake."

Jennifer Lake's story interested Moira, but she had yet to find complete information. According to what they already found, Jenny Lake was the only person who claimed to have faced the Abrams Witch and survived, though her infant son did not. Unfortunately, Jenny Lake was also mentally ill. Paranoid schizophrenia was the popular idea, but they didn't have access to her medical records to know for sure. The court sealed her records years ago, as she was a minor when she stood trial for her child's murder. That Dani had found any viable information was groundbreaking for their project, provided they could make something out of it. It could also be a welcome shift from just reading old newspapers and county records, though all the information about Celeste Martin was an eerie change itself.

"How did you find her?"

Dani gave a series of exaggerated blinks. "Because I'm amazing. Duh." She smiled. "And Rodney is a bitchin' lawyer who can make some things happen when effectively motivated by an exceedingly charming and ridiculously beautiful little sister."

"That's amazing!" Dani's smile meant that there was more for her to tell. "And?" Moira asked.

"I even tracked her down. She lives in a group home near the Cities. I have a brief in-person interview with her and her caregiver next Tuesday."

"Shut up!" Overjoyed, Moira threw her arms around Dani and squeezed while hopping on her toes. Now she had something concrete to bring to prove to Zebka that Dani was pulling her weight on the project. "This is even more reason to celebrate! I just want to brush my hair first."

"Sure. Let's go in. I'll even brush it for you, if you're buying my mimosas."

Moira was searching her bathroom for a decent hairbrush when she heard Dani give a pained squeal. Near the bed, Dani, her face a mask of shock and accusation, pointed at the overturned laundry hamper and the stuffed purple pig under it.

"You put Mr. Piggles in jail?" Dani's nostrils flared. "How dare you?"

Moira smiled and said in her worst Russian accent, "He is in gulag for insubordination. "Rooting around where he wasn't supposed to. It's a good thing he has you as his protector, otherwise I'd have eaten his bacon."

She let Dani spring her partner-in-crime from prison.

Dani cradled Mr. Piggles in her arms. Her face lost a bit of mirth when she looked at Moira. "Now that we're here, maybe we could do something a little different instead of going to the bar for brunch? It's expensive, and it's been stupid hot and dry for the last week of April, so the idea sitting outside kind of seems like a bummer. And I don't want to stink like stale beer."

"Okay. What did you have in mind?" Moira asked while brushing out snarls. "I don't have any finals until tomorrow."

Dani reclined on the bed like a still-life of a dark-skinned Cleopatra, Mr. Piggles cradled protectively in her arm. "Maybe we can close the curtains, change into some cozy clothes, get a pizza, eat a couple of gummies, lay on the couch, and watch scary movies?"

How Dani looked at her made Moira shiver in a way she liked. "Yeah," she blurted. *Don't complicate anything, Moira.* "Yeah, I want that."

Moira made it through two pieces of a thin crust pepperoni and black olive pizza and maybe thirty minutes of the second movie before her body became heavy and floaty like she was a sleepy piece of driftwood riding the surface of a lazy river.

At some point, the woman on the screen had entered the creepy house and Moira had cocooned herself in a knitted afghan blanket and leaned into Dani, who pet her hair and chuckled at the hapless teens being systematically slaughtered.

Moira was not having as much fun. Whenever she tried to fall asleep, shadows played in the darkness behind her eyelids. Another set of eyes, blacker against the black, watched her from a distance. Staring back at them brought the sensation of an unexpected drop, and she shivered awake each time.

Moira looked up to make sure Dani hadn't fallen through the

floor. Dani blinked through heavy eyes, and Moira could tell she felt as floaty and buzzy as her. "Mo-mo, never say 'hello' to a haunted hallway. That's how they get you."

"Yes. You are wise." She held on to Dani's hand while the women on the screen screamed and ran away.

Near the end of the movie, Dani asked her, "What're you more scared of, Mo: monster, ghost, or psycho killer?"

She barely heard the question, but mumbled, "Uncertainty."

"That's not a monster."

"Aren't monsters extensions of our own weaknesses brought on by a primal fear of the unknown and the uncertain?"

"Don't big brain me. I'm too high for that."

Moira pulled the blanket closer, suppressing a shudder and reminding herself the paranoia will pass. "Why do we do this to ourselves?"

"Desensitizes. So when a chainsaw killer comes after us, we won't run screaming into his basement. We'll kick the shit out of him instead."

That made sense. Dani, for all her goofiness and joking, was practical and forward-thinking. She also dabbled in martial arts to both stay in shape and protect herself. Moira thought she was brave. "Aren't you a ninja or something? Couldn't you fight the bad guy?"

"Judo is ineffective against werewolves, vampires, and most incorporeal entities. It's kryptonite to creepers and serial killers, though."

Moira nodded. "Well, if creepers and serial killers show up, you're in charge of saving us."

Dani's head swiveled on a wobbly neck. She tried to give Moira an agitated expression. "Sounds like work. What're you gonna do when I'm saving us? Watch me get beat up?"

She shrugged mentally. "You're the superhero. I did cheerleading in high school, so I'll just be your cowardly sidekick screaming encouragement from a safe distance."

Dani kissed her on the soft part of her face, just outside her ear. "Best sidekick ever."

Moira awoke with the sun. She was laying in her bed next to Dani; their arms were around each other. Mr. Piggles was smashed between them. They were still wearing their clothes. The floral comforter covering them was a shell of warmth that kept out the chill and made everything inside puffy and wonderful.

A long exhale escaped Dani's lips. The warm pink under her light brown flesh looked soft and kissable.

The first time Moira kissed another girl she was 11 and at her first and only summer camp. Her name was Juanita, and her lips tasted like strawberries warmed by the sunshine scent of her skin. The first time she kissed a boy was her freshman year of college at a party. His ashy tongue slapped awkwardly at her lips while his hands fumbled at her crotch. She gagged a little in his mouth.

She met Dani the next day during a partner assignment in English class. She was hungover and needed another shower. Dani, on the other hand, was upbeat and smiling. "What's up, buttercup? Signing up for a Friday morning class was a huge mistake, huh?" They'd been friends ever since.

Dani stirred and wet her lips before sinking back into the mattress. Moira eased her face closer and let her lungs fill with vanilla and coconut while her petal soft lips tingled, hovering an inch from Dani's mouth.

She leaned away before making the very mistake she wanted to. Instead, she opened a secret door at the far end of a little forest cottage hidden in her imagination, a place where a Sleeping Dani rested on flower petals, hands folded atop a lacy pink bodice, while beams of sunlight bathed the curls of her hair in sparkles. Moira kissed that Dani, her mouth lingering on a plump, caramel lip.

Careful to not wake her, Moira crawled over Dani and turned her alarm off two minutes before it went off. She washed up in the bathroom sink, deciding she would shower later, and wore her hair up in a tail. After brushing her teeth, she was checking to make sure she had her paper in her backpack when Dani's sleepy voice said, "Byou leabing?"

"I have a final."

"You rwant me to leeb? Imma go."

"No, no." Moira settled Dani back into bed. She went down without a fight. "You stay. I'll be back in an hour or so. I'm gonna lock the door, too. You want donuts?"

"Mlike dunnuts."

Moira giggled and pushed a curl of hair away from Dani's nose, purposely brushing fingers against her cheeks.

Dani smiled and mumbled two words Moira did not quite hear, but hoped she understood. Probably not, though.

She said, "Bub you, too," and stepped quietly out of her studio.

After Moira left, Dani shoved Mr. Piggles out of the way and buried her face in the heat of Moira's pillow.

After an hour, Moira was back with two coffees and a half dozen donuts. Any hope she had of sneaking back into bed next to Dani disappeared when she saw Mr. Piggles and the warm smile waiting for her on the futon.

"Good morning," Moira said.

Dani sipped her glass of water and paused the video she'd been streaming. "Mr. Piggles was lonely. He said they don't have cartoons in the gulag."

Moira pursed her lips and nodded. "But they have donuts."

"Oooo!" Dani traded Mr. Piggles for breakfast.

After they ate, Moira finished packing with Dani's help. She grabbed three bags of clothing, her electronics, makeup, a few books, everything she had on the Abrams Witch, her own pillow, a blanket, and two sets of cheap cotton sheets. They loaded everything into the trunk of her car.

Once they tidied her apartment and locked it up, she sent Dani an email with the information for the place she was staying, as well as her grandmother's phone number and address, in case of an emergency.

Moira shouldered her backpack, did a final check that everything was in order, and locked up.

Dani waited for her in the parking lot. "Call me when you get there. Okay?" Dani's hand pressed against her upper arm.

"I will." Moira tossed her backpack onto her passenger seat. "When you interview Jenny Lake, will you ask if you can record it so we can reference it?"

Dani nodded. "I didn't ask when I talked to them. She's a vulnerable adult, so I'm not sure if there are any legal hurdles."

"Then do it only if you think her story is impactful. You take good notes, so I'm not worried."

For a moment, she thought she saw Dani blush in the sunlight.

"Can I give you something before you go?" Dani asked.

"Sure." Moira unconsciously ran a tongue over her lips to moisten them.

Dani dug around in her purse and pulled out a little green tube on a key chain and handed it to her.

"Um, what's this?"

"Pepper spray. It's the strongest stuff I could find. It probably won't blind a bear or a witch, but it might make them reconsider eating you."

Moira laughed. "The Witch isn't real. And what if bears secretly like spicy food?"

"Bears don't like spice. The Witch might not be real, but creepers and weirdos are. Aim for the face." She showed Moira how to use it. Just twist and press. When she fumbled, Dani asked, "You wanna take Mick, instead?"

Mick Dagger was an eight-inch knife with a handle, pommel, and cross guard made of rose gold Dani bought from the Renaissance Festival three years prior. It was expensive and handmade, yet she kept it in her glove compartment in case she needed to "get stabby." As tough as Moira knew her to be, it was hard to picture Dani hurting anyone.

"Mick should stay with you," Moira laughed. She thanked Dani and wrapped her in a lingering embrace. Dani's lips swept past her cheek. Moira leaned in, then immediately pulled back, unsure of what to do. "I should go. I'll see you next week."

Dani smiled, a sliver of disappointment in the corners of her eyes. "Drive safe."

Chapter Three

The drive was long, boring, and flat. The rolling farmland and the lakes were pretty and sometimes quaint, but they were also unbearably constant. Very brown, very constant, very same. The worsening drought from the previous summer carried over through the brown winter and into a sepia-saturated spring. Everything looked dead. Even the dirt looked lifeless and light, piles of dusty husks releasing cloudy souls to the wind.

Farther north, the evergreen forests thickened and encroached on the highway like fingers folding over the road to make a green and yellow tunnel. When she reached the parched wetlands, the pines browned and lost their foliage. Fingers turned jagged, rheumatic, oppressive.

Moira turned up the volume on her audio book and closed her windows.

The sun eventually came out from behind dark clouds. The trees thinned into marsh and farmland. To her right, railroad tracks followed her past tall grass, collapsed sheds, and through two small towns until her GPS had her exit onto another road fenced by fields of desolate earth and brightly colored houses.

A sign read: Abrams Pop. 1486.

Abrams itself appeared to be a cheery town, if a small one. There was a small community park—barely half an acre in size—with a rose garden and pruned crabapple trees surrounding a white and green gazebo. Several businesses hugged the sidewalks: a small car dealership, what looked like a boat or pontoon repair shop, a cafe, and grocery store, and a bank. Of course, like many small towns, there were two bars, a gas station, and a liquor store.

Moira turned left at Marie's Bridal Shop, drove past the butcher and the laundromat, and kept on for a mile, passing several pretty houses and a few drab ones, a mobile home court, and the expansive Evangelical Church. She made a mental note of that. The corner of Central and Byron.

County Road Five appeared to be the boundary of Abrams' town limits. Each road leading farther away was gravel and surrounded by cows, corn, and the smell of manure. Moira drove on to the edge of town, took a left on the main street that she could have stayed on to begin with, had her GPS not led her in a giant circle, and continued for two miles until she reached the Abrams Motel.

The clerk Becky, a stout, good-humored woman, said she didn't mind taking down information while Moira stretched the knot out of her spine and the soreness in her hamstrings. "I know what that's like. Just wait until you get my age. Ha!" She reminded Moira of someone's favorite aunt, the kind of person who could purposely look captivated whenever a first grader told them about what happened on the playground.

"Those long drives are killers. My back aches for you, dear. You just passing through? An overnight stop before heading to the cabin?"

"I'd like to stay a few days, actually. I'm doing some historical research for a college project about rural Minnesota stories. Old stories, tales of families settling, and towns being established. Things like that. It's a mixed bag of Cultural Anthropology and Humanities."

"You heard we have a witch, right?"

Moira didn't expect that level of openness from anyone here, especially not after the last email she received. "I may have heard a thing or two but didn't think it would be very sensitive to lead with that in conversations with people I haven't met. Sorry."

Becky clicked her pen and gave a dismissive wave. "Don't even worry about it. Plenty of folks come through each year asking about it. They usually leave disappointed. It's mostly a kid's story now. Stuff emo high schoolers talk about when they're in the woods smoking weed and hating their parents. I should know. I did the exact same thing when I was their age."

Moira grabbed a pen and her small notebook out of her purse. "Would you happen to have any information about the Witch's origin story? Where she originated, what people think she's doing here, what she might represent?"

Becky filled her cheeks and blew out the air in one long breath. "That's outside my wheelhouse. I just remember people saying there was a scary witch who lived in the woods and would eat you if you stayed out too late or didn't do your homework. Tiny stuff. If it's in-depth stuff you're looking for, I can get you the number for our local historian."

"Reverend Hopkins?"

"You know him?" Becky gave her a warm smile. "He's going to be your best chance at finding out the folklorey stuff about Abrams. He also has a bunch of old town records at the church, if it's not just the Witch you're interested in."

"Excellent!"

Moira signed the receipt for four days and followed Becky to a small, but thankfully clean, room. Number Five. Becky gave her three days' worth of bleached white linens, two extra rolls of toilet paper, and a metal key with a half of a cedar roof shake as its key chain.

"Makes it easier to not run off with it or lose it."

It was too big to slip into her back pocket, so she shoved it into her purse. "Certainly does that."

Becky gave her a rundown of the general rules, check-out times, where the vending machine was, and the hours her office was open. "You don't seem like the type who's planning to have crazy parties, but please keep the guest count to four or less. Also, don't skip the cafe. It's got the best pie in the county. And the Belgian waffles are huge."

Moira thanked her and headed to her car to grab her bags. Through the reflection in her windshield, she thought she saw Becky's smile instantly vanish into a scowl and her eyes harden when Moira wasn't looking. She looked back, but Becky was already halfway to her office.

Strange, she mused, and shrugged it off as a misunderstanding—just a trick of the light—and she carried in the last of her bags.

It came as no surprise to her that Abrams seemed strange and insulated. Customers at the gas station and the grocery store were friendly but slightly cold; one old woman was downright brusque, having pushed through Moira to get through the door. The people that crossed paths with her on the sidewalks gave forced smiles that dropped quickly when they thought she stopped looking. A pair of conservatively dressed, middle-aged women stared at her through the bank's dark windows as she crossed the street toward the cafe. At least they turned away when she caught them looking. The teenage cashier watching her through the window of the hardware store just kept staring, mouth partly open, freckled face slack and colorless. Even after she waved at him, he didn't move or blink.

"I ain't dyin'." An elderly man, tall and slender, wearing black slacks held up too high above his loafers by suspenders over his white shirt, shook his cane at her and stumbled forward. Flaccid skin jiggled below his enraged, yellowed eyes. "I ain't dyin'!"

Moira stepped back. "Are you okay? Do you need help? Is there anything I can—Hey!"

The old man snatched her wrist with surprising strength. Thin, steely fingers bit wrapped around her narrow bones. The voice warbling out of his flimsy windpipe boomed with extraordinary energy. "I ain't dyin'! You hear? Not for you!" He raised his cane above his head with a shivering arm. "I ain't waitin' to die!"

"Chuck!" yelled a deep voice from behind her. A police officer wearing a dark blue uniform reached around her, pulled her wrist free of the old man's grip, and pressed the man firmly against the brick wall of an antiques stop. The officer was stocky, about three times the size of the lanky man, so he easily held him in place. "Chuck!" the police officer shouted, inches from the man's face. "Look at me, Chuck. Do you know where you are?"

The old man wiggled, wormed, and whined. Quickly, his struggles slowed, and his gaze shifted between Moira and the officer.

She couldn't see the officer's face or hear his whisper, but what ever he said made the old man shake and his bottom lip stuck out. As he huffed and wept, Moira thought how much he looked like a child with his wispy, chalk white hair sticking straight up from the middle of his head.

His eyes cleared, and from a full throat, he grunted, "I'm sorry, Jeff. I'm sorry."

Her heart went out to him.

The officer hugged the old man, patting his back and letting him cry into the shoulder of his uniform.

A purple SUV pulled up to them, and a middle-aged woman with red hair and a patterned shirt stepped out. "Thank you so much!" she said to the police officer. "Come on, grandpa!" she nearly yelled. "Let's go home!"

Moira stayed around long enough to watch them load Chuck into the vehicle and drive away. When it moved, Moira saw that the boy in the window still stared at her.

"Sorry about that, Miss." The police officer wiped tears and snot off his chest with a handkerchief. "Chuck has had quite a, uh, quite a past couple of years. Dementia." He hopped the curb and gave her a quick, tight-lipped smile.

"I'm sorry," she said. "I didn't realize."

He waved it away. "No apologies. There's no way you could have known. If anyone should apologize, it's me. Someone should be caring for him all the time, but he's not a puppy, you know. There's still a lot of the man in there. Chuck liked to walk through town with his wife every day. Now that she's gone, it seems cruel to make him break the habit. We just kinda let him be."

Moira nodded. She saw a flash of Rachel's face in her mind and swallowed a lump of worry. "Yeah. I can't imagine what it would be like to go through something like that."

"And that one," he pointed to the boy in the window, "don't worry about him. Tommy's a good kid. He's just a bit slow. His daddy owns the hardware store and gives him gainful employment—stocking cleaning up, greeting customers. Sometimes he gets distracted by a pretty face." The officer waved. Tommy smiled, returned a half-wave, and walked back into the aisles. "He's harmless, I promise."

"I'm sure he is. I just wondered if he even saw me." Moira admonished herself for not remembering disabled people exist in small towns. "Everyone else seems to be curious. I feel like I'm being watched everywhere."

He smiled, the wrinkles at the corners of his eyes deepened like cuts that didn't bleed, giving a dark and threatening quality to his eyes that appeared years younger than his gray eyebrows and leathery skin showed. The policeman was tall and graying. Sharp features pinched at his nose, and he squinted like he constantly started at the sun. His wide belly brushed against her arm as he leaned in. "First time in a small town?"

A sudden sense of revulsion wormed its way up Moira's stomach. "First time in Abrams." She extended her hand out of habit. "Moira."

"Jett Lake. Chief Lake, if you prefer." The stiffness of his fingers and the rigidity in his glare told Moira that it was what he preferred. "Reverend Hopkins told me he was working with a Moira about some sort of college research project or what have you. That you?"

Something about the air around made her queasy. Something hot and oily and humid, like being trapped in a raw sewer without her sense of smell. Touching him made her nauseous. It took effort to slip her hand out of his and much greater effort to not scrub her palm on her pant leg. "That would be me. I thought I would explore a bit of Abrams and catch up with Reverend Hopkins tomorrow, since it's getting late."

Chief Lake cocked his head and stepped away. "Don't worry about bothering the good Reverend. He's usually at the church well past supper. Hell, he might even have more time for you tonight if you're still eager to see him."

Salty sickness filled the back of Moira's mouth. Blood rushed from her face. "I am. I'll visit. The cafe is this way?" She pointed and stepped away from Chief Lake.

"Indeed it is," he said as he turned away and walked toward his cruiser.

Moira hurried around the corner. She needed to get away from him and find a quiet place to throw up. The faster she walked, the better she felt physically, but she doubted any amount of walking would erase the overwhelming disgust she felt just being in his presence.

What the hell was that about? When was the last time she had been sick? Three, four months ago after eating poorly prepared cafeteria food? She ran through several likely scenarios—hangover, bad donuts, motion sickness—but her every instinct told her none of those were true or rational. It was him. The cop sickened her for some mysterious reason.

She took three breaths and spit the salt from her mouth. Her stomach finally calmed. She was glad to have not vomited in public.

Across the street, eyes stared at her through the cafe window. Forks of pot pie filling floated halfway to open mouths. Fingers rubbed condensation from glasses of iced tea. A server pretended to write in her pad but used the wrong end of her pen. After a moment of suspended animation, everyone in the cafe went back to eating, drinking, and ignoring the woman outside the window.

Moira blinked, unsure of what she just saw was real or an illness-induced hallucination. Whatever it was, she didn't want to be there anymore.

The setting sun cast tall shadows of thin pines over the church as Moira pulled into the parking lot. A single light glowed from within. Moira had never been to church and wasn't sure if that meant someone was inside. Her parents were staunch atheists and Rachel told her, "Any real god wouldn't give a damn about what building you talked to her from," so she had little experience she could rely on. She just assumed they closed after five.

Feeling awkward, she got out of her car and checked the door. Unlocked. Given the general sense of security or captivity Abrams gave off, she wondered if it was the type of town where people didn't lock their doors. It was a frightening concept. Keeping the deadbolt unlocked in a college town was something she'd never done and would never risk doing. Then again, maybe she just didn't understand, didn't click with the small-town mentality. She'd been a suburban kid all of her life. Perhaps something positive could be said about everybody knowing everyone where they lived?

Maybe. It didn't make walking into a church at night, uninvited and unannounced, feel any less invasive.

Dim fluorescent bulbs lit the entrance. A row of coat hooks ran along the wall to deep shadows hanging like enormous bats in the corners. In the center of the far wall, a bulletin board announced baptisms, births, and potlucks. Moira jotted down her name in a sign-in book.

The doors to the nave were open, and she heard footsteps on polished hardwood coming from within. She followed the sound into an expansive room with rows of padded pews and a wooden and brass octagonal font in its center. Colorful banners depicting Jesus and the apostles hung in the darkness where tear-shaped lights didn't shine. Frosted windows admitted dying light in yellows and golds. At the opposite side of the room, splitting the pulpit and a lectern, sat a wide altar covered with a white cloth trimmed in blue and gold. Atop it rose an enormous wooden carving of Jesus, arms raised and frowning over a three-foot-tall crucifix. A thick Bible sat open at his feet. On each side of the altar, brass candlesticks stood unlit.

Moira noticed a pair of doors on either side of the altar and walked to the one marked Office, acutely aware of how the dark eyes of the Christian savior appeared to follow her. She knocked. The volume and persistence of the echo made her frightened stomach jump.

"How may I help you, miss?" A voice thundered from the entrance. A tall man, face swathed with shadow, prowled into the nave. Narrow lips surrounded a wide mouth like a cartoonish outline. White teeth flashed in the dark.

Moira stood breathless for a startled moment before managing a weak, "M-my name is Moira Clarke. I was hoping to find Reverend Hopkins," and unconsciously calculating just how fast she could sprint toward the door.

Shadows pulled up from the floor and between the pew to attach to his lanky frame, making him appear to grow taller with each silent step nearer the font. "I am he." Reverend Hopkins gave her a nod. His solid white clerical collar hung loose around his slender neck. "I've been eager to meet you, Ms. Clarke. Though I truly didn't expect you until tomorrow. Did you just arrive?" Once he stepped into the light nearest the altar, the shadows drew back slowly like cold rubber and the bulbs glowed brighter.

Moira exhaled an anxious breath. Other than his sunken cheeks and eyes and the sheen from his heavily gelled hair, he looked positively ordinary. "No," Moira said, the confidence in her voice returning to its usual depth. "I've been here a few hours, taking in the sights and such."

"And what do you think of Abrams?"

Moira swallowed. His eyes were captivating, almost fearsome. Two dull, mahogany orbs surrounded by rings of iron. The way they didn't reflect the light shook her, but she couldn't turn away. "My plan was to stop by tomorrow, but Chief Lake said you'd be here. So, I thought… I'm sorry. I feel like I'm intruding."

"Nonsense." The easy wave of his hand blocked her way past him. "Chief Lake is correct; I am usually here late, though I was just leaving for the evening. Perhaps you wouldn't mind walking me to my car? We can discuss how I can help."

There was a smell, a stink, to him and his cologne. Cold concrete with a chemical, watery sweetness painted over it. She tried to give a cheery, "Absolutely!" but it creaked out like a loose floorboard.

She felt much better outside, enough so that they made small talk once they exited the church. They talked about how her drive was, how she liked college, what her future plans were, mundane things. Moira answered with little energy; she was just thankful he kept his hands to himself. The idea of being touched by him after her experience with Lake affected her at a primal level, as if she'd been pricked by a cactus or scarred by fire.

"What are you looking for with your search, Moira? Something of a more spiritual nature?"

She shook her head. "Purely academic. No offense, but I've never been a spiritual person, and religion to me is just a historical circumstance. I'm more interested in how things like religions, stories, superstitions have defined people and cultures. And I like to know why those stories persist, even after facts or events have disproved the possibility of their actual existence."

"So this is a search for meaning? In your own way, of course."

"To a degree. I like to think I search for facts that explain metaphors. Vampires as the manifestation of rural worry about uncleanliness leading to communicable disease, or the importance of maintaining cultural burial rites. Werewolves as an exploration of the monstrous behavior brought out by rage over isolation, or how we view actual murderers as animals and beasts. Those sorts of things. I want to know the 'why' behind the superstitions."

The corner of his mouth curled up. "You don't think the Witch is real, or that there is actual truth behind her story? Do you?"

"Witches, vampires, and werewolves don't exist, Reverend.

They're just archetypes, things people have used to communicate complicated emotions and events. I want to know the facts behind the Witch. I want to know how she became, how she evolved. Because once I understand the facts, the truths of who she is become evident."

The Reverend gave her an appreciative glance and nodded. "You're a very interesting young woman, Moira Clarke. Come by after breakfast tomorrow. I think I know exactly what you need."

Moira nodded and said she would. Reverend Hopkins wished her a good evening and walked alone toward a cluster of houses in the nearby cul-de-sac.

The shadows of the parking lot settled around her like a blanket weighted with the last of winter's chill, and Moira wrapped her hands around her shoulders. The weather was so strange. "Of course. This is Minnesota," Rachel would tell her, and then change the subject. But there was something different about the temperature and the air. It was feverish. Hot in the days and cold in the evenings, as if the world around her was sick.

Moira shook her head. It was pointless to dwell on it. Control what you can control, she told herself before looking up to the filling moon, getting in her car, and driving back to the motel.

Chapter Four

The next morning, Moira felt as if she hadn't slept—weak, drained, and like somebody poured glue into her eyes. Her mind was slower than usual. It was only about fifteen feet from the bed to the bathroom, and she bumped into at least three different things, including knocking her hipbone into the bathroom doorknob.

A hot shower should smooth the edge off the tiredness.

Steam quickly filled the little bathroom, and Moira felt suddenly aware of her surroundings. Her ears perked and she held still, a rabbit sensing a predator hidden in the trees. The lack of windows told her it was silly to feel as if she were being watched, yet the tickle of eyes on her back persisted, even after she wrapped a towel around herself and checked that the drapes were drawn and the door locked.

She inspected everything. The soap dish wasn't a hidden camera, the hair dryer was not a listening device, and the light was just a bare bulb. Just to be thorough, she stood on the toilet and shined her phone into the vent. It was empty save for the lines of lint trapped in its metal fins.

Her phone buzzed. A text from Dani with a winking emoji read: *What're u wearing?*

She smiled and sat down on the toilet seat. *Off to church. Got my red robes and white bonnet.*

A moment later: *LOL. Tell jesus i'll fight him if he touches u. I know his abs r just 4 show.*

Moira smiled, tossed her phone onto the bed, and jumped into the shower unable to shake the sense of eyes hovering over her.

The sunshine prickled on the skin of her neck, forecasting a hot spring day even though the scent of the north wind still carried the tang of snow.

A blue pickup truck idled near her car. Its driver exited the office, carrying a black toolbox. He was older, at least fifty, dressed in dirty blue overalls that stretched around his beer belly, worn boots with more paint on them than leather, and a black cap with a fishhook on the brim. Despite his beard, Moira could tell by how his lips worked in a circle that he was chewing on the inside of his cheek with agitation. Something about him seemed familiar.

The pit of her stomach squeezed a warning.

"You must be the young lady Rev Hopkins is helping," he said when he found her staring. "Amanda, right?"

"Moira," she corrected. "Nice to meet you."

He nodded and leaned against the tailgate of his truck, trying to appear relaxed. "So you're staying here long? A few days, maybe?"

"Maybe." She brushed the tickle of an insect off of her wrist.

"Lot of history in this town. Might take you a while to get through it all."

She opened her car door and tossed her bag into the passenger seat. "Right. Well, I should probably get started."

"Yeah, sounds about right. I've got a full day myself." He nodded toward his truck. "Say, why don't you hop in, and I'll give you a ride to the church. No sense in wasting your fuel while I'm headed that way."

She didn't like that he knew where she was going. "I'm good. Thank you." Steel teeth bit into her thumb as she squeezed the key.

His complexion darkened with a scowl. Sunburned skin turned a shade of brownish purple in the shadow of a white pine. "Nah. Abrams is a friendly town." He bit down on the word friendly. "Taking care of each other is something we do. Come on, I insist. I just need to move stuff around." His door opened with a rusty squawk; things rattled out. He dove for them, fumbling and swearing. From where she stood, Moira saw oily orange rags, a box overflowing with empty beer cans, a coil of rope, a white running shoe crammed under boxes of garbage, and a lever action rifle sitting on the back seat.

Moira said, "Thanks, I better go!" In one well-practiced motion, she was in the car with the engine started and the gear shifter already in reverse. She backed up far enough to see him through her windshield just as he picked up the roll of duct tape that had fallen out of his truck.

He called something to her as she pulled away, but she was already running the stop sign on her way to town.

She took a roundabout route through town, exploring much of Abrams inside of an hour. Down the road and past the water treatment facility, sat the brownstone high school with its multiple baseball fields and a recently constructed football field with a tarmac running track. Farther down, the elementary school and its brightly colored playgrounds greeted passersby with a sign covered in painted handprints, "Abrams K-5 Elementary Welcomes You!"

A side street led to an area of subdivision housing with two-tone houses pained the same brown and cream. The end of that road opened to the parking lot of the Abrams Event and Community Center. Moira gave the folks in the lot a friendly wave as she turned around and drove toward the Vast Manufacturing building and the main street leading back to the heart of Abrams. Once on the road to the church, she rolled past the clinic, a tall brick apartment complex, and an electrical station. Taking a left on a county road brought her to a public storage facility painted in a gaudy orange.

Overall, she considered Abrams to be a cute town. Houses had interesting architecture and expansive yards—some surprisingly lush, considering the drought. The main street businesses were quaint, and the roads well maintained. Her only criticism was the unpleasant and languid tang of manure in the air. She never liked it as a young girl and had not seemed to grow out of it.

Moira reached the church and opted for breakfast from her purse: a dense protein bar with chocolate the consistency of sand. The parking lot was empty save for one other car, yet she made sure she parked under one of the security lights. While she didn't have any notions of staying there past dark, she wasn't about to park in a place where someone driving a blue truck could jump out of the shadows and grab her.

Finished chewing, she slung her bag onto her back, put her keys and pepper spray into her pockets, and headed inside.

Reverend Hopkins was a completely different person from the night before. Physically, nothing had changed other than the absence of shadow. He was the same thin man with sunken eyes and a light complexion but without the intimidation she experienced the night before.

"Moira!" He walked up to her with a quick smile and an extended hand. "I'm so glad to see you again. How was your morning? Was the motel comfortable enough for you?"

His hand felt warm and soft in hers. She felt no nausea or anxiety, smelled nothing strange or sour. He was smiling, warm, kind. Worse, there was something almost charming about him, in a public figure sort of way. "Yeah... um, yes. Yes. It's been very comfortable. Thank you."

"Rebecca takes pride in our little stop, even though Abrams isn't exactly a roaring tourist destination. The community does what it can to keep her afloat. No doubt you saw people setting up chairs, running lights, and such on your way here. All of them are volunteers for our spring dance. They take time out of their week to help make our celebrations seem bigger than what our humble town can provide. That's something we truly pride ourselves in, the power of community. We can truly work miracles when we pull together to do what is necessary to take care of one another." He turned to the altar. "With His help, of course."

"Of course." Moira smiled, hoping she wasn't about to have a conversation about conversion.

"Come this way. Let me show you where we keep our history."

Reverend Hopkins led her past the pews, through the door opposite his office, and down a set of carpeted stairs that led into a dusty sub-basement lit only by golden sunlight from frosted windows.

"Please forgive the state of the place. The previous town historian passed away four months ago. She used to keep the dust down and the files cleaned. The Lord didn't see fit to instill in me the same exuberance for cleanliness as he gave her."

"It's next to godliness, right?"

If the Reverend heard her joke or found it amusing, he made no indication.

The wooden door at the end of the hallway opened with a quick squeak. Inside, steel shelving units sat in perfectly arranged rows, each stacked with banker's boxes labeled with years and different ranges of letters spanning the alphabet. Boxes and fat manila envelopes had been arranged by year. Plat maps with fading blue ink dangled from their corners by hooks screwed into the wall. A larger map, one of the entire town of Abrams, hung by pins to a corkboard and displayed prominently above a resin table with fat three-ring binders stacked next to a brass lamp with a green shade. Running along the ceiling were old aerial pictures of farms, their barns and silos carefully arranged around tall houses.

Hopkins folded his hands behind his back and nodded proudly. "Here it is. There isn't much history in Abrams. Certainly not as much as pioneer towns. But we like to think the quality of our community trumps the quantity of its years."

"Wow," she said. "I wasn't expecting it to be so—"

"Organized?"

She stumbled over her words, finally saying, "I hope that doesn't sound insulting."

"Oh, don't let the illusion trick you. Boxes are easy to label with tape and markers. What's inside could be an absolute mess."

Moira gave an involuntary chuckle. "I know exactly what you mean. My grandmother had shoe boxes of photographs stacked in her attic for decades. It took me all summer to arrange them by year and put her favorite ones in albums." When she considered it, the little closet held nearly as much about Abrams as Rachel's attic and basement had about their family. Her inner project manager started asking questions. "Is this everything? All the history since the beginning of Abrams?"

"As far as I know. Though I haven't cataloged everything."

Moira let her backpack slip off to one shoulder. "How about the records kept in public offices? Mortgages, divorces, birth certificates?"

"Everything that wouldn't be considered invasions of privacy are here. Anything else would be with the county records." Hopkins' angular features sharpened as his lips pursed. "Though I don't see how birth certificates and such would help you study this witch."

Moira nodded and assured him they didn't. "I just want to be thorough. If I run into something that suggests the Witch might be an actual person who lived in Abrams, I may go looking, but I'm not diving into people's private lives without permission."

Hopkins raised an eyebrow. "Even though you are diving into the private lives of Abrams by searching through this?"

Moira considered that. He was right. She was. "But if it was something you felt strongly against, I doubt you'd have brought me here and given me permission to look."

"Quite right," he said, hands folded at his waist. "I have a brief meeting with a few parishioners before lunch with the mayor." He gave her a shrug. "Seems like now is as good a time as any for you to ply your trade. I'll leave you to it. Don't worry about locking the door. I'll check on it before I leave."

"Thank you." Moira breathed in the musty air with a smile. Her fingertips sang with the anticipation of flipping through old pages and dusty photos. Part of her wished she hadn't worn her contacts, since they dry out so easily when she's reading, but she could just trash them and throw on her glasses in a pinch.

She surveyed the room. It would take her two, maybe three days to skim through all the boxes and narrow them down to pertinent information. Another two or three to make her way through those stories she considered relevant. Maybe a few more to go through what she skimmed past. She could easily be through it in a week. If she worked long hours, she could probably cut it down to five days. The thought of thumbing through history, secrets, and the stories of a strange town made gave her a rush of anticipation.

Before he reached the end of the hallway, Moira called out, "Excuse me, Reverend Hopkins." He stopped. "I understand this town has had some unfortunate events take place in its history, and I want to assure you that my goal isn't to glorify the negatives. I want to focus on what's made Abrams Abrams, not what has made it a, uh—"

"A cursed town?" Hopkins nodded toward her. "Like you said, Moira, if I had any sign that you weren't the right person to illuminate Abrams, I would have never unlocked that door."

Moira dove into the files. By the time the Reverend stepped out for lunch, she was through an entire shelf of old newspaper clippings, pictures, plot maps, heirloom diaries, and property documents. When he came back, she was through another. At two o'clock she took a quick break to assess her work. She'd taken close to one hundred snapshots with her phone and twenty full pages of handwritten notes.

Apparently, the story of the Abrams Witch originated with a young woman named Korrine or Karina or Korey—it was hard to tell from ancient handwriting—who supposedly went mad, ran into the woods to mate with wolves and consort with demons, and was ultimately called into the service of Satan himself, leaving behind a grieving husband and a shocked and terrified community. It sounded a lot like a horror movie trope. What bothered Moira the most was the lack of variation to the stories. There was eerie uniformity to each tale, as if the few people in Abrams who wrote about the woman, the 'Witch' kept the same journal.

Nothing else she found spoke of the Witch's origin, only her existence. Everything in the records between the 1920s and 1940s related accounts after the Witch was already rumored to haunt the Abrams woods. Diaries and stories mentioned farm blight and diseases blamed on the woman's angry spirit, which could only be appeased by sacrificing a ewe within the first month of spring. From there to the early 1980s, the Witch became the hyper-misogynist scapegoat for miscarriages, equipment failure, an increase in the wolf population, livestock disease, crop death, blizzards, a freak tornado, brush fires, impotence, lightning strikes, strong-willed women who voted without consulting their husbands, a lesbian, cousins caught fornicating in a barn, two reports of rickets, and three cases of rabies. There were even spells that could summon the Witch. Though Moira doubted many people gathered the 'heel of a jackal' and the 'thumb of a walrus'.

By mid-afternoon, her backside had become so sore, she pulled off her hoodie and used it as a cushion. The t-shirt Dani lent her but forgot to take back still smelled like vanilla and rose. Sweaty and caked with dust, Moira decided she spent enough of the day doing serious searching. Besides, she was eager to take her notes and pictures back to the motel and look more closely at the history of Abrams.

As she lifted a box overhead and returned it to its shelf, she caught the muffled metallic sound of Reverend Hopkins' voice coming through a metal vent. She wasn't one to eavesdrop, but the weirdness of this town had her curiosity practically alight, so she climbed up on a shelf and leaned her ear as close to the vent as she could.

"Like I told you, Matthew. The Lord will provide."

"I'm running on fumes. It's been almost ten goddamned years since you fucked up. You know what's happened? Everything's died. My farm is dying, Dan. We need to do something soon."

"If my memory serves, it was you and your impatience who fucked up, Matthew! And mind the blasphemy. As I said, the Lord will provide for us. In *time*."

"Fuck time, Dan! My seed molded. Half my yield was dust last season and the year before was the same. It's gotten nothing but worse and worse. You said last fall that this year was going to solve everything."

"And it will."

"When? When, Dan! This shit's on you and your brother. I've been you and your brother's bitch for almost forty years. Forty fucking years! When do I get mine? When do I get my piece of the pie?"

"Haven't we made you wealthy? Through all the drinking, the sloth, the hunting, and the womanizing, haven't you prospered?" The Reverend's footsteps crossed his office. Moira had to strain to listen. "Of those forty fucking years, Matthew, how many have been successful? Give it time." He bit off each word. "Remember that this too shall pass. Everything is going according to His will. His plan. Once our work is done, things will return to the way they used to be." There were more footsteps and mumbles she couldn't hear clearly. It ended with the *thunk* of a closing door.

Moira waited for thirty seconds of silence before lowering herself down.

Who talks to a pastor like that? And what were they doing to make themselves wealthy? It seemed out-of-character for a pastor to focus on generating wealth. Unless, of course, they were up to something villainous. What was going on in this town?

A flash of shadow crossed the wall in front of her.

Moira spun. "Hello?"

There was no one down the gray hallway when she looked.

She found she could see beyond the doorway if she stayed near the shelf with the Ms and Ns and faced the hall. Everything was silent for minutes, and she had trouble focusing on her task. It was her own fault for her sudden paranoia. If she hadn't been nosy, then she wouldn't be creeped out by the shadow of a person or bird moving in front of the window. Because that's all it was, just a shadow from outside. She repeated this to herself while she examined folders of plot maps and seed inventories; it did nothing to ease the feeling she was being watched from the shadows.

Inside a box from the 1980s, she found an empty folder for Celeste Martin. The rest were mostly obituaries, old deeds and permits, along with what appeared to be clippings and pictures of people considered local celebrities: sports players who went on to famous colleges, a couple of young men who served in state government, and a blue-ribbon Best Pie Award. Nothing related to the Witch.

She swore at her growing impatience, shoved that box back onto the shelf, and grabbed another. C through G.

A folder fell out when she lifted the lid. Gardiner, Veronica. She wiggled it into its place and began thumbing through the other folders from the beginning, freezing when another shadow passed through the room.

The door at the end of the hall echoed a metallic click.

"Hello?" Moira called as she slid the folder into her backpack, then closed her fingers around the pepper spray.

The faint breeze from the ventilation that spun motes of dust into the rays of melancholy sunlight made the only reply.

It was time to leave. She wouldn't be able to focus like this. Moira zipped up her backpack, put the box back on the shelf, slipped her hoodie on, gripped the pepper spray in her front shirt pocket, and stepped into the hallway. From what she could tell, she was alone with the mustiness of old cardboard, the faint scent of cigarettes, and the hollow, tunnel-like fullness in her ear. There were no other doors that someone could have cracked open, and the hazy frost coating obscured the windows enough that nobody could look inside. Yet again, there was no shaking the sensation of eyes bearing down on her, appraising her like a wolf stalking a fawn through tall grass. Someone else had been in the hallway. She was sure of it.

Hair on her neck and arms raised atop her gooseflesh. With wide, shifting eyes, Moira headed toward the end of the hallway, keenly aware of the shadows widening at the end of the hall where the doors sat recessed. She pressed her shoulder against the wall, dragging it quietly along the paint, finger tickling the button on of the pepper spray.

"Hello?" she whispered, then swallowed, moistening her tight throat. "Hello?" she said louder.

Again, no response. A chill washed over her like she stepped under a waterfall. Now she was positive something was watching her.

Shadows from within the storage room curled and crawled against the walls and ceiling behind her, following her every step.

Four or five more tentative steps turned into a dozen. Two dozen. After thirty steps, she hadn't made any headway. It was impossible for the hallway to be growing longer, stretching out imperceptibly in front of her, but that's exactly what was happening. Either that, or the floor became a giant treadmill. Yet, she was still passing by windows. The same four windows glowed with afternoon sun. She counted them as she passed. One, two. She stopped and appraised everything around her. There were two more windows. Two more before the shadows, before the eyes and teeth hiding just around the corner. Before the blood and pain.

Get a grip, she told herself. Lingering terror sat heavy in her jaw, and she bit it down. Her next few steps didn't have the confidence or command she desperately tried to instill within herself, but the hallway stopped stretching, the windows still held their places in the wall. Three, four. As she concentrated on those, the surreal feeling of her essence being pulled forward and away from the rest of her lessened. The shadows in the doorway didn't eat her. There was no attack.

A dark blue pocket folder and a little red box waited for her on the floor in front of the door.

Moira shoved the door open until it slammed against its stopper, a crunching echo that reverberated through the vacant church like a dog's bark. "Hello?" she yelled to the empty pews and lonely golden glow from the windows. Not even the Reverend stepped out of his office at her call.

She knelt and opened the box. Inside was a leather-bound journal with a faded pentagram etched into the cover with permanent marker, a small cassette tape, and an older voice recorder. She hadn't seen an analog one in years. It reminded her of the cassette player in her great-grandmother's house.

There was a tape inside. Moira pushed the play button.

A young woman's voice, stern and determined, spoke.

My name is Gogo Jocelyn Ylva. Gloria to you knobs. If you're hearing this, then I'm right. There's a curse in this town, and it doesn't have anything to do with any goddamn witch. Whatever it is, it's evil. It's in the woods, and it's the reason they've been secretly killing people in Abrams.

Chapter Five

The next day, Moira returned to the church to speak with Reverend Hopkins about the storage room and the Gogo's box. Gloria Ylva was another missing child. From what Moira pieced together, she was a sick girl who disappeared from the woods around Abrams in the spring of 1998. The police recovered her clothes, but her body had never been found.

Moira's stomach trembled with the thought of what may have happened.

Reverend Hopkins was in the middle of a fiery sermon when Moira stepped through the open doors of the church. Three large oscillating fans stirred the sweltering air and blew her hair into her eyes. It was hotter inside than outside, and the dung-scented humidity within made her skin damp and uncomfortable. Considering how many people packed in the pews and stood along the walls, she preferred to not think about where the moisture came from.

She found a spot to stand in the back near the doors. A young man next to her nodded politely and turned his attention back to sweating Reverend Hopkins and his message of sacrifice.

"… the hand that provides is the same had who holds back the rains. Yet those same hands pour out bounties of goodwill and reward for our sacrifices. We should not question from where these bounties come but kiss the fingers of the hands who provide it. We do not question how the Lord supplies our salvation, we merely humble ourselves before His glory and wisdom and continue to sacrifice to earn his reward. Sow and reap…"

A sudden pain lanced through Moira's skull between her right eye and the bridge of her nose and brought with it a steady ringing which grew louder and louder, until she could barely continue paying attention as the sermon reached a crescendo. She'd never been prone to headaches, especially ones so sudden, and the nausea and dizziness soon had her jamming her thumb and forefinger into the corners of her eyes. Her back bounced against the wall and Hopkins' voice dampened to a distortion of warbling nonsense and reverberations. A moment later, she felt a pop in her sinuses. The tickle of fluid warned her in time to catch the rush of blood pouring out of her nose in her palm.

Moira wobbled away from the sermon and stumbled toward the restrooms. Her senses returned enough for her to elbow open the restroom door and rush over to the sink. First, she washed her hands. Then, she bunched her hair into her fist, pulled it aside, and let the blood drip freely into the sink until the tickle in her sinuses eased and the flow slowed. The paper towel she dabbed at her upper lip was rough and scratchy, and it left her skin pink and irritated when she finished wiping away the blood. She turned the faucet's handle slowly, making sure not to splash, and cupped her hand under the cool water, spreading it around to clean the ceramic basin.

With the last traces of crimson gurgling down the drain, a sudden burn tickled her nostrils. She barely had enough time to grab a handful of towels and sneeze into them. She groaned at the embarrassing thought of spraying blood all over herself and the countertop.

Once she was sure there wasn't a follow up sneeze coming, Moira pulled her hands away and inspected the towels.

A dark red and purple blob of clotted blood rested in the center of a spray of scarlet. It was about the size of a dime, bigger than she expected something coming out of her nose to be.

"Ew," she said. Then she looked closer.

The clot moved.

Purple pulsed within the red like a shimmering caterpillar wriggling within its translucent cocoon. The clot bulged and grew to twice its size. Crimson fluid sweat and bubbled off the surface and the clot's inner core pressed outward until it finally split open like a ripped balloon and a wheel of silky wings unfurled from within.

Moira gaped. They weren't wings; they were petals. Delicate petals in the shape of hearts, purple with blood red rings at their centers. It was a flower. A pansy.

The door opened. An older woman wearing a cantaloupe orange

dress and her hair in a perfect bun jumped when she saw Moira hovering over the sink. "Oh! Hello. Are you alright, dear?"

Moira tipped her hands away, hiding the flower. She smiled at the woman. "Just a nosebleed. It's the dry air, I think."

"I understand. My husband has the same problem in winter." She gave Moira a kind nod and stepped into the stall, closing the door behind her.

Moira turned her attention back to the bloody towel. The flower, what she thought was a flower, gone. In its place was merely the impression of a flower in the slowly spreading blood. She held it closer to the light, tipping her palms this way and that, trying to recreate the illusion. All she conjured was a sense of foolishness.

With a huff and a moment of self-admonition against letting her imagination get away from her, Moira cleaned up her mess and left the bathroom.

She drove back to the motel for a nap and ibuprofen, but she couldn't relax. To distract herself from the dull throbbing in her face, she spent her entire day going through Gloria Ylva's diaries, listening to her voice recordings, and arranging her pictures into a cohesive story so she could better understand what happened and why Gloria disappeared. Questions fired from all corners of her mind. Who left the box? Why did they leave it for her? Could they have been hiding it this whole time? What kind of person would hide this evidence for over two decades? If there was anything, *anything*, that suggested a connection to missing persons or murders, she was going to take it to

Chief Lake, regardless of how repugnant she found him to be.

That was something else she needed to explore. Of the few Abrams people she'd interacted with, why did she have such a visceral reaction to Reverend Hopkins, Chief Lake, and the man in the blue truck? What is something subconscious? What was she not seeing?

She studied the pictures of Gloria. Gogo. Moira liked that name. It suited her, too. Outside of Halloween, there weren't many goth kids at her high school, so she didn't know when the fashion died out. Whenever it was, it was certainly alive when Gloria's pictures were taken.

In most pictures, Gloria wore heavy white makeup, black lipstick and eyeliner, and muted red eyeshadow that made her look either constantly tired or like she just finished crying. She had long hair that was both red and black. A spiked leather collar ringed her neck. In every photo, she wore blacks and reds trimmed with steel and lace. Sometimes it was leather, others it was velvet. Moira wondered if the girl ever smiled.

There was another picture. One small enough for a wallet. It was of Gloria when she was much younger. Her hair was short, and she wore thick glasses. Her expression was slack and sad. Moira didn't have to wonder why. Children were often cruel to people who looked different. And for all accounts, Gloria looked like any young girl. She was pretty, with full lips and deep, coffee brown eyes. But there was no ignoring the heart-shaped birthmark, purple and angry, puckered over her left eye like a patch.

Moira admitted she would have worn the makeup, too.

With everything spread out on the bed, she took a drink of beer and an aggressive bite of pizza. Things were coming together. Dates were matching, pictures and loose pages were falling into order. Her thumb hovered over the play button on the voice recorder.

She decide to take a break before playing it. Eager energy buzzed in her neck and shoulders after the morning's headache and nosebleed, so she bought herself a rare treat. It was waiting for her in her purse.

Beer in hand, Moira stepped into the shadows behind the motel.

She lit the cigarette with a match, blew a lungful of smoke into the woods behind, and almost immediately felt dizzy, a little sick, and wonderfully anxious. It was her first cigarette in four years. Smoking never grew into a teenage addiction for her, it was more of a rebellious curiosity. She kind of liked it, but it wasn't a habit she wanted to fall into. This one was purely reactionary. The scent of smoke in the hallway and all over Gloria's journals clicked a button inside her stomach, and she bought a pack at the liquor store.

Smoking in the dark like a teenager hiding it from her parents eased her anxiety about Abrams, and eating half a pepperoni pizza brightened what was an already troubled day. But all of it wasn't enough. A perplexing hunger lingered from the moment she picked up Gloria's things. A throbbing that started at her stomach and radiated to her lower back, around her hips, and up to her breasts. It didn't help that every time she squeezed her eyes against the gnawing, she thought of Dani. Masturbating in the shower took the edge off, but the ache was still alive in her blood.

Her phone vibrated. "Speak of the devil…" She answered it. "What's shakin', bacon?"

"Hey! How are you?" Dani replied.

Something was off. "Good. How about you? You sound tired."

A sudden movement from the woods stole her attention. She waited, silent.

"I had a weird day at work. People are just… gross. I can't wait until we graduate, and I'll never have to work another weekend again."

Moira kept her eyes on the wall of year-old brown leaves and dried vines in front of her, waiting for her eyes to adjust to the darkness, until the orange halo of light from the parking lot behind her was barely a glow in her periphery. "Tell me about it."

Dani talked about her day. She worked at a clothing shop at the local mall and hated every minute. It was understandable. Dani was one of the smartest women Moira knew, destined to be a doctor or an extremely expensive lawyer, not working the floor in retail for a manager who spent most of his day glued to his phone rather than supervising his subordinates.

While Dani talked, Moira sneaked closer to the trees, feet crunching along dry ground. A chill breeze blew parallel to the wall of dead forest. Something else shuffled within the leaves. She forced her eyes to remain locked on that single spot in the darkness and stepped closer and closer until she felt the tickle of a dry leaf caress her forehead and the layers of forest behind the leaves came into focus.

Two little glowing spots flickered in and out of the darkness.

A single word blew along the wind.

Moira

Her heart hammered into the back of her throat as an owl hooted inches from her face.

"Jiminy fucking crickets!" Moira let the air explode from her lungs.

"Holy shit!" Dani exclaimed. "Are you okay?"

Heart still racing, Moira managed a shaky laugh. "I'm fine, fine. Did you hear that? Jesus. There's an owl staring right at me."

"Did you hand it the phone? That was loud." Dani chuckled. "You better be careful. You're in another world now. The animals there are crazy. They're taught forest kung fu when they're babies."

The owl clicked and ruffled its feathers on the same branch, staying a foot beyond the trees and just below eye level. "I'm going to hold still and try to get a picture when we hang up."

"I can hang up if you want. You can call back right after."

"Nah. I'm all shaky and bluh, right now. Probably couldn't take a good picture. Keep talking. I like talking to you."

That usually made Dani smile.

She could tell when Dani smiled on the phone by the way she breathed through her teeth. She wasn't smiling. "Did you try calling me earlier? From another phone, I mean. Maybe from the motel?"

Odd. "No. This is the first time I've used my phone for anything other than taking pictures of papers today."

"Somebody called me from there. There was no number. It just said Abrams."

"Did you answer it?"

Dani sounded worried. "Yeah. It was just whispering. You know how you're trying to tune in to a radio station, and the closer you get, the more you can kind of hear the station, but not really?" Her voice lowered to a near whisper. "I thought I heard it say my name."

"The whispers said your name?" Moira swallowed. "Creepy."

"Yeah. And normally I don't think that would bother me, but it made me feel…" She breathed into the phone twice, gathering herself. "It was scary, you know. Eerie."

Moira took another sip of beer and a drag on her cigarette. A sudden anger clawed at her cheekbone. "I think I have an idea what that's about."

"You do?"

Moira explained to her about the email she received before leaving for Abrams. "There's this super creepy guy here who tried to convince me to get into his truck this morning. Then I heard him cursing out Reverend Hopkins about something. If there's any shit head with access to the church's computer, it's him. I mean, how do you confuse my name with 'Amanda'?"

"Who's Amanda?"

"He was so full of shit. I bet if I ask around, I'll find out he's the local pervert or something. Anyway, I'm pretty sure I put your contact info in my original email. That has to be how he got your number. And he's probably the same asshole who sent that messed up email telling me to stay out of town! Ugh! I should've guessed."

Dani made a disgusted noise. "What a freak. Ick! You should've taken Mick."

"How ridiculous would I look wearing a dagger on my hip?"

"There are witches there. Seems like a perfect place to be carrying around a sword or a magic wand."

Moira laughed. "I suppose. Maybe she'd show up and just tell me why she's here. Why her? Of all things and monsters this town could have picked, why a witch? Why not a demon or a devil or some other monster? It's not like is has some kind of historical link to Salem or paganism. Well, that last part I'm not positive about. Abrams' history is still a very boring mystery to me."

"You know who might know?" Dani teased. "Hooty the owl."

"The owl?"

"Yeah! Don't witches have owls and black cats and stuff? Familiars that do their bidding?" She added, "You should ask," in a sing-song voice.

It was silly, but Moira was enjoying the conversation and didn't want Dani to hang up. "Okay. I'll ask Hooty. Hooty, tell me about the Abrams Witch."

The owl said nothing.

Dani offered, "You should be more grandiose with it. Sound all stern and powerful and huffy or something." She dropped her voice an octave. "Blah! Reveal thyself, witch! Moira the Mighty demands an audience."

Giggling, Moira spread her arms and said, "Speak to me, oh frightening witch of the Abrams woods. Show yourself, oh creature of the night, and tell me all your spooky secrets!" She paused, slowly returning her phone to her ear while listening to the rustle of wind ferry her echo through the branches.

"Anything?" Dani asked after a few seconds.

"No. Looks like I'll have to go back to reading."

"Damn the bad luck."

They talked longer, changing the subject to Gogo's journals and Dani's questions for Jenny Lake, and joking around to extend the call and hear each other's voices.

It was coming upon midnight when Dani said, "So, I have to get up early. I want to keep talking because, um, there's been some stuff on my mind that I want to talk to you about. I just don't... I don't want to do it over the phone."

"Yeah? What kind of stuff?"

"Just stuff." Dani was smiling now. "Maybe we can talk about it when you get back? I thought that we'd get dressed up and go somewhere nice. When was the last time we got real dolled up?"

"Freshmen year." There was an unspoken party tradition on the weekend before finals and the weekend after the first week of finals finished. "Yeah. We should do something. Together." Her throat dried. "I want to talk about stuff." She hoped Dani noticed the emotion in her voice.

She did. "Me too."

Five minutes later, Moira ended the call with a hopeful smile and clicked on her camera's light. "Alright, you nosey noserton. Gimme a smile."

She aimed the phone into the woods. Her phone flickered. The screen went black.

A figure moved in the shadows. Something darker than the moonless night and larger than an owl.

Another movement. Then another. Sounds wheezed past the trees. Snarls. Growls and hissing. From the center of the black, darkness grew outward. Thin tendrils like empty veins wiggled through the trees as if the night tore away from the sky and pressed outward at her.

It was a trick of the light. Staring too hard caused her vision to dance. It wasn't real. It couldn't be real.

Moira squeezed her eyes shut. That just made it worse. She still saw them through her eyelids. And the noises they made were familiar, horrifying gurgles like infants choking on their spit.

The sounds from her dream of Celeste Martin in the circle.

The owl hooted from behind her. A patch of something rough and sharp reached out and dragged itself across her skin.

Moira pulled herself away, dropping her bottle and leaping backward. She sprinted around the corner, not looking back until she reached the patch of wildflowers growing against the outside wall of her room and the darkness dispersed by the glow from the parking lot lights. Behind her, the shadows of the forest slithered back into the dark.

She burst through her room door and slammed it shut. Her heart hammered. All she could hear was the pressure of her blood squeezing into her ears. She barricaded the door with a padded chair and an empty dresser.

She waited in the middle of the room as silence crept in.

When nothing burst through the door or pressed its face against the window, Moira put her arms at her side and tensed her shoulders, imagining her sudden fright melting away.

Dani was right. She was in another world. Another world populated by creepy owls, giant deer, and where the wind played mind tricks to trap you long enough for the poison plants to leave pink burns all over your arm. Even her grandmother's home, a little hobby farm a few miles from town, didn't have the wildness of Abrams. There were no thick woods, wild animals avoided nearby farm equipment, and the marsh collected more birds than mammals. Again, she just let her imagination run away.

She ran her arm under the cold bathroom tap until her skin was numb. At least she'd find out if she was allergic to poison ivy by morning.

Determined to prove there was no monster outside waiting for her, Moira slid the furniture away from the door and stepped back into the night, phone flashlight guiding her around the corner of her building. She hadn't noticed the wildflowers before. Tufts of orange, white, and purple stuck out of half-closed calyxes like colorful squinting eyes peering at her from a bed of dead grass.

It was curious, she thought, how a knee-high bush of wildflowers could grow and bloom in the shadiest area of a building during one of the worst droughts in state history. Perhaps Becky had a green thumb?

The crunching of tires beyond the trees caught her attention. Her flashlight wasn't bright enough to illuminate the road, but from what little light came from the small parking lot, Moira just made out the faint outline of a truck, headlights off, inching away before it gunned its engine and drove off.

The Howling

1

My name is Gogo Jocelyn Ylva. Gloria to you knobs. If you're hearing this, then I'm right. There's a curse in this town, and it doesn't have anything to do with any goddamn witch. Whatever it is, it's evil. It's in the woods, and it's the reason they've been secretly killing people in Abrams.

I don't want to sound dramatic, but if you're listening to this, they found me and they killed me, too. I just hope I went down fighting and not from this fucking tumor.

I'm hiding this tape with the rest of my journals and diaries and notes, just in case somebody out there can stop this weird-ass cult in Abrams. And don't think I'm crazy. I'm not crazy. This isn't some sort of new-age, X-Files, southern-educated wacko, Satanic panic, Christopher Lee movie, Baby Boomer conspiracy theory bullshit. This is the real thing. Real people are dead.

I don't know who I can trust. Brittni is on her way to college. Dez is a burnout. Staci moved away last year and hasn't called since. My dad might be involved, and I don't know if my mom can handle the truth.

Whoever you are, I'm sorry I'm dumping this on you, but you need to read everything. Go through my notes. But don't stay to figure this shit out on your own. Get out of town. Run! Go to the State Patrol, the FBI, the National Guard—anyone with guns and handcuffs. Save people. Even if you have to torch this place.

The recording squeaked. A girl's voice sang along with Mötley Crüe's "Home Sweet Home". Moira kept it running while she grabbed the first journal, careful not to let its loose leaves fall out of place. Considering how she came about the mysterious box, Moira felt a renewed commitment to uncovering Abrams' secrets. There was something harmonious about searching for folk stories and discovering what was essentially an oral telling of someone's tale. Wasn't that just like an old story, too? The girl finds the forbidden thing and becomes a cautionary tale?

Most papers had dates on them. Others were notes on random pieces of scrap. Sometimes the writing looked shaky and jagged as if she wrote on top of a washing machine on its spin cycle. At least Gogo had good penmanship. It was going to be difficult to read, but nothing she wasn't used to. However, she wasn't accustomed to the sense of intrusion tingling in her stomach. These were a person's personal journals—Gloria's innermost thoughts put to the page, possibly her hopes and fears. Smears of black ink left thumbprints in the margins. Thinned dots of black that warped the paper in spots may be her tears. Dusts of what could be makeup clung to the binding like memories refusing to be forgotten. It was intimate.

Thinking of that word, of Celeste Martin, made Moira shiver.

The idea of multiple unreported murders had Moira casting worried glances toward the door every few minutes. Did Gloria uncover something? And did she disappear because of it?

Moira opened the journal and read.

October 14, 1995

Dear Douchery,

I don't think Mr. Little has ever seen tits before. All the other girls say the same thing. He likes to make us stand in front of his desk and pull our papers closer to him, so we have to lean in to look at them. I caught him staring at the LADIES in History. Pervo.

Anywho, we're going to a farm party at the Miller's this weekend. Gonna get druuuuuunk. Have to watch out for Jillian's uncle Matt, though. I heard he slips girls sleeping pills in their drinks so he can fuck them easier. He's been nothing but nice to me, so I don't know. Now that I think about it, he gives off mad creepy vibes.

Be careful. Open your own beers, girls.

Jillian tells me her sister told her something about there being an old story about the Abrams Witch being seen on that farm in the 80s. Said she has a friend from the cities who knows how to conjure her or talk to her ghost or something. Real magic spells, not like fantasy book stuff. Real stuff. Like some X-files shit.

I'm totally summoning a demon to give me wishes.

December 18, 1995

Report: Cat farted, and it made mom puke eggnog all over the kitchen floor. Christmas came early.

January 25, 1996

Dear Dorkery,

You should see how freaked out the people in town are every time they hear the wolves howl. Good ol' Gertrude Bodeen and her half-idiot, half-yorkie spazzed out in the graveyard when she was visiting her sister. Again. You'd think with all the cool ghosts in there, she'd get the idea that her sister was hanging out with better company and didn't have time for her.

Anyways, she just about flew out of her diabetes socks when they howled. That old bat can haul ass when she needs to. Shows you just how bullshit her whole "You're a devil worshipper, Gloria Ylva, and I'll pray for you" crap is. If these good xtian idiots were really scared of Satan or witches, you'd figure a little ol' woof in the woods would be old hat. But nooooooooo. Hear one dog getting boned in the trees, and it's three seconds from a risk of heart attack and/or stroke.

Too bad the devil isn't real. He'd probably be cool to hang out with. I bet he likes wolves.

April 25, 1997

College day. Dez wanted us to just skip and get blazed in the graveyard, but Brittni and I decided that we wanted to actually visit a school or two. Mom wouldn't let us drive to Mankato—said it was too far—so that ruled out Iowa, too. But we went, anyway. We picked a Friday and made it a road trip under the pretense that I was staying over at her house, and she was staying with her cousin in Rochester. Easy win.

The drive took about a year and a day, but it was worth it. The campus is so beautiful. Nothing like the community colleges around here. Not that I want to learn welding or accounting, anyway. Mankato's got these huge hills and these old brownstone buildings that make it look like something out of a rich person's 1920s wet dream. I want to go there so bad.

The Professors we met were super nice and super smart. They have an English program where all they do is read and write. There are poetry classes and fiction classes and all of these other classes where there are only 10 students. And I don't have to wake up early. DO YOU HEAR ME? NOT. WAKE. UP. EARLY!!! These fucking headaches make it impossible to go to bed early enough to get up for school and feel my subhuman self.

I'm stressed. If I go there, I think I could be not stressed.

There was even this super beautiful older—not too old—woman there who must have been a former student or something visiting the campus with the group. She said she just liked to 'visit her old haunts'. She wasn't a teacher or anything. She was just there. Brit thought she was weird, but I liked her the instant I saw her. She didn't stare at the gob of shit on my face like everyone else.

She was a historian, or whatever. But she knew a BUNCH about witches and monsters and shit. She even knew about the Abrams Witch! Can you believe that? She bought me lunch and talked to me about how there might be witches everywhere and how they can be scary and beautiful at the same time. Gorgeous and horrifying—some leveled up girl power shit. I hope that someday there will be a surgery that can make me beautiful and horrifying instead of just horrifying.

But she was amazing! So easy to talk to. Not like mom. I didn't have to sit there and listen to her preach. She listened to me talk when I wanted to talk. I don't normally get diarrhea of the mouth, but I could have told her anything. I think I did. I can't remember. Weirdo Gogo showed up and just kept babbling on.

Anyway, she said that not all witches are bad and that maybe MAYBE they aren't evil at all. She said, 'Look at those lovely little gargoyles and grotesques on old churches and castles. They were put there to be so frightening that they scared demons away.' I asked her if God is so super powerful and devil-hating, then why would he need to have priests put monsters on his churches to scare away other monsters? She said something about wolves in sheep's clothing. Makes sense.

I think witches kill demons. I think they're the good guys. I want to be a witch. A REAL one.

July 25th, 1997

Dear Diarrhea,

Went to Ozzfest with Brittni, Staci, and Dez. Type O and Fear Factory were cool. Machine Head sucked. Ozzy's looking hot. Would've been funner in Somerset, but too many uptight bible thumpers sent it to the dome. Cheeseheads. Was glad for Dez's van since it gave us a place to crash. Don't have my license, so Dez only let me drive it for an hour outside the Cities. Pretty sure it doesn't go over 65. Think Brit gave a handy to an old guy for a bag of mostly stems and seeds and a cheap bottle of merlot. She argued with me over whether or not smoking actually opens up your lungs and is good for breathing. I used to run track, so I know it makes your lungs basically collapse.

Whatever. I had a good time with some awesome people. Abrams is such a backwater shitburg. I can't wait to leave. Brit wants to go to college together, but I don't know. My grades are bad and I'm a family embarrassment. Maybe if I started running again, I could get a scholarship. Or not. Sounds like work.

(No Date)

Ran for the first time in six months. I think I might be dying. My legs feel like bags of shattered glass and my lungs might be rusting from the inside. I submit this as scientific evidence that smoking does NOT open up your lungs and make you run faster or more efficiently. Dr. Gloria Ylva, reporting.

August 4, 1997

He touched me. That fucking pig cornered me in his little church office and stuck his hand up my dress and I'm NOT SUPPOSED TO TELL ANYONE?!?!? That fucking sicko and his beady little weirdo eyes in his scrawny little head and his bony freak fingers. FUCKYOUFUCKYOUFUCKYOU I swear to fucking god I'll kill him if he touches me again. I'll fucking kill him. Tear him apart. I'll cut him to pieces with scissors in his sleep and I don't care if I go to prison or to hell. I'll do more than just shove my fingernail into his other eye and kick him in the balls again. I. Will. MURDER. Him.

FUCKYOUFUCKYOUFUCKYOUFUCKYOUFUCKYOUFUCKYOU

Fuck you too, mom. You molester-enabling WENCH! Dad's the one related to him, so what's your excuse? Did you just marry into it being okay that your daughter is nearly molested by her uncle? WHAT'S WITH THIS TOWN'S OBSESSION WITH FAMILY SECRETS?!?

(No Date)

Mom still doesn't believe me. Says I exaggerated that he touches everyone the same way. She made me repeat it, over and over. But you know what, mom? He DOES touch other girls the same way. Millie Canby says he has a hidden camera in his office and in the bathroom so he can record us. THE FUCKING PERV RECORDS US. Mom says I can't say a word to anyone else or the Witch is going to take me into the woods and leave me, just like she does every year. Nobody believes in your stupid Witch mom.

But that got me thinking. Every year someone disappears. Every year. And everyone gets real quiet about it, like everyone knows. Even the way mom talks about the Witch is like she knows something. Everybody around town gets all whispery and shit about it. They keep talking about this witch like she's real. It's not like we didn't try contacting her with a ouija board and a seance. It was a real seance. We even used tarot cards Staci stole from her sister.

Nah. There is something more going on. There's more going on. And I know where Uncle Creep keeps all his old town records. Mom and dad are going to the Rockies for a week for a second honeymoon or some garbo. They don't know that I know how to get into that crawlspace.

Oh, and next time I'm in the church, I'm going to shit on the floor. Let him show the tape to anyone to prove I did it. That'll just show everyone he's got a camera in the ladies room.

(No Date)

Who was Celeste Martin? Inquiring minds want to know.

2

The things Gogo said and wrote made Moira uneasy. It was easy to brush off the allegations of a cult operating in Abrams. Sure, small, tight-knit communities with a single church and a decidedly conservative lifestyle could display cult-like behaviors to some. Towns like this were prone to containing echo chambers that regurgitated the ideologies of parents, grandparents, and town leaders. In her opinion, those kinds of places were harmless. What turned Moira's stomach were Gogo's accusations of abuse at the hands of her uncle, whom Moira presumed to be Reverend Hopkins.

Abuse wasn't something she had prepared for. Yes, there were old tales of people abusing people and blaming the devil or one of his agents—usually witches. But those were old tales, not ones where the abuser still held power and the abused no longer had her voice. And for her mother—her own mother—to insist Gogo forget the entire thing out of fear of a fictional character? Madness. Absolute fucking madness.

At least she had one certainty: Hopkins would never have left this box for her to find, not with these sorts of charges leveled against him.

Even with those accusations, she had to admit the academic in her found the story interesting. Heartbreaking and disgusting, if true. But interesting.

Keep your proximity, she reminded herself. Observe and record. Don't pass judgment.

Yet for all her personal declarations of impassivity, Moira spent the rest of her night tucked in her own sheets, the chair pushed firmly against the door, imagining a teenage girl quietly sobbing into her journal, the only thing that could give her any solace from an attacker that would go unpunished, possibly forever.

What would she do if everything Gogo said and wrote was true?

The next day, Moira couldn't shake the dark cloud of her memories as a lonely teenager.

For the year after her parents' accident, Moira locked herself in the little room in her grandmother's house and sunk into shadows and rough carpet. Rachel kept her distance, yet was always available for a little girl's screams, made herself a target for thrown pillows and stuffed animals, and had the softest arms to cry into. The following spring, though, Rachel practically dragged her out into the flower garden to help stick tulip bulbs in tiny holes and mow the lawn. When that wasn't enough to cool the angry fire in her throat, Rachel strung a hammock between her trees, dropped a stack of Nancy Drew books in Moira's arms, and locked the front door until she finished tending her herbs and vegetables, usually around mid-afternoon.

In the cooler months, they abandoned Rachel's hobby farm for a suburban apartment so Moira could continue going to the same school. Something about that change made her grandmother wilt, the leaves of her own flower closing around her. They would go on long walks in the fresh winter air until the moisture crystallized in their noses. Those seemed to help raise Rachel's spirits. Not long after, though, she would sink into her chair and wither. It wasn't until Moira was older that she understood Rachel had never properly mourned for her own dead daughter. She had to raise a terror of teenager, instead.

Being cooped up inside and away from anything quiet and green made them both restless. Moira hid herself in history books and social studies; Rachel adopted hundreds of potted plants from the local garden center. It wasn't the same. Everything felt too artificial, like air without wind or water that didn't splash when you hit it. Once she was old enough to drive, Moira suggested they move back to the farm, permanently.

After her shower, she texted Rachel to ask how she was, hoping the communication with her grandmother would give her something soothing to pass along to Gogo's spirit. All Rachel replied with was a silly message: Full moon soon. Be careful. Awoooo!

By 9AM, Moira felt restless. She determined she needed sunshine and people—even if they were decidedly strange people. So, with her arm slathered in cortisone, she walked the two miles into Abrams to experience the spring celebration Reverend Hopkins spoke about.

She spent her morning walking up and down the streets in the cool humidity. After several exploratory passes through the heart of Abrams, Moira concluded that small town gatherings and dances are just like they are in the movies. Flags hanged from every pole. Red, white, and blue bunting crisscrossed with blue and gold along the brick buildings. A huge banner suspended between the crosswalk lights—there were no stoplights in town—read 'Happy Abrams Spring Days!!! Brought to you by Abrams Area Elementary K-3' in massive crayon lettering. Wood barricades striped with orange and white paint closed off the street so children could safely scribble chalk drawings on the road and middle-aged women in cardigans could carry foil pans to the resin tables set up in the bank parking lot. In the narrow adjacent park, three old men crunched around the dry grass as they set up a tall counter with a faded 'Beer Garden' banner across the top. Across the street, in an empty space next to the pizza pub, sat a raised stage with large speakers and balloons. Pickup trucks loaded with heavy beams of wood and scaffolding creaked and puttered around the detour. She assumed a second stage was going up somewhere, but the trucks headed out of town. Probably scraps.

Gogo was right about there being a gloss of happiness in a town where people regularly went missing and blamed a fictional witch. The entire scene put out a very Stepford vibe.

Occasionally, Moira would catch someone eying her. She pretended to not notice, adjusting her ear buds as nonchalantly as possible to give the impression that she was in her own little world, but the moment she turned and caught their eye, they either turned away quickly or they gave her a wide, forced smile and went about their business. The fact they watched her made her skin crawl.

Listening to Gogo's voice diary wasn't helping. Every half mile or so, she needed to turn it off and absorb what she said. Sometimes Gogo read her own poetry. It wasn't the worst Moira had heard; definitely written by an angsty teenager with a fair degree of natural talent. Longer conversations had to do with an argument between her and Dez regarding Nu Metal being inferior to the New Wave of British Heavy Metal. Loud music wasn't her thing, but she respected Gogo's passion.

Sometimes Gogo made outright accusations that Reverend Hopkins, Chief Lake, and a farmer named Matthew Miller were all a part of a cult that sacrificed a person every year to ensure a bountiful harvest. That was something Moira had a hard time reconciling with the obvious drought and reports of poor harvests in both Abrams and the surrounding areas over the past six years. Nothing in the County's online records supported so many missing persons before or after Gogo's disappearance, yet there were still enough accidents and other disappearances in the 90s that could trigger a teenager's imagination. However, Gogo's earnestness gave Moira the chills. Worse, if Moira counted correctly, someone in Abrams went missing or had a fatal accident every other or every third spring. Gogo insisted that Chief Lake was covering it up. Whether or not she had proof remained to be seen. If she did, Moira decided she would take it to the county police when she was finished in Abrams. Gogo deserved that much.

How do you think they handled missing persons before computers? Everything got typed up in a smoky room, just like an Al Pacino movie. All Lake had to do was not type. And of course he wouldn't. Nobody wants their dirty laundry aired out in this town. Nobody wants to know about how the teachers touch the kids. Nobody wants to know about the alcoholics who beat the shit out of their wives. Nobody wants to know that shit. Because the moment one person's garbage gets dug through, then everyone else is going to protect their shit by letting other people's shit slip first.

The neighborhoods other side of the railroad tracks clearly enjoyed greater wealth. The houses were nicer than those on the downtown side; their stucco wasn't cracked. More than just a few lawns were free of weeds, though the grass still struggled. Every sprinkler was tap-tap-tapping arcs of water. Seemed like a waste of water for a nice-looking lawn. So many curtains moved just as she looked at them. An old man burying seeds and small vegetables leered at her until his wife slapped him on the shoulder with a hand towel and waved at Moira. Each car that passed her had at least one person who seemed to stare at her, though it was hard to tell in the sun's glare off the windshields.

Gogo's story only added to her already growing paranoia about this town.

She found a wooden bench in a small community park and sat in the shade of a nearby oak with tiny leaf buds on only half its branches and hid her face under the hood of her shirt.

I'm not trying to say the Witch isn't real. She is real. She is. I'm saying that she's not the problem. There is something else here. Something out in the woods near the Miller farm. Something that isn't right. I don't know if Celeste Martin found something or if something found her, but I don't believe for a second that she just disappeared. I don't even believe that Jenny Lake went nuts and killed her kid. That poor girl was messed up to begin with, thanks to her dad, but it wasn't like she was insane. Nobody I talked to said anything bad about her, they were just sad about her. At least that's what it they made it look like. But who knows what's real in this town?

Moira refused to allow herself to belittle a town's celebrations. She always found the 'your way of having fun is wrong' mentality to be small-minded and tasteless. That being said, watching 21st century teenagers square dance to polka was the most ridiculous thing she'd seen in a very long time. Worse, they looked like they were enjoying themselves.

The spring celebration started mid-afternoon. Tiki torches spilled smoke into the air and charcoal grills sizzled and flared as thick cuts of peppery steak dribbled melted oil and juices into their fires. People laughed and gathered in little groups, occasionally splintering off to visit booths with face painting, pies for sale, free punch and lemonade, and where lengths of thin ribbon were tied into children's hair. One young man with shoulder length hair paid a frowning old woman to tie one in his hair, which she grudgingly performed to the delight of others.

Moira kept to the street, admiring the children's chalk art on the road. Flowers, shining suns, green stars, mushrooms, blue bonfires, and countless stick figures ran along the street in a broken mosaic alongside unfinished games of tic-tac-toe. One kid must have lost a game of hangman by only a few letters, leaving ' _o o d _ y _, _o_ _ a' next to an unfortunate stick person. They could've tried harder to save him.

"Good to see you, Moira." Reverend Hopkins stood like a thin shadow in the middle of the cloudy day's sleepy glow. His eyes had dark rings around them like he hadn't slept, and when he took a sip from his paper cup of cider, she could see grime under his fingernails and tiny scratches on his knuckles. The way he stared at her, unblinking, like he was trying to exert some sort of college boy masculine dominance over her, was unnerving.

Bile rose into Moira's throat at the sight of his disgusting fingers. She forced a smile. "Hi, Reverend. I'm sorry I didn't notice you there.

Just catching up on a podcast."

His head bobbed with an apathetic nod. "It's nice to see that you've decided to indulge in our little celebration. It's a very important week for our community, where we come together and enjoy one another's company. I hope it's not too distracting for you."

"Not at all. It looks like a lot of work went into this." Moira felt compelled to hide her earbuds behind her collar. As she did, she glanced past the Reverend's shoulder and noticed three men staring in their direction. Like always, they looked away when she caught them. "Out of curiosity, what do you think about all of this? Your celebration? I thought spring dances were frowned upon by most churches for skewing too closely to the heathen or pagan. It seems pretty progressive for a town like Abrams."

He laughed at that. It was light and full of good humor, almost contagious had it come from anyone else, anywhere else. "While there are denominations of our faith that would see it that way, there haven't been any lightning strikes or plagues that have struck people for simply celebrating their earthly connection to their Creator. We are as He made us. He created us with the biological need to sustain ourselves off of the land and its animals, so enjoying ourselves in His name can hardly be considered a sin. So long as those who partake do not stray too far into the realm of worshiping nature rather than simply respecting it."

"Interesting."

Reverend Hopkins stepped onto the sidewalk and stood too close to her. "I understand you're agnostic. You view religion as, what was it? Historical circumstance? But I'm sensing you don't subscribe to the tenets of our beliefs, even without the faith. Is that accurate?"

"Depends on the tenet. I'm all for loving one's neighbor and thou shalt not kill, but faith isn't for me," she answered. "I've seen entirely too many bad things to think that anyone, creator or otherwise, who planned them ever had good intentions. But I'm not the kind of woman who would begrudge someone following the traditional beliefs and practices, insofar as they're keeping their hands to themselves and aren't hurting themselves or others." She stared at him.

Hopkins gave her a nauseating grin. "Fair enough."

A petite, full-figured woman strolled up to them, a group of children in tow. Reverend Hopkins gave Moira a slight bow of his head. "Good evening, Miss Clarke."

"Good evening, Reverend." Moira choked down a sourness as she watched him grab the hands of two children and walk over to greet a group of students. There wasn't a fiber of her body that found his dark, Byronic figure act at all appealing. She wasn't exactly sure his motives for it, but she was certain that every movement, smile, and open display of warmth was a carefully practiced performance that worked on the people of Abrams like a magic spell. Every piece of her screamed Hopkins was dangerous. She'd best keep on her guard.

Open your own beers, girls.

Moira spent her day walking around town, watching people watch her. Eventually, she took refuge from those prying eyes in the center of an undeveloped area near the gas station and under a couple of wooden picnic tables beneath a rickety cabana. There she sat and read from a thin stack of pages browned with dirt and dust.

3

(No Date)

Dear Dipshittery,

Celeste was mom's friend. She didn't write much about it, but from what I found, she's guilty about treating Celeste like shit. She says she loved Celeste like a sister, but it looks like she used to bully her in high school and make Celeste carry her books and tell her she was a queen and whatnot. Sounds about right. Mom is kind of a bitch who lets retrospective guilt beat her up.

Everything else was just crazy talk. Some crap about a radio playing tapes backward, sticking Celeste in the middle of a road, sex with dad (ew!), searching for Celeste, and then not telling the cops everything. That explains why dad's a lawyer. If he's my real dad, anyway. Do they have tests for that?

(No Date)

Holy Clitoris! Mom was there the night Celeste Martin went missing! She kept all her old shit in a box in the crawlspace filled with random stuff from grandma. I doubt even dad knows about this.

ADDITION: DAD WAS THERE TOO!!

Did they kill her? Are my parents responsible for Celeste Martin's disappearance? It sounds like mom was really broken up about it, though. Maybe she wasn't faking. Matt Miller was involved, too. It was on his farm. Did he poison her, kill her, and hide the body? Did they help?

And why is Uncle Creep involved? Why am I the only writer in the family, mom? Gimme some details! I wonder if I should ask her about it.

(No Date)

So, there's this shitty storage room right behind Uncle Perv's office, and it has a vent in it. I was fucking around and picked the lock (cuz I'm a BADASS like that) and snuck in. There's nothing in there but some old files and stuff, but there is this vent that leads right to his office. And he was in there with Ginny Taylor talking about some kind of "Great Working" he was trying to replicate. Casting magic spells and shit. Granted, it sounded pretty cool at first. But when he started babbling about knocking her up in order to create some kind of magic baby to keep the town going, it made me want to barf. What kind of pickup line is that? But get this: I think they started having sex! GROSS! She's like a senior in high school! Fucking freak!

Anyway, glossing over that shit, this got me to thinking. Everybody whispers about Jenny Lake. She was like 15 or 16 when she got pregnant and then completely disappeared. People say that she went crazy and smothered her baby, Ollie, so they carted her off to the loony bin. What if Uncle Perv had something to do with Ollie Lake's disappearance. They never did find a body. The poor thing. And Jenny Lake's in the wind. She's gone forever.

If they're trying to make a magic baby for the Witch, then this is some dark shit. DARK. And that's coming from me, the Queen Bitch Devil Mother of Abrams.

Shit. Maybe the Witch isn't good, after all.

Time to start digging harder.

(No Date)

These headaches are so bad! I want to take dad's drill and just open a hole in my temple to let the demons out, like they did in Greece or wherever. I don't mind them every once in a while. Honestly, the weird halos of light around everything can be kind of cool at night. But do they have to be EVERY damn day? What the hell? I wonder if it's this big purple crap on my face eating its way through to my brain.

Moira was walking back to the celebration when a body blocked her path. Thick hands held two plastic cups of beer, offering one to her. At first, she didn't recognize the rolled sleeves and furry, well-tanned arms, but when he said, "Hey!" she recognized him as the man in the blue truck. The one who tried to give her a ride.

He wore Abrams casual attire: a blue-collared shirt with the sleeves rolled to the elbows tucked into dark, almost black jeans. Artificial sandalwood percolated from below his collar. At least he was clean.

Her reaction was to grab the beer, and she immediately regretted giving the impression that she was open to whatever social obligation taking it meant.

"I didn't know you were in such a hurry the other day. Next time, I'll make sure I clean my truck out for you." A reddened nose sat in the shadow of the curved bill of his Miller Lite ball cap. Through the dim glow of the strings of lights dangling from the buildings, Moira thought she saw a wink.

"Uh, yeah. Sure. Sorry about that. I'm on a pretty tight timeline for this project." She didn't feel bad for lying. The way he gawked at her, the angry scar above his eye, his smile just a fraction too big, and how he leaned too close, too familiar—there was something predatory about him. There was one around every corner. The same type of guy in every bar.

She said nothing, nor did she drink her beer. She knew better. She also hoped the awkwardness would chase him away.

"I'm Matt." He bumped his cup against hers.

"Miller?" she blurted. His was the voice with Hopkins' in the church vents. Her stomach fell, and a buzzing crept up the back of her neck. The farmer. He was there when Celeste Martin disappeared.

"Yeah! You'd probably heard I've got the biggest farm in town. Family's been here for generations. Probably read that in those records, too. Right?"

She nodded as she fought the urge to run away.

"It ain't polite to not drink after a cheers." He knocked his beer into hers, spilling a little on her finger. She took an exaggerated step back, laughing when he laughed. "That was close, huh? Bottom's up!" He took a long drink, looking at her and moving his hand in a "Come on!" motion the whole time.

Nobody around them seemed to pay attention to her anymore. Instead, the crowd congregated around the stage. Moira slowly realized just how alone with Matt Miller she was quickly becoming.

"Don't worry, I'll drive you back to the motel. You don't have to walk back." He urged her by lifting her hand to her mouth, spilling more beer onto her thumb.

Her frightened thumb squeezed a depression into the plastic. He knew she walked into town.

Her mouth went dry. She almost took a sip. "I'm not a beer girl," she said. Before he could say anything, she raised her voice a little louder than the music demanded, and asked, "You knew Celeste Martin?"

"Who?"

"Celeste Martin. She went missing on your farm in 1984. You're that Matt Miller, right?"

He blinked, clearly caught off-guard. "Uh, yeah. She was a friend. Ran away or got ate by a cougar or something." His nonchalance was astounding. "Come on, drink up! That's a good girl."

She set the beer on a nearby brick ledge and pulled the notebook from her back pocket. "Can you tell me more about that night? After you left her at the crossroads?"

His jaw flexed and the air around him darkened. He swayed at the hips, looking away. "Too good to drink that?"

Moira felt herself slinking backwards.

"What the shit is with women? It's like you think every guy is trying to get into your pants. Someone brings you a beer to be kind and welcoming—hell, I even offered you a ride, too—and you automatically think I'm trying to fuck you? How arrogant are you? Abrams is a friendly town. We are friendly people. So, when people like you come in here and act like you rule the fucking world, it just fucking pisses me off!" He yelled the last, fists balled, face burning red in the orange light.

People were looking now. She doubted they would get there quickly enough to keep Miller's fists from doing any actual damage if he wanted to use them. It was a risk to keep him talking, but she took it by instinct. "Can you at least tell me about the whispers? The ones you heard the night Celeste disappeared."

His eyes unfocused for a moment, confused. Then his cheekbones slackened and his shoulders deflated. "What? How did—What whispers?"

"The whispers you said you heard when Heather and Brian were driving Celeste to the crossroads. Do you think that's why people blamed the Abrams Witch for her disappearance?" She checked her notes. "You said in the paper that you heard—"

"No." He shook his head. "No. No, I never told anyone about that except for Heather and Brian. Did they tell you?" He took a threatening step toward her, his bulk casting a violent shadow over her. "Did she tell you? What else did that weepy slut tell you?"

Startled, Moira backed away from the intensity of his shouting. Her elbow scraped against brick and knocked into her cup, splashing its contents onto the sidewalk. "You know," she held her hands up and slouched to look smaller and less threatening, "we should probably talk about this when you're less angry."

"Oh, I'm not fucking angry. You don't know angry." His thick fingers clamped around her wrist like steel shackles. She knew she could never struggle away. He could snap her arm like a toothpick. Maybe if she screamed, someone would come to help.

"Problem here, Matt?" Burning white light jumped from her eyes to Miller's face. He dropped her arm to block it.

"Jesus, Jeff! Put that down."

Chief Lake lowered the light to chest level, but lights still danced around the darkness of her vision. To Miller, he said, "Dan wants to see you."

Miller huffed. "Bullshit. I'm busy. Fuck! I'm just talking to her, Jeff."

"Come on, Matt."

"Fuck you, Jeff! I'm just talking to her."

Lake shined the light in his eyes again, then pointed in at a spot on the sidewalk ten feet away. "Come over here and talk to me. Matthew! Come here and talk to me."

Miller ground his molars, shot Moira a dangerous look, and followed Lake.

Moira hurried across the street and sunk into the crowd, keeping herself under the brightest areas of light.

The street dance was in full swing. The band played a lively bluegrass song through a set of loudspeakers. Women in flowing sun dresses whipped their hemlines around and kicked, while men in checkered shirts and slicked back hair orbited them. Everyone smiled and looked to be having a good time. Moira made sure she stood far enough away from the streamers and road cones that made up the border of the dance area, so nobody else 'friendly' would get the impression she was at all interested in dancing.

A tall man in a starched shirt and tight-fitting slacks made his way from person to person, shaking hands and smiling. Based only on his smile and how upright he carried himself, Moira suspected he was Brian Hopkins, the mayor of Abrams. The dark-haired woman holding his arm was pretty, willowy, and just as tall as he. Plastered on her face was a brilliant smile, but her eyes were joyless and tired. It was the sort of smile usually reserved for funerals where people were expected to put on a strong face. The pair strutted into the center of the dance area until their faces became blurs between swinging arms and crowding people.

At the far end of the stage, Miller was having an animated discussion with Hopkins while Lake hovered close by.

Moira put some more distance between herself and the dance area by buying a cup of thin beer and wandered from tree to tree, hiding in the shadows. But there was no hiding at all. Wherever she walked, a pair of eyes followed her.

She buried herself in the shadow of a tall bush until the glances and gazes eased and people went back to enjoying the celebration. Children danced and played games. The mouth-watering scents of barbecue sauce and fried onions poked at her belly. A pie contest had just finished, and a strawberry rhubarb was proclaimed champion and its baker given a blue ribbon and a gift card. When it was done, slices of pie were dished out in little paper bowls.

Two older men ambled close, voices low. They stopped on the other side of the bush. "Who's to say what's blasphemy and what's not? Not us."

"That's a load of shit. We read the same book."

"Who are we to question the servant of God? Hasn't he kept the town afloat?"

A scoff. "You think consorting with witches is a Christian act because some skinny prick told you it was okay for him to do it? Next thing you're gonna tell me is marriage ain't a union between a man and woman."

"I think it's okay because it's worked."

"Don't be talking so loud, now."

They lowered the voices further. Moira strained to listen, but the music and the rustle of dry leaves made them sound like old television static. Instead, she focused on writing a quick note in her book.

Hopkins consorting with the Witch? What could this mean? What is Hopkins up to? Does it have anything to do with the disappearances?

Over where the dance wound down, Reverend Hopkins took the stage with his arms raised in a wide Y above his head. People clapped and cheered.

"Well," one man grumbled. "Time to do the thing, I guess." They walked away from the bushes and into the gathering crowd to join with polite clapping for their spiritual leader.

Hopkins spoke without a microphone, and Moira stood too far away to hear him clearly. When she stepped closer, a moth fluttered in front of her face. Its gossamer wings beat against her lips and flicked tiny clouds of powder in her eyes. She spat and sputtered it away. Then a mosquito flew into her ear with a reeeeee that made her shoulder involuntarily flex into her ear. She cursed and slapped it away.

By the time she could focus her attention, the crowd had backed away from the center, forming a U-shape. A group of children and teenagers stood in the center. Each one wore a white choir robe and their hair was combed and set perfectly, shimmering with hairspray and gel in the streetlight. A woman placed a steel bucket at the Reverend's feet. Another placed what appeared to be a broom or brush made of unlaced threads of wicker into his left hand. He dipped the broom into the bucket, reciting a prayer Moira couldn't hear until the crowd muttered "Amen."

She guessed it was water in the bucket, perhaps for some odd ritual baptism, but when Hopkins dipped it in and raised it, she watched red shower the children with every muttered blessing and flick of his wrist. A dip, a prayer, a flick, and splotches of crimson covered their white robes until they group looked like someone fired a shotgun into a crowd of angels. Each flick was another spray of scarlet on pristine white. Children flinched and spit, but none moved to avoid the spray.

Moira crept to the edge of the crowd, amazed that nobody rushed out to shield their child or grandchild from an obviously vile display. Before she reached the backs of the people in the farthest row, a snarling Doberman off its leash intercepted her and pressed her back into the bushes.

She stepped carefully, struggling to show no fear the way Rachel taught her. Paying the dog the respect it demanded, she slowly backed away until the branches of the bushes stabbed her in the neck.

Hopkins continued to spray the children with blood.

Then the dog sat, quietly waiting. Close enough for her to pet.

"My daughter loved these."

Moira's stomach leaped. The mayor's wife stood next to her, alone, a plastic cup of beer held in both hands. She wore a sad, distant smile, and seemed oblivious to the aggressive animal at their feet. "The dances, I mean. Not this mess. She would've hated to get her makeup wet."

Moira's eyes bulged. "Wet? It's bl—".

The crowd erupted in cheers. The teens and children hugged and kissed each other and their families. Each of them was damp with liquid, but there was no sign of blood. As a joke, a pair of teens picked up the bucket and dunked the Reverend. His annoyance sharpened, but then relaxed as he laughed, wiped the water out of his eyes, and joined the festivities.

Moira blinked hard. The dog pattered away.

The woman spoke. "When she was little, she'd let me pick her up and swing her around. She really loved the Oak Ridge Boys. Elvira was her favorite. It was old music, but it made her so happy she'd smile and laugh. She always had these chubby cheeks that balled up really tight against her ears when she giggled. I'd pick her up, and she'd lean back and let her arms just float behind her, like she was falling but she knew I had her and wouldn't let her drop. And we'd dance all night. Even when she was a headstrong teenager who hated me, she would still come down here with her friends who were too cool and mature to dance. But whenever she thought nobody was looking, I'd still see her swaying in a little circle. I like to think she was having good memories."

The heavy emotion in her voice made Moira feel a throb of guilt and nostalgia. She suspected she knew who this woman was. Instead of walking away, she said, "I don't think she hated you. I was an angry teenager once, too. I didn't hate the people close to me, but I wasn't always kind to them. I just trusted them enough to let them see me angry. Did she move away? School in a different state?"

The woman nodded, the focus in her eyes waxing and waning. "Move?" She looked at Moira as if seeing her for the first time. "Yes. Yes. She could always move so fast. Even when she was a baby, she was always going and going. She hopped like a frog instead of crawling. Those chunky little legs would kick and kick and kick. Once she took her first steps and got her balance underneath her, she was unstoppable." She laughed, and a tear bubbled out of a heavily mascaraed eye. "I had to put up cages around the apartment—those silly plastic baby cages people use for pets—I had to put up dozens of them, like a maze, just to keep her curious little brain occupied. She would wake up with that big, beautiful smile, and she'd just go. Just go and go and go. That's how she got her nickname."

Moira's heart slid downward. She whispered, "You're Heather Ylva. Gogo's mom. You left me the box?"

Heather nodded.

"Why didn't you just come talk to me?"

Heather ignored the question. "She let me hold her one more time. When we knew she was dying." Her forced smile became a wince of pain. "I wanted so much to carry her like I used to. To bounce her on my shoulder and tell her it was going to be okay, that I was going to take it all away like a good mom." She spooned a tear in a fingernail and flicked it away. "I could've been a better mother. I could've protected her better."

Heather poured her beer into the grass. Gently, she guided Moira's wrist closer and pressed something into her palm. "I have to, um, go. To go. I have to run." She locked eyes with Moira. "You know. Run."

Gently, Heather's hand slid away, and she glided back into the crowd, smiling and shaking hands as if she hadn't spoken to Moira at all.

Gogo was dying? Moira fought the urge to follow Heather. Instead, she quickly unzipped her purse and made a show of pulling out a pair of dollar bills while secretly dropping the object inside. She stood in line for a beer, paid, and took a few sips before stealthily walking into the shadows between buildings where she dumped out her cup and jogged toward the motel.

Out of breath and sweating, Moira slid the chair in front of the door, made sure the curtains were closed, and turned on every light in the room. There was nobody hiding under the bed or next to the ironing board in the small closet. She didn't question the sudden paranoia, she merely acted on its demands.

Satisfied the room was safe, she dumped her purse onto the little dresser and searched for whatever it was Heather handed to her. It felt like a coin or a pendant.

It was a key.

A strange key, to be sure. It was a size between a house key and a padlock key. Its top was round and orange, with the number 34 carved into the center. Only one place had the same color orange: the self-storage buildings just outside of side of town.

4

She'd never driven at night with the lights off. It was frightening and exhilarating, like she'd become a spy or secret agent in a matter of moments. Security lights along the county road leading to the storage facility illuminated most of the road, so it wasn't completely black. Yet, when she parked on the dirt road outside the entrance to the storage building, her hands buzzed with exhilaration.

Unfortunately, the automatic door had a keypad, and she didn't have a number. 34 wasn't enough digits. There was, however, a fence and a lack of visible cameras surrounding the rows of brown buildings and orange garage doors. This wasn't a problem for Moira. She spent two years as a high school cheerleader and had a childhood of experience climbing trees and fences. With the headband Rachel made of her pulled over her nose to hide her face, Moira scaled the fence.

It took a little longer than she hoped, and her fingers were nearly numb from the cold aluminum, but she was soon inside and jogging past the rows, looking for number 34, which was easy enough to find. Her heart beat faster when the key slid in and turned with a click. The rolling garage door made a horrifying, mechanical roar that echoed into the fields of tall grass between her and the cornfields.

Inside, a rectangular black box held together with masking tape waited in the center of the concrete floor.

Moira watched enough movies and read enough books to know better than to casually saunter into a dim storage room to claim her object of desire. Her phone's flashlight searched every corner inside and down both directions in the aisle of doors outside until she was ready to dash inside. In a flash, she rushed in and snatched up the object. Then she ran out before anyone could sneak up from behind and trap her within.

Nobody waited. The door didn't close on its own.

The door rumbled closed. Moira pocketed the tape and scrambled back up the fence, eager to get back to her room and listen to whatever secrets Gloria or Heather recorded for her. Perhaps some evidence of Hopkins' and Lake's involvement in the disappearances and deaths? Something more about Celeste Martin?

Moira's surge of excitement distracted her from watching the ground as she finished the climb down, and her shoes hit packed with a hard, awkward thump.

A low growl brought her pulse to a standstill.

An orange-eyed gray wolf, twice the size of a mastiff with shoulders as tall as her hips, stood inches away. It growled low and threatening.

Heart hammering in her throat, Moira tip-toed along the fence, pressing and dragging herself against the coarse chain link to get out of striking distance from one of the biggest animals she had ever encountered.

The wolf sniffed the air twice but didn't follow.

Don't run, she told herself. Don't run and it won't chase. She hoped she was right. Just because a dog wasn't barking didn't mean it wasn't about to tear your arms off. And this wasn't a dog. It was a wild animal who had taken an uncomfortable interest in her very tender self. Part of her hoped someone saw her hop over the fence and had called the police. She knew she couldn't count on that. Slinking away toward her car and willing herself to become invisible was what she had to do.

The wolf plodded after, staying within a couple of feet of her.

"Good puppy," she breathed. She shoved her hand into her pocket and pressed the unlock button on her fob, causing the wolf to jump a little and nip at the flashing lights. "Shhh. Easy, puppy. Good girl."

Moira's fingers felt around for the door handles. Her eyes never left the wolf or the shine of its massive canines in its panting mouth. When her hand brushed against something solid and soft, she spun.

Another gray wolf, this one with angry, green eyes, stood between her and the car door, growling through salivating fangs. Behind it, a dozen or more pairs of fiery white lights watched her from the shadows.

Moira forgot to breathe. She wasn't sure if her heart shuddered or if the world around her shook. Her first thought was to climb up onto the trunk and get to the top of her vehicle, but green eyes growled, and orange eyes lunged closer, pinning her against her car. Terrified, she pleaded. "Go away. Please go away."

The wolves stood still. Their cold noses poked at her exposed flesh.

She couldn't wait. They would tear her apart and eat her if she just stood there. She considered screaming, but she couldn't catch her breath long enough to fill her lungs with any meaningful amount of air. She pressed her thigh against green eyes, trying to coax it out of the way with a body part not as easily edible as the soft tissue of her stomach.

Green eyes snarled, snapped its jaws at her belly, and leapt. The press of muscle and fur rocked her backwards. Giant paws pinned her shoulders to the car. Its weight pressed the air from her chest.; the creature had to weigh more than she did. Crooked and pale teeth hovered inches from her face. Hot air from the animal's mouth stank of meat and something vaguely fecal.

The cassette and key slipped out of her hands and clattered to the rocky ground.

Growling, wet and glottal and warm, bubbled up from the wolf's throat. Its nose brushed against her cheek like a fat, black ice cube. It smacked its lips and sniffed, then sniffed again at her ear and shoulder. Protecting the veins and arteries in her neck, she trapped her ear deeper into her shoulder each time the wolf tried to force them apart with its sloppy tongue. Green eyes gave up and sniffed along her chest and armpits, to her chin and nose, and then back to her neck as it searched for an opening.

A distant howl rang through the night, stealing the wolves' attentions. Each went dead silent, listening.

Another howl.

Green eyes released her and retreated into the darkness with the others as if Moira was just another part of the landscape.

Moira snatched up the keys and cassette and jumped into her car, locking the doors. Once the engine started, she hugged the steering wheel and gave herself a few minutes to shiver, breathe away tears, and thank whatever deity, spirit, or witch for not letting her get ripped apart by a pack of wild animals.

On her way back to the motel, she drove with her high beams on, watching the ditches for any glowing eyes.

(No Date)

They're keeping her sick! Something else is in there with her. There's a pit in the woods. The Pit. A hole where they take all of the missing people and kids to sacrifice. I dreamt it, but I KNOW it's there. I don't know how, but I just KNOW. I dreamt that they were pouring blood into the Pit and whatever is in there, whatever evil thing is in there, it's getting stronger, and it's keeping her sick. They're killing people to keep HER sick! I knew something was fucked up in this freakshow town. I'm right! I know I'm right! I'M FUCKING RIGHT!

I have to stop them.

But what happens if I let her out? What if she's evil? What if the old woman was wrong?

Dear Deathery,

Well, the secret of the headaches has revealed itself. It's called a glioblastoma, if that's even how it's spelled. However it's spelled, it's not as scary a word as 'inoperable' was. There was a second where I thought he was kidding, where I thought I didn't want to die, but whatever. Everyone has to go someday, right? At least I'm getting some bitchin drugs to help with sleep and pain.

All mom has been doing is crying. I don't know why. It's not like SHE has brain cancer. She ugly cries, too. Real bad. Like she looks like a turtle straining to shit. Dad's been on the phone all day with specialists, Reverend Pervert, the insurance company. They're talking about chemotherapy and radiation. It's like they didn't get the message that 'inoperable' means it can't be dug out of my brain. I hear they shave people's heads when they cut them open for brain surgery. I wonder how I would look with a shaved head. Probably pretty sexy. Maybe I have another birthmark shaped like a giant middle finger on the top of my head.

Shit, that'd be almost reason to live.

At least it's got 'blast' in it.

(No Date)

I'm going to die. I am going to die. I will die. I am dying.

Maybe I deserve this? They say kids can be horrible. I did some bad stuff. I bullied kids on the playground. Shoved Denny Anderson into the lockers every day for a year. I've wished my mom was dead and I lived on my own. Maybe I should have been a better person. I could've been a better daughter.

Everything is heavy. Some days it's hard to walk straight, like there's a rope pulling me down on one side. I tried talking the other day, and my mouth was just mushy and stupid and felt like it was full of warm, chewed gum.

I hope it doesn't hurt, doesn't feel like fire. I hope it's so cold I won't want to move, won't have to move. Lying here hurts. Feels floaty. I'm a crumbling leaf, and the wind is pain carrying me into the darkest part of the woods. I don't want to suffer. I want the numbness. I don't want to wither in a bed like grandma.

I don't want to be dying.

(No Date)

I'm so scared.

(No Date)

Mom told me everything. She wants us to leave. To run. To leave dad here and take off the hell out of Dodge. But she doesn't think they'll let us go. The truth is fucked in the head.

There is some kind of cult in Abrams. Something to do with the Witch. There are a bunch of farmers, retired folks, store owners—everyone in town is a part of this thing. It's like some kind of creepy cribbage club and farmer's market rolled into one. And not even in a cool Satanic way.

Mom says that Uncle Dan is behind the whole thing. Huge surprise. It was obvious, really. What real difference is there between a church and a cult? Good marketing? Anyway, she suspects they are the reason the town has done so well over the years. She thinks they sacrifice people at this old place in the woods on the Miller farm, a pit by a half-burned tree. A Pit like in my dreams. But they only kill outsiders or people already dying. They do it every spring and fall. And every year they forget or don't do it, the ground goes bad or there's a drought or something. Dad might be a part of it. She didn't say.

It started a while ago, like a looooong time ago. I guess there was a crazy woman who could talk to animals and predict the weather who got chopped up, raped, and burned before she was drowned or something. My head hurts thinking about it. It hurts regardless. Whatever. Drugs help. There was some more detail in there, but mom had a bottle and a half of wine in her and wouldn't slow down.

Long story short: they've been killing people. Sacrificing them to some kind of beast or demon for good harvests on every Flower Moon—the first full moon in May. That must be what keeps Her sick. Mom wants to leave because she thinks if word gets out that I'm sick, they're going to come for me. We can't call the police. Lake is part of it. That explains what happened to Jenny.

For now, I can't tell anyone I'm sick. I'm going to hide all of this in case they do get me. Maybe someone else can stop them, if I don't. If I have to die, then I'm taking a couple of them with me.

Next: We're doing a seance to summon the Witch, even if she's evil. If they're keeping Her sick, then she's gonna be pissed.

(No Date)

Update: Ouija boards are bunk. Staci's sister's friend was full of shit. Like she's the only one in the universe who owns and burns black candles and pretends to speak in tongues. Brittni was right: this chick is a ditz.

She had us all sit in a circle near the bonfire, holding hands like idiots, and sober as judges. SOBER? Who does this shit sober? Isn't that why they dropped acid in the 70s? To not be sober and contact the spirit world? I mean, the government gave people psychic powers through LSD and some other secret shit. Being sober is the opposite of having spiritual focus. Whatever.

When the candles were lit and she was all concentrated, we

jumped on the Ouija board and tried to contact the Abrams Witch. It took about four tries. Pfft. She couldn't even tell when I was moving the planchette. C-O-C-K. I knew she was a fake when we started in for real. Everyone here knows the Abrams Witch doesn't have a name. She's just a ghost, a powerful thing that is above names. Transcended them. She just IS. This dunce could have at least done some homework and spelled out Celeste instead. What kind of grandma name is Korey? Shitty name for a witch. It's a boy's name, anyway.

Anyway, the Witch said she's coming for me. I'm pretty sure that was Staci's sister's subconscious lesbian desire for me manifesting itself on her glorified Monopoly board. Either that or she was pissed that I was moving the planchette and called her a fake. She'll get over it.

(No date)

I'm hiding this. No more written records. If they can't fix me, then I'm going to get help from the witch. Maybe I can convince her to save me. Maybe I'm a fucking idiot.

Please don't let me die.

Moira neatly stacked Gloria's journals and papers and gently laid them back into their box, silently wishing there was something more she could do for Gogo than read and listen to her story, wishing Heather would have done more for her daughter. Was that all she could do? Wish? Wishing was almost as useful as people's thoughts and prayers after a hurricane.

Gloria's story wasn't over. Moira slipped the last cassette into the player.

What is this?

A tape recorder, dipshit.

Not that! This, ass? What is this? Jesus Christ, Gogo! Is that blood?

Take a pill, Brit. It's not human. Though it probably should be. My cousin goes bowhunting deer every year, and he kept some warm for me.

I'm—I'm not drinking that.

We don't drink it, airhead. We need to pour it out.

Good. I don't like it out here. This place gives me the creeps.

It should. It's where they kill all of the kids and visitors. What? You don't think that all those missing persons are just people getting out of Abrams or random wolf attacks? Dude, they kill people. Sacrifice them. We're going to find out to what.

Oh god... Gloria, I don't—

Chill, sister. It's only a little bit.

Can we turn that off? I don't want my mom finding out. She's born-again.

Yeah. Mine too. Three or four times already. But we need this for posterity. We need evidence for the attorneys.

Your dad?

No. Not him. Someone else. Someone who isn't involved.

(silence)

Alright Brit. You ready?

Are you kidding? This is fucking freaky, Gogo! I wan—What the hell was that?

Just wolves. They're fine. They're active in the spring, not this late in the summer. And I thought you wanted to help with this? What happened to all that talk about finding the Witch or finding a murderer? What about burning this shitty place to the ground and get all these child predators and weird cultists out of here? Don't look at me like that—you know it's true. Everyone knows! But nobody says shit. We just keep it quiet because nobody's gonna believe a kid, and our parents are in on it.

We don't know that! It could be anything. It could actually be wolves and accidents. We don't have anything that proves anything. All we have is a bunch of scary stories and a mason jar full of deer blood out in the middle of the thickest part of the woods. Where the shit even are we?

I told you. It's where they take people to die. Where the sacrifices are made.

I don't wanna be here.

Don't worry, Brit. You don't have to do anything. Just watch.

(A pause, then a retching noise)

That's disgusting, Go.

Fucking stinks, right?

(silence)

(A sound, unintelligible.)

What?

Brittni!

What? What did you do?

Stand up. Stand the fuck up right now.

What is it? What the fuck is it!

Run!

(silence)

The recording ended with a click. Moira flipped it over and played the other side.

(Gogo breathing hard.)

He knows! He sent them. He knows, and he sent them after me!

(Howling. Snarling. Animals panting.)

Oh god! Ohgodohgodohgod! Somebody please help me!

(More running. Heavy breathing. Gogo crying.)

Alright. Okay. Okayokayokay. If they're going to catch me, it'll be in the Pit. They can find my body there… oh, mommy, I don't want to die. I don't want to die. Please don't kill me.

(A crash. She screamed. Scraping and grunts. Running. The howling, the snarls closer.)

(Paws galloping along the ground.)

No. Nooooo…Nnonono. Get away from me. Get away!

(Snarls and barking. The clack clack clack of teeth. A scream followed by a series of light thumps. Gogo's voice getting farther away.)

Fuck you!

(A hollow sound like a muted drumbeat. A cracking noise followed by a yelp.)

Go away! Please. Please, please, please, go away.

(More guttural snarls and the snapping of teeth. Gogo screaming. The tearing and ripping of cloth.)

Moira held her breath. Fingers trembled at her lips as Gogo wailed and shrieked for her mother, over and over, and the wolves tore at her, ripping and howling. An animal instinct urged Moira to run, to drive her car out into the woods, back in time, and pull Gloria from bloody jaws and razor-sharp claws. But she could only keep listening until there was a horrible, final silence.

She let the tape run, holding the recorder's speaker up to her ear. Willing the hiss of the cassette formed words in Gloria Ylva's voice. She wanted her to say something, anything to let her know she survived, that the fight within Gogo manifested into something barbaric and powerful that gave her the strength to beat a pack of wolves into submission.

For several agonizing seconds, Moira thought she heard sounds that weren't the sniffing and wet licking of canine tongues. Wanted to hear anything but the wolves feasting.

She couldn't take anymore, and she let her quivering thumb slide down to the STOP button.

Wait.

Moira froze. Her muscles filled with electricity.

Who are you?

It was Gogo. Her voice was shaking and thick with tears.

Who are you!

Was she talking to herself? No. There was whispering. She couldn't make out the words, but there was definitely someone else there with Gogo.

No, you're not. No, you're not. You are not.

(A pause.)

I don't want to die. No. No, I don't. I want my mom. I want to go home. What do you mean? I want to go home! My home!

(Another pause. Whispering.)

Whatever was said brought Gogo to desperate, frightened tears.

No. Please, please. No.

The lights in Moira's room dimmed. The air thickened with silence.

Why? Why me? Special how? No… No, I don't. I don't care about that! Whatever they—I can?

(A longer silence.)

The whispers sounded soothing but insistent. Moira fought to hear them but couldn't tell the difference between the whispers and the ambient hissing of the tape.

(Gogo sniffled.)

What do I have to do? Why? Why? Why do I have to—If I do, will you promise that nobody else will get hurt?

Moira swallowed. The hairs on the back of her neck stood tall. This was the same kind of conversation Celeste Martin had in her dream. Gloria Ylva was speaking to the Abrams Witch. By the way it sounded, she making some kind of a deal.

That? Promise me that. That! Promise.

Moira's heart sank when Gogo said, *Okay. Okay. I will. But you promised me.* Gogo's words slathered with rage. *Remember, you fucking promised me.*

A skin-rending scream knifed into Moira's ear. She threw the player onto the bed and covered her head to quiet the ringing. The little speaker frizzled in its own metallic agony as Gogo's tortured and garbled screams threatened to rip through the cassette and tear down the motel room walls.

Just when shrill sank needles so deep into the back of Moira's neck she couldn't take anymore, the pained moans shifted into something else entirely. Gogo's cries of misery changed to gurgles, to groans from a throat bubbling and frothing with blood, to a bestial roar of animal fury, to the howling of a wolf.

The tape clicked to a stop.

Chapter Six

Moira spent a second night in a nearly sleepless stupor of nightmares. Every time it was quiet and she was just about to drift off into sleep, she heard a howling in the distance and movement outside her door. With the lights off and the glow from the parking lot seeping through the curtain, shadows writhed along the window like steam cooling on cold glass, so she kept all the lights on and covered her eyes with her headband.

When she finally slept, she dreamed of her mother.

Moira sat in the backseat of their car, sulking because they didn't wait. They were on their way home after picking her up from summer camp, and her parents refused to wait for her to have a chance to say goodbye to Juanita and get her email address so she could write. "An hour is long enough, love," her mother told her. In hindsight, Juanita had most likely left earlier that morning.

Memory and the dream always converged on the same image. Moira's eyes followed the seam of the seat to the gear shifter where her mother's and father's fingers interlaced, mom's thin thumb caressing the knuckle of dad's pinky. She imagined a pair of light brown fingers gripping hers, white knuckled, desperate, and unsure.

Blue digits on the dashboard read 3:13.

Dad moved his hand to the wheel and merged onto the highway. The hot sun moved out of the windshield and off her bare knees. Mom reached back, offering a sympathetic hand. Moira didn't take it at first, but eventually slid her own fingers, moist with tears, into her mother's palm. A lock of hair swung past mom's eye and down her shoulder, hovering in the pine-scented breeze of the air conditioner. Mom always wore her hair down. They shared the same auburn, but hers never glistened quite like her mother's, never had the same gossamer lightness that seemed to float like a ruddy wedding veil. Mom was the most beautiful woman in the world.

The drunk driver jumped the median and hit them head on at 60 miles per hour.

There was no sound. Never was. There was only the impact that twisted her world into a sudden rise of blue and black. Everything slowed. The hood bent. Spider webbing raced along the windshield. Dad's face bent the top of the steering wheel into the gauge cluster, killing him instantly.

Her memory flooded with grays and half-images, as if she were spinning underwater. But in her dreams, her mother always moved so fast.

A sudden lift forced the world down and back. With impossible speed, mom slid her arm out of the seat belt and threw herself in front of Moira and held her fast, protecting her from the invisible hand pulling her into the sky. Her face was always the same: mid-scream, brown eyes bulging with terror.

The nightmare shifted. Freckled cheekbones birthed tiny flowers, pink and white valerian. Mom's hair whipped like a cloak in the wind, and became a mossy blanket of furry green angelica and spikes of purple burdock that covered Moira in its suffocating damp earth and bouquet of springtime decay. There was no world, only a moment of quiet existence and the *thud, thud, thudding* of heartbeat.

Fire erupted on Moira's forearm, searing flesh to bone as if her skeleton was overheated cast iron. She woke up shrieking, bound in sweat-soaked sheets, pawing at the weeping rash sizzling on her skin.

After freeing herself from her damp cocoon, she shoved her arm into the bathroom sink and ran icy water over the wound. She leaned there, half-asleep and propped up by her elbows, head against the mirror, struggling to hold on to what she remembered.

Dani's phone call was as much a relief as it was a weight around her neck.

"Jesus, Mo. You sound like hell. Are you having fun out in the sticks without me?" Her cheerful voice pinched Moira's chest.

"No. Not really."

"Hey… are you okay, Moira? Do you need me to come up there?"

"No!" she nearly shouted before flexing her toes into the thin carpet, composing herself. As much as she wanted to be next to her, to sleep in her arms, she couldn't endanger Dani. If there was any real danger at all. Damn it, what the hell was she supposed to believe? "No. I'm just… drained, you know? It's been a long couple of days. There's so much more to this story than we thought. I think I might be digging too deep. But I'm not sure I want to stop." Thoughts of howling wolves and blood nauseated her.

"I'm not surprised. That's you, isn't it? For as long as I've known you, you've been the queen of persistence. Once you get started, you just keep going and going until you have all the answers. Jeez, lady, you sometimes don't even stop there. That's why you can be such a pain in the butt as a project partner."

"Ugh. Don't remind me."

"But you're my pain in the butt."

Moira wanted to laugh, to kiss Dani through the phone. If only she didn't feel like a paper bag filled with air.

Dani's voice softened. "It's not a bad thing, Mo. I think more people would benefit from having someone like you with them. Someone with your attention to detail. You're smart. You're the best listener. I think everybody needs someone who can read between the lines and hear what someone's trying to really say." Dani's smile through the phone brought her a much-needed touch of relieve. "You make me want to work harder, be smarter. You know? That's why we're so good together. Remember freshman year? Team Awesome Sauce?"

"Yeah. Team Awesome Sauce."

They talked a little longer. Chatted about home, television shows that Dani liked and Moira didn't, and what they wanted to do with their summer. Dani knew just how to distract her. Listening to her talk was a salve to her sore brain. She laid on the bed, letting playful laughs ease their way through the cracked walls in her tired mind.

There was so much she resolved to tell Dani when she left Abrams.

"Are you sure you're okay? You don't normally let me prattle on like this. Did you fall back asleep?"

"I'm awake. I'm just still exhausted, is all."

"Moira." Dani's voice was serious. "Are you crying? What's wrong? What happened?"

"I'm just a bit overwhelmed. Kind of freaked out about a few things. Nightmares again."

"Maybe you should come home? Or if you're tired, I can postpone the interview with Jenny Lake, and we can meet somewhere north of the Cities. We can get a room, eat some garbage food—"

"Don't do that. We need Jenny's story." Steely resolve returned to her bones. "I have to know hers. I have to."

"Alright, putting my foot down." Dani put on what she called her 'smotherly' voice. "What's going on?"

"You know when I said there was more to this than just the Witch?"

"Yeah."

"What if she's real? The Abrams Witch? What if she's a real thing? Not in a supernatural sense, but real in the sense that there is someone here who is killing people and using her as an excuse?" She put her lips closer to the phone and lowered her voice. "Dani, I think they hurt people. They might still be hurting them. I don't know for sure, and I don't have any proof, but I think there is something going on besides a folktale."

"What? Like an active serial killer on the loose?" Alarm thinned Dani's voice. "Are you safe? Are *you* hurt!"

Moira itched her sore arm against the knee of her pants. "I'm fine. Promise."

It took Moira 40 minutes of cajoling to reassure Dani that everything was fine, that it was her nightmares and stress-induced anxiety making it difficult for her to concentrate. She admitted to finding accusations of sex abuse, as well as Gogo's idea of there being a cult in Abrams, but she left out everything about her final cassette tape and the wolves. In the end, Dani demanded Moira at least make an appointment to have her arm looked at and take it easy that day.

Moira promised she would.

Abrams didn't have an urgent care facility, so when she called to make an appointment about her rash, it shocked her when the receptionist said she could be seen that morning. She hoped the urgency didn't end up being too expensive. Rachel took care of the medical insurance, covering every copay and deductible, regardless of what it was or what doctor she saw or how expensive the procedure was, but that was no reason to not be frugal.

"This isn't a reason to not take care of yourself, Moira. I haven't lived this long by the grace of a clinic alone. Eat vegetables, don't drink, don't smoke—don't think I can't smell it on you—and get exercise. Get outside. And for heaven's sake, take birth control. I don't care what you use—it's your body—but be on something. Don't jeopardize your education for a man who will love you and leave you just as quickly as he would a properly made sandwich. Your mind and time are too important to be distracted by early motherhood. Be free."

Moira wanted to argue Rachel's argument had a distinctly non sequitur stink to it, in the personal control sense, but she didn't. As always, Rachel was trying to protect her. The generational difference in their language was sometimes difficult to navigate, but Moira knew Rachel's advice was coming from a place of love and, she suspected, no small amount of fear. Rachel had her first child at 17. It had been a difficult childbirth, and the baby passed away.

They're keeping her sick. Gogo's voice continued to whisper in her ears, even after she packed the tapes away in the small pocket of her backpack.

An ear-shattering shriek made her jump in her seat and drop the magazine in her lap.

Across the waiting room, a woman with three children shushed a swaddled baby.

Moira breathed a light laugh and locked eyes with the little boy in a striped shirt who was drawing with coloring crayons at a nearby table. She smiled.

The boy stared, unblinking, while his little fist drew furious circles on a piece of thick paper.

Moira went back to the article about sensible socks for autumn wear and continued to keep a close eye on the strange child until a nurse cracked a door and called her name.

"Well, it's definitely some kind of rash." Dr. Gorman, a kind-faced elderly man with a shockingly thick mane of white hair, inspected her arm through his otoscope. "I'm not ruling out poison ivy or sumac."

"How could it be poison ivy if there's nothing growing in this town? There's hardly any green here."

An image of the wildflowers outside her room flashed in her mind.

"Hardly? Heck, there's nothing. The past few years have been rough. My wife can barely grow tomatoes, and she's the one with the green thumb. But some tougher stuff seems to survive each year, and not all of it good." Fluffy eyebrows worked like inchworms above his eyes. "Are you allergic to poison ivy?"

"I don't know. Never had it."

Dr. Gorman grunted. "I think perhaps it may be. Does it hurt when I do this?" He rubbed his thumb over it. It felt irritated but not painful. He nodded. "You know, southerners call poison sumac 'thunderwood'."

Interesting. "Why is that?"

He shrugged. "Probably because you yell when you touch it." Dr. Gorman's quick smile and friendly eyes made her laugh. "It's most likely because of the pain you described. Those who are most sensitive to it may experience these sudden shocks of fire and pain that eventually subside." After another minute of careful examination, he clicked his ballpoint pen and started drawing on her arm. "This is what we're going to do. I am going to connect the outer edges of this with my trusty pen. If you notice any continued growth out of the boundary within the next twenty-four hours, come back and tell Sylvia at the desk that I said to ask for me." When he finished, it looked like she had a red spider in a black web tattooed on her forearm.

He ripped off a page from his pad and handed it to her. "Ointment. It's a steroid cream with a bit more kick than over-the-counter cortisone. Don't cover this with a bandage. Don't itch. When you pull up your sleeves, do your best to not drag it up your arm. Poison ivy and sumac typically blister, and if you pop the blister and smear the ooze, the rash can spread to other areas of the skin. Be careful. If I don't see you again, then I will assume you have been cured of all ailments and have returned home in better physical condition than when you arrived in Abrams."

His smile held all the spectacle of a comedic stage actor.

"Thank you," she said with a smile of her own.

Feeling better for having one mystery solved, Moira signed out on the clipboard at the desk and related Dr. Gorman's message to Sylvia, who made a note.

As she turned to leave, the boy in the striped shirt handed her his folded paper with a quiet, "Goodbye," before following his mother through the door to the exam rooms.

The paper crinkled when she opened it. In the center was of a brown-haired woman, mouth agape in a perpetual scream, surrounded by sharp, thorny circles of black and green tipped with crimson.

With a smile to Sylvia, Moira folded it back together and left the clinic. She tossed the drawing in a garbage bin on her way out.

Moira browsed the pharmacy aisles while she waited for her medication. The happy blond with the name tag "Denise" told her it would be less than ten minutes.

This pharmacy had the same clinical white and blue color scheme as major chains, but with fewer odds and ends being sold on endcaps or stuffed on the tops of shelves. Here, they sold only medicines and toiletries, no groceries or sweatshirts that proclaimed love for the state of Minnesota. The shelves were well-arranged and completely stocked. Considering the only other customer in the store was at the counter flirting with Denise, Moira figured they must not do much business on Tuesdays.

She checked the label on some Benadryl for something to read other than old greeting cards or animal calendars in aisle five. It was over a year expired. She brought it to the counter.

"Hi. I'm sorry to interrupt, but I was just wandering around and saw that this is expired." Moira kept her voice conspiratorially low.

Denise gave a guilty smile. "Thank you!" She took the bottle. "I think your medication is ready, too. One moment."

Denise stepped around back, leaving Moira alone with the man at the counter. Moira smiled politely at him but preferred to keep her eyes focused across the counter at the multicolored boxes of allergy medication. He wore too much cologne, as if he bathed in leather and dirt that morning and coiffed his black hair with something that smelled vaguely of shoe polish. The crisp collar of his green and blue flannel shirt hugged the folds of his neck while its midriff held back a doughy belly with the help of a thick belt. It wouldn't surprise her if his blue jeans still had the tag on them.

He smiled back, shamelessly tracing the outline of her body from head to foot with his eyes.

She wished Denise would hurry.

"Getting some medicine, huh?"

"Yeah."

"Sick?"

Moira kept her voice even. "It's personal."

His laugh was the kind of breathy giggle that older men had when they confused their ignorance for charm. "Yeah. You ladies got your secrets, for sure. I know all about that lady stuff." His exaggerated exhale told Moira exactly how much he knew. "Grew up with three sisters and a mom in the same house. They were some firecrackers, I tell you."

Denise sure was taking her sweet time.

"What's that you got there?" He scooped up her arm and lifted her sleeve over her rash. "You should get that looked at."

"Excuse me!" Moira ripped her arm out of his grasp. "That's none of your business."

"Whoa, whoa, whoa!" He raised his hands in the air. "It's okay. I'm just friendly. We're friendly here in Abrams. I'm sure you're not used—"

"I didn't ask." She pulled her sleeves down. If there was one thing she had no time for, it was a strange man putting his hands on her. Impatience and anger came quickly. Especially after the lack of sleep, the pain in her arm, and how terrible the secrets in Abrams were revealing themselves to be. As far as she knew, this man could be a killer masquerading as the Witch.

"Hey now! Calm down. I said it was okay. I know you're not from here, but—"

She snapped, "I don't give half a shit where you think I'm from. Friendly doesn't mean you get to touch women or strangers without even giving a moment's consideration to asking for permission. Or didn't your mother and your sisters teach you that?"

His face flushed.

Denise slunk back around the partition splitting the counter from the pharmacist's area and handed Moira a narrow yellow and white cardboard box. "Here you go," she said with a wide-eyed and nervous expression.

"Thank you," Moira replied. "Is there a copay?"

"No, sweetie. You're fine."

Moira stuffed the box into her purse and turned away.

"I'll be glad when you're gone." The man's porous face was red. His shoulders flexed upward, and his fists tightened around his pockets.

Moira rolled her eyes. "I'm glad I can contribute to your happiness." And she left the shop without a second glance at him.

In her car, she sent Dani a quick text to vent. *I swear this town is stuck in 1985. Some jackass told me it was okay for him to touch me because he had sisters.*

By the time she reached the motel, Dani had sent: *jesus. What a freak!! Did u punch him?*

No.

Wnat me to kick hiss ass 4 u? Cuz I will <3 <3

I know you would. :) I think I embarrassed him in front of his girlfriend. The shame should be punishment enough.

K. Am staying on 'kicking ass 4 Mo-mo' standby. >:D

Dani's stomach felt cold and stony after she sent the text. Moira sounded tired, sad, and afraid on the phone that morning. That meant Moira *was* tired, sad, and afraid. And after Moira told her she thought the Abrams Witch might be real, Dani also felt tired, sad, and afraid. It only amplified the nervousness she already felt about the interview with Jenny Lake.

Dani distracted herself by playing music and singing obnoxiously loud in a blazing hot shower until the tingling on her skin melted its way past her muscles and settled into her bones.

After drying herself and her hair, she put on her makeup and got dressed. She chose the white shirt she borrowed from Moira a month ago after assuring her she would have it dry cleaned or wash it herself on a gentle cycle before wearing it.

The daffodil scent of Moira's perfume still lingered on its collar.

After dressing, she spent a half hour practicing her interview questions. According to Marco, the group home supervisor, Jenny Lake was a very delicate woman. Tone of voice was something she was sensitive to. Too forceful, and she would lock up and withdraw within herself. Too saccharine and she would simply walk away, disinterested and untrusting. Jenny had been through six psychiatrists in the past three years because each pushed a wrong button. "It's not a matter of her not wanting to tell her story; it just depends on the person she's telling it to. It's taken a lot of time for me to earn that level of trust from her, so don't expect her to respond to you like everyone else. And don't expect me to ask these questions for you. There's no way I'm jeopardizing her trust for someone's term paper. I'm only doing this because she's excited to talk to you about it."

Dani understood Marco's reticence. She also didn't want to let Moira down by either not asking good questions or by screwing up this opportunity and scaring away the only person who faced the Abrams Witch—or whatever the witch manifested as in her mind—and didn't end up dead or missing.

A shiver ran up her legs. Dani wasn't religious, but she silently prayed to someone that Moira wouldn't turn up dead or missing at the end of this. Not after their last conversation.

She squeezed her eyes shut and forced positive thoughts into her brain. Everything would be alright.

When she felt calm and centered, she gathered her things and left for her interview.

It was an uneasy two-hour drive to Jenny's group home, and when Dani got there, she took a breath, and readied herself like she was about to take a test, by imagining her middle was a steady ocean and her body was rock on the shoreline. She knocked solidly on the door.

A heavy-set man with brown skin and a close-cropped hair greeted her with a big smile. "Danielle?" She recognized Marco's deep voice.

From inside, a woman's voice asked, "Is that Ronnie? Is that you, Ronnie?"

Marco called back. "It's Danielle. Remember? From the phone?"

Dani thought she heard an excited gasp from inside.

She introduced herself and offered her hand. Instead of shaking it, Marco stepped out of the house and closed the door behind him, his brow creased with apprehension. "Before you talk to her, I need to tell you something. Something about Jenny's past. It's not going to be easy to hear. I just don't want it to surprise you if it comes up."

"Sure. I understand. What is it?"

Marco chewed on his lip. "Take a walk with me for a minute."

The Devourers

1

Moira hated every second of her ice-cold shower, but it helped chase the numbness and fog from her mind. She would have preferred a lava hot bath with Epsom salts and a bath bomb like she planned, but the brown rust ring around the tub didn't look inviting.

Twice she called her grandmother before the meeting with Jenny Lake. The first call went to voicemail, the second was just empty air. She had full bars, so she guessed it must've been on Rachel's end. She'd try later.

She put on a patterned shirt and thumbed through more records while she waited for Dani's call. When the chime rang, she clicked the green button.

Her smile started as forced but changed to a genuine grin when she saw Dani, hair loose and wavy at her shoulders and wearing the stiff-collared shirt she 'stole'. Even through her solemn frown, the serious furrows in her brow, and the darkness in the room, her eyes sparkled.

"Is something wrong?" Moira asked.

"Check your email."

Moira caught the anxiety tightening Dani's voice and checked her email.

Mo,

Jenny is a special case here. She responds well to therapy. Her medication dosages are small from what I understand. But there is someone adamant that she stays here. It's not her family. Marco, her caretaker, has standing orders from her benefactor, some guy named Ronnie, to keep them away from her. Sounds like Ronnie thinks she's in danger. Marco doesn't want me to tell you why via email. Says it's up to Jenny to tell. He summarized things for me.

Don't mention anything about her family unless she says it first. I honestly think it will be better if we didn't say anything until she was done talking. I'm going to record the audio only.

Mo, I'm really worried about this.

—D

She nodded into the camera, and Dani adjusted her computer until a yellow-haired woman in a blue sweater came into view.

"Moira, this is Jenny Lake. Jenny, this is Moira, our project leader. She's who I was telling you about."

Jenny gave her a big smile and a wave. "Hello, Moira Clarke! It's so nice to finally see you." Though in her mid- to late forties, with her high cheekbones, pale skin, candy-sweet voice, and radiant smile, she looked much younger. She was beautiful. If they would have run into each other in person, Moira would have easily mistaken Jenny for an actress or a news anchor in a comfortable sweater on her day off.

"It's nice to meet you, too." Moira waved back. "How are you? Are you well?"

"I'm very well, thank you. Dani Olsen says you're looking for stories about the Witch."

Moira nodded. "I am. I'm actually in Abrams right now. I've been going through some old files and visiting some places. There was a street dance last night. Did you ever dance?"

Jenny's face darkened, as if the shade over the window in her room had been drawn. "Are you careful?" She whispered, "Are they after you? Chasing you?"

Moira swallowed hard. "Who's that, Jenny?"

Jenny's eyes lost their glimmer. She stared at a spot past the computer's camera. "They chase you; they always chase. The shadows. They chased me. Caught me. When I was a little girl, they caught me."

Moira swallowed against the burning in her chest. "What shadows, Jenny?"

Jenny's lips moved, but there was only silence, as if someone had taken her voice. Dani gave her soft reassurances off camera.

Finally, Jenny spoke.

"It didn't always hurt, wasn't always a punishment. Sometimes it was wonderful, even gentle. It was probably their way of trying to convince you they weren't monsters, that they weren't giving you a soul and a heart just so they could rip it away. Then you learned that being gentle was their way of buying silence.

"People knew, though. They always know. There are no real secrets in a small town, especially one like Abrams. People knew, but they didn't do anything. They didn't interfere. It simply isn't done." She pounded the table with her fist for emphasis. The way she lowered her voice an octave told Moira that Jenny recited someone else's words. Perhaps her father or a teacher. "Because if they interfere, if they reveal anyone else's secrets, then all their secrets could be told. No more hiding in houses or little castles when everyone knows everyone's every secret. No one is safe once those walls come down."

"What did they know, Jenny?" Dani gave Marco an uncertain look. He gave her a wave to tell her it was an acceptable question.

Jenny leaned in closer, imparting her secret to Dani but loud enough that Moira could still hear. "Who the shadows were. The devourers. The ones that feed on the young and the weak. Everyone knows who they are, they just don't want to remember. They want to forget, even when there aren't any memories for them to forget. It's like they forget beforehand."

Moira forced the question on her lips into silence, as Dani suggested in her email. Jenny was obviously fragile. Regardless of how lucid or cheerful she appeared at first, the more she spoke, the more vulnerable and hesitant she became. So, Moira kept her mouth shut. Had to control herself, to not jump in and demand answers. Because if anyone could calm another person into talking to her, it was Dani. But the look on Dani's face made her even more uneasy. Always stone-faced and stoic during their interviews, Dani looked shaken when she glanced at the camera, her shoulders stiff and her elbows held close to her ribs like she was mid-flinch.

Moira kept herself still.

Dani slid her hand under Jenny's. Her voice cracking, she asked, "Will you tell us about the shadows? The devourers. You can tell it however you want. You don't even have to tell us if you don't want to."

"Oh, No. I'm not scared. It's okay." Jenny scratched at her cheek, just below her eye. "I want to. I want to. I think she wants me to. Ollie would want me too." She made a little 'hoot-hoot' sound to herself.

After a moment of tense silence, Jenny's fingers curled around Dani's hand.

2

You can't always see them, but you always feel them. Feel them in your heart or where it hurts, places where forgetting them isn't possible. They're always there. There's no running because there's nowhere to go. They're everywhere and nowhere at the same time. If older people can see them or talk to them, they don't tell anyone. Try to tell someone and they'll tell you to stop making up stories. To shush. Don't you start spreading rumors like that! They say they don't believe you, but they know. They all know.

They like young ones. Nobody knows why because nobody's ever said anything about it. But it's always the young ones they talk to. Make promises to. And you can't get away from them. Not when you run, not when you hide. Especially if you're special; they like the special ones. And it doesn't matter if it's a boy or a girl, so long as they're special. A fast one. Tall one. Ones that look older than the rest. But their favorites are the pretty ones.

I was pretty once. Long hair, thin. Big, blue eyes that always glistened like water. Like a lake. A lake a-lake alake. So pretty. Soooo pretty. Such a pretty thing, they'd say. A pretty, pretty, pretty thing. They'd say a lot of things like that. Always reminding you of how pretty you are. Reminding you that pretty things get pretty things because pretty things never tell.

Swimming is fun. Do you like swimming, Dani? I miss swimming, the smooth, floating hug of the water. I was so fast. The water loved me, I think. It always wanted to pull me down, and I always wanted to go with it to find the bottom, to find its heart. I could hold my breath for two minutes before the first grade. Momma didn't like it, but I knew the water was safe. So, I practiced. Counted. One thousand, one… One thousand, two… One thousand, three.

One time when I was little, I went into the lake and held it for thirty-five minutes. They said it was a long time, but it felt quick and quiet. Like sleeping.

I did it because I wanted to see the others.

Oh? Oh! Do you know that when you stare into the deep water when the sun is just right, you can see the others? The others are the spirits of the other children. The other special ones. When they whisper, it's always in this ear right here. That's how you know it's them. Right here. And they were always so nice. 'You have the prettiest hair, Jenny. Do you like how the sun smells like flowers to you? If you touch that, you'll taste chocolate.'

Do you like chocolate? Me too. Marco, can Dani please have a chocolate with me? You'll like these. My friend Ronnie sends them to me. She's very nice. Like you, Dani.

Thank you, Marco.

The spirits went away after you told; they don't like it when you tell. Nobody in Abrams likes it. But that wasn't the reason they left. It was because *they* came and chased them away. The devourers.

Breakfasts got crunchy and bitter after the doctor said the others weren't real. Momma cried a lot about it. She didn't like hearing that breakfast makes your brain wobbly and your knees feel fuzzy on the inside, not when Daddy works so hard to keep a roof over our heads. You should be more grateful.

Momma had to take medicine that helped her sleep because of

you. She would just sleep and sleep all the time.

Daddy said it was hard for him to sleep, but it was nice that he could sit up and watch TV with his little girl. To cuddle up. Snuggle bunny. Someday, you'll be too big to be a snuggle bunny. Do you know how pretty you are? Just as pretty as your momma was. Do you like being pretty? Hold still. Close your eyes. Daddy's just going to take a quick nap. Don't move too much. That's my pretty little thing.

You were ugly when you cried. Not pretty. Saying you didn't want to be pretty anymore meant that you made Daddy mad, made him sad. Made him wish he wasn't there anymore. But you didn't care. You didn't want to take anymore naps. They felt wrong. He wasn't supposed to be whispering those things and moving against you the way he did. It made you feel dirty inside.

It was fine. It's okay. It's okay. No more naps. It's okay. Just remember to never tell.

Memories are strange. You know? They're a lot like water. Floaty, wavy things that come and go. When you think you catch something in the reflection, in that little shadow between the waves, they disappear, or maybe there is another one that's more interesting just over there by the flowers. They're hard to follow, but if you really, really try, you can catch one floating back to where they're made, to where they sound like autumn leaves being swept along the road by a chilly wind.

Be careful which ones you chase down, Moira Clarke. Not all of them are good. Because that's how they find you. When you're a bit older, that's how they find you. Things with teeth that look like Daddy and Pastor Dan. They hide in the dark and tell you what you like to hear. They tell you that you have the prettiest hair, the prettiest face. It's okay if you're tired, just relax. You have an old soul, don't you? Growing into a fine young woman.

They say it's okay; it's just a dream. This is just a dream. Just dreams. Dreams don't hurt. It's okay. Just a dream. Safe in your own bed.

And you believe them. For a while. That it's just a dream. Even when you get a little older and things start getting clearer in your head, you tell yourself it's just a dream… It's only dreams.

B-bu-but you know. You know. You know.

May I please have a glass of water?

3

Things change. It's hard to remember how or when, but they do.

There were times it hurt, when you were afraid. Those times it wasn't him, it was the shadows. A beast. A thing that haunted the house, haunted only your room. It came to visit you every few weeks, every full moon. It looked for girls like you, taller with longer legs that still had soft, tiny hairs on them. Little breasts that didn't know what it was like to be touched, to be kissed. The more you shove or fight, the more it hurts. The more you want to scream. The more you wished you were powerful. Stronger.

Those were the years you learned you could hold your breath until the stars twinkled behind your eyes and made you dizzy. Learned what whiskey and cigarettes tasted like. Learned to relax, to go somewhere else in your head. A beautiful place where little angels flew around and put yellow flowers in my hair and carried me down a warm river of cinnamon and butterflies. And I could be there for as long as I wanted, with angels kissing my fingertips, tickling my belly and neck, and balancing on top of my breasts on their little feet. Sometimes, they would whisper, 'We've been waiting so long for you to find us. You're special, Jenny. You're going to be the most special because you're strong in your own way. Someday, we'll take you home. We'll keep you safe.' And I wanted them to. I would have given them anything if they would have taken me away then and there. Just to be in the beautiful place forever.

But they said no. No, they couldn't take you. Not yet. And it made you so mad, so angry you could have just grabbed them… But you couldn't hurt them, wouldn't hurt them. They were innocent. It wasn't their fault. But it hurt. The anger hurt so bad.

The hate had to go somewhere.

You learned a lot. Learned a lot. Little noises in the house that used to be warnings turned into the little angels' laughter. The click of the doorknob down the hall didn't scare you anymore. When you heard the creak of the third floorboard in front of the bathroom door, it wasn't frightening. It was exciting. But you kept your eyes shut. Pretended to sleep. When the shadows came to the door, you still pretended.

And you waited. For the smells. For them to slip under the

sheets, to feel their weight on top of you. It wasn't frightening anymore because you learned. You learned that it can be whatever you want, whoever. Those smells could be anything. Whiskey could be butterscotch; cigarettes could be spring rain. Even the rough fingertips could be flower's petals on flesh. Puppy kisses.

They told you it was okay. It's okay. It's always okay. It wasn't hurting you. It was taking back its snuggle bunny. Its pretty thing.

When the shadows started to stay longer than usual, it was harder for them to be anything but him. It was a struggle. To keep the hate down, it was a struggle. You couldn't hate him. It was wrong, lying in his arms, bathing in the warmth and closeness, the sweat. But you still couldn't hate him. You couldn't hate him, because you learned that there was something missing in you, something that only the shadows could fill.

But you learned. You learned that all men have weaknesses. That it's better to not tell anyone what happens. To protect your family. Because you were special. You learned to let the shadows come at night, not because you were afraid anymore, but because you found a place in your mind to put the hate. Learned to make it go away. The shadows were coming anyway, so you learned to let them. Learned to hold them closer each time, to feel their heartbeat against your cheek, the roughness of the hair on their legs against yours. He didn't like it when you squeezed him and pulled him in deeper, but you did it anyway. Did it and hated yourself for it. Hated the little girl that was afraid of the dark. Hated Momma for sleeping. Hated that you sometimes forgot to close your eyes or to go to the beautiful place. Hated that you sometimes did it on purpose, that you embraced the shadows for what they really were. Hated yourself because you started to like it. Because it didn't have to hurt.

Things don't stop, they just change. People stare. They look at you differently, but then they turn away when you look. They forget. The Reverend comes over for dinner more often, and sometimes he stays a little later to have a drink with everyone. When Momma goes to bed, he sometimes sneaks you a little glass of whiskey or some wine and tells you how ladylike you look, how adult you've become. Probably the most mature girl—young woman—in high school. Here, have another one.

And you feel like the lady they say you are. Start to feel things like a woman. Warm things in your body. Something that's like desire but different, dirty. Like if desire came in from a hard day in a dusty field. You drink with Pastor Dan even though it makes the shadows different, makes them hurt a little more. But it's alright. It's alright. Shhh.

Breakfasts get quiet.

Then one day, Momma stops being Momma; she's just the other woman in the house. You don't have to listen to her anymore. You're grown.

There are fights. Quiet ones. Loud whispering in the kitchen, angry whispers. It's hard to make out the words, but it's easy to get their meaning. Anger, rage, worry, fear. It's all the same for months, but the arguments get louder. Right after dinner, in the kitchen. 'She's not my daughter anymore. That thing in there is not my baby girl, it's some kind of monster. What did you do? Tell me! What did you and that bastard do?'

You felt the slap more than you heard it. It had to be the first time Daddy ever hit her. Of all the times they fought, all the stomping and shaking in the house, all the shattered dishes and tears, he never hit her. Never even hit any of the kids. Not until she said something about you. He did it for you.

He did it for you. That's what you told yourself. Then you realize that wasn't true. Wasn't true at all. You learned how to lie. It was easy since you already knew how to believe your own.

May I take a break, please?

4

One morning, you wake up sick. It's like a little flu. Just a tiny one. A little belly bug that'll pass in a week or two.

But you know. And you don't tell.

You weren't allowed to go to the lake alone. Couldn't go anywhere alone, even before you were showing. But you managed to by pretending to take your pills at breakfast and shutting yourself in your room. People get use to patterns, you see. If they think they know what you're doing, then you can do anything you want.

At one point, Momma and Daddy were never home as often as they used to be. There were more and more meetings to go to, arguments with angry people demanding to know why everything is so dry, why the soils are dusty this year. The town changed in a strange way that year, but the lake was the same.

I remember it being a hot afternoon. Muggy. The kind of hot day where your sweat makes your skin feel hotter and you can smell the sunlight baking the moisture out of the dirt. It was only about four miles to the lake, and I still had my bicycle, so I made good time. Road grit and barley dust caking to my skin. I kept pushing, pumping my legs, because the faster I rode, the clearer I heard the others calling out to me. They were my friends, and they missed me.

By that time of the summer, the lakes are overgrown and mucky. There are no shorelines like there are on TV lakes. Wading in is like stepping on hot peanut butter. Not many people like it, but I always liked how it tickled to squish it between my toes. I called it Lake Jenny because nobody else liked to go there.

I hung my dress and my undies on a tree and splashed in. The water was cold, but that perfect kind of cold where it was warm when you held still but was nice and cool when you moved. I remember because I was worried that I had forgotten how to swim. But I'm like a fish, Moira. It was as easy as jumping in and letting the water hold me up, clean me off. I floated on my back for hours and hours, listening to my friends—the others—tell me about how glad they were to see me. And I was glad to hear them. I missed their little whispers, the little hugs in my brain.

When I heard the other splash, I was scared. It sounded too big to be a beaver and too small to be an old log, so it shocked me a little. Bears here don't swim to eat you, and the wolves had been quiet for a few years. I started treading water and looking around. I didn't see anything, so I assumed it was my imagination. But my brain couldn't explain the ripples at the other end of the lake.

The wind got cooler, and birds circled above me, but the trees didn't sway in the breeze; they stood completely still. Little fish swam up from the bottom and nibbled at my toes and slid against my legs and tickled my sides. And I knew everything was fine. They didn't tell me 'Shh. It's okay.' I just knew that, because they were there, everything was fine.

They wanted to swim with me, so I dove and held my breath until my lungs burned and my nose tingled. When I went back up for air, the wind was spinning and spinning, but the trees still didn't move. It was like they were made of those rocks in caves, stalagnites? Stalag… mites? Are you sure? Oh. Because mites crawl on the floors. Ew, Dani! You're silly. Stalagmites. Mites, mites, mites.

Anyway, everything smelled fresh and a little tangy, almost like milk that was just a little old, only sweeter. Birds swooped around in circles, some even landed and splashed themselves clean and flew into low branches where they scared the poor little squirrels back into the woods. The voices got so loud, kept telling me to swim with them, but I was getting so tired. I'd been out there so long I didn't know what time it was or when my parents might come home. I didn't want to get caught or make them worry, but I wanted to stay with my friends. My little brothers didn't like talking to me. I could never have any other kids over to my house. All I had were the others.

I said one more time wouldn't hurt, and I dove down.

And I was glad I did, Moira. Very glad. Because that was when she spoke to me for the first time.

It was dark. I could barely see up. The weeds caught on my ankles and held me down when I swam too close. Everything was fine for a moment, but then my lungs started to tickle real high up, here, right below my throat, and I wanted to cough. I started to choke. I was scared.

Then there were arms around me. "Hello, Jennifer," she said. I don't know the last time someone called me Jennifer. Not even Momma called me Jennifer. But everything went calm, and I could breathe, so I didn't care.

I wasn't sure if I could talk, so I just said *'hello'* in my mind, and she heard me. *Who are you? Are you a new friend?* Because I didn't know who she was just then, but I knew she was real. She wasn't like the others. I knew she was real because I could hear her in both ears. And I remember everything she said to me.

"Perhaps. I would like to be your friend. How can I be a friend to you?"

I don't know. You can be my friend if you're nice. Are you nice?

"I try. But sometimes being nice is an obstacle to kindness or doing what's necessary to help people. Do you understand that?"

Kinda. Where are you?

"I'm right here."

I can't see you.

"Here." She slipped her fingers into mine. Her skin was like something hot being cooled by the water around it. Fire and ice water. "I'm right here."

But I can't see you.

"I don't want you to. I don't want you to be frightened."

There isn't much that can scare me. I'm brave.

"I know. That's why you're special to me. Why you can help where others cannot."

Because I'm brave?

"Because you've endured so, so much. So many horrors that no child should ever have to experience. You've faced a thousand terrors forced on you by those you love. Horrors meant to break you, to kill your mind. Yet all that's remained is strength and kindness. You're too full of the milk of human kindness, as they say. Kindness people don't deserve. But it's your strength that makes you special."

I don't understand.

"Existence is pain and strife. Even in the smallest of things, there needs to be endurance. Life is that endurance. Humanity has shown time and time again how capable it is of destruction, but humanity overlooks the true strength of life: change. To go from one thing to the next. To evolve. Just like how volcanoes turn fire into earth, and that earth into food, with time. Or how water wears rock into a haven for bacteria to multiply. How even something as delicate as a flower can burrow through concrete to give its pollen to bees."

I didn't know what she was talking about. I still don't. The way she said it sounded pretty. Her voice was pretty and kind. When I think back on good days, I hear her voice instead of Momma's.

I asked her, *You said I can help you. How can I help you?*

"You can help me. I know you can help me. But you have to want to help me. To be strong. To endure one more horror, one more terrible, terrible thing. For me. For everyone that's come before. For the other children."

I don't know. I don't want to anymore. I don't want to.

"I know. I understand. But I can give you something. Something wonderful. Do you remember the time you were very little, when you were never afraid? When you didn't need to talk or listen, you could just feel your mother's heartbeat and it was like something was plucking the strings of your soul, and every note was warm love, a chill of safety, the beautiful ache of a full belly? I can give that to you. Forever."

It sounded nice. I didn't remember ever feeling like that, but I wanted to. I still do. I still want to.

I'll help you, I said. *What do you want me to do?*

And she wrapped her arms around me, held me close, and told me a secret. Whispered it into my ear.

"It's a secret. I can't tell you, Dani. I'm sorry. I'm so sorry. If I tell you, it won't be a secret." Jenny looked frantic, frightened. Her eyes were large and unblinking. She breathed like she had just finished a sprint.

Marco stepped into view but stopped when Jenny reached out for Dani. Dani calmed her by petting her arm and saying, "I believe you. Your secret's safe. Keep it. I don't need to know. I never need to know. You're a good friend for keeping her secret, Jenny."

Moira stayed quiet. She dug her thumbnail as hard as she could into the cuticle of her opposite thumb to keep herself from crying. Lake and Hopkins were monsters for what they did to Jenny. Worse than monsters.

Dani made soothing sounds and said gentle words until Jenny caught her breath and took a drink of water. "I'm a good friend."

"The best friend." Dani nodded toward Marco. "We don't have to keep going if this upsets you, Jenny. We can talk about something else if you like."

Marco reached over to take Jenny's hand, but she pulled away and gripped Dani's hand and arm until her knuckles went white. "No!" she cried. "No! You have to know. I'm supposed to tell you more. You need to know about my little angel, Ollie. I have to tell you. I have to tell both of you. She said so. That was the other thing I had to do."

5

So… so, so, I um… I… Marco please! Stop telling me I don't have to. I know I don't have to!

Sorry.

I… I think people aren't happy when you get caught being different, and it's worse when you're already different. When they know.

It looks like so much fun when they did it to the other women.

Hugs. Pet their hair, saying, "Oh, you're so beautiful. You're glowing. Is this your first? You always remember your first. You don't need to buy anything. You can have all of little Luke's old things." They touch their tummies and smile. You want to be one of them so bad. You want the smiles, the hugs, someone to touch your hair and hold the door while you get in the car. But it's only for other women, not for you. Everyone's happy when it's anyone else; they're not happy when you're already different.

But that's okay. It's okay. It's easy to be happy in your room, imagining it's Momma or somebody else rubbing the bump as he gets bigger and bigger. He's so funny, too. Always hungry. Always… What's that word when you wiggle around all the time? Restless! He's so restless. And he's so warm it's like squishing a puppy so hard that it slips into your belly and sleeps in a little ball. On the nights when he can't sleep, you can't either, but you don't want to. Those are the nice nights. When they leave you alone.

Momma stopped talking. Daddy slept on the couch a lot. There were some nights where he tried not to, but the door stayed locked. All of them stayed locked.

Pastor Dan stopped by every few weeks to say a prayer and drip oil and rub. His hands were always so cold and rough. Slimy. So gross. He'd just sit there and stare… and touch… and…. He was awful. Just mumbling strange words, drooling, eyes rolled up into his head, and shivering.

You have to let him. You have to let the Reverend do it. It's not godly if you fight. Be a good Christian, Jenny! Let him do his great working. If you don't stop fighting, I'll hit your belly with my belt.

Crack, crack, crack.

I had to protect Ollie. My little Ollie, Ollie, Owlie. Hoot. Hoot.

No, Marco! I'm fine. It's not time for them to go! It's my turn to tell my story. You're supposed to be here to help me when I need help to do things, and I need help telling my story to Dani Olsen and Moira Clarke! Stop it!

I'm sorry.... Yes, I would like a fizzy water. Thank you.

Do you like cherry or lemon, Dani? Ha! Red isn't a flavor, silly goose. Well, then green is my favorite flavor.

Abrams babies are born in Abrams, nowhere else. Those are the rules. That's why Momma gets the hot water and the towels ready. Extra sheets. More women, strangers, fill your room to the walls when your insides felt like an angry fist squishing a ball, over and over. They fill the bed with pillows and bring cool apple juice from the harvest. They don't say the nice things you thought they would. "You're fine. Stop complaining! I had my first at sixteen too, and I've done this four times. You're just being dramatic. Such a big baby! Don't you know women younger than you have given birth for centuries? You should be happy you're young; your bones aren't stiff. This is what you get for spreading your knees like a whore." They stop talking when the pain comes, when things get dizzy. They just stand there and stare at the space between your legs, whispering.

But She didn't. She talked. *Shhh. Breathe, dear. Breathe. Let your body relax. He wants out, and he'll find his way out. Let him find his own way. Don't force him; guide him. Squeeze right there. Take another breath. Push.*

When it was over, it was like ice breaking away from a lake in spring. Or like a river finally burrowing through an old dam. And he was so loud, Dani. So loud all the other women had to cover their ears and leave. He heard what they said to me, how they talked about me, and he let them hear it until there was nothing they could say to each other that could keep them in the room. So much sound coming out of that itty bitty body.

Daddy and Pastor Dan were mad he was a boy, said that they failed somewhere but that he should be good enough to give them years.

Momma smiled for the first time in forever. It was just for that day, though.

They wanted him named after grandpa, but that wasn't his name; he didn't want to be called August when he was born in November. I asked him what he wanted his name to be, and he just kicked his legs and said, "Hoo-oo, hoo-oo, hoo-oot," like a little owl. Little owlie Ollie. Hoot. Hoot. He sometimes comes to see me still. He'll pop up just outside the window. He's such a good boy. So brave.

Momma didn't like the name, said it was stupid. "A childish name from a child." That was fine. She wasn't Momma anymore, anyway. So, when she tried to make you take the pills again, all she could do was yell about it. She couldn't make you.

For Ollie's first Christmas, I made him socks for his hands so he couldn't scratch his face, a blue bonnet for his head—his hair is light and thin like mine—and I cut my favorite blanket in half and made it into a smaller one so we could be the same, so we'd know what each other was feeling when it was cold.

He has the prettiest blue eyes, like sunlight shimmering off the lake in summertime.

Hoot. Hoot.

6

In the spring, the shadows came for him. The devourers. The things that eat.

They slither through the windows at night and watch him in his crib, whisper things to him. They tell him he's naughty and that he has to come with them, to live far away from his mommy. But you won't let them. You're not going to let them fucking touch him. He sleeps with you now, out of his crib, away from the windows, behind locked doors. He cries at first, but then he gets quiet, drinking everything in with those big blues. Such a good boy.

You think you might not have heard them right. Tell yourself they maybe weren't really there. But you know. You know. There's this feeling. This awful, sinking feeling in your stomach, and you know, you just know that they want him. They want to take him, make him stay in Abrams. They want to make it so he can never leave. But you can't let them. You can't. So you run, even though there's nowhere to go. Anywhere can be somewhere if you're with someone you love, and I was with Ollie.

The shadows came in the morning, slithering through the windows and under the doors, searching the house from the bottom to the top for a little boy bundled in his crib. Thick strands of black crawling along the floors, avoiding too much light through the windows. They don't like much light; they're terrified of fire. Nobody knows that, so don't tell.

You made sure there was plenty of darkness in the hallways leading to the crib. Closed all the curtains, turned off all the lights, shut the doors except one. Pretending to ignore them was easy, since they're used to being ignored. Nobody wants to see them. Maybe you're the only one who can, but they don't know that. They don't know you can see them, hear them whispering in their language like little snakes hissing with steam. Don't know you've been waiting, planning, packed all of Ollie's warm clothes into one of Daddy's bags. You bundled him up in his car seat half an hour before and hid him on the porch while you stole the keys out of Momma's purse.

He's so quiet. Such a good boy, my Ollie. He didn't cry once. He just smiled his little toothless grin when I buckled him into the car, slowly backed away from the house, and drove toward the highway out of town. The farther we went from the house, the more he just laughed and laughed. Hoo-oohoo-oohoot. Hoo-oohoo-oohoot.

We were out. Gone. We had no idea where we were going; we were just going. Leaving. Out of Abrams for good. We thought that maybe we could find a warm place to live, somewhere with lots of sunshine and grass for Ollie to crawl on. Maybe even have a puppy.

I thought that maybe I could be a waitress somewhere, a nice restaurant with big plates of french fries. Ollie likes french fries. I could drive him home from school and go swimming on the weekends. We thought we were out.

As soon as we reached the edge of town, he started screaming. Shrieking. Like nothing… If you don't know what it sounds like when your baby is in pain, it's like someone dragging your soul across broken glass and cutting you in half, stabbing and stabbing and stabbing. And he got louder and louder the farther away from Abrams.

There was no stopping the bleeding. He was so tiny and there just was so much… What are you supposed to do when…

Your only choice is to drive back, to get him back inside Abrams. And it works. He stops screaming, stops bleeding enough for you to wipe it off him so he isn't drowning in it, but he keeps crying. So scared. He just hurt so bad.

The shadows must have heard it, because now they're chasing you. Running up from the ditches, sliding along the road, reaching out from the trees. You can only drive so fast. They chase and chase and chase all the way through town, past the farms, toward the forest, and just when you think you're away, they grab hold of the car and choke the life out of it. They're on the ground and in the sky. Everywhere! All you can think of is to grab Ollie and run. Run toward the lake, toward the Witch. She could help.

They chase you, Moira.

The forest is still so wet and cold in the spring. Your feet are numb. Lungs burn; you're breathing knives. Branches cut and tear your skin like icy hooks scratching at your eyes. You keep running. Even as the shadows twist and crawl alongside you, you run. Poor Ollie is so scared he can't help but cry so loud. You press him closer to your heart so he can hear it beat, so he knows it's going to be alright, that mommy has him and is going to bring him somewhere safe. Each time he cries, the shadows get closer. You hold him tighter. "It's okay, Ollie baby. Mommy's got you. It's okay. Hush, hush for mommy. Be brave. Be brave."

And he's so brave. He hushes. So quiet and so brave. So quiet. He doesn't scream when you do. Doesn't scream when you realize you've been running in the wrong direction, that the shadows have chased you somewhere else, some place in the woods you've never been. Doesn't scream when the world turns blurry and the air from your lungs explodes into the sky as you hit the ground.

There's Daddy, standing over you. You think he's come to help, come to take you somewhere safe, but he doesn't. He rips Ollie from you and hands him over to Pastor Dan.

You scream and kick and punch, but you're not strong enough; hands and shadows hold you down as Pastor Dan takes something long and shiny out of his belt. The shadows laugh and roll and curl into a huge ball over a dark pit in the ground, and Dan holds Ollie's little body overhead, offering him to the shadows.

You scream. You scream so hard. No matter how hard you yell, how loud you scream, "Daddy! Daddy, please! Please don't let him hurt my baby!" he doesn't listen, he just ignores you and stands there like he doesn't see you, like you're just another squirrel barking from the tree, some other distant forest noise that men can easily ignore.

There's nothing. But you can't quit; you have to fight. For Ollie. For those little hoots. Hoot-hoot.

You tell him the truth. The truth you suspect he already knows, hoping it will help him change his mind. "Please, Daddy! Please don't kill our baby. Not *our* Ollie. Please, Daddy, please don't. He's your son."

He knows. For a moment, you thought it would shock him into doing something. It doesn't. He just ignores you while the Pastor holds your naked little Ollie by his feet in the cold.

Such a good boy. So brave and quiet. He didn't make a sound when the flash of sunlight came down.

I saw his little spirit fly away. An angel with polished glass wings picked him up in its arms and lifted him over the pit and up into heaven to play with the other angels.

That's when I knew the Witch wasn't evil. No evil witch would ever call the angels to save Ollie. She did it because she's good, she protects. She saved Ollie from the monsters because I couldn't. Because I was too afraid and too weak.

But I saw them. I saw the monsters, the ones that eat you, devour you. The shadows knew I could see them, and they were afraid. So afraid that they forgot I was so fast. That I could bite and wriggle loose. That I could run. And I ran straight out of their world so fast I knew they couldn't catch me.

Don't let them catch you, Moira. Never let them catch you.

Moira couldn't stop the shaking or the nausea. A sharp ball of unwept tears clung to the walls of her throat. All she wanted to do was reach through the computer and hold Jenny, tear out her horror and agony and watch it blow away like ashes in the wind. The only thing she managed was a croaky, "Thank you, Jenny. Thank you for your story." A hot tear cut a burning river across her cheek to her chin when Jenny smiled at her.

"You're welcome, Moira and Dani. I'm very tired now. May I take a nap? Ronnie's coming soon."

Marco told her he'd get her a blanket so she could sleep on the couch.

Dani, eyes rimmed with red and near bursting with tears, told Moira, "I'll call you later tonight. Okay?" Then she reached over and folded Jenny into her arms.

They hugged until Marco came back and gently suggested the interview was over. Jenny said a quick, distracted goodbye, adding, "Be careful, Moira Clarke. They know you know. They always know."

Jenny's warning turned to ice her Moira's veins as Dani disconnected the call and the screen went black.

Chapter Seven

After crying until her eyes burned and the light was too bright, Moira called the police via the State Police's non-emergency line and told them everything about Jenny Lake's story, about Gloria Ylva, and her suspicions about Chief Lake and Reverend Hopkins. It took her several minutes to convince the woman at the other end that it wasn't a prank, and even then, the phone call lasted all of fifteen minutes and proved entirely fruitless.

"No. There's nothing we can do. All I can do is take down your information and pass everything along to my supervisor. Maybe it ends up with a detective, maybe it doesn't. Unless you have solid evidence of a crime being actively committed, there's really nothing we can do. Try the local police."

"The local police are involved! The police chief in this town is the one taking part in the abuse and murders. That's why I called you."

The line was silent for a while. "Again, Miss, if you suspect one of the officers of engaging in illegal activity, you need to go to your county seat and fill out a complaint."

"A complaint?"

"Yes. It's a formal— "

Moira hung up.

That was the benefit of being in power. You could do anything you wanted, and nobody would care. Sure, they'd make it sound like they cared, like something could be done. Yet it was always the same line of bullshit that led to this procedure or that form, which were only distractions, anyway. Ways for them to navigate around actually giving a damn or potentially being held accountable. Bastards.

Moments later, Dani called.

"Hey."

"I am so, so pissed off right now." Dani breathed hard, her voice thick with emotion. She had been crying, too. "How could someone do that to their own child? And what kind of terrible place would let someone do that and get away with it? This… criminal puke raped his little girl, and everyone knew and nobody said anything, and all she wanted to do was grow up and have friends and love her baby, and the people who were supposed to love her most abused her for years and murdered her baby. Murdered, Mo! That's what she meant by the angels taking him, right? They killed little Ollie!"

"I know they did. I know, Dani." Moira said it, but she wasn't sure. Something about how Jenny talked about Ollie picked at a dark area in her mind. *So quiet.*

"Can you imagine having all of that pain in your head for so long, just to have some stupid college brat come knocking and asking a bunch of personal questions? Ah, fuck. And all I did was reopen the wound."

Moira calmed her. "Don't blame yourself for anything they did, Dani. It wasn't your fault. You didn't push, you didn't pry. She chose to tell us her story."

Dani sniffled. "I hugged her for so long after that. She cried a bit. But then she just suddenly brightened up like nothing happened, and went to take a nap. Just like that. What the hell do we do, Mo?"

"I called the state police— "

"Fuck the police!" Dani shouted. "You think they care? Jenny's dad is the cop who did it and covered it up. All those bastards do is protect their own; they don't care about who or what gets hurt, so long as they don't have to admit they did anything wrong or hurt their precious reputation with each other." Dani seethed. "Oh god, Moira. If was a boy, I would sneak in through his bedroom window, nail his hands and feet to the floor, and burn his house down around him."

Moira collapsed onto the edge of the bed. "They hid it. They all hid it. The entire town's complicit in her abuse. Dani, how many other children have been hurt here? Hurt and then poisoned with over-medication and cast away like garbage to keep this dump's evil secrets?"

"I don't want to know," Dani whispered. "Not right now." Dani and Moira breathed together in silence for a long time, crying quietly.

"What did they say when you told them? The police?"

"They said it was out of their jurisdiction. Said if I have evidence, I should go to the local police or the county sheriff first, since they're the ones who would have to request additional resources from the state police or any federal authorities."

Dani scoffed. "Of course." After a pause, she said, "I'm scared for you up there, Moira. Are you coming home soon? Please come home soon."

"I want to. I really, really want to. I've had enough of this." She'd been in Abrams barely a week but it felt like a month. "There's just so much more than I thought there would be. All I wanted was to find some scary or strange stories about a witch in the woods that a small community used to scare each other. Celeste's story wasn't… It wasn't Gloria's or Jenny's." The tape recorder fell out of her bag and onto the floor when she sat up.

Dani sniffled. "This is usually where you say 'but'."

"What if you're right? What if the police can't help, and we need something more?"

"Rodney might be able to do something," Dani suggested.

"Rodney needs evidence." Dani's brother would do anything for her, but even he was shackled to the law's red tape. "We don't have enough. All I have are newspaper clippings, redacted copies of police reports, journals, notes, and a couple of strange recordings."

"We have Jenny," Dani said flatly.

"And we have to take into consideration how her and her story would be viewed in a court."

Dani gave an exasperated growl. "You heard her! How else could it be viewed?"

"She's sick, Dani. We know now that Jenny was diagnosed with paranoid schizophrenia, and she's had other hallucinations."

"They faked the diagnosis and drugged her to keep her quiet!"

"We don't know that. You and I can come to that conclusion and feel like we're right, but we need to have evidence to back it up if we want a court or law enforcement to do something about it. We also have to contend with whatever her conviction was. It's going to take more than we have, Danielle."

"What the hell are we supposed to do?"

Moira sighed. "I don't know. I don't know. There is more hiding here. There was something in Gloria Ylva's journals about Oliver Lake and other children. I guess Hopkins was trying to cast some sort of spell or something. Some kind of weird sex ritual that was supposed to create a magic baby, or some nonsense. He also records things, so he might have something on his computer."

"A moon child?"

"A what?" Moira asked.

"A moon child. It's this old Aleister Crowley sex magic crap from way back in the day about a bunch of wizards trying to impregnate a woman with a magical angel baby or something. But it's not real. It was totally a fiction novel. Those old pulpy books."

"What were they trying to get out of it?" Moira wondered.

"I dunno. Power or something? More magic?"

"How do you know this, Dani?"

Dani laughed. "What? A girl can't like Pokémon and weird occult shit, too?"

Moira's stomach bunched. "This is a real thing?"

"It's not real; it was a book. There's no such thing as magic. All those people were a bunch of crazies who made a club to get drunk and high and screw each other senseless while cosplaying as wizards and stuff. It's not real."

"But what if he believes it?" Moira posited. "If he believes it, then who knows how many people he's hurt or killed?" She swallowed hard.

Dani was quiet for a moment. "Then you need to come home. Like you said, this is over our heads."

"What if I can get more?" Moira stared at the rash on her arm, her stomach sinking. "If I can find more, maybe get a recording of someone admitting something. Could that be enough? I know that it's not our responsibility to collect evidence, but if this might be our last opportunity to get Jenny and Gloria some kind of justice. Isn't that the point to all of this? Uncover the truth behind the Abrams Witch?"

The hesitation in Dani's voice was clear now that her anger cooled. "Can't you do that from here?"

"Maybe. Maybe not. Give me another couple of days to check into something. I'll know for sure what I can do." Moira shook her arm until her sleeve fell to her wrist. "How many more days until the Flower Moon?"

"What's a Flower Moon?"

"The first full moon in May." She left out that it was also the day on which Gloria claimed they sacrificed people. Her plan was to be gone from Abrams well before then.

"Two days. It sounds pretty. You should come here and see it with me."

"Yeah." The air in her room felt suddenly much heavier than it had all afternoon. "Listen, I'm going to send you a few things—pictures and files. If you can get them to Rodney, see if he can get something started, or if he can help us."

"Why don't you just bring them home?"

"I will, Dani. I promise. I just want an electronic record of everything. If there is something we can do to help bring whatever evil is in Abrams to light, then the sooner we start, the better." Moira grabbed her keys out of her purse. "Besides, I think there's someone who can help."

Moira stomped up the driveway to the Hopkins' house, her face a mask of determination in the unnatural heat of early May. Confronting Heather while angry may not be the best approach, but whatever kindness Moira had brought with her to Abrams was ground down to a nub by Jenny Lake's story, by Gloria Ylva's, by this stupid town and its people.

While there were things she couldn't explain, what happened on Gogo's third tape being chief among them, but she wasn't about to pass things off onto a supernatural being. There was no Abrams Witch stealing women and whispering secrets to them, no supernatural being or demon trapped in the woods. There was only a handful of very fucked up people in this town who killed people, either their own dying or outsiders like her. This wasn't a school project anymore. It was a mission to avenge three dead children and a broken woman. Whoever the Witch was—Hopkins or Lake or both—they were going to answer for what they've done.

The waxing gibbous moon hung in the late afternoon sky like a sleepy eye as she shouldered her way past a tall arborvitae and approached the front door. A motion sensor flicked on the light. She pounded on the metal frame of the storm door and rang the doorbell.

Brian answered with a confused smile and a glass of what could have been whiskey or apple juice. "Good evening. How can I help you?" His smile quickly faded.

Moira kept her words measured and calm. "I would like to speak to Heather, please."

"I'm sorry, she's busy. Who are you?"

"You know who I am." Impatience hardened her voice. "This whole damn town knows who I am. Your wife, Brian. I want to talk to her."

Brian's face went rigid. "I said she's busy." He slammed the door.

Moira swore and raised her fist to pound again, maybe this time on the glass. That would get his attention.

Several quick clicks of plastic on metal caught her attention. From the right side of the garage, a cone of cigarette smoke billowed out from between the tall hedges.

Moira walked toward it.

Waiting for her in the evergreen shadows on the other side of a white picket fence was Heather Ylva, her face illuminated by a slight orange glow as she took another drag of her cigarette. She put a finger to her lips for Moira to keep silent. Heather blew out another lungful of smoke and watched through the window as Brian poured himself another drink and went upstairs. "His office is on the other side of the house," Heather whispered. "Walk around the hedges to the back corner. There is a little space between them where we can talk."

Chapter Eight

The hedges were almost taller than her, yet she still ducked her head and sneaked around them just in case the neighbors were watching. Near the very back of Heather's yard, Moira found a narrow separation between hedges. The smell of burning tobacco paper reminded her of the woods behind the motel, and an uneasiness about being pinned between thin branches filled her belly. She chewed on her lip and wrestled her way through the hedges up to the fence. It was dark, almost sundown. Darker in the hedgerows.

Heather sauntered past her flowers, around a wooden windmill, and stood by the three-tier fountain for two drags, yet she never took her eyes off Moira. She held up a finger.

A light on the second floor brightened the beige curtains. Brian peered between them. Moira leaned into the shadows.

"Babe, I wish you'd quit those. They stink when the wind blows this way."

"Yes, my love." Heather waved at Brian.

The window closed with a *shish* and a click. The curtains went dark.

Heather twirled the fire off her cigarette, stomped it out in the perfectly manicured grass, and lit another. She approached Moira casually. "What do you want?"

"You're Gloria's mother. You were there when Celeste Martin disappeared."

"Yes." Heather's jaw clenched. "And you're the girl I told to stay the fuck out of Abrams. Why did you come here? Why couldn't you just stay away? Why didn't you run?"

Moira's stomach fluttered. "Because I can't run from this. I can't leave when I know they're killing people. I need to know what the hell is going on, and I'm guessing you might be the only one in town that will help me."

Heather looked every month of her 50 years. Deep lines cut into the corners of her eyes, darkening blotches of brown and red kissed her cheeks, and the sagging skin under her jaw looked more at home as a frown. Yet underneath all of that, she still looked like the girl from Moira's dream. "Because I gave you the box? You think I gave you Gogo's story so you could stay here and play hero? I told you to run!" A fortunate gust of wind masked the volume of Heather's harsh whisper. She glanced at the house. None of the curtains moved. "You could've taken her away. You could have taken my baby's story and told the world the truth about this place. That Abrams is cursed by madmen who have no qualms about slaughtering babies to some evil thing in the woods. A demon. And the people here all know about it. We know. We all know, Moira. There are no secrets in Abrams."

"Demon?" Moira stiffened.

"You don't understand, do you? Haven't you noticed how there are no poor people here? The houses aren't half as run down as they should be. Nobody's ever sick. The ones who are, are…" Her lips trembled and her throat worked itself. "This place is a blessing for many, but a curse for everyone. In the winter, we don't even have to put salt on the roads. We plow the snow and what's left melts. There is no ice buildup. All the flowers bloom. We don't have to pick weeds out of our vegetables. All of this because every year, every Flower Moon, a sacrifice is made to keep the fields fertile and the water clean."

Heather blew a cloud of smoke in Moira's face. "I told you to run, and now you can't leave. What do you think I can do?"

Moira huffed away the smoke. "I can leave tomorrow, Heather. I can take everything you give me and be gone by morning. I've already talked to the State Police."

A bitter laughed creaked past Heather's lips. "It's too late. You can't leave. We all know about your arm."

"What? This?" Moira pulled up her sleeve and inspected the red lines circled in ink on her arm. "It's poison ivy."

"That's a mark." Heather pointed at Moira's arm. "This is why you can't leave. It's marked you. You're the next offering to the Beast on the Flower Moon."

Moira pulled her arm away. The sun dropped behind the peaks of nearby pines. "What the hell are you talking about?" A surge of panic and desperation shot through her arm. In a flash of movement, she had Heather's wrist locked in her grip. "Heather. Tell me everything."

Heather ripped her hand away and lit another cigarette, shaking. "You don't understand. We have to do it. As much as it may kill some of us to let it happen, we have to. It's the way it is, the way we have to live now. If we don't, we all die." She gestured at her lawn. "We have to water this all day to keep it green. We haven't told anyone that we'll be out of water by the end of the month."

"God damn it, Heather!" Moira hissed. "Will you please make sense?"

Heather scowled. An angry tear rolled down her eyes. "Nobody can leave Abrams and live for long. Nobody. We're cursed here." Her face scrunched with sadness and shame. "Look." She held out her left arm and clicked on the flame from her lighter. Moira's eyes adjusted quickly. She could just make out the thin, white scar running from the heel of Heather's hand to the middle of her forearm.

The flame went out. "When Gloria went missing—when she died—I couldn't take it. It took my baby from me. It made her sick. It let her be sick, so it could take her away from me. And I wanted to be with her, with my Gogo. She was my everything. When it was cold outside but warm in bed and I didn't want to get out from under the covers, she was the reason I crawled into the cold. Even when she was thirteen and thought everything I did was to hurt her, when she called me whore and a terrible mother, she was still my reason for breathing.

And it took her away."

Heather sniffled. "Brian shaves every morning. He's an old-fashioned person, like most people in Abrams. He uses a straight razor. So one morning, I went to where they found her clothing, way out in the woods. I brought her favorite stuffed bunny with me. I found the tree where…" Heather took a breath. "I took Brian's straight razor and went to be with my baby girl." Tears glittered orange and silver on Heather's cheeks. "It was two days before Matthew Miller found me. Two days," Heather repeated. "I bled for two days, Moira. And I didn't die.

"None of us can die here. If I leave this town for more than a few days, I start to bleed. A couple of the other women in town choke. One took a vacation to Florida and her heart exploded." Heather's eyes filled with terror. "Imagine a place where you never have to die. You age slower than the rest of the world. Farms produce more than enough, even though the rest of the world could be turning to dust. Nobody needs to worry about not having anywhere to sleep or not enough to eat. Do you know what people would do for that?"

They'd kill innocent people. Moira nodded, though the thought made bile rise to her throat. "But the droughts?"

"Because one offering escaped. She survived."

"Who was it?"

"A forester. A woman named Veronica Gardiner."

The name sounded vaguely familiar. "If nobody can leave, how did she survive?" Moira asked.

"I don't know."

"Did you help her?"

"I can't help you, Moira." Heather shook her head. "I'm so sorry."

Moira's pulse raced. The pressure of her own heartbeat in her skull was like a steel ram battering open a door. "So who is it? Who's the Witch? Hopkins? Lake?"

Heather shook her head. "There's no Witch. We made it up. Brian, Matt, and me. We made it up to scare kids at farm parties. It was just some stupid dream I had when I was little. A witch in the woods eating kids in the dark. When Celeste disappeared, it just started running on its own steam. It was before all of this." She pointed at her wrist.

"Bullshit!" Moira hissed. "What about the tape? Who was Gloria speaking to?"

"I don't know what you're talking about."

"The tape in the storage room! The one you gave me the key to. After the wolves caught her, Gloria was making a deal with someone." Moira's throat tightened at the horror on Heather's face. "There was more at the end of the tape, after she was chased. Who was it?"

Heather shook her head. "I don't know what you're talking about. There isn't anything more. I listened to that tape over and over. All of it. Both sides. There was nothing else." The look of pure desperation on Heather's face disarmed her. "What did you hear?"

Moira chewed on the inside of her lip. She told Heather everything. "If there is no Witch, who was she talking to, Heather? Someone promised her something."

"I don't understand. Promised her what?"

"My guess? Revenge. Justice, maybe. Some way to get back at Hopkins for what he's done."

Heather's eyes dropped. "Or me for not believing her." She nearly collapsed but steadied herself on the fence.

Moira put her hand on hers. "Heather. Tell me who it is. Which one of them is killing people? Who's the Witch?"

"I told you it's a demon. It's the Beast." Heather searched Moira's eyes for something. It was as if she couldn't talk, couldn't find the words. At last, she said, "Dan's just its servant. I don't know if it's really a demon, the devil… Hell, for all I know it really is a witch. I just call it the Beast."

"What is it?"

"I don't know!" Heather bit her lips so she wouldn't yell. "It's something evil. Something real, Moira."

"Show it to me, then. Where is it?"

"Where?" Heather asked, no longer whispering. "It's everywhere. It's Abrams. It's here in the dark, listening. It can hear every word we're saying. Don't you ever see the shadows crawling around where they shouldn't? Maybe something moving out of the corner of your eye when it's dark out?"

Moira looked around and noticed a faint aura surrounding everything, as if a child went through and outlined the night with a marker blacker than black. The sensation of eyes upon her prickled the flesh on her shoulders and the mark on her arm burned.

"Like I told you, there's no escaping. It has absolute control."

"Prove it to me. Where's the Pit? The Pit Gloria and Jenny Lake talked about."

"You know Jenny?"

"I know Hopkins killed Oliver Lake." Heather trembled; Moira grabbed her hand with both of hers. "Heather, listen to me. The reason I read books and hunt down old stories is because I'm always afraid. I'm afraid of failure, afraid of being alone in a city at night, afraid of falling asleep because all I see are nightmares. Stories have always taught me that there are things stronger than fear. That for every monster, there is a knight or a wizard or a pissed off princess with a knife who faces the evil and comes away victorious and unafraid. They've shown me that no matter how bad it gets, there is always something we can do." Moira squeezed her hand. "Please, Heather. I don't know what this Beast is, so I don't know if it can be beaten. But I'll be damned if I'm going to be something's lunch without trying to choke it to death on my way down."

Heather seemed confused and scared. Rightfully so, Moira thought. She was a prisoner her entire adult life, shackled to this town, her husband, and the men who would have killed her daughter for a good corn harvest. It was clear that fear kept her silent.

Moira pressed her. "Heather, please. What is the Beast? What can I do to stop it?"

"You talked to Jenny Lake? Today?"

"Yes," Moira answered.

"Oh God." Heather hand went cold. She trembled. "I dreamed… I didn't think it was you. I thought it was someone else. A black girl."

Dani. "Why? What happened to her? What did you dream?"

Her voice tight, Heather said, "Hide. Never let it in."

"What do you mean?"

"Run." Heather pulled her hand away from Moira and started taking panicky steps away. "Run back to your room and don't answer your door. Don't turn off your lights. Stay inside after dark tonight."

"Why? What are you people planning?"

"Shh! I had a dream. It's going to come for you tonight. Don't let it in. Don't let it touch you again." Heather turned around and headed for her door. "Never let it in."

Moira returned to her motel room just as it got dark. Once inside, she barricaded the door with the chair, and turned on every light. She was in the middle of folding clothing into her suitcase when her phone rang. On the other end, Danielle was breathing hard.

"Mo? A-are you coming home soon? I tried calling you earlier."

"I was out. I'm packing right now. Sweetie, are you alright? What's wrong?" She put everything down. "Talk to me."

Dani paused for a long time. Her breaths uneven and strained. "I don't know what it was, and I know how crazy it sounds, but I think something was in my room last night."

Moira's skin rose. "What was it? What did it look like?"

"Shadows, just shadows. They could talk. They whispered things to me. Terrible things. They told me you… that you…"

"What, Dani?"

"They said you were doing things you weren't supposed to do, that you were going to hurt more people. They said everything you were doing would end up costing people their lives. Innocent people who didn't deserve to die." Dani started breathing faster, gasping for breath. Her voice strained until she was crying. "They said you wanted to hurt me. You're going to hurt me, Moira."

"No. No, don't listen to them. Whatever they're saying, it's a lie. Don't believe any of it."

"Why are you going to hurt me, Moira? Don't you love me? Don't you want to hold me?" Dani's voice smoothed to the even, calm breaths Moira wished whispered in her ear. "Don't you want to let me in?"

The sounds of scratching on the door turned Moira's spine to steel.

"Let me in, Moira."

The skin from her legs to her neck stood up in cold waves. Dani wasn't crying; she was laughing.

"Who the fuck is this?"

The response came from the door. Three quiet taps.

She looked at her phone. The screen was blank. In her call history, there was nothing. There had been no phone call.

The world felt like an elevator that had stopped three inches too low, then slowly crawled up to come even with the floor.

Another knock. The same three quiet taps. Same rhythm, same strength.

Moira swallowed. "Who is it?"

"It's me." Becky, the clerk, called. "I think there's a problem with your credit card. Do you mind coming to take a look?"

Moira looked at the clock. 11 PM. Becky hadn't stayed past 9:30 the whole time she'd been there.

"What kind of problem?" She picked up her phone and checked her credit account and found the payment for the room had already cleared. She texted Danielle. *Are you okay?*

Three more knocks. No answer.

"Becky?"

"It's me." Same voice, same tone. Every shadow in the room darkened. Lights flickered.

"I don't see one on my end. Can you quickly explain it while I get dressed? I just hopped out of the shower."

"Do you mind coming to take a look?"

No way was she opening that door. "You know, I'm super tired right now. The bank isn't open until nine. Do you mind if I stop by first thing in the morning and we look at it together?"

No answer.

After a minute of steady silence, Moira exhaled and the prickles on the hairs of her neck settled down.

A shadow passed in front of her window. A thin body with long hair back-lit by orange-yellow light.

"Mo?" Dani's voice sounded hollow through the glass.

Her blood tingled with static electricity and shaved ice.

"Mo?" Shadow Dani pressed her hands against the window. "Let me in."

"Get the hell away from me." Moira rushed over to the door and slid the chain in place. Her voice shivered. "I'm not letting you in. I don't give a shit who or what you are. You're not getting in here." She grabbed the only things she thought were useful: her keys and the pepper spray.

"I love you, Mo. Let me in."

"Get away!" She yelled, pressing her body into the darkest corner but never looking away from the shadow.

"I love you."

Moira wanted to scream, threaten to call the police, anything that she thought would frighten away a normal person, but settled on silence. Whatever it was, it wasn't human. It knew she was in there and it needed her to let it in. If she didn't, maybe it would get bored and leave instead of standing there, staring, completely motionless. It wasn't even breathing. It was more a Dani-shaped cardboard cutout than a person.

After a long minute, a brief hiss, almost a laugh, blew against the glass, and the shadow stepped away from the window, dragging a clawed finger across her door and along the brick outer wall of her room where it faded into silence.

Chapter Nine

Moira considered herself a sensible woman. The following morning, she decided the most sensible thing for her to do was pack her stuff, get in her car, and speed away in the direction that got her out of Abrams the fastest. Whatever this Beast was, it was real, it was some kind of monster, and the only thing that mattered was getting as far away from it and Abrams as humanly possible.

She took a deep breath. *Think simply. You're leaving. Pack your stuff in the car, get in, drive away. Don't stop. Don't wave goodbye. Don't look anyone in the eye. Just drive. To grandma. To Dani. Get away.*

When her phone buzzed, Moira let out a tense squeak and checked the room. There was no noise from the other side of the door, no shadows hiding in the morning light oozing through the orange curtains. Nothing that would reasonably react to the sound of vibrating plastic on paper.

It was a message from Dani: *No. was just about to text you. jenny lake is gone.*

Gone? Like dead?

disappeared after we left. marco said it was like she just vanished

Fuck. How?

dunno. when r u coming home?? I don't feel good and don't want to be alone anymore.

Packing now. She decided to not tell Dani anything about what Heather had said or about the shadows from the night before. Instead, she wrote, *I'll be home soon,* and then immediately texted Rachel the address of the motel, even though her grandmother rarely used her cell phone.

Gamma. I love you. Am staying at the only motel in Abrams. I'll be home soon. If I'm not home in a couple of days, then

She didn't know what else to say. What would not unnecessarily worry her grandmother?

I love you and will see you soon.

Moira went back to shoving her clothing into her suitcase. Stuffed her sheets and blankets into her own pillowcase. All the information and evidence she found about Abrams and its witch, she carefully slipping into her backpack. When she was done, she threw everything into her backseat.

She tossed the room key on the dresser next to a torn hunk of paper with *Thank you!* written on it. If she owed anything more for the room, Becky could charge her card.

The tires squawked against the highway leading out of town. She headed north with the intention of then driving as far west as was necessary to skirt the town by a few miles, then drive straight south back home, avoiding as much of Abrams as she could.

A tingling anticipation ran through her body when the sign that marked the town limits came into view.

Before she reached the sign, there was a bump under her tires, followed by the sound of small explosions underneath. Her steering wheel vibrated so violently that by the time she pulled over to the side of the road, her knuckles were white, and her palms cramped. The dashboard lights flickered; her radio volume went wild. Everything electronic in her vehicle acted on its own until she turned off the engine and removed the key.

Breathless, she opened the door and felt her heart plunge at the sight of two blown tires. She nearly wept when she found her passenger side tires to be flattened as well.

There was a movement in the ditch in front of her—shadows pulling back into the forest.

That was the moment she understood Heather was right. Abrams would not let her leave.

She rattled around the console for her phone and found that it was dead. Of course it was.

A rush of anger tangled with fear in her chest.

Moira shouldered her backpack and slammed her door shut. The road north was a straight line of gray-black pushing through thick trees.

She knew it wouldn't let her leave. Whatever was in this town—Witch, cult, demon—it wouldn't let her go. Abrams was a trap. A prison. Part of her toyed with the temptation of walking out, just taking the road on foot to wherever it led and figuring out her situation from there. But she could see strange wavering in the distance, as if the road ahead ended in some kind of clear veil waving in the wind. She knew, instinctively, she knew she could never get past it.

She tried anyway.

It was like walking through glue or running within a nightmare. Everything became slow and sticky. Her legs protested with each sluggish step. Not thirty feet beyond the sign, the corner of her vision wobbled and shifted like a carnival mirror until her stomach felt full of needles. She folded forward, covered her mouth, and retched.

She pulled her hand back and gasped at the smear of blood on her finger.

Another step forward, and she vomited a mouthful of blood onto the pavement. The trickling of fluid tickled her every orifice. A bloody tear rolled down her cheek.

The primal drive to survive forced her legs to carry her back to the car. She leaned against the hood, struggling to breathe through the clogging in her nose and the ache in her lungs. After a minute, her entire body felt perfectly normal.

Just like Oliver Lake, whatever had a hold of her was going to kill her if she left. There was no escaping Abrams.

Moira didn't look toward the sound of another vehicle coming to a stop behind hers.

"Good thing I was headed this way." It was Miller in a rusty red tow truck. "Otherwise, it'd be a long haul back to town." He hopped out of his vehicle and inspected hers. "Hoo! I don't know if I have tires this size. Might have to order them. Could take a couple of days. Tell you what, I'd be beside myself if I didn't have any of my vehicles working." He gave her a knowing smile. "Thinking about it makes me feel kinda trapped. You know what I'm saying?"

Moira ignored his comments, noises of surprise, and questions while he circled her car. The Flower Moon was tomorrow. Thursday. Today and tomorrow. Two days. Two days to figure out how to save her own life.

Miller came around to face her. His yellow smile and the manure smell of his clothes threatened to gag her. Dirty fingers gave her shoulders a gentle squeeze. "How about that ride now?"

Moira's hair whipped around her face in the dry wind. She stared past Miller like he was a ghost. "Tow it," she spat, and then tore herself away from his heavy hand. "I'll walk."

A quarter mile from Abrams' boundary, Moira's phone screen blinked on. It was around 9:30 in the morning when she reached the motel parking lot. Miller honked as he drove past with her car on his flatbed.

Her head was numb, and her heartbeat raged against her throat as she stepped past the withered wildflowers along the wall and entered the motel room, barricading the door with the desk and a chair behind her.

Rivulets of browning crimson left trails on her face from her eyes, nose, mouth, and ears. The ache in her stomach told her she'd swallowed too much of her own blood, which she vomited into the shower drain.

She sat in the steam until the water went cold.

Whatever it was, it existed. Witch, demon, monster—it was real. Not only was it real, but it was strong enough to reach into her and squeeze her life away if she tried to escape. It could kill her if it wanted. It was killing her. It was killing her, and there was nothing she could do about it. Nobody she could tell. Her phone worked, but who was she going to call? There was no way she would endanger Dani or Rachel by calling them for help. The police? They had made it clear they would not get involved. Even if they did, she still couldn't leave Abrams without bleeding to death. Whatever it was, this thing, this Beast, it didn't care that she could call anyone and everyone and tell her story, because in the end, it wouldn't matter. She would still be dead. She could run and die. Or worse, she could run and either Miller or Lake would bring her near lifeless body back into Abrams to be sacrificed. There was nothing she could do.

Like Heather said, it had complete control.

Moira allowed herself to cry in the shower, so long as she kept thinking. What did she have that it couldn't take away? Anything?

She dressed in the only clothes she had left, leaving her bloody underwear in the wastebasket and getting as much wet out of her jeans as possible by squeezing handfuls of toilet paper along the seams. Apparently, she had bled from everywhere.

When she finished, she called Dani.

"I need you to take everything to the police. Right now. Take it to the police and tell them they're murdering people in Abrams."

"What the hell is happening, Mo? Why do you sound sick?"

"I had a bloody nose again." Moira kept her voice even and calm, even though her chest filled to the point of bursting. "Dani, listen to me. I want you to take—"

"I'm not doing a damn thing until you tell me what's going on? You know, this whole time you've been up there, you've been different. For as long as I've known you, you have never lied to me, never sidestepped any of my questions. You've always been open, and you've always talked to me. Every time you've ever lied or bullshitted your way through something, you've told me about it, so I know when you're lying, Moira! Why the hell have you been lying to me? Why are you hiding things?"

"Dani, it's not like that."

"Then what's it like? Huh? Tell me what's going on. All of it. Right now."

Moira chewed on her lip. She knew Dani would come running if she knew the truth. She couldn't allow that. "Take everything to the police. Tell them they're killing people."

"I'm coming up there. Today."

Moira held the phone away from her ear and talked into the screen. "No! Dani, listen to me. It isn't safe!"

"Fuck you, Moira. I'm driving up right now. I'm punching out and I'm getting in my car."

"Don't you dare! It's not safe, Dani!"

"And you're going to tell me everything, and I'm going to drive you out of that town, even if I have to strap you into my trunk."

"Danielle Rose!" Moira screamed. "Stay the fuck out of Abrams! Stay the fuck away from me. I don't want you here." She choked on the last word, barely getting it past the tears she was tired of crying. Her voice softened. She added, "Get everything to the police. Never call me again." She hung up, saying a final "I love you" to the blank screen before turning her phone off and stuffing it into her backpack.

She wiped her eyes and flipped her hair through her grandmother's headband and marched out of the motel room and toward the office where Becky was sitting on her tall chair, reading a thick romance novel.

"When did you know?" Moira tossed the key onto the desk.

"I'm sorry?"

She stared hard at Becky. "When did you know they were going to kill me? Hopkins, Lake, and Miller? When did you know?"

Becky's cheeks went white.

Moira kept staring. Her nails dug into the meat of her fists until a precious drop of blood peeked out of her skin. Every fiber of her body tingled with a rage which she imagined as invisible lightning firing into Becky's wide eyes, burning away her strength to resist and giving in to Moira's will. "Fucking tell me, Becky."

Becky's face and body turned as if to run, but her eyes were transfixed. "The d-day before you got here. Reverend Hopkins told me. Said that you were coming to end the drought."

"What the hell is wrong with you people? How many people have you killed for that thing in the woods? How do you live with yourself, knowing you took away someone's child, someone's love?"

A tear dribbled past Becky's cheek. She hadn't blinked in so long. Moira wondered if any of the other offerings confronted the people of Abrams this directly. "We have to," Becky said with a shrug. "It's God's will."

Disgusted, Moira considered slapping her. Instead, she asked, "Where is it? The Beast? It's supposed to be in some kind of pit, right? Tell me where it is."

Becky shivered. "I don't know. In the woods outside the Miller farm. I've never… I don't watch. I don't want to."

"Where can I get clean pants?"

"The hardware store?"

Moira leaned in, cinnamon eyes burning. "Get in your car."

With a strange compliance bordering on obedience, Becky gave her a ride to the hardware store and told her about the round rack of clothing in the back of the building before she drove away, leaving Moira standing on the sidewalk in bloody clothing. The two people peering out of the window of the insurance sales building looked away. A middle-aged couple carrying bags of produce spun around and headed back into the grocery store when they saw her.

Moira marched to the back of the store, ignoring Tommy and the customers at the counter as she tore open a three pack of underwear, ripped the tag off a pair of green 'tactical' pants that were close enough to her size, and changed right in the middle of the floor. She didn't have the patience for shame or modesty.

On her way out, she grabbed a black-handled knife off the shelf and started tearing apart its plastic packaging.

A middle-aged man, an employee judging by his red apron, walked over to where Tommy pointed. He cleared his throat. "Miss, can I help you? I can't just let you—"

She pulled the knife out and tested the blade. It was razor sharp. "This is mine now." She stuck it in the front pocket of her hoodie and pushed open the door. Nobody followed, they just eyed her from a distance. People hovered at the windows of the apartments above the seamstress. Cars slowed so children could look. Two women who were sharing a cigarette near the light pole in the bank parking lot stared in her direction. Some faces held a hint of guilt and sympathy, while others glowered with outright hostility.

That was it, she realized. Even with all its power, the Beast wouldn't take away its own sacrifice. She bet nobody in Abrams would dare touch her; they were too afraid to upset either the Beast or Hopkins. Still, she needed to be careful. Two large men with rope could make it certain that neither she nor anyone else hurt her.

It was a risk she needed to take. Whether it was the Beast, Hopkins, Lake, or the entire town of Abrams, she would not let anything kill her without a fight. And she was going to start her fight at the church.

Chapter Ten

The sun, high and bright in the noontime sky, threatened another abnormally hot spring day. Moira reached the church, sweat dripping down her back, pulse racing in her ears, and lavender wafting from the little twist in her headband.

Reverend Hopkins and Chief Lake waited inside. They looked surprised to see her.

"Good morning, Moira." Hopkins glided away from the altar. "How is your research going?"

"I know." Her stomach jumped at the powerful echo of her own voice wandering between the pews. "I know everything you're doing."

Hopkins and Lake shared a short laugh. "Everything? My, my. I'm impressed. Would you like to share how you came about this sudden omniscience?" His mock empathetic demeanor made her stomach roil. "You look like you're carrying quite the burden."

She rolled up her sleeve, displaying her mark. "What's in the woods outside the Miller farm?"

Hopkins' face kept its smile. Lake stepped forward, patting the sweat on his face and neck dry with a cloth. "Trees, animals, a variety of plant life, I suppose."

Moira scowled at him. "You know what I mean. What's out there? Where did you take Jenny and Ollie?"

"What?" Lake's eyes darted between her and Hopkins.

"Your daughter. Your son and grandson." She choked back a rise of bile. "You monster. You absolute fucking bastard. How could you do that to her? Your own child?"

Lake's face went slack before it flexed with anger. "Who the hell are you to go digging through my personal life? My family's? Who told you about her?"

Moira gave him a sour smile. "Pretty things never tell."

"If you know where she is, you tell me right goddamn now!" Lake's booming voice rattled against the rafters. He stomped toward her. "Right goddamn now!"

Moira took a step back. Her fingers tightened around the knife.

"Relax, Jeffrey. I think Ms. Clarke is a little confused about what's happening in our little community," he added with a grin, "and her role in it."

"Oh, I know plenty. I know about the tape you gave your brother. He played it on the night Celeste Martin disappeared. I know about Heather and Brian. I know about what you did to Gloria Ylva, about the cameras you installed in the bathrooms so you could watch little girls. The weird sex rituals or whatever the hell you do with those girls in your office. I know that you've got the people in this town brainwashed into thinking murder is an acceptable means of praising Jesus or whoever. And I know I will not be your bullshit cult human sacrifice to whatever god, demon, or whatever you freaks worship."

Hopkins nodded to Lake, who walked past through the back exit. Moira kept her eyes on him the whole way. Hopkins said, "The truth is difficult. Separate what you think you know from reality. Things like gods, angels, devils—call them whatever you like; they are all spirits. Childish concepts such as good and evil are beneath them, and they've no need for worshippers. The truly powerful have no need for the triviality of worship. They simply take what is theirs, what they need to fulfill their purpose, their will. One of these spirits, the thing my brother's wife insists on calling 'the Beast,' lives in the Abrams woods." He opened his arms and turned his eyes heavenward. "A spirit sent to us by the Almighty to preserve our town and our way of life."

"You kill people so you can have street dances and expired medication?"

Hopkins dropped his arms and looked at her with disappointment. "Oh, Moira. Surely, you understand that wasn't a celebration for Abrams. It was a celebration for you!" He shook his head. "I suppose not. There's so much about Abrams I wish I could have shown you, about its people, about who we are: a good, humble, friendly,

God-fearing community of hard-working people who choose to embrace traditional family values and purpose."

The laugh left her lips before she could catch it. It almost didn't sound like her own. "You're murderers. You sacrifice innocent people to some kind of shadow monster."

"That's the problem with humanity, Moira. You're conditioned to believe in stories that make you feel special, singled out." Hopkins paced between pews, never coming closer to Moira than the font in the center of the room. "You cling to old-fashioned notions of innocence and guilt, good and evil, darkness and light, because they magnify your own sense of self-importance, until you feel a sense of elevation and superiority over everyone else. Yet you call this spirit, this holy vessel, a monster for preserving the lives of a thousand good people and their children?

"This spirit you call the Beast is a giver of life, a true sustainer. Where else have you gone where the old need never get older, where the young are never sick, where mothers don't have to die in childbirth? Farmers in Abrams need not worry about toiling in the fields and praying for rainy days. The grocery stores are never short of produce. Livestock is free of disease and deformity. No one goes hungry."

"Nobody going hungry in a prison, Daniel!" The skin on her arms crawled with thousands of cold insect feet. "Can you imagine how frightened most of them must be? What about the ones who have family on the other side of the world they can never see again?"

"Prison is a subjective term. For eons, humans and animals have carved out swaths of land and marked them with signs and piss scents to keep others from encroaching on their territory. Don't you surround your homes with fences to protect yourselves and demarcate what you consider yours? It seems hypocritical to carve out spaces of your own where you can engage in self-determination, then turn around and vilify another for doing the same on a larger scale. Then again, that sounds perfectly American, doesn't it?" Hopkins raised a thin eyebrow. "Remove the board out of your own eye, and then you can see clearly enough to remove the speck from mine, Moira."

"This all sounds a lot like blasphemy, Reverend."

A condescending smile spread across Hopkins' face. "I decide what is blasphemy."

Moira knew trying to convince him of anything other than what he believed was pointless. The religious weren't people who would change their minds in a moment, unless it supported what they already believed. Zealotry was unyielding. She wouldn't survive by talking. It had to be done with blood.

She pushed the knife out of its sheath. "So, where did it come from? Did you summon it or something?"

"The spirit?" Hopkins turned his back to her and began lighting candles. "It's always been here. We are its followers, gifted our right to subservience by virtue of God's will. Since the birth of Abrams, there has been a Hopkins devoted to caring for it." His laugh was short, humorless.

Moira ignored the jab meant to distract her. "Why? Why you?"

"I just told you."

"That's not what I mean." She stepped past the font and freed the blade, her right hand clasped around the handle. "If it's so powerful, if God himself sent it down from upon high, why does it need you and Miller and Lake to care for it?"

He glanced over his shoulder. "Just because it's sent by God doesn't make it God."

"Wouldn't Jesus disagree?"

Hopkins turned and barked a full belly laugh that resounded throughout the chamber. The way he leaned against the altar, ankles crossed in front of him, it was like he didn't care. There was no emotion, no guilt, nothing that would betray any amount of emotion for what he and Abrams had done to countless people. He made Moira sick.

"I liked that. I liked that." He nodded. "The spirits of heaven and Earth are very much like humans when it comes to following paths of least resistance. While they don't have need for worship, should a group of desperate people treat them as gods and provide them with what they need—sacrifices, offerings of gold, sex—then why shouldn't they take what is offered and demand more? What hungry creature would turn down a free meal, and then do everything it could to ensure they would never go hungry again? No stray animal refuses a free meal."

Moira took another step closer. Her thighs flexed in anticipation. Sweat slicked her palm, but the stippled rubber of the handle clung to her flesh. "You don't seriously believe that, out of all the religions on this planet, this is a Christian monster? Doesn't murdering people to appease an evil spirit make you a sinner, according to your little rulebook?"

"Of course I believe it." Hopkins clasped his hands together and gave them a venerable shake in the cross's direction. "Everything I've done, everything my family has done, has been in His name. The Lord saw fit to give me a tool to shepherd this small flock, a tool greater than He has given any other man, save His son and the saints. I'm merely using what He has provided to sustain the faithful and punish the unbelievers, the infidels. As far as your concern about sin, I have transcended it."

"What about the Witch? Is she a spirit, too?" She was close enough to smell the heat of his cologne. "How does she fit into your fairy tale, Daniel?"

"Of course! The Abrams Witch." He smiled and took a half-step closer, his narrow body vibrating with power beneath his black suit.

She flinched and stepped backward.

"Such a terrifying word, witch. An unfair moniker given to anything that small-minded fools desperate for salvation apply to anything or anyone that runs counter to their perceptions. How dare you outlive your reproductive usefulness yet teach our daughters how to keep from getting pregnant? Witch! How dare you find your spiritual solace in nature and not the austerity of the church? Witch! You make your medicines when it should be through our prayers that the Almighty heals us. Witch! Are you smarter than me, stronger than my sons? Do you question my version of the truth and counter it with evidence? Witch! Witch! Witch! Simply put: if you don't understand it and it has tits, it's a witch."

Moira didn't respond. She closed her mouth, too late to hide her surprise when he laughed.

"Did you not expect that?" he asked. "Did you expect me to praise patriarchy? To tout male authority as divine providence?"

"No," she countered, thinking as quickly as she could. "If we're past good and evil, then I imagine we're at a point where we're above little things like gender-based social authority or male hegemony."

"Interesting." Another step closer. One more and he'd be close enough to sink the knife into his stomach. She hoped the blade was sufficiently sharp, her arm strong enough. "Not everyone thought this way. At one point, even in Abrams, anything claiming to be against established authority, such as the church, held a certain appeal for those most easily swayed. Those of weaker constitutions needed to be identified. The chaff amongst the wheat, if you will."

"You're telling me she was some kind of test? An invention to weed out people who would follow the Beast from those who wouldn't carry out human sacrifice?"

"Promises of power to use against the powerful are tempting. Even the spirits have a sense of self-preservation."

"But the woman? Korey? What about Heather? She said she made it up."

"Kernels of truth slip into stories, don't they?" His eyes widened with surprise. "Ah-ha! Therein is your fairy tale, Moira. Behold!" he spread his arms with a dramatic flourish. "As my fathers before me: I am the Abrams Witch."

Moira shook her head. "You're insane."

He held up a finger. "I am one with the Most High."

She gripped the knife in her fist. Resolve steeled the muscles in her shoulder. "You are not a god, Daniel. You are a sick, sick man who has convinced other sick men to do horrible things. You are a murderer, not an apostle. I don't know how, and I don't know if I'll live to see it, but I swear on everything I hold dear in this world, I am going to stop you from killing any more people. I *will* stop you, Daniel, and whatever evil is out in those woods."

"Oh Moira. This is God's will. It cannot be stopped."

A series of rapid popping noises clacked from behind her. A pressure against her lower back released what felt like a thousand bees composed of lava underneath her skin, all stinging at once. Blue light buzzed in the periphery of her vision, and the muscles in her back, shoulders, and butt seized so hard it felt like her spine would snap.

Her arm went limp. The knife clattered to the church floor.

Moira floated in an agonizing world of blue-gray television static. Her body felt heavy and compressed, squeezed into a small ball of something gooey and lifeless. Slowly, the goo solidified, and numbness blazed into a persistent ache spreading up her tail bone to around her throat. Pressure flooded her head. The back of her neck burned terribly. Something had a hold of her, twisting her feet and forcing her knees apart.

A surge of horror and adrenaline drove her legs into a frenzy, as if she could swim away from the danger if she just kicked harder and faster. Lights sparkled in her eyes and her lungs filled with needles instead of air as she kicked and kicked and kicked at Lake's hands while he tried shoving her the rest of the way into his car by her ankles.

Her bottle of pepper spray rolled to the floor.

"Stop… fucking kicking… little bitch…"

Lake pulled his stun gun, its two metallic points rattling with bolts of blue lightning and aimed it at her stomach. Her body curled into the fetal position to protect her core.

Instead of bracing for the impact and pain, Moira kicked out with both legs with all the strength she could muster, landing a solid blow to Lake's upper chest.

The stun gun clattered to the pavement behind him.

"God damn you!" he coughed. Lake's eyes filled with menace. One large hand clamped all the way around her ankle, the other balled into a meaty fist.

An engine roared through the parking lot.

"About goddamed time!" he yelled. "Dumb son of a bitch, I told you to bring your truck, not your—"

There was a sudden jerk, followed by the crashing of exploding plastic, glass, and metal. The fluid in Moira's head whirled violently in her skull. An invisible hand plastered the side of her face into the leather seat.

Then everything settled down to a rough rocking sensation and a wailing screech in her ears.

Hands around her feet yanked her backward. A woman's voice yelled, "Get out! Get out of the damn car!"

The wind still hadn't entirely returned to Moira's lungs. Her protesting arms refused to work, which made the woman angrier. She jerked against Moira's backpack until her head swam.

"Stand up! Give me your arm. Your arm, woman!"

Something dull and painful slammed into her wrist bone. Her vision cleared just as the woman spun her around and clicked the handcuff on her left wrist. "Get in the car."

"What are you doing?" Moira was half-dragged over to another car and pressed into its door. Her vision cleared.

The woman's black hair sat up in a red band. She wore a green, military-style jacket that hung loosely around her shoulders. Dark features sharpened into a snarl, her brown-eyed gaze piercing and determined. She shoved the barrel of a revolver into Moira's face and whipped open the door. "Get in the fucking car."

Moira climbed into the rear passenger seat. The car smelled like an ashtray.

The woman reached behind her and tied the chain of the cuffs to something in the back seat. She ran around to the front, jumped inside, and drove off with a slight screeching of rubber.

Panic welled up in Moira's chest. Her bonds were too tight to struggle against. "Wait," she begged. "Wait! If I leave Abrams, I die."

"Be quiet!" the woman demanded, her focus on the rearview mirror while she sped down the tarmac and made a left turn onto an unimproved gravel road. After she put a wide distance between them and the rest of Abrams, she tossed the revolver onto the passenger seat and turned her attention to Moira. "Sit still. This is going to be uncomfortable."

The Roots

1

Her wrists and shoulders screamed against the handcuffs as the old car rattled and creaked along the dirt road. Moira hissed but said nothing. It was useless to scream and, judging by the dirty rags and rope on the floor, pissing the woman off didn't strike her as a wise move. Every ounce of bravery she gathered in the church was a fading memory.

The woman glanced at her in the rearview. Moira turned her head away.

"I'm sorry," the woman said. It sounded genuine. "The road's going to get rougher before we get there. I can't have you jumping me from behind and driving us into a tree."

Moira flexed her jaw and stretched her shoulders as best she could. Absently chewing on her tongue helped fend off angry and frightened tears.

They drove down winding road after winding road. Moira was completely lost to begin with, but now she had no sense of direction, no idea where Abrams proper was. There were farms, swamps, open fields so closely manicured they looked as if a giant lawnmower ran through them. After a couple of turns, the electrical poles all but disappeared and a dense forest dominated the scenery.

They hit a monstrous bump that shook the car and sent Moira crashing face first into the back of the front seat.

The woman stopped the car. Steam hissed out from under the bent hood. "Are you alright?" Her concern seemed earnest. "I forgot about that one."

"I'm fine," Moira said as she sat back. Her eye hurt and her cheek burned where it rubbed against the cloth. She wasn't sure if the tickle down her face was blood or a tear.

"It's just a little farther."

"How did we get out of Abrams?"

The woman drove slowly. "We're not leaving Abrams; we're going deeper into its heart. Most of what's out here is early Abrams land, before the town. It's mostly state forest, tax forfeited plots, or abandoned. These are the old lands." She pulled up the sleeve of her jacket. Her skin was darker than Dani's. On her forearm was a patch of discolored skin, scarred over. "But it's not like there aren't ways out of this place."

Moira said, "You're Veronica Gardiner. The offering who escaped."

"You know me? Did she tell you?"

"Heather Hopkins told me a woman escaped." Veronica looked surprisingly clean. No way she had spent the past six years hiding in the woods. "How did you get out?"

Veronica regarded the scar on her arm for a moment, then pressed the accelerator. "She saved me."

"She?" It came out as a half-sob. "Demons and witches and cults. I should've never come to this fucking place."

"I know." Veronica reached back and gave her knee a sympathetic squeeze. "But you had to. She's been waiting for you."

They left the road, turning onto an old logging trail that ended near a long recreational vehicle in the middle of a crunchy forest clearing. Veronica parked the car behind it.

Moira's stomach knotted when the engine stopped and Veronica stepped out and walked around to her door, opening it, pistol in hand.

"I'm not going to hurt you. I just don't know you, and I don't know if I can trust you yet. You can get out and walk around while I take care of a few things, but I'm going to keep you cuffed. We're in the middle of nowhere, and nowhere to run that you'll live through with your hands behind your back. If you attack me, I'm going to shoot you in the leg." Veronica flashed the revolver at her. "It hurts more than you think. Behave and we'll talk, okay?"

Moira couldn't tear her eyes from the gun. She nodded and

leaned forward to allow Veronica to unhook her. "I'll have to pee soon. I can hold it for a while longer, but not forever."

Veronica nodded. "There's a toilet in the camper. I'd let you piss out here, but then I'd have to tie a rope or something to you. Or watch. I'm bladder shy, so I wouldn't do that to you. It sucks." She stuffed the gun into her waistband and eased Moira out of the car.

Even though her shoulders and hips felt like they were going to explode, Moira was glad to be standing.

Veronica gave her an apologetic look. "Just a few more minutes. Promise."

She wanted to tell Veronica she wouldn't run away or jump her from behind, but she decided it wouldn't be worth the effort. Instead, she walked around the small clearing while Veronica untied a pair of green ropes connected to a length of netting covered with leaves that closed like a curtain over the road, camouflaging their entrance. It looked like good concealment, yet she doubted it would stop a truckload of curious cultists wondering where the fresh tracks leading off the dirt road went.

"Do you have more guns in there? Heather said the Beast can see us, all of us. If it knows where we are, then Hopkins and Lake probably know, too. They're going to come for me." Her throat went dry. "I really don't want to die without being able to fight back."

The look on Veronica's face made her heart sink. "Not here. But we don't have to stay long. Tomorrow is the Flower Moon. We just need to make it through tonight." Veronica pulled a knife from the sheath on the back of her belt.

Moira took a step back, worried the blade would find her throat.

Veronica held up her hands to ease Moira's sudden fright. "I'm not going to hurt you. I just need you to watch this. Okay? Just watch." Veronica drew the blade across her palm until a line of crimson beaded up from the slice. Blood trickled down her wrist. She angled her hand to catch most of it, walked over to a tree, and pressed her bloody hand against its bark, saying, "Mother, guard us from our enemies. Protect us while we rest."

A gust of wind whispered through their hair. The ground rustled with the sounds of hidden creatures scurrying beneath dead leaves. Roots from the trees on both sides of the path burst up from the earth, curling themselves around trees in a lattice pattern, whipping from tree to tree, forming a wall of earth and brown and red tendrils all around the clearing. Flowers bloomed from sudden buds. Hundreds of butterflies and winged insects burst from the bushes, fluttering around them in a great circle, upward into the tops of the trees where they spun and dove in and out of the woods in a kaleidoscope of color.

As terrifying as it was to watch, something about the scene seemed right, natural. A wall of nature growing around them to form a wattle fence covered in wildflowers. Moira shuddered. It was beautiful.

Veronica stared, equally taken by the extraordinary display. Tears and sweat glistened on her brown cheekbones. "I didn't know that was going to happen."

"What did you think was going to happen?"

"No idea." Veronica shrugged. At some point, she tore herself away from the wonder and wrapped a clean rag from the front seat of her car around the cut in her hand. "I just knew I had to do it."

"How did you do it?"

"Magic."

"Magic? Sure. Why not?" Moira flinched when Veronica stepped toward her. "Are you the Witch?"

"No." Veronica shook her head. "But it was a gift from her." She sheathed the knife and pulled her keys out of the pocket of her pants.

The cuffs being removed sent hot knives grinding through her shoulders and up Moira's neck. Her fingers went from cold to warm and full of needles. She shivered in the heat. "That's how you escaped? She gave you magic?" She shook her head, half wanting to disbelieve what she saw. It was real. In the very thrumming of her soul's heart, she knew it was real. "That's a hell of a gift," was all she could manage to say.

Again, Veronica shook her head. "It's not a gift for me, Moira," she said. "It's for you."

2

The RV was more luxurious than Moira expected. It had a full kitchen with a gas stove and sink, a separate dining area with a table and bench seats, and another area in the back separated by a folding door that muffled the dialogue and music of what sounded like a children's movie. In the front behind the driver's seat was a small bathroom area with a shower head and a composting toilet that smelled like a chemically disinfected portable toilet—significantly better than Moira expected. Unfortunately, the one window inside was clearly too narrow to fit her shoulders or hips.

So much for escaping out of the bathroom.

As she washed her hands in the little plastic sink, Moira considered whether she wanted to escape, not if she was capable of it. What she had just watched Veronica do, her magic, was beyond extraordinary. It was the stuff she wished she could do as a little girl. Silly, secret dreams that she carried with her into high school after her parents died. One reason she studied fairy tales and folklore was because she loved the idea of magic, wanted to know more about it to the point she still, in the quiet places of her imagination, hoped it might exist. To watch it unfold before her eyes gave her a sense of elevation, as if she climbed a tall fence and looked over the top to find a place like Avalon or Tír na nÓg on the other side, knowing she could fly there if she just learned how. It was both wonderful and immeasurably frightening.

"It's for you," Veronica had said. The Witch gave her a gift. Why?

Moira finished and stepped out of the tiny bathroom as Veronica said something to another person behind the folding door and shut it behind her. She still had the gun in her pants.

"So, is this thing all yours?"

"My ex-husband was useful for something when he wasn't drinking away our savings. I've been putting all my money toward taking care of a friend, so this has been house and home for a long time." Veronica pointed toward the table. "Sit down. Please," she added.

Moira did. Veronica cuffed her left hand to a metal bar on the wall. Unlike the cuffs she used in the car, this one had a two-foot-long chain attached. "Is this necessary?" At least she kept it loose around her wrist.

"For now." Veronica opened the small refrigerator near the oven and dug out a couple of square plastic containers. "Hungry? Even if you're not, you should try to eat something."

Moira shrugged and nodded at the same time. "Yes, please." Regardless of what happened, she was going to be polite. It still wasn't clear what Veronica's motive was.

"Vegetarian?"

"No."

Veronica smiled for the first time, a wide grin that curled upward and revealed dimples at the corners of her eyes. Moira guessed Veronica couldn't be much older than she. Maybe only by a few years.

She brought Moira a snack box of lunch meat and crackers, a sparkling water, and a bag of generic nacho cheese chips. She set a rectangular dish of chopped vegetables in the middle of the table and sat across from her with her own modest prepackaged meal.

Moira took a few bites, even though she lost her appetite almost immediately after seeing the food.

"You have a family? Husband, kids? That sort of thing?"

Moira shook her head. She still didn't trust Veronica enough to tell her personal details. "I'm focused on school."

"College?" Veronica's eyes brightened. "Nice, isn't it? I studied biology. You?"

"Double major in Anthropology and English." To Veronica's quizzical look, she added, "It's sort of a soft degree in folklore. I like old stories."

"Are you one of those rich girls who studies what she wants without needing to worry about picking a major that gets you paid after graduation?"

Moira bristled and scowled.

"Your shirt's a nice label. You don't look hungry or too fat from eating a bunch of junk food. There's an air of superiority about you. College is expensive, and you don't look like the type to have a sugar daddy. But I've been mistaken in the past." Veronica popped a piece of cheese into her mouth. "That's a nice scarf, too."

Moira forced a sour smile. "Thank you. My grandmother made it for me. She's taken care of me. We have plenty, but we aren't rich. My parents had to die so I could go to college, eat well, drive a reliable car, and rent a small apartment while other kids struggle. Yes, I know how crippling debt is going to be for a lot of people. Yes, I recognize how other people are being taken advantage of by a predatory system designed to hurt poor people. But if you think I wouldn't suffer through all of that just for the slightest possibility of having them back, then you are sorely fucking mistaken, Miss Gardiner."

Moira jerked against her chain, hoping old memories would give her the strength to tear it off the wall. When the steel just bit into her wrist, she deflated and stared at the wall.

Veronica's shoulders slouched forward. She bit down on her bottom lip. "I'm sorry, Moira. That was cruel. I'm… I'm sick, and I get these terrible mood swings since I've quit my meds. I haven't had a lot of human interaction…" She slid her hand across the small table, but Moira pulled her own away. "Never mind. That's no excuse. I didn't intend to come off as a heinous bitch and hurt your feelings. I'm happy you get to go to school, but I wish you didn't have to pay that price. And I wish I didn't pick at that wound. I'm sorry. Truly, I'm very sorry."

Moira sniffed away tears. "Forget about it. We have other things we should talk about. Like how you know my name. Have you been following me? Did Heather talk to you?"

"No." Veronica took a bite of celery. "She told me about you. In my dreams. She talks to me in my dreams."

The Witch. Moira stiffened. "She's real? What is she like?"

"Like hearing my grandmother yell. This beautiful and frightening thing. When she talks to me, I want to run and I want to stay at the same time. I remember when I was a little girl, there was this dog. It was one of those cute, little furry things that run around back and forth like they're crazy. So cute and so fast. All I wanted to do was give it a hug. One day, I gave in and cornered it. I was going to give it a hug. And when I did, it bit me on the face. Right here." She pushed her hair to the side and pointed at a scar on her cheek near her ear. "I bled so much. I screamed. You know, the kind of scream that only little kids can belt out. Like I was on fire. Anyway, I was terrified of that dog after that. But I still wanted to pet it, to hug it, to let it lick my face and play with me." She chewed on a carrot stick. "That's what she's like." Veronica grabbed a sketchbook and a tin of charcoal pencils from a cabinet behind her, flipped open the cover, and started drawing.

Rachel could be like that, Moira thought. Beautiful and intense. She carried that sort of authority only found in a grandmother who cared enough to not coddle. "So, what is she to you? The Witch?"

"Like I said. She saved me from the people in this shit town."

3

It's not my story I want to tell you, but we've got to start somewhere. I've been playing this out in my head for months, and now that you're here…

Sorry if I seem nervous, I've just been waiting for this day for a long time. It's just… The dreams. I've had so many dreams about her that I'm worried about what's going to happen when they stop. To have that constant in my life taken away. To feel like I was the one who gave it away. Which is weird for me; I don't usually go for constant. I prefer consistent over constant.

I'm a biologist by trade. Well, at least I wanted to be. I never got to finish school because of this shitty town and that asshole Hopkins. I've been spending the past few years as a forester and an arborist. It's good money, and I get to drive a big ass truck around. Isn't really conducive to a stable, three-bedroom, two-bathroom house in the suburbs lifestyle, though. But I've never wanted to put down roots somewhere and just stay. My dad was in the Army, so we moved around a lot. Besides, I wonder if I lived like that—a house in town and an office job or something—if Hopkins or Matt Miller would've already tracked me down and killed me.

No. No, they've never found me. I thought they were on my trail once, but that stopped when I found my now ex-husband. These fools can talk all the shit they want, but these Minnesota farm boys are all scared of an angry black man. Looking back, it was probably just some lonely trucker following me around. Still, I had nightmares. Always thinking there was someone behind me, waiting for me to fall asleep. Seeing shadows in the woods creeping at me.

You saw them, too? That's... it's whatever that thing is out there. What that Heather Hopkins lady calls the Beast. Where did you see it the first time? The motel? That place is seedy. Lucky you don't have bedbugs. Ah, I'm joking. You're right, though. It is kinda gross in a creepy way.

I got this in a wildlife management area north of the church. Right here. That's where it marked me like it marked you. I thought it was poison ivy, too. Maybe a nettle burn or something. I don't know. Anything other than some supernatural, people-eating monster's evil brand.

So, before all of this, I was lucky enough to get an internship with the Department of Natural Resources. Paid. Oh yeah, I loved every second. Until Abrams. Pay me to study fungus and take soil samples all day? Pfft. Don't threaten me with a good time. There was one day where all I did was walk around the woods and count flowers. I was one smiling woman for a semester.

Right after finals in the first week of May, I got assigned to do some drought measurements and take some soil and water samples around Abrams, to measure the impact that climate change was having on widespread soil erosion and what the runoff from the farms was doing to the waters in the state forests and management areas. Since I was just an intern, they didn't give me a truck or per diem or anything. I had to figure that stuff out for myself. That didn't bother me since I like the sort of camping where you have to haul everything in on your back and dig your own toilet. It's so nice to just get away from everything, the cities, the sounds. A place where the wind stinks like pine and mud and animals, where I could just lie on my back and let my heart beat in time with the turning of the earth and the singing of the birds. Ha! Yeah, a real poet. Right.

I did that a lot as a little girl, lying on the ground. It felt right. You know? Nature. Maybe it was because I spent my childhood with my grandma as a chubby farm girl while my mom waitressed us into a cheap apartment. I don't know. The sky was bluer back then when I think about it.

Sorry, I don't mean to get all misty-eyed and nostalgic. It's been a rough couple of years, and I'm tired. It's almost over, though. Just keep pushing, girl.

What? Oh, uh, yeah. I was up here taking some samples and eventually had to run into town for gas, water, wet wipes, and food. And, you know, I'm used to being gawked at by old white women, but that day at the gas station, their stares were strange; just so intense and awful. My grandma grew up in Mississippi and she told me about people who looked at her like that in the sixties, where it's like they're just staring naked hatred at you, hoping you catch fire on the spot or something. They don't even hide it here.

I should've known better than to trust Miller, but I was stupid. "Just ignore the old folks in town," he said. "They're terrified of anyone browner than a paper bag, and everyone in this town is so insulated that they freak out when they see on out-of-towner."

"Everyone except you?" I asked. I used to make it a point to be friendly. Kill people with kindness, so to speak.

"Me? Oh, I'm terrified." He laughed, so I knew he was joking. "You're going to be testing my soil. I own the farmland next to the State land you've been running around in."

I tell you; I wish I would've known about him then. In hindsight, I should've dumped gas all over him and lit him up. But stupid me kept talking. Gotta make good relationships with the farmers in the area, since they're already strained with the State and we can't make them worse. Need to regain their trust. What a waste. But believe this: he invites me to have lunch with both him and the mayor, who just happens to be his childhood friend, so we can discuss how Abrams can help me. I agreed because free lunch, for one. For two, maybe I could springboard it into something else—the intern who earned a town's trust or whatever. Such an idiot.

You met Brian Hopkins, right? Looks like a mayor. Super-white smile and bullshit promises. You'd think that a little hole like Abrams wouldn't need to have that kind of guy in charge, but I guess that just shows you how dug in the cult of personality is in this country when these folks are supposed to be the sensible 'salt of the earth' ones.

Probably the rudest of awakenings for me.

I made it to the cafe before both of them and sat down at a high-top table so they couldn't squish me into a booth—I learned that lesson in college—and we had a really nice lunch. They were open to me coming onto Miller's land to test soil in different areas. Brian even offered to contact a few of the other farmers and convince them to give me access to their fields.

This was a huge deal for me! All I heard were horror stories about farmers chasing people off their lands, because of course they don't want to have the State tell them that their fertilizer or chemicals are poisoning public waters and habitat and they have to pay to dump all that product and possibly pay a fine. I thought that maybe if I had a regular contact with a town and things went well, the DNR would think that I was more useful than just an internship. It was perfect.

We planned where I would meet Matthew on his farm, and from there we would ride out to the edge of the management area and basically gauge the areas most likely to have runoff.

I should have known better because I slept really well that night. One of those stress-free sleeps where nothing can wake you up. Even the burn on my arm, the mark, stopped hurting so much.

4

Long story short, Miller took me out to these woods the next afternoon. I met him out on his farm. It's a really beautiful place, too. Idyllic. Looks like the kind of place they use for movie settings—perfect plowed rows of dirt, apple trees with pink flowers, and those big oaks that look professionally trimmed. Nothing like the run-down barn, empty silo, and ragged trees and overgrowth I grew up with. It was almost enough to distract me.

I didn't know what Miller has done to people, to women, children, not until She showed me. He drugs them first.

We drove out to these woods, not far from here. He brought a couple thermoses and a big bag of cookies to dip in his coffee. Said it was an Abrams Brunch for a cold afternoon. A picnic for two on the hood of his vehicle. The way he smiled—all teeth, wide eyes, this air of expectation about him like it was a foregone conclusion that I was going to giggle at his whole picnic idea—it made me sick, watchful. He thought I didn't see him pour himself a coffee from one thermos and another from that stainless steel mystery container when my back was turned. Like I don't know how to use a car window or the glass on a picture frame at a bar as a mirror when I'm alone with a man I don't know.

I could tell he was pissed and trying to hold it in, but he stayed nice, joked around about it. "You out-of-towners don't know what it's like to be in a friendly town, do you?"

I sometimes think I should've run then and there. Stupid me.

Then again if I had, I'd never have met Her.

He took me out to the woods, laughing and joking the whole time. Talked a lot about his farm and how important he and his family were to the town. We walked for an hour before he showed me the Pit.

I didn't know what to make of it, I just knew that it was wrong. Instinctively. I knew it in my soul that thing was just plain wrong. The air around it felt like poison; heavy, horrifying, and it stunk like rotting meat and human shit. You know how you just need to get away from someone, can tell they're dangerous and they want to do you harm? Multiply that by a hundred. Being there made me feel this overwhelming anxiety, like I needed to run in any direction as long as it was away from that place.

I remember Miller looked over my shoulder into the Pit, gagging. Damn near threw up on me. "What do you think?" he asked.

"I can't be here," I told him. "This isn't natural."

"You'll change your mind when you're dead." And he smiled at me. Smiled. Like he told a joke or something. Then he said, "Take off your pants," as if I'd already agreed to do it.

"What?"

He punched me in the stomach so hard I felt it in my throat. I folded in half and fell to my knees, my face hovering over that Pit, that stink. I thought I was falling in. Part of me—a small part—still thanks him for grabbing a fistful of hair and dragging me away like I was a sack of potatoes. Being near that thing was like… it was like it wanted to turn me inside out, pull me apart. I'm not a Christian, and

I don't believe in much, but I could only think about how I needed to protect my soul from this thing. It wanted me, wanted the thing inside me that made me, me. And Matthew Miller was going to give me to it, just as soon as he was done getting what he wanted.

When my eyes opened and I caught my breath, all I saw was the barrel of his rifle. "Take off your fucking pants, whore!"

Now I've never been raped, thank heavens, but there was a moment in my mind where if it came down to him raping me and being any closer to that Pit, I would've gladly let him rip me to pieces. Who thinks like that? How bad does something have to be for your brain to go there? I don't know. But me being me, I figured if he was going to do that, I was going to make him regret trying.

Whenever I go into the woods, I always carry two knives: a folder and a fixed blade with four-inch blades. They're good for cutting wood and cord and digging little soil samples. The only person I had ever cut with one of them was me. Now he might've taken my good knife, the one like this that I always kept on my hip, but he didn't know about the folding one I had hooked inside my belt, right over my back pocket. This one here. A good one, too. It's got a spring assist, so I only have to do this with my thumb, and it's open. And I keep this thing sharp.

Now, when a man gets all hot and bothered, he gets impatient. Starts yelling. Breathing hard. Shaking. They're like puppies like that. So, I started untucking my shirt real slow. It helped that I was scared and hurt; kept me tense. I think he liked it, too, because he started taking off his belt real fast and mumbling about how he was going to do this and that—I'm not going to get into the details with that. And I saw he couldn't manage doing that and balancing the gun at the same time. The moment it slipped a little off his shoulder, I grabbed that thing, pulled hard on it, and swung my knife. Cut him right across his stupid face, right down the eyebrow. Then I ran like hell.

I know guns, but I'd never been shot at before. See this? This engraving on the frame? I won this at a shooting contest. Champion, three years running. You give me a handgun, rifle, shotgun—I can do crazy shit with a gun. Wild shit, like Annie Oakley. At thirty yards, I put a 22 right through a bottle laying on its side. Right through the opening and out the back. Perfect. I used to shoot all the time. But no one ever shot at me before him.

I used to think when a bullet goes by it makes that high-pitched Hollywood *viiiing* noise, but I was wrong. It sounds like an angry bee. *Vzzzzz*. Makes the hair on your neck stand up. I bet if I didn't get him over his dominant side, his shooting eye, he would've shot me dead.

The bullets weren't the scariest part, though. The shadows were. Once I saw them, those octopus arms stretching up from the Pit and chasing after me like fast little ropes, I found another gear in my legs I didn't know I had. There was a point I was running so fast I thought that if I jumped, I'd fly. Jet off to some other land, some other forest to hide. Anywhere. I didn't look back. Not once. I didn't want to see those things coming after me.

The worst part about the forests up here is that they're thick and flat in a lot of areas, and when you get to the hilly parts, things thin out. Makes it hard to run and hide, especially when it starts to get dark.

You know what it's like to be scared, Moira? Truly scared? Probably not. And that's fine; it's not a judgment. Fewer people need to be afraid in this world. But you've seen animals frightened, scared for their lives and running. Nature shows are brilliant for that. They show you the little bunny hopping along the prairie, eating clover, not giving a damn. Then it's a quick shot to a coyote stalking it from the tall grass or a bunch of trees, all hunkered down, ears perked up, eyes laser focused. Isn't funny how they never tell you that the coyote is hungry and that if she doesn't eat the bunny, her babies will starve? I was a fat kid who liked to eat, so I could empathize with the lions and tigers and bears, even though the message is that you're not supposed to. Everything with teeth is evil. Only the cute ones can be the victims in Disney cartoons, and the victims always won. Everything else is vile. Anything else trying to survive is the enemy.

When the coyote moves in, the bunny bolts. Just tearing ass through the brush, trying to get an angle. Rabbits are fast, but they can't out-sprint a dog. The coyote pushes the bunny into the trees, so it can't maneuver as well, slows it down even more. The bunny has to dodge and jump away from snapping jaws. Maybe the coyote snatches a bite of white fur in its teeth, just to show how close it is to catching the bunny. Snap, snap, snap. The coyote catches the bunny by its leg. The bunny screams that piercing squeak of theirs. But the coyote can't hang on. It slips on some leaves or loose dirt or something, giving the bunny a chance to run away. But no. The bunny is injured now. One leg doesn't kick quite as well as it did. The forest is getting thicker. There's no way out.

Luckily for the bunny, it's small and it can blend in. It's got some space between it and the coyote, and it hides. Stumbles on a little hole in the ground, maybe a ball of roots from a fallen tree where it can just squeeze through, but there's just the one way in and the one way out. And it waits. It doesn't shake, doesn't shiver. It can sit death-still until the coyote loses the scent and gives up.

People are just like those animals. We all run when we're afraid, Moira. All of us. But what they don't tell you in those nature shows is that when we get scared, we get stupid. Our brain panics and our body pisses itself. We can only run so far and so fast. Unlike the bunnies, we don't know the forests. Getting lost adds to the panic. Everything shuts off. All you hear is your heartbeat in your ears because you're running so fast. Because you're so scared of the man who wants to beat and rape you before feeding you to some kind of demon-monster-thing hidden in the woods. It's mindlessness. Pure terror erasing every rational thought in your head. My lungs and my legs couldn't keep up with how scared I was, though.

Bunnies have natural colors, camouflage. They can just sit still and disappear. It was getting dark. The forest was thickening; the shadows were everywhere. For some reason, my brain told me that it was a great idea to hide instead of running. So I did.

I found this tree. It had fallen over in a storm or something, years and years ago, but it was still alive. Half of its roots were still in the ground, the other half grew into this jumbled ball, all crisscrossed like a chain-link fence. It was tight, but there was just enough room for me to squeeze my narrow, college ass into. I pressed myself in there. Didn't even care how bad the sharp ones cut me. I forced my body back in there and hid.

What they don't tell you about those nature shows is that they don't film the same bunny and coyote, they just film the same habitat. There are probably five or six different bunnies being chased by five or six coyotes, maybe more. Whatever it takes to put together a more compelling narrative, because the coyotes almost always catch the bunnies. But they can't show that to kids.

I knew it, too. I knew. When I calmed down a little, I knew he would find me. When the shadows pressed in, I heard his footsteps. I knew the shadows were leading him to me. There was no way out. I just covered my mouth and shut my eyes and held my breath.

I heard more footsteps. Someone else was in the woods with us. For a second, I thought it could've been someone that'd help me. Maybe that it was Hopkins or a hiker. Somebody who could get me out of there. I started crawling out, pulling my way out of the roots. Almost took a breath to scream.

She found me first.

I felt these arms pull me closer into the tree, farther away from the roots. I almost screamed, but she said, *Shhhh. It's alright. You're alright. Hush, hush, hush.* And she held me. Just held me. God, she sounded just like my mother.

I don't know if it was the fear, or if it was the sound of her voice, but I leaned back and kept quiet while she held me, brushed my hair, and told me it was going to be okay. It could have been the devil himself speaking to me, wrapping his arms around me, and I wouldn't have cared. I was warm and safe. I could feel the strength in her, you know. She held me and I liked it. I never wanted to leave. Even when Matthew Miller stopped in front of me, pants still unzipped, rifle at his side, I was calm. I didn't move. I just curled up like a little ball in her arms.

But he could still smell me, knew I was close.

He shot in the air to get me to scream. Called me every horrible name you can think of. Whore. Cunt. Nig—you get it. All of them. Said he was going to fuck me in the ass with his knife when he caught me. He said all the horrible things. All I really heard was her voice. *Shhhh. Don't be scared. Just hush, hush, for a little longer. There, there.* She hummed this old lullaby I remember my grandma singing to me before putting me in my crib. I didn't even know I had that memory before she started humming it, but I remembered it. I remember it now. They say babies don't have memories, but I don't remember a time when I didn't know what mommy was, even if I didn't know the word.

The other one, the hiker? Turned out he was with Miller. He was pissed at him, too. Kept telling him that he should've waited, should've kept his stupid hands off me until they were ready, until it was time. I guess Miller took me out there a day too early. The full moon wasn't that night. Lucky for me he couldn't keep it in his pants for another day, right?

They argued right in front of me for what felt like an hour. Damn near threw hands, too. Whoever that other man was, he did not like Miller one bit, but he was still in on their plan to kill me and feed me to those shadows, the Beast.

On and on they went, but she just talked to me the whole time. She hummed, I listened, and they left. Only the shadows stayed behind, and they knew exactly where I was. Could see me. But they couldn't get past the roots. She held them away.

Eventually, I fell asleep. When I woke up, everything was black. I thought the shadows had me, thought I was in some kind of Hell. It took me a minute to realize where I was. It was nighttime, but I wasn't cold. She was still there. She stayed with me, holding me until dawn, until the shadows were gone. I was safe. For a while, I just relaxed and felt like I was with my mom again.

I was crushed when she told me I had to leave.

Don't think I didn't fight or put up an argument, but you try arguing with the supernatural. She let me go and said, *No. I need you to go. I need you to wait for me, for a special moment when fate will bring us together again. Shhh. Hush. It's alright. I'll call to you, in your dreams, when it's time. But be brave. Our enemy is powerful, ruthless, and undying, so I may ask you to put yourself in danger. Be brave, my lovely little girl. Be brave, and I will see you soon.*

Then she was gone. I crawled out of the roots, and I ran the hell out of Abrams.

5

"That's it. That's my Abrams story. Thanks for coming."

Moira smiled briefly at the joke. She suspected there was more Veronica wasn't telling her. "And you never told anyone about Miller?"

"Of course not! Who would I tell? The cops? The local Conservation Officer?" Veronica's head fell into her hands. She closed her sketchbook and pulled the band from her hair, letting it fall around her face. "As far I as knew, everyone was after me. I've just been so paranoid about everything for years."

"So why you? Why now?" Moira pressed. "You said she came to you in a dream. What did you dream?" There was a sound from behind the curtain, tiny marbles rattling in plastic. Her eyes immediately shifted between Veronica's wrist and the bandage on her opposite hand. Poking out of her jacket was a thin, white strip of paper with letters and numbers printed on it.

"Wait." A piece of a puzzle fell into place. "Oh, my god. You're not sick, you're dying." She reached over and pulled Veronica's sleeve up, revealing the hospital wristband. "Aren't you? You're dying. Celeste Martin had a heart condition; Gloria Ylva had a glioblastoma. She only takes the dying."

Veronica let her hand fall to the table. The date on the band was from a week prior. "Ovarian cancer. They thought they got it all when they pulled everything out five years ago, but it's in my bones now. The pills were just to take the edge off while I wither away. 27 years old."

"But Ollie Lake wasn't dying until Jenny smoth…" Realization widened her eyes. She pointed. "Veronica. Ronnie!" Suddenly, Moira knew who was on the other side of the curtain. "Son of a—Jenny!" she called.

"Leave her alone."

"Jenny!" Moira leaned around the small table, the handcuff biting into her flesh. "It's me, Moira! We talked the other day. With Dani Olsen."

A moment later, a set of fingers reached around the curtain and eased it aside. Jenny Lake poked her head into the kitchenette, a guilty look on her face. "Hello, Moira Clarke."

Moira's breath caught in her chest. "You took her? Why would you do that? Jenny's not dying! She's done with this! How much more could this place possibly take from her?"

"It's okay, Moira," Jenny said with a sad smile. "Don't be mad at Ronnie. She's my friend. I dreamed about her, and she saved me from the hospital and helped me live with Marco and the others. Now she's taking us home." Her hands trembled. "I know about Ollie. I'm not so…" She poked a finger at her temple. "I know what I did to Ollie. I always knew." Quietly, she added, "I died a long time ago, Moira."

Moira turned her focus back to Veronica. "What did you dream?"

"When? All I've done is dream about her. For the past six years." Veronica opened her sketchbook and stared at the page before turning to Moira. "A woman," she answered. "Covered in flowers and chained to a tree. She had a baby in her arms. In one of its hands was its own bleeding heart, in the other was a sword. It poured the blood from the heart onto the chains, and they melted away like the blood was acid. There was a storm, and there was a fire that burned the world." A haggard and tired look darkened her face. "It was beautiful."

A woman in flowers. Just like her own nightmares. Veronica's drawing was beautiful, indeed. One of the best charcoal sketches Moira had seen, even compared to the most talented students at school. The only thing missing in the drawing was a clearly defined face. "Tell me what she looked like. Her face." Her gaze landed on the sketchbook. "You drew her. Show me."

"Hold on." Veronica lowered her head. "There's more." She picked up the gun.

Moira felt the blood drain from her neck.

Jenny reached and easily, as if taking a broken toy from a baby's hand, slipped the gun out of Veronica's fingers and put it on the counter behind her. "No, no, no, no, no. Look at her." She sat next to Moira. "You scared her again." Jenny wrapped her arm around Moira and pulled her close, fussing with the headband around Moira's neck until it was resting correctly. "It's okay, Moira. We're just going home. It's not far. There, there."

Veronica lowered her eyes. She was on the verge of tears. "I was just putting it away. It's not even loaded. None of the bullets I have are for you, anyway." She reached into her pocket and slid the handcuff key across the table.

Jenny took the key and removed the cuff from Moira's wrist, but held on to her, gently rubbing and cooing away the red welts on her wrist.

Moira swallowed. "Why you? Why me? Why any of this?"

"I don't know. I don't know what I'm doing, Moira. Honestly, I don't. I thought I was going to die before she called to me, and I didn't. I thought I was going to have to break into the house and steal

Jenny, but she was just standing there at the end of the driveway, waiting for me when I pulled up. I didn't know what I was going to do or where I was going to hide here. I didn't know how I was going to find you. I didn't know how I was going to get around if we had to wait for weeks. I really don't know what I'm doing. All I feel is pulled. Pulled to Abrams. To here. Pulled to Jenny, to you." Veronica's face hardened. "All I know is that if I have to die, I'm taking that asshole with me."

"Matthew Miller?"

"Miller. Hopkins. Lake. They're never going to touch another woman, child, or person ever again. Ever. I'm going to make sure of that while I can still breathe."

"But you can't do that if the Witch kills you," Moira ventured. "And you can't help the Witch if they kill you."

"She's not going to kill me."

"Do you know that for sure? Has she told you what she wants or where she is? You don't know what you're waiting for! How do we not know this isn't all some collective hallucination?"

Veronica slammed her fist into the table, rattling its thin legs. "You know it isn't. You have to by now. She's real, Moira. Look outside. You think I can just conjure a wall of plants just by wishful thinking and a few drops of blood? She is real. And we're going to find her because she made a promise to me, and I believe her."

The Witch made promises to each of them, told them secrets. "What did she promise you?"

Veronica took back her sketchbook and drummed her thumbs on the cover, her gaze cast to the wall of flowers outside the window. "I've always loved the idea of magic. I read a lot of fantasy books when I was little. Grew up on Disney cartoons. I got into biology because I think life is magic. How everything from ecosystems to cells interact is beautiful and mysterious to me. I know how cells reproduce and replicated and grow from seed into tree, but there's still a magic to it for me. Yet no matter how badly I wanted anything magic to be real, I always knew there was a line between reality and fantasy. Like you with your stories, I've dwelled in that transition between fact and possibility, trying to suss out what's possible in the impossible. Now, that line is gone. Magic is reality. She says I can be a part of that. I can be a part of that magic. That's why I'm doing this."

Veronica's hand sank to her stomach. "I've always been barren, Moira. Endometriosis when I was barely out of high school. Cancer, now. I wanted to be a mother. I get the biology, and I'm not fool enough to believe that having a baby is some kind of divine miracle, but I still wanted to feel it, that little magic life growing inside me.

"You don't know what it's like to touch her, Moira. To know her. Not yet. All of that power. Everything we've grown up seeing in movies and TV and books has been strength reserved for angry men who need to kill or destroy. It's different with her. It's all that energy condensed into a warm hug. Something supportive, creative, but still angry. Righteous anger, though. Anger that means something. She's an angry mother bear shackled to a cage and forced to watch her cubs be tortured. She reminds me of my grandma's love, my mother's. I miss that. I miss the days when I thought I could be that for a daughter or a son. She said if I do this, I can be a part of that. I can be that. She didn't promise me vengeance or murder; she promised me life. The power to create and maintain it." Veronica's eyes filled with moisture. "Vengeance, too. Against Miller and Lake and the rest of the bastards in this town. For everything he did to them before feeding them to whatever's out there. For the kids who died before me. For Jenny," she added with a whisper. Moira didn't need to ask why. "What would it take for you to believe me? What's enough for you?"

"Oh, I do," Moira said. "Oh god, do I believe you. So much. But the only thing that I am positive about, the only thing that I have no question about, is that there is something in those woods. Something evil. Something that needs to be ripped out like a rotten tooth and burned into ash. I've seen it, I've felt it. But I still don't know what it is. I am having so much trouble connecting dots. I need things to make sense."

"What more do you need?" Veronica asked.

Moira clasped her hands over her face. "I don't know. Magic? Witches? None of this is supposed to be real. I have spent the entirety of my possibly brief life studying stories, myths, folktales, all these little fantasies, and I've tried to understand what about them makes them seem real to us, as humans, people, cultures. Now that there is something real—really real? I mean, how does this go from a dream about Celeste Martin to a town of evil-worshipping murder-cultists? Why me? Why am I supposed to be here? Why do I have to the next offering to the Flower Moon or whatever?"

"You have dreams? Like mine?"

Moira told her. "A woman dressed in flowers. We don't talk, she doesn't say anything, she's just… there. Burning the world. Sometimes, she's my mother. Protecting me."

"I understand. She's sometimes my mother, too." She tapped her sketchbook. "But she's shown me other things, too."

"Like what?"

Veronica reached over and gave Moira's arm a quick squeeze, then she stood and walked over to a cabinet and came back with a thin plastic square. "This is what I've been doing for the past six years. This is what she asked me to do."

"What is that?"

Veronica's eyes narrowed. "Don't you try to fool me into thinking you don't know what a CD is."

"That's not what I meant."

Veronica tapped the case against the back of her hand. "I've spent nearly every day since I escaped trying to figure out what the Abrams Witch is, who she is, what she wants. I've been all over, down every rabbit hole on the internet and in every library. I even tried to come back here, once, about three years ago, just so I could break into Hopkins' little church library of town secrets and see what I could dig up." She lowered her eyes. "But I didn't have the stomach for it. Seeing that thing, the Beast, that little veil of black hovering over this place. I knew that if I came back, I'd never leave. Nobody would ever know what happens here or what they're doing to her."

Moira remembered Gogo's diary. "They're keeping her sick."

Veronica bit her lip and nodded slightly. "She's not a witch, in the sense that you and I think. Witches are different. She is some kind of spirit, something that has always been here."

"Hopkins said the same thing about the Beast. He also said the Witch was made up by his grandfather to weed out nonbelievers."

Veronica tapped the plastic case on the table. "There are spirits living among us, things of the earth and sky, who care for the land and protect the natural cycle of life. Just like everything else, there's an opposite. Call them demons if you want, but whatever they're called, they're evil energies that exist only to feed on the souls of innocent people. Both spirits and demons will sometimes choose people to serve them, to help one battle the other in a quiet war that has been raging since the beginning of everything. Abrams is just one of many battlefields." She slunk down into her seat. "And she chose us to fight with her."

Veronica handed her the disc. "These are all old files I pieced together. Stuff I copied from other people who claimed they had a story about a witch or demon, things I downloaded from paranormal websites, or outright stole from state and county records. I got some stuff randomly emailed to me earlier this year."

"From the church?"

Veronica nodded.

"Heather Hopkins."

"In a dream, she said I was supposed to give that to you. Something else, too, but this first. You got your laptop?" Veronica asked. "I don't suppose it has a CD player?"

Moira asked for her backpack, which Jenny happily brought to her, and pulled out her laptop and clicked open the disc player. Cold excitement breezed through her. She popped in the CD and searched through files.

Veronica continued. "There are other places, other towns and countries with things they call witches or demons or spirits. I know you already know this kind of stuff from myths and folklore, but this still feels new to me. Even after I got out of this town and to somewhere safe, it took me a long time to not think I was crazy. Who dreams of ghosts telling them their backstories? It's ludicrous."

Moira half-listened while she browsed files and skimmed the text. She was impressed by Veronica's level of organization. Everything was arranged by topic, from 'Academic Sources' to 'Zoogeography', and pertinent sources of information were referenced and cross-referenced in an impressively long text file that, at first glance, read like the first draft of a graduate thesis or a professional academic paper preparing for peer-review. At the top of the page, in larger, bold font, was the question 'Who or What is the Abrams Witch?'

"Your brain is amazing, Veronica."

"I like it when things make sense, too. Before I knew what to do with it, I wanted everything to be easy to follow for whoever found it, you know, for when something happens to me."

Moira kept her focus on the paper, reading it as fast as she could. There were so many unsubstantiated details on the first few pages, bits and pieces of information that didn't have any supporting documentation beyond Veronica's repeated use of 'she said this to me in a dream.' It was frustrating to see, especially when there were references to solid evidence like newspaper clippings, journals, and pictures in other folders. However, it wasn't like any of them could prove the existence of magic and spirits in the woods of Abrams, Minnesota.

"Page twelve starts a more narrative version if you don't want to skim through the beginning. I've never been much of a storyteller, so I'm sorry if it's not engaging. I don't think I have a bestseller in my blood." Veronica's voice dropped to a near whisper. "I'm only really good at drawing people, not writing about them."

Moira ground her molars to distract from the falling sensation in her stomach, took a deep breath, scrolled down to the break in the document, and read aloud.

6

Her name was Korey. She was born around 1920 to a small family of European immigrants who came to America to build a farm and avoid the aftermath of the first world war. She grew up in the small town of Abrams, in Minnesota.

Korey was the first person to speak with the Spirit of the Abrams woods.

They spoke to each other in dreams, when Korey was young and liked to run into the woods and nap in a particular tree with a crooked, U-shaped branch that held her body just right, just like a Goldilocks bed.

The Spirit only ever spoke to her during the warmer months. Once the north winds carried their chill into Abrams and the trees yawned gold and brown, the Spirit became silent and only visited her in her deepest sleep. Those winters were lonelier, the fires colder without the Spirit. So much so that her family noticed just how affected she was by the absence of summer. But they couldn't do anything to cheer her up. Korey simply endured in her own silent way. Each day that passed was another day she longed for spring, when the men started tilling the soil. Another day closer to when she would be soothed by the warmth of her secret friend's embrace.

When she was old enough to understand death, the Spirit made her watch as wolves chased down and killed a fawn that had become separated from its mother. Life on a farm accustomed her to the sights and sounds of animals being slaughtered—her mother had dispatched her fair share of chickens for dinner—the fawn's helpless, unanswered cries shook her. She begged the Spirit to stop, to let it run away. The Spirit refused and made her stay and watch. The Spirit didn't show Korey the blood or the gore; it didn't force her to watch the mess of biological death. Instead, it showed her death in its truest, purest form.

While the fawn's terrified cries and struggling body lay helpless in the maw of clacking teeth and bestial snarls preparing to fight over hunks of muscle and organ, the Spirit secreted away part of the fawn's essence, a fragment of its soul, and gave it to Korey.

Suddenly, Korey could see the light of the fawn's soul pass into the bodies of the wolves, seep into the ground, climb into the beaks of birds, and finally absorbed into the squirming forms of grubs and insects feasting on the remains.

They did this with fish in the lake, pigs and chickens at the farm, squirrels and field mice, even flowers and other plants, until Korey realized there was no such thing as death as she knew it. There could only ever be life with a thousand different forms, a thousand different faces.

In the summer of her thirteenth year, Korey could see and understand the souls of every lost animal, every eaten plant, each pile of dried feces turned to soil, as if each one tethered to her memory like the touch of her mother or the scent of burning wood. By her fourteenth, she understood how each plant and root had certain qualities that could ease an old man's knee pain, make the delivery of a child less painful, or make an unwanted pregnancy end. These secrets she never told to anyone. Instead, she hid them within the fragments of her own soul.

With each passing year, each new learning, the Spirit grew quieter. Spring and summer were sad, lonely, and silent. Korey was getting older, spending more of her time with the other women, minding her siblings, and taking care of the farm. She begged for the Spirit's forgiveness. Promised to spend more time with the Spirit in the woods, if it would just be with her the way it used to. But the Spirit couldn't make that promise. It was fading.

It wasn't her fault, the Spirit assured her. As in nature, all things must die so that others may live. Death brought purity to the land.

Korey understood, though part of her didn't want to.

One day, nearing the fall of her sixteenth year, Korey was in the woods foraging mushrooms when a familiar sight approached her from the shadows. It was the wolf who fed on the fawn whose soul she first saw.

The years had taken their toll on the old thing. It was gray-faced and lame. Skin clung weakly to its ribcage and hip bones. Teeth that were once frightening and terrible, like sharpened pearls, were now brown with rot or missing altogether. If anyone else were to have seen this wolf, they would be frightened—starving animals are desperate and can attack anything they could consider food. But Korey knew the old wolf was safe. It was weak and came to ask her to sit with it, to watch as it died.

She did.

On a cool afternoon, under her favorite napping tree, Korey sat beside the dying wolf, massaging its paw and petting its ears, because she knew it had never had its ears scratched or its paws rubbed before. With its last breath, it thanked her with a lick on her arm.

Korey never thought about burying it, to give it a proper funeral, as her father would say. She knew better than to do that. The bugs and scavengers were already on their way to take the wolf's essence and pass it along to their children and the rest of the forest.

Being young, her heart large and aching with loneliness for her missing Spirit friend, Korey stole a little of the wolf's soul to keep with her always.

One day in summer, her parents gave her to a man she never loved no matter how much she tried. Their wedding was small and quick. At the bride's request, they did not hold the ceremony in the church, but at the foot of her favorite tree. Many of the town elders silently protested the strange request, but they shrugged it off and charged it to the caprice of youth.

The couple started a farm next to her family's. The land was fertile, and Korey wished to not be far from her family. For the first years of her marriage, she was a dutiful wife. But to her family and the people of Abrams, duty wasn't always enough.

Her mother told her often she should be warmer, less distant from her husband. Winters were already cold and difficult on their own, and a man needed a good wife to keep his heart and hearth warm during the dark months. Korey tried demure. She tried to be pleasant to her husband. She tried kindness and a sort of detached affection; warmth with her body, but never with her soul. No matter how ardently she tried, how hard she prayed to be a better wife, her heart could give nothing more than a familial love to her husband. The emptiness within her left behind by the absent Spirit of the forest was too great to overcome.

Her husband was not a wicked man, but he was proud, young, and easily swayed by others, especially his own father, a great bellows of a stonemason who was stern and demanding.

When his son came to him in the spring asking for husbandly advice about what he could do to make his wife love him, his father took a meaty hand and slapped him in the ear, calling him a fool. Husbands were the heads of their homes, the closest to God—they didn't ask for what they were owed from their wives.

Filled with shame and rage, her husband burst through his front door, pulled Korey to the floor by her hair, and forced himself onto her. He ignored the screams, her pleading, her entreaties to God and the Spirit, and he did as his father instructed—what he did wasn't against God; he was simply taking his wife back from whatever darkness chilled her heart to him.

It was two months later when Korey's pregnancy was revealed. Her parents rejoiced. The only joy Korey felt was the relief her husband would not touch her, as he had become shaky and skittish since that awful day.

It was during those quiet months that something found its way into Abrams. A sinister force hunting for dark hearts to latch onto and feed upon like a leech. How or why it picked Abrams is a mystery. Maybe it was the harsh winters and the years of blight, perhaps even the absence of the land's Spirit protector. Whatever its reason, it chose Abrams as its feeding ground.

On the hottest day of summer, Korey walked into the woods to harvest flowers and roots to cool the burning in her throat and the ache in her belly. Mostly, she hoped the Spirit returned to take away her gnawing melancholy. Near the lake where a particular purple flower bloomed, her husband's father, who had declared himself the local pastor, approached her. Suspicious and angry, he accused her of hunting for the herbs and flowers she needed to make the potion that would cause her to deliver her baby too soon for it to live.

Korey was a kind woman, quiet, but she was neither kind nor quiet in her response. With a spit and a slap, she blamed him for putting evil into his son's head. She called him weak, womanish, and a child for being afraid of his daughter-in-law.

He grabbed her and pressed his thumbs into her windpipe until she collapsed against the tree.

The Spirit returned to her a final time.

The morning winds blew, the wolves howled. The lake reached out beyond the reeds and soaked into the large man's boots. A raven the size of a house cat barked from the top of a cedar tree and swooped down, digging black claws into the soft flesh of his right eye until all that remained was a mess of meat, fluid, and screams.

Injured and frightened, her husband's father fled the forest in terror and agony. Korey stayed until dark when her mother and father found her resting against her childhood tree.

For weeks, her husband's father suffered from his festering wound. Her own husband was furious, beside himself with worry, and exhausted from having to work both his farm and his father's smaller one. He blamed her for the attack, berated her for not being warmer and friendlier to him and his family. Korey simply stirred the soup, swept the floor, and hummed old songs to her growing belly.

It wasn't until his father was near death that her husband begged for her help. There had been whispers among the women that she knew secret cures, potions that could give life and health, and he begged her to give one to her father. Korey agreed, provided he never touch her in that way again, that he be happy with having only one child, and if his father ever threaten her again, she wouldn't cure him of what would happen.

To these, he agreed. The next day, Korey found the ingredients to make a poultice that, after three days, cured the infection in her husband's father's eye. Unfortunately, her kindness raised the suspicions of everyone else in Abrams.

As her husband's father got healthier, Korey's health declined. The difficult pregnancy left her bedridden. Her mother was too old to take care of her, and the last of her sisters died a year earlier. The other women in town were too scared to help, because her husband's father had spread rumors of witchcraft and Satanism.

While there had not been a church-sanctioned witch trial in the United States since the 1600s, they could not ignore the proof of her power or the burden of their Christian duty. Instead of a public trial, the people of Abrams tried her in the silence and insulation of their homes and prayer groups. They decided that once she had her child—as it was sinful to kill a woman with child—she would be dealt with, and her child would be immediately baptized and given to another couple who struggled to conceive. Everything that would happen would stay in Abrams, among the people of Abrams. This was their pact, witnessed and blessed by the demon living in the shadows of their homes.

Korey's health worsened as winter breathed its chill. There was little snow that year, but the cold was bitter and bone breaking. Even with the horrible cold, Korey's fever had her sweating through her thin sheets and wool blankets for the last months of her pregnancy. The lavender oils and tinctures she taught the other women to make couldn't calm her. Elderflowers and willow bark did nothing for the fever. There was no help for her. The local doctor refused to see her, and her parents and husband did not have access to a motor vehicle. She was dying, and she knew it.

Using the last of her savings, her mother contacted a prominent midwife from St. Paul and begged her to come to their town and help. The Midwife took the next train north, bringing with her a medical bag, personal luggage, and her own suspicions regarding the rumors about Abrams.

Abrams did not welcome her. It was no longer their way to be inviting to outsiders.

The Midwife arrived on the morning of the first full moon in May, just as Korey's child struggled to free itself from her belly. Sheets bloodied, bed soaked with sweat and fluid, the Abrams women railed in panic. The Midwife was a pillar of calm they needed in the center of that storm. She ordered clean towels, boiling water, alcohol, any ice the town could scrounge together, an ambulance, and the local doctor's presence.

It appalled her when the local authorities refused the doctor. The ambulance would take hours to arrive.

There was no time to argue; the baby was coming.

The Midwife ordered the men and half of the women out of the house. Unless the husband was going to help, he could also leave, which he gladly did.

The Midwife immediately tended to Korey.

Knowing the fate that was about to befall on her and her child, Korey begged the Midwife to listen to her story. Korey pulled her closer and whispered her secrets into the Midwife's ear. Just as she finished, her daughter slid effortlessly out of her and into the Midwife's awaiting arms.

Weakened from the struggle of her labor, Korey could only manage enough strength to hold her child with one oiled arm, to smell her, and put her first and last kiss on her daughter's forehead before handing her back to the Midwife and begging, "Please, please, save her. Save my little bunny. Please."

A commotion erupted downstairs when the women announced the child's birth, though the sounds were far from joyful.

When the people of Abrams came to drag Korey out of her bed and into the woods, the Midwife hid in the closet, the silent baby clutched to her chest. There's no knowing why the people didn't immediately search for her, but as soon as they were gone, the Midwife swaddled the child in the warmest, softest fabric she could find, slipped dried lavender next to its nose to calm it, and ran down the road until she met the arriving ambulance, whom she ordered to drive her as far away from Abrams as they could.

Within the woods, in the presence of the people of Abrams, including her own parents, and before man, God, and demon, Korey was denounced as a witch. They beat her, carved her hair off with her husband's knife, held her face under the lake until she was nearly dead. Finally, they strung her up to the branch of her favorite childhood tree and hanged her by the neck until she stopped kicking. They then dumped her body, upside down, into a pit dug at the base of the tree, and her remains were burned with the wood they cut from its branches.

As her body burned, Korey's own spirit sunk into the earth and spread as far as the smoke brought her ashes. Instead of feeding the land like the souls of the animals and people before her, her rage at Abrams cut its life away. Drought spread from the woods outward. Farms turned to dust. Hundreds of people died in the extreme heat. Wells dried to sand. Animals barely bred. Wolves returned and dragged away the old and the infirm. People began suspecting black magic, blaming one another for inviting evil into the community by either killing Korey or allowing her to live as long as they had. Family fought family. Abrams fell into decay.

Korey's husband and his father, the soils of their farms blowing away with the wind, heard the call of the demon from within the Abrams woods and answered it. Life for a life, it demanded. It would save their town from Korey's spirit, and allow Abrams to prosper, in exchange for a sacrifice every Flower Moon or until Korey's child was brought back to Abrams and the last of her soul destroyed.

Their agreement was the genesis of the Abrams curse.

Chapter Eleven

Moira's throat went dry. It was painful when she swallowed. "This is terrible." She quickly added, "Not your writing. This story—all of their stories—just… It puts a lot of hate in your heart." Scrolling to the top of the document, she asked, "She told all of this to you through dreams?"

"Mostly. I found a lot of things in the county's records, but other stuff sort of fell into my lap." Moira scanned the story while Veronica spoke. "The Midwife's name was Annabelle Mitchell. She was a nurse from Cottage Grove. I don't know much more than that. These old records are a pain to navigate. Um, she had three kids of her own—boys—one sister, was married to a banker who came out of the depression better than he went in. One sister died of tuberculosis. The other one was hard to find anything on; it doesn't look like she ever worked or married. This was also before social security numbers, so who knows? I like to think she was one of those lounge singers or was part of the war effort, like Rosie the Riveter." Veronica flexed her biceps and put on a smug smile. "There's a little more information on Korey's daughter. There's a scanned copy of a scrap of an adoption record in one of the folders."

"They found her? Was she alive?" Moira hurried through the folders and files. There were so many names. "Which one?"

"In the Cs," Veronica said. "It's under Cordelia Clarke."

Moira froze. "What?"

"It's her name. Cordelia Rachel Clarke."

Moira shivered and kept scrolling, half-hoping to not find that file. When she found it, she couldn't bring herself to open it.

"As far as I know, it's the only copy. Somebody mailed it to me three years ago, and I scanned it before burning it. I don't know how they found me unless she told them."

Moira ran a sandpaper tongue over rough lips, and she clicked the file open. It was an email attachment but not from the county's records. It was from Hopkins' church. "Heather," Moira said. "Heather Hopkins used to work at the county records before she quit to stay in Abrams and work for the church. What's her role in all of this?"

"Can we focus on the important detail for a moment?" Veronica tapped her knuckles on the table. "You're a Clarke."

"Coincidence." It didn't sound as convincing as she hoped. "It's a common name."

"Witches are a bloodline, Moira. That's what everything and everyone has told me. The power of a mother is in her blood. A piece of Korey's soul was passed on to her daughter. This isn't a new concept!"

"This isn't a storybook, Veronica! Besides, just because a Clarke adopted her doesn't mean there is some magical bloodline."

"Are you telling me you don't believe your own eyes?" Veronica held up her palm. Where she had sliced into the meat, the skin had healed into thin line of slightly paler flesh. "This is real. *She* told me to show it to *you*. You. There is no coincidence."

"Are you telling me she brought me here in some kind of cosmic, metaphysical… Moira-heist? A witch so powerful she can infect dreams and move people around like pieces on a game board, but she can't stop a town of assholes from killing innocent people? Why? Why me? Why you and Jenny? Why all of this?"

"She needs all of us," Jenny said. "She can't save herself alone." She squeezed Moira's hand. "But you're her family. You're the most important of all of us."

"And the one person the demon wants dead." Anxiety bobbed up and down in Moira's stomach.

"Or the one thing that could free her." Veronica shrugged. "I don't know about Jenny and everyone else, but she's giving me something to fight for, instead of laying down and dying."

"She's going to take me home with her." Jenny rested her head on Moira's shoulder and held onto her hand. "I get to have my Ollie again."

"And you said she promised something to Gloria; Celeste Martin, too," Veronica reminded her.

"Dreams," Moira responded. There was more she wanted to say, to argue, but she grew weary of talking and reading and wondering. Tomorrow was the Flower Moon. Hopkins, Lake, Miller, and the Beast were all looking for them. How does someone hide from a demon?

The thought of dying pressed freezing dread against her intestines. She desperately wanted nothing more than to be sitting on her grandmother's couch watching re-runs of courtroom dramas and procedural television shows while munching on buttered popcorn and drinking sparkling water. Dani could be there, too, next to her, so close she could feel the warmth of her leg against hers.

The thought of never seeing Dani again sent a hot tear of fear and anger to her sliding down the side of her nose.

Jenny rubbed Moira's shoulder and handed her a napkin. "You should show her the other thing, Ronnie." To Moira, she said, "I made Ronnie draw me another one when she told me the story. She's so pretty. It's exactly how I saw her in my head."

Veronica slid a small manila envelope past Moira's laptop. "I drew this five months ago." The envelope's adhesive seal was intact, the two copper pins bent open and held down with a piece of clear tape. A square of floral postage stamps covered the upper corner. The address had no name, only a post office box. The red stamp from a post office in Montana showed it was mailed in January. "She said you'd know her."

Moira ran her trembling finger over the tiny feathers on the fraying edge. A hollowness opened within her, as if all the cells in her body collectively held their breaths. "I can't." She slid it back to Veronica. "I can't."

Veronica slid her knife through the seam. Jenny asked if she could open it, and happily did so when Veronica handed it to her.

She removed a piece of sketchbook paper and unfolded it. "This one is my favorite."

Moira stifled a sob.

It was a sketch of a woman. Tiny wildflowers and thin vines intertwined the long braids of her hair, which were pulled back into a crown that draped past her lithe, bare neck. Her shoulders were thin and strong. Even though the drawing was black and gray, her skin held a luster that brightened the whiteness of the page. Thin lips parted into a tiny smile. High cheekbones sat beneath a soft gaze directed past the right side of the page. Other than a rounder jaw and sharper eyes, the woman was the image of Moira's mother.

"That's Korey. That's why I know it's not a coincidence that you're here."

Jenny unfolded another sheet. "You didn't show me this one."

"Because she said I wasn't supposed to show anyone until Moira came."

"Is it her momma?"

Moira looked over Jenny's shoulder. What she saw made the floor of her mind fall away.

"No," Veronica said. "It's her daughter."

It shouldn't have bothered her as much as it did, but it bothered her all night long. It still bothered her. It wasn't the "stay the fuck out of Abrams" part. It was that Moira said she didn't want her. "I don't want you" echoed over and over in her mind. Between being pissed off, crying into a pillow, and throwing the shirt she took from Moira into the trash—then removing it—Dani didn't get a wink of sleep. On top of that, Marco called her that morning to question her about Jenny Lake, who had vanished from her group home. Apparently, Jenny's civil commitment was commuted several years prior, and she had been voluntarily staying at the group home ever since. Since she effectively released herself from the home, the police said there was very little they could do until after 24 hours, even for a vulnerable adult. The entire morning just wanted to squeeze her every heartbeat through her throat.

Now she was at work, worried and angry, leaning against the glass case in the jewelry section with a tissue balled in her hand, trying to not cry anymore because her face felt like an overstuffed bean bag chair. No amount of makeup helped the bags under her eyes. After she punched in that morning, she'd basically been hiding from her supervisor, Jeff, as well as all customers. Nobody bought jewelry in the middle of the workday, so she figured she was safe.

"Danielle!" Jeff called from the perfumes. He waved at her, the ever-present steel clipboard cradled in his arm. "There are customers over in women's that need help."

Dani moved the rag on the counter in little circles. "I'm cleaning the glass and setting out the necklaces. Can't Terri or Steve help?"

Jeff's cheap shoes squeaked along the tile floor. He leaned his elbows on the counter until his silver watch clicked against the glass. "We're a family here, Danielle. We help each other." The authoritative glower on his face was diminished by spiked hair so gelled it could pierce skin. "You've been cleaning this glass for the last half hour when there are customers in other areas of the store that need help. Get moving."

That was his default. Everyone is family here. What a dysfunctional way of thinking. Family meant that people could do or say or take advantage of your kindness with impunity. This was a job, not Thanksgiving dinner. Besides, she didn't think she could carry on a friendly conversation with another middle-aged customer obsessed with their jeans size. "Jeff, I don't know if I'm in the right shape for people-ing today."

"Why? What the hell is wrong with you? Have you been crying?"

"I kind of had a bad night."

He immediately waved his questions away. "You know, whatever. I'm not your therapist. God, you college kids are all the same. Working for an easy paycheck during the summer and barely lifting a finger in the fall." He pointed toward the wall of blouses with his clipboard. "Be a professional for once. Stop taking your handout and go make money for the store. Keep your relationship problems at home."

Her nose and eyes felt brittle, and she worried that if she moved, she'd shatter. But after more of Jeff's harsh, whispering insistence, she stepped away from the counter and took the long way through the racks of bras and underwear, stopping near the clearance sweaters to take a deep breath and exhale slowly, fighting back the burn of another set of tears and hoping someone else had already reached whoever waited for her so she could hide in the bathroom.

I don't want you.

What the hell was she doing here? She should have called in sick. Should've just quit.

"That was excessively rude. Don't you think?"

Behind her, an elderly woman in a thin, green dress examined a cashmere sweater.

Dani cleared the thickness in her throat with a tiny cough. "I'm sorry. I didn't mean to keep you waiting. How can I help?"

"Not you. The way that awful man with the silly hair spoke to you."

The counter must have been at least 30 feet away from where they stood. Did this woman have superhuman hearing?

While Dani considered that, the woman hung the sweater back on the rack. "Dearie, have you been crying?" The concern in her voice dripped honey sweet off her tongue. She pulled a silk handkerchief from her brown handbag. "Here, lovely. Take this."

Dani forced a smile and held up her hand. "No. Thank you. I'm just… I have a, um, naturally watery face. It's a condition."

The woman laughed, deep and sultry. "Do you now?" An easy

smile and bright eyes gave her a youthfulness that contrasted with the head of thick, downy white hair she wore down in a long ponytail. The scent of dewy earth and flowers in the morning swirled around her in the gentle breeze flowing past the automatic doors. The cut of her green dress was a lower in the chest than Dani imagined a senior citizen would dare. A chain of knotted bronze diverted attention away from the spotty skin on her breasts rather than accentuating it negatively.

Dani liked her instantly. Her style, her smile, her familiar cheekbones. Everything.

Sensing a bright spot in her day, Dani gave her a genuine smile. "I'm sorry. I've had a morning. Can I help you find something?"

The woman smiled in a way that said she would not let the matter drop so easily.

A black woman in a flowing blue sundress and a hat adorned with what appeared to be real flowers walked over and showed the older woman a graphic t-shirt with the phrase I WISH YOU WERE PIZZA printed on it. "She'd think this is funny." Hearing Dani giggle, she turned and nodded. "I know that look. Red eyes, biting the inside of your lip. He said something stupid, huh?"

"It won't be the last time, dearie. Believe me."

Of course, it looked obvious. If she wasn't so damned touchy, she wouldn't need too much makeup, or too much trying to bring down the bags with ice packs over her breakfast of dry toast. Now she had to navigate nosey people intent on helping her cope. At least these two seemed nice. If another man tried to 'save her' on a bad day, she would lose her mind.

"Danielle, this is my sister, Caroline."

"Sisters?" It must have been through marriage or adoption.

"She has a keen eye for fashion, as I'm sure you can tell." The older woman leaned in. She smelled like lavender and something else Dani couldn't place. With a conspiratorial hand against her mouth, she whispered loudly enough for Caroline to hear. "Watch out for this one. She's practically clairvoyant. Sees everything."

"Practically?" Caroline lifted an eyebrow.

"Mmhmm." The woman smoothed out her ponytail. "So, Dani. Tell us, who is the lucky fool that has your eyes simmering like that?"

Dani shrugged it off. "I don't know. It's just a... maybe just a silly little crush. It's nothing. You know how they are. Temporary."

"Nuh uh," Caroline said, pointed at Dani's eyes. "Those aren't the kind of angry eyes I've seen come from a little crush. Somebody you love hurt your feelings."

"Indeed," the woman said.

The world dropped an inch under her, and her chest was a glass balloon rolling on the tip of a needle. Moisture brimmed painfully in her eyes. No, it wasn't a crush.

"Now, now." The woman patted Dani's arm and held her wrist with warm fingers. "Nothing that's nothing can make a young beauty like you daydream stars so bright that I can see them in your eyes. Tell us this boy's name, so we can have a little chat with him. Straighten him out."

Cool calm ran up Dani's arm from where the woman touched it and tickled the top of her stomach. The balloon tilted back to a precarious but sure balance upon the needle. This woman reminded her of how her grandmother covered her sourness with sweetness. She had a good-natured aura of flower gardens and a kitchen filled with Christmas cookies. These two were so kind to be concerned. Everything was safe here. Women their age had secrets and advice. Ways to make hurt flutter away like a startled butterfly. There was no harm in just talking a little.

Hell, she could tell them just about anything.

"Moira," she breathed. "Her name's Moira."

The sheen in the woman's eyes shifted. Her stare hardened into cinnamon-colored marbles. "Moira? Isn't that a beautiful name, Carrie? Dani and Moira." She turned the words over in her mouth as if they were a candy to be savored. "I know a Moira, as well. Of course, not your Moira. Couldn't be."

"Couldn't be," Caroline echoed, rolling her eyes.

"And here I was telling Carrie that there was no need for us to come into town this morning—what with online delivery and all—but she insisted. Very strongly. Now that you're here, I'm very glad, too. Look at us. Strangers in a store, sharing memories of our Moiras. Don't you just love these happy coincidences, Carrie?"

"You know how I love a good coincidence."

She couldn't help but smile at the two women. Though she

wasn't sure they were sharing, exactly. What was it about their Moira they told her?

"Tell me about her." The old woman gave Dani's arm a reassuring squeeze. A chill warmth ran through her body as if her soul walked back in from a frosty winter evening. "Is your Moira as beautiful as her name?"

Dani's body felt hollow and stiff, a metal watering can that, once asked a question, let answers pour into the flowers.

"So beautiful. She has this auburn hair and these brown eyes—" Dani nodded like an eager child, glad to know the women wouldn't judge her for the way she looked at another woman. "She's like autumn. You know those days when the air is just getting chilly and the clouds are puffy and cottony and purple and red, and you can't tell if it's going to rain or snow but everything is so green and brown, like the world is a fresh painting and it looks like the sun is rising all day?" There was a flash within her, as if her soul was a great eye that just blinked. She felt suddenly self-conscious. "I don't know what I'm talking about. I babble sometimes. I don't think she even likes me like that."

"Nonsense." The woman cocked her head. Fingers, so tiny and frail, flexed against Dani's wrist with a surprising amount of force.

Everything was alright. Things would be fine. She wouldn't need to cry again today. Probably didn't even need a nap after work.

"Why don't you know?" the woman asked. "It seems to me that anyone who would have such an effect on me, well, I'd be sure he or she didn't like me the same. Moira." The woman's hands slipped down Dani's wrist, cradling her hand in both of hers. She edged a step closer and seemed to grow taller, glowing with more radiance. Her voice dropped an octave, became commanding, as if age was just a thin fog obscuring a completely different woman within. "Names are like stories and stories are magic. Do you know what the name Moira means?"

Dani swallowed hard. "It means destiny. Fate."

"Absolutely correct." The woman nodded, eyes glowing with pride. "You are very smart, Dani. Carrie, don't you think Dani is just as smart as she is beautiful?"

"I miss being young and pretty."

The woman smiled. Her finger feathered the back of Dani's hand. "Lovely. So very, very lovely."

Dani floated, a puff of dandelion in a soft breeze. She liked being called lovely. Moira called her lovely.

"Tell me everything."

Dani left out no detail. From the moment Moira told her about the Abrams Witch; the nightmares she confided in Dani; about Celeste, Gloria, and Jenny—Dani spilled everything. Jeff walked past them twice while she told her story, yet he said nothing. Didn't even look their way. Like they were invisible.

When she finished, the woman asked, "Are you brave, Danielle?"

"I don't know. I want to be." She once broke a guy's thumb for grabbing her ass at a bar. Tough, maybe. But brave? Not so much. She still kept a stuffed bear on her bed and felt safest when she was cuddled against Moira.

As if reading her thoughts, the woman said, "I think there are two kinds of courage, Dani. The courage of those who run toward danger, and the courage of those who run toward love. Running toward danger, well, that's just simplicity, isn't it? You pick up your sword and armor and dash into battle, thinking you're invincible. But love? Nobody runs toward love while wearing armor. No, we drop our swords, unstrap our shields, peel away our flesh and bones until all we are is who we are, and we run naked and vulnerable toward the monsters, into the fire. We hold our hearts in our hands like we're carrying the last piece of bread into a den of starving thieves, armed with their daggers and their teeth, and we don't even think about survival. All we want is to wrap ourselves in it, to feel complete. To be whole again. With all of that in our midst, only the bravest of us run toward love.

"Fate." The woman slid a finger past the sensitive tissue inside Dani's elbow, up her shoulder, and down to her breast. "Don't you think we should chase destinies, Dani? Sister Carrie, what do you think?"

"Ran down to the end of the earth, Sister Rae."

The woman unhooked Dani's plastic name tag from her shirt pocket. "To the end of the earth. Until there is nothing between it and you but the brightest burning certainty. Isn't that what you want, Dani? To be brave? To run toward your autumn day? That fresh painting of purple clouds and auburn hair?" She fingered a curl of Dani's hair. "Oh, if someone talked about me like I was living art, and then you asked me if I'd let that go without a fight, I'd tell you three words:

Fat fucking chance."

Fat fucking chance. Dani really liked this lady.

"I'll ask again. Dani, are you brave?"

Dani nodded. "I can be brave."

The woman's smile was both warm and frightening, a lioness smiling. "I know you can."

Dani suddenly found herself laughing along with the two of them at some meaningless joke friendly strangers tell each other. Everything felt light and fresh as the first warm morning after a spring rain, and her worries trickled away.

"Thank you so much, Dani. You've been such a great help. I think we'll take this one." The woman draped the t-shirt over her arm. "It's perfect for my granddaughter. Absolutely perfect."

"Sure! I can ring you up, up front."

"Oh, that's unnecessary, dear. You've been more help than that slacker and his clipboard." She lowered her voice. "Do men bathe in cologne these days?"

"Cologne? I'm pretty sure it's bug spray."

The women cackled, their voices carrying across the store.

"You go ahead, dear. We'll find someone that works here."

Confused, Dani looked down at her chest and saw her nametag was gone. Odd. She must've finally mustered the nerve to quit that morning.

"You have a wonderful trip now."

Dani nodded, said goodbye, and carried the women's kindness with her out the door and toward her car where she made a list in her head of the things to pack before making the drive to Abrams.

Chapter Twelve

They ate hot dogs and potato chips outside as the sun set over the Abrams woods. Jenny stayed inside, preferring to watch Veronica's DVDs instead of sitting on the rough ground with nothing more than Moira's sweatshirt or Veronica's jacket for padding. Several vehicles rumbled in the distance, but none came near. Veronica thought it safe enough to run the RV's engine and charge her battery bank while they had dinner.

Moira managed three bites before her appetite disappeared. She wished the bottled water was vodka, but Veronica didn't drink. The best she could do was a lime soda that Moira turned down.

Finally, Moira announced, "My grandmother isn't a witch."

Veronica nodded as she chewed. "Again, I'm not saying she is. All I've been trying to tell you is that you and she share Korey's blood. Whether that means you inherited anything the Witch gave her or not,

I don't know."

"Right. Because *She* told you in a dream that witches are bloodlines."

"I know how it sounds."

"Do you?" Moira dropped her plate into the shadows at her feet. "Maybe you do. I don't know. All I wanted to do was write a paper so I could get into graduate school and not burden my grandmother anymore."

"Is she one of those grandmas that holds things over your head and makes you feel guilty about being alive?"

"No," Moira answered. "She's a saint. She's sacrificed so much for me and has only asked that I do my best in school and be independent. Never made me do anything I didn't already want to, unless it was yard work."

That got a laugh from Veronica.

"Why wouldn't she tell me? We've practically shared everything for the past ten years." She took a sip of water. "If Rachel is a witch, why would she keep that from me? Why would she let me come here? If they know me, then they have to know her. If she's what the demon wants, then why would she let me leave her all alone?"

Veronica shrugged. "Just because she's Korey's daughter doesn't mean she knows. If she does? Maybe she can't do anything about it. Maybe it's not her who can do something about it, Moira. Besides, it's you the Witch needs."

Moira threw her hands up, exasperated. "For what? What am I

supposed to do about a shadow demon thing, a murdering pastor and his pet cop, and a town filled with cultists who would happily kill all of us to maintain their near immortality?"

"I don't know. She said you'd know what to do." Veronica dropped her own plate. "We've got until tomorrow to figure it out."

"You know where the Pit is. Why can't we just go now?"

"It has to be tomorrow. On the Flower Moon. That's the last thing she told me."

A joyous laugh sang from out of the camper. Moira's heart sank. "This is so fucked. None of this is Jenny's fault. Not Gogo's, not Ollie's, not Celeste's. Even Heather is practically blameless."

"Sounds to me it's mostly guilt that's got her helping us."

Moira begrudgingly agreed with that.

Veronica picked up her plate and shook the dirt and dead leaves off her jacket. "I'm gonna turn in. There's room in there, but it's not a motel. We'll have to sleep close, but I can keep it running for the AC. Coming?"

Moira shook her head. She wanted to be alone with her thoughts and her laptop. "I think I'll just sit here for a bit."

Veronica nodded. When she reached the door of the RV, she said, "Moira, everything I've told you is the truth as I know it. I wish I could tell you more. Believe that I'm trying to help all of us." With a resigned smile, she added, "Please don't run."

Moira shook her head. Where would she even go? "Wait," she

said. "With everything we know, with how little we know, how certain are we that the Beast isn't masquerading as the Witch? How do we know she's even real?"

Veronica hesitated at the top of the folding stairs. When she answered, it was with a sad smile. "Because she is. I know she is." And she walked inside, leaving Moira with her thoughts.

Moira reclined against a thin tree wondering, waiting for the inevitable supernatural aid that usually arrived when the hero needed it most desperately, until the milky white light of the nearly full moon replaced daylight. This was when some magic helper was supposed to show her a solution to her problems. The indispensable sidekick with answers. Of course, there was never a time in her life when she wanted to be the hero. She preferred the fairy godmothers and the wizened farmers. As a girl, she imagined herself as a huntress cloaked with the forest, appearing only in times of someone's greatest need, when they needed to be shown the path to greatness or pulled away from it to wander among the trees and the fairies forever.

Like a witch?

She squeezed her eyes shut and wished she could be anywhere else.

Nothing happened. When it was dark and no one arrived to save them, she considered prayer. The only other time in her life when she prayed was right after her parents' funeral. There was no answer then, and there would be no answer now. Instead, she sat in front of the blue glow of her laptop and typed two goodbye letters. One to Rachel, telling her everything and apologizing for not being as strong as she always told her to be. The second was to Danielle, telling her she had always loved her, always wished she could have figured her life out differently, maybe thought less about school and more time holding her hand when they ate lunches at the blue picnic tables outside the library. How she wished she'd kissed her on so many occasions—the movies, the zoo, that time they had dinner at Olive Garden and had too much wine and fettuccine. *I would have totally Lady and the Tramp-ed you.* She even wrote her a secret, a little thing she carried out of the little forest cottage hidden in her imagination.

I thought that if we were good together, we would get married someday. Maybe by my grandma's house near her flower garden, or by a lake somewhere at sundown. A really pretty spot with a long beach and clear water we could swim in afterward. We could have flowers, garlands, the white arbor decorated with roses—all of it. We wouldn't wear white. No way. We'd wear red or purple. Paint our nails the same color. You'd have to do our hair, because I don't know what the hell I'm doing with my own half the time. I thought that instead of hyphenating our last names, we could just pick a new one that we both liked, like Raspberry or something silly like that. Mrs. and Mrs. Raspberry. Dr. and Mrs. Pancakes.

I hope you read this. I hope you read this, and you think happy thoughts. I hope you read it and cringe about how stupid I am and laugh at the idea of us being together. I hope you forget me. I hope it's easy. And I hope you find someone who you love as much as I love you.

Moira let herself only cry for a minute before removing the lock screen password, shutting off her computer, and navigated her way to a narrow bed near Jenny. There she laid down, face buried in her headband, and fell into an anxious, dreamless sleep while thin shadows swam in angry circles above the clearing.

Dani pulled up to the Abrams Motel on Thursday morning. Moira's car wasn't there. The only other vehicle in the parking lot was a rusted blue pickup.

She remembered Moira telling her there was only one motel in Abrams, but to be sure, she went inside to ask the clerk.

A woman with Becky on her nametag greeted her. "Well, hello there! How are you today?" Becky pointed at the larger gentleman kneeling on the floor and examining a pipe. He smelled like raw pig shit. "Sorry about the maintenance here. I've been having a bit of a water issue."

"No worries. Is this the only place to stay in Abrams? I'm looking for a friend of mine, and I didn't see her car outside. I just want to make sure I'm in the right place."

Becky gave her a warm smile. "Sure. This is the only place in Abrams, unless she's staying with family or a friend. We had someone check in last week. What's your friend's name?"

"Moira Clarke."

Becky's shoulders tensed, and she checked her book. "Yeah. She's staying right—Matthew!"

A dark shape flew down past Dani's eyes. Before she could react, a thick arm wrapped around her neck and applied tremendous pressure.

"What are you doing?" Becky gasped.

The voice behind Dani growled, "Dan's taking too long to find that bitch. We can use this one."

There was an argument. Sounds. Dani felt light and puffy. Her throat wiggled for air. Then the world went black.

The moon wouldn't rise until after supper, yet they struck out for the Pit early that afternoon based on Veronica "feeling it was the right time to leave."

Moira didn't argue. She felt the same tingle in her chest pulling her into the forest.

"Moonrise begins early," Veronica tried to lighten the mood with a smile and a nasal voice. "So technically, the Flower Moon started rising at five this morning."

Moira couldn't bring herself to smile. "I don't think we're going to beat a demon based on semantics and an astronomical technicality."

Veronica's smile faded. "It won't get over the horizon until after supper." She stuffed packages of food and bottles of water into her backpack. With her lips tightened and concerned, she asked, "She say anything to you?"

"I didn't dream."

"I dreamed my stomach hurt," Jenny said, as she slid her own backpack of food and water onto her shoulders. "My stomach still hurts."

Veronica wrapped Jenny in her arms and rocked back and forth for a minute, whispering soothing words in her ear. It was a touching moment Moira didn't want to interrupt, yet she ventured, "Jenny was never marked. She could leave Abrams. Forever."

"No." Jenny shook her head, mashing her cheek against Veronica's shoulder. "I promised her I wouldn't leave. She promised me, and I promised her, and we keep our promises here. Right, Ronnie?"

"Right, Jen-Jen." Veronica patted and kissed Jenny's hair. "Why don't you wait for us outside? Maybe some fresh air will help your stomach?"

Jenny nodded and stepped out of the camper. When she was gone, Veronica whispered, "Will you do something for me? If something happens and it comes down to saving me or her, save her. Leave me."

Moira wasn't sure what or where Veronica expected her to go if something went wrong, but she agreed and followed Veronica out into the afternoon.

When they were ready, Veronica tossed her backpack onto her shoulders and said, "I assume they have to make their sacrifices near nightfall."

"It doesn't like light or fire," Jenny said, her eyes glazed and distant.

Even with that possibility, Moira wasn't brimming over with confidence. "I don't suppose you have another gun, or maybe a group of large male friends with years of combat experience?"

Veronica pointed at the holstered revolver on the waistband of her backpack. "I have this and a rifle stashed out in the woods with some ammo and food. You know how to shoot?"

She admitted she didn't. There was never a time in her life where it was practical for her to use, own, or consider shooting a firearm until that morning. If she was honest with herself, she didn't want to learn, even now.

As they approached the wall of vines, Moira expected they were going to have to cut their way through. Instead, Veronica pulled the knife from the sheath on her belt, sliced her palm, and pressed it to the barrier. The moment her blood touched the green, it came alive, whipping and curling and sprouting more tiny flowers. One vine slipped down from above and slid its tip along Veronica's cheek as if it were aware and recognized her.

Once the opening was large enough, they walked through.

The air was heavy with moisture. Dry earth breathed its sandy stink into the air. They'd only been walking for an hour, and they were already breathing heavy.

Veronica showed them how to walk silently in the forest. Jenny excitedly accepted Veronica's gentle coaching on how to walk quietly. "Toe to heel when we go slow, like this. When we're just being kinda quiet, we're going to walk like this," and she helped Jenny balance while stepping slowly forward. Moira watched just as closely, but Jenny caught on more quickly. This was her home, she reminded them.

Their brief training session did little good in the dry woods. The moment Moira's calves ached, it seemed every leaf crunched, and every twig snapped and popped under her feet.

Movement was slow, and she didn't know how far they had gone. Every hundred glacial steps uphill in the thickening humidity felt like half a mile. Her legs groaned, the inseam of her jeans wore against the skin inside of her thighs, and newborn blisters buzzed on her heels. Watching the other two women, she was certain she was the weak link. Veronica navigated the terrain like a cat. Jenny seemed to float.

Moira slipped her headband up off her neck when she realized she'd sweat through the collar of her t-shirt. The smell of her grandmother brought her a sense of calm as the dying afternoon light turned the browns to grays and the shadows deepened among the shattered boles and desperately thirsty trees struggling to cling to the fuzzy bulbs at their tips.

Veronica slowed. Her shoulders tensed beneath her brown shirt, and she trembled.

"What's wrong?" Moira asked, as Jenny put a hand on Veronica's arm.

"We're close. I remember running past that fallen tree over there." She pointed to where a massive tree had fallen over, its roots standing tall like the headstone of an open grave.

"You okay?" Moira asked.

"I just need a sec."

Moira kept watch while Veronica drank water, and Jenny rubbed her shoulder.

Veronica announced she was ready to move on, but Moira held up a hand. "We're close, and we still don't know what we're going to do when we get there. I think we might—"

An ominous rumble echoed across the sky.

"Thunder?" Moira asked. "They said it hasn't rained in Abrams for almost a year."

Howls responded in the distance. Nearby, an owl gave five quick calls. *Hoot-hoot hoot. Hoot hoot.*

Jenny covered her mouth with both hands and made a noise between a laugh and a sob. "Ollie? Ollie!" Her call echoed. She rushed away from them.

"Shh!" Veronica hissed, "Jenny, be quiet!"

The crunches and shuffles of Jenny's footsteps were louder than they should have been. They echoed from too many directions. When she stopped and the noises didn't, Moira whipped her head around to face the nearest noise.

Five men dressed in dark clothing ran at them, rifles in hand.

"Run!" Moira screamed, but when she took her first steps, powerful hands closed around her legs. The impact of the fall forced the air from her lungs. More hands pinned her to the dirt. A rope wound its way quickly around her wrists and ankles.

A gunshot rang out. One man fell, his body collapsing downward as if all his bones had been suddenly removed.

More shots and a scream. Moira looked up just as a bullet tore into Veronica's chest. She kept her feet, firing once more before turning around and sprinting into the woods, dribbles of blood leaving a trail behind her.

One man took aim with his pistol and fired. Jenny pulled on his arm, and his shot went wide.

A shrill scream of horror pierced through the gunpowder fog. "Daddy! No!"

Chief Lake stumbled backward, his eyes wide with shock.

Moira choked out, "Jenny, run!"

Lake stood stock still. He stared at Jenny's mortified face for a long, breathless moment, then he simply said, "No," and shot his daughter in the belly.

Moira screamed. Something was stuffed into her mouth. It tasted like hay, and its rough surface burned the corners of her mouth.

"Jesus Christ, Jeff," Miller sounded amused. "That's cold."

The other two men agreed.

Lake spared Moira a final, shaking glance before turning around and running in the opposite direction.

"Where the hell is he going?" asked one man.

"Who cares? We have two offerings this year, boys."

They laughed. Fingers and leers found their way along Moira's neck and lips, into her ears. "We gonna have fun with her first?"

Thunder growled in the distance.

"Nah." Miller sounded disappointed. "The storm's getting close and I'm not about to waste another year growing dirt and weeds for you ungrateful fucks. Leave that one to rot. You two get after that other bitch. We get her and that's three this year."

"Man, she's already got a head start." This voice was younger, a teenager. "It's hot."

"Shut up and go!" The violence in Miller's voice made Moira's stomach jump. "She's hurt, and you've got a rifle. It's not like we need *you* there."

With a whine, the boy jogged after Veronica.

Miller flipped Moira onto her back and straddled her chest. The stench of his body odor and stale cigarettes wrestled with the bile and terror in her throat. "See this?" He pulled a large knife from his boot. The tip poked at the soft skin below her left eye. "If you struggle, if you fight, or if I even get the idea that you might run, I'm going to fuck you with this before you die. Understand?"

No matter how hard she tried to keep still, Moira shivered. The rope bit into her wrists and ankles. Her eyelid twitched and the sharpness bit a little deeper.

That must have been enough for them. Moira was jerked to her feet and dragged up a hill, deeper into the forest to be sacrificed to the Beast of the Abrams woods.

Chapter Thirteen

The sun hid behind the gnarled branches. Gray light dimmed to a brown haze. The trees thinned and became increasingly unhealthy, some having shed their bark to reveal the ash gray wood beneath. Wood smoke and the tang of fresh pine sawdust lingered within the gloom.

The two men shoved Moira forward toward the smell of burning wood and the chattering of impatient voices. Dozens of people cheered and sang praises and hymns when Miller called out to them. "Looks like the good Lord giveth today. Eh, Reverend?"

Orange and white lights dotted the landscape. Torches and flashlights swayed this way and that around a tall structure with a flat platform of freshly hewn planks overhanging the jagged corpse of a half-blackened and petrified tree mostly sunk into the hard-packed dirt to its thick U-shaped branch, the only one that remained. The ground surrounding it looked like a swamp so black neither light nor life seemed to touch it. When Moira was dragged to the ground at its edge, she could tell it was a vast hole lined with sticks stripped of their bark. She looked closer.

Not sticks. Bones. A hole held together with dirt and bones of all sizes. Thin and thick. Little round skulls shared a grave with pelvic bones, like the ridges of so many teeth.

Her stomach lurched.

Miller gagged and spit as he walked past the Pit. "Dammit. Every time." He pulled a cloth mask up over his face.

Moira only smelled fire and flowers. The chunky aroma of fresh, wet earth.

Miller pulled her up by a fistful of her hair. With his knife, he pointed to the top of the platform. "Here's a surprise for you."

Near the edge of the platform, a figure struggled to stand. Her hands were tied, elbows pinned to her sides, curly hair bunched tight to her neck by a length of rope connected to a blackened branch.

Dani screamed from behind her cloth gag.

The callused hand clamped around her throat silenced Moira's scream.

Thunder shattered the sky. Miller and the other man pulled Moira up a set of makeshift stairs, never letting her feet touch the wood. She recognized the boards from when they were driven out of town, away from the stage. They were building a second one. For her.

The robed man who waited at the top moved a squat stool next to Dani's and held the circle of a knotted rope open.

"You look like an idiot, Doc," Miller jeered.

Dr. Gorman snapped, mouth muffled by a cloth mask of his own, "Have some respect for tradition. We wouldn't be in this state if it wasn't for you." He wrapped the rope around Moira's neck, pinning her headband between it and her skin in an empty display of mercy, and pulled the rope until the toes of her shoes reached the stool. When she nearly fell, he held her fast. To Miller, he barked, "Now get the hell off of my stage."

"Listen, you old fuck! I don't wan—"

"Matthew!" Reverend Hopkins' voice boomed unnaturally from the center of the crowd. His dark figure parted the crowd like the shadow of a blade. Hands folded in front of him in supplication, he calmly commanded, "Come forth."

Miller growled, mocking the Reverend's call, and walked down the stage.

"Christ, it stinks." Gorman freed her ankles. "Hold still. Balance as best you can," he said, before letting her go. "Don't let yourself fall off just yet."

Moira twisted on the balls of her foot until she faced Dani. Her eyes were bloodshot, her face sticky with dirt, grime, and tears clumping on her cheeks. Two dark blobs of scabbed blood collected on her chapped lips. They'd hurt her.

Moira shook her head, hoping the denial would whisk Dani away to safety or reverse time to their last phone call, so she could warn her not to come, tell her about the real danger in Abrams, anything that would have kept her away. She should have known, should have reminded herself about Dani's fire and headstrong nature. Now, there was no saving her.

She flexed her arms against the ropes, digging upon an inner reserve of impossible strength to rip through her bonds so she could reach Dani, to touch her one last time if she couldn't free her. They only dug deeper into her skin.

"Easy, now." Gorman whispered and turned them to face Reverend Hopkins.

Flashlights clicked off. The torches moved into the outer ring of the crowd. Hopkins opened his hands, his body a dark crucifix in the dim of the coming evening.

"We blessed few bear witness to this great work of our Lord. We humbly ask His blessing as we call upon His holy name! Send us your messenger, O Lord! We beg you: send forth your angel to accept this humble offering from our community on this holy of nights, the night of the Flower Moon, and bless us our fields and our bodies with health and prosperity, our souls with your gentle hand of salvation. Come forth! Come forth and receive our offering as we receive you!"

Red lightning flashed, illuminating the shadows. The air charged with electricity and the stink of ozone. Thunder pealed in a drawn-out and bestial growl that echoed through the forest, unending, as the shadows of trees and the gathered people peeled away from their backs and feet to coalesce into a rumbling mass of serpentine black fingers twisting and swimming around each other like earthworms packed too tightly together within a crystal ball.

Overwhelming dread pressed down into Moira's bladder, pushing her screams through her chest and stomach until urine ran down her legs.

The shadow of the Beast swirled above them, blocking out the last of the waning sunlight. Dani struggled against her bonds, tears and spit turning the orange rag in her mouth to a blood red, the small stool under her toes making a *clack-clack-clacking* as it wobbled against the wood. Moira yelled for her to stop, to hold still and not do anything that would cause her to fall into the Pit below, but her own gag choked her to silence. All she could do was weep and push herself higher onto cramping toes while her fingernails bent at odd angles and ripped against the knots.

More thunder rumbled in the distance.

"It's working!" Miller yelled. The others nodded to each other, some even smiled, but all their faces tensed with trepidation at the sight of the churning black mass hovering and whispering overhead. Doubt and fear clear in their eyes. "Get ready, Doc!"

Hands press against the middle of Moira's back.

"Hold yourself until it is time!" Hopkins pulled Miller aside by his elbow and spoke to him in an animated whisper.

Gorman held Dani still, pushing down on her until the knot tightened around her neck and she choked. "Hold still, now. Don't let this be a wasted sacrifice. At least die knowing that you saved a community." To Moira, he said, "I'm sorry. Truly, I am. I tried to convince them to burn you. The fire would have been faster; I'd have drugged you, so you didn't feel anything. The smoke would have made you pass out before you felt much more than your legs burning. But the Reverend said it had to be slow this time, to make up for our last failure. Just try to relax. Have faith that you're going to a better place. You'll be together again soon."

His obvious sincerity made her sick. Sick and angry.

A flash of lightning illuminated the Pit below. A heavy peal of thunder shook the ground, pouring sand onto the skulls and bleached bones littering the roots of the old, burned tree like some perverted imitation of Christmas.

Miller stormed off to the side, leaving Hopkins at the edge of the Pit. He faced the crowd with his hands stretched high above. "O, Father! For love of us you came to earth, gave your life for us. Every day you give us now, we give back happily. Take all our laughter, all our tears. Take each thought, each word, each deed, and let them be our prayer to you, to help our homes in need."

He faced Moira and Dani. There was no coldness in his eyes, no calculation, only a stoic mask of duty and unquestioning purpose in the shadows of his eyes.

He nodded once and began to pray. "Our Father, who art in Heaven, hallowed be thy name."

Moira barely noticed her bladder release a second time. She stared at Danielle, beautiful and innocent, eyes spider-webbed and ringed red with terror, the pink burning under her glistening almond skin. She said, "I love you," through the coarse rope in her mouth.

She knew Dani heard her, knew the words. But when Dani took a breath to speak, the rope cinched an inch tighter, the stool casually kicked from under her feet, and the rope lowered again until the toes of her shoes pointed downward like a ballerina. Her eyes rolled up into her head, and her shoulders trembled as if she were being electrocuted—her body's instinct to survive taking over, becoming the very thing that ensured a slow, torturous death.

Moira screamed and wrenched against her ropes. Gorman's hands held her fast and made her watch Dani kick and struggle; tears and snot blowing out of her nose with gurgling, animal grunts. Moira fought to push the stool into the Pit, because she would rather die with Dani than watching her suffer, but his hands were too strong, easily knowing when to push, pull, or hold. She was helpless against them.

Above, the Beast coiled and uncoiled like a ball of twisted rubber bands being stretched and relaxed between a child's hands. Moans and hisses of rapture boiled off its formless surface.

A crack of lightning and thunder brought gasps of fright from below.

Dani kept fighting. Tears rolled down her face like raindrops. Her stomach lurched and flexed, her knees pulled up to her waist and kicked. The rope's teeth cinched tighter, twisting and folding the soft skin around her throat.

Another crack bit through the air. The Beast roared. Blood splattered across Danielle's face.

The hands around Moira slipped away. Dr. Gorman fell to the

stage, the top of his forehead bloomed open like a rose, fragments of his skull dotted the gore like seeds.

Tendons in Moira's hips screamed as she fought for balance. The rope tightened around her throat. Out of the corner of her eye, she watched Veronica work the lever of her rifle and fire another shot.

The bullet buzzed and whistled past her head. The branch above her cracked and sprayed chips of blackened wood into her hair. Her toes dropped a fraction of an inch. Dani's did too, but it wasn't enough for her to balance on her toes. Her face was a juicy berry, ready to burst.

A gunshot barked from the middle of the crowd. Fabric ripped away from Veronica's arm, trailing a line of crimson behind. She stumbled, turned, and fired three quick shots into the crowd, taking Miller in the stomach with one. He fell to his knees, and his gun went off. His second shot caught an old woman through the neck in a gout of blood.

Veronica aimed. The unsteady barrel sent the shot wide and into the trees.

Balanced on one foot, Moira screamed and kicked her other foot at Dani's arms, hoping to hook one in her elbow and pull her closer to the stool, but she only spun her in a half-circle.

Dani's kicks weakened, the fluttering of her eyelids slowed, her shoulders went slack, and her neck tilted at a sickening angle. Moira thrashed until the knot around her own neck squeezed the rope taut against her windpipe.

Another gunshot. A quick, pained yelp.

Moira whipped her head around. Despair squeezed her heart in its fist.

A black dot poured scarlet, bubbling blood down the front of Veronica's shirt. She stumbled forward.

From his place on the ground, Miller gave an angry shout. "Yes!"

Veronica barely held her balance at the edge of the Pit. The light and focus waxed and waned in her eyes as she raised the shaky barrel directly at Moira.

A sob caught against the rope. Moira shut her eyes and waited for the bullet.

A crack.

A buzzing.

Splinters of wood rained down.

Miller's third shot burst through Veronica's left eye, spinning her completely around. The pink mist of her blood formed a halo around her skull just before her lifeless body fell and crunched into the bones at the bottom of the Pit.

Hopkins gave a victorious scream. Wolves howled in the distance.

The branch holding their ropes creaked with a *crick-crick-crick*. Dani's body wiggled as the last of her life began to escape.

Moira didn't pray. She didn't scream. She did the only thing she could think to do. With all the force she could muster from her numbing calves, she leaped forward into the air. When her stomach jumped to catch her fall and the rope pinched against her throat, she went limp and kicked downward, driving all her weight into her feet.

The branch shattered. Moira and Dani fell headlong into the Pit.

Hopkins roared. To the Beast, he screamed, "We've given you what you want, demon. Feed!"

The Beast groaned its sinister whisper and sank into the Pit after them.

Fingers of fresh earth massaged the inside of her nostrils. Pine, wildflowers, and berries brought memories of dewy mornings in Rachel's flower garden, of picking tomatoes and cucumbers in August, of the tickling spice of nasturtiums at a lake where frogs and grasshoppers leaped around marigolds at sunset. Turning the garden soil in the fall. Adding the compost in spring.

These were not dreams.

Dazed, Moira slumped onto her side. The knot was tight, but not tight enough she couldn't breathe.

Next to her, Dani's face swelled like a dark balloon.

She rolled onto her knees and threw herself at Dani's neck, biting and tearing at the knot. It slipped away from her teeth. She couldn't get a hold of it. She buried her face in Dani's curls and chomped like a wolf tearing at the intestines of a fallen fawn, but the knot didn't budge.

The shadows of the Beast reached down and licked at her shoulders, tasting her.

It didn't matter. She wouldn't leave Dani. Not like this.

Moira dove backward, jarring her shoulders and biting her tongue. She crawled like a worm toward Veronica's body, and used her teeth to free the knife from her belt.

Living roots slithered out of the hole in Veronica's head, lapping the fresh blood and brains until they grew longer and thicker, curling through her clothing, along her skin, their tickle caressing the tears on Moira's cheeks.

The knife pulled free. She stretched and spun on top of it, numb fingers fumbling at the blade. When she had it, Moira worked her already burning shoulders up and down, not caring how coldly the blade bit into her flesh.

The ground beneath her rumbled with rage. The Beast sank closer and closer.

Moira worked even harder to slice through the knot. When the Beast's many tongues fondled Dani's limp body, Moira screamed, "Get the fuck away from her!"

The knot broke and Moira's hands slung free, sending drops of blood arching into the dirt.

The world shook. Thunder from the earth below her shattered the steel of the heavens above them.

The Beast recoiled.

Knife clasped in her fist, Moira dove at Dani and cut through the rope around her neck and arms. The coppery taste of blood from where she bit her tongue filled her mouth. "Baby, baby, please don't be dead. I've got you. I've got you. Please, please, please, please."

She didn't know CPR; she just did what she remembered seeing in movies and videos at camp. Crusty dirt mixed with salty blood and tears as she put her mouth over Dani's cold lips and breathed.

Dani remained still. The faint memory of a heartbeat pulled desperately at Moira's fingertips.

She breathed again, ignoring the tangles of roots running past her socks and against the skin of her thighs, tugging her away.

"Dani, please," she wept.

Above her, the Beast trembled, almost orgasmically.

Moira breathed again, letting the blood trickle past her tongue and into Dani's mouth.

The gurgle before the scream was the most beautiful noise she ever heard.

Moira turned Dani onto her side and held her as she vomited blood and mucus into the dirt. The earth quaked and rumbled in response. Three ragged breaths, the sound of cracking glass, escaped Dani's throat before she heaved again. When she was done, her ragged voice whimpered, "Mo? Help… me."

"I'm here." She smoothed Dani's filthy hair, her blood a choir of ghostly lights. "I'm—"

Black tendrils pulled against Dani's legs, hoisting her half into the air. She screamed. Roots yanked Moira away, separating them.

Moira slashed at them. The knife hacked against jeans and vines, slicing deep into the side of her leg. Like long leeches, the roots shrank against the open wounds, pulsing and drinking.

Lightning blasted into the tree, splitting it lengthwise in a shower of smoldering ash. Super-heated bone burned with orange and black.

Instinctively, Moira knew she should have been blinded, knew the light should have stolen her sight and blanketed her in a world of darkness, but she saw. She saw everything. A faint blue glow painted every bone in the Pit, whispering to her in a language she felt but didn't hear. Voices long dead spoke horrors, whispered visions of pain and terror, of begging and pleading. Of children abandoned, left to the merciless strike of a blade or the fangs of fire. Daughters screaming for their fathers' forgiveness. Sons calling out to their mothers. Of animals' wild, sense-starved demand to survive, no matter how the rocks carved their skin to bone. They all screamed, and she screamed with them.

Roots pushed through Veronica's body and sprouted from her limbs like a waking giant, twisting and turning around one another to form whip-like branches out of her outstretched arms and legs, raising her corpse from the ground and into the sky where the thorny branches snapped skyward, biting into the shadows with their wicked light.

The Beast roared and dropped Danielle, turning toward the new danger.

Moira looked at her bleeding legs and the roots drinking her.

Blood. The blackened tree.

Veronica's voice echoed in her memory, "The power of a mother is in her blood."

Blood. A fruit. A kiss on the lips of a sleeping princess. All parts of every witch's story, only this one screamed ice into the marrow of Moira's bones, crying for a different ending.

And like Celeste Martin, Gloria Ylva, Jennifer Lake, and Veronica Gardiner, Moira felt the presence of the Spirit of the Abrams woods, and she realized why it called to her. Why it needed her to crawl through the bones and earth and blood.

This wasn't a pit. This was a trap.

Frantic, she lunged away from Danielle and swam through earth, fire, swirling winds, and bone, pulling herself along the roots to the base of the tree where Korey was loved, embraced, kept safe, and ultimately massacred. With a steadying breath, she drew the knife along her palm, barely feeling the cut that awakened an angry pool of crimson in her palm.

She smeared blood along the tree and remembered Ronnie's words. She could barely speak past the pearl of fear lodged in the throat. "Please guard us from our enemies… Please protect us." Blisters from the Beast's nightmare heat bubbled and split on the back of her neck. The stench of burning hair filled her nostrils. Moira pressed her body against the dirt, but never let go of the roots. With a whimper, she begged, "Grandmother, Sprit, whatever you are, please wake up."

The Witch

1

The impact from the explosion ripped the air from her lungs and thrust her back against the wall of the Pit. Loose hunks of earth rumbled from the edges and down into the belly of the Pit where it bounced and skittered against a shivering mound of earth growing skyward in an upheaval of rock and bone. An infant's skull rolled down at their feet. Above, the shriek of an owl pierced the sky.

Moira cut away the last of Dani's ropes. The burns on her skin were already healing from red to a pinkish brown.

Dani threw her arms around Moira's neck and pulled her mouth into hers. She pulled away and, with a scratchy voice filled with tears, said, "I love you. I love you so much."

Moira kissed her, bled a part of soul into her. "I love you, too.

Climb me."

Cheerleading taught her how to turn her body into stairs. Kneel, back straight, cup your hands, squeeze your butt, lift with your thighs. When Dani was on her shoulders, she pressed upward, using the wall of dirt for stability until Dani pulled herself over the lip of the Pit.

Dani reached down for Moira, but she rolled back when the Beast struck out at her. Dirt and rocks fell into Moira's eyes and mouth. She ducked and covered her head.

Thunder pealed.

The earthen mound at the center of the Pit rose and rose, a great belly bursting toward the Beast. The flesh of Veronica's body unraveled, shooting vines and roots outward, thin strands of brown and green weaving around the Beast like ropes. It fought, bouncing back and forth, snapping branches and roots, but it couldn't keep up. Every severed vine split off, forming two more that reached out and grew into its neighbor, spreading along the Beast's surface and creating a ball of roots, prison bars tightening around it like a pair of hands interlacing their fingers.

The Beast screamed.

Moira watched as the figure of a person, backlit by the fire raging in the tree's hollow, clawed its way out of the top of the mound.

Hands, bloody and caked with fresh dirt, punched through the surface. They stretched and pressed downward, dragging a skeletal head and torso out of the mound. Thin strands of long hair hung limp from a crown of decayed and desiccated flesh, the empty sockets of its eyes emotionless. Tattered remains of a rotted dress drooped from bony shoulders and fell away from the wrinkled and pruned skin of its grayed breasts. Limp legs dragged behind as the thing climbed what remained of Veronica's body, clamped its chapped mouth over hers, and undulated like it was drinking, chewing.

More dried vines shot upward, completely entangling the Beast. Its roar was the tortured sound of screaming elephants and lions.

Moira screamed and dug her fingers into the earth, intent on climbing her way out of the Pit even if it ripped her fingernails away. She slipped against a stone and nearly fell, but Dani's hand latched onto her wrist, giving her enough strength to pull herself up over the edge and onto the dried earth of the forest.

Matthew Miller was waiting for them.

Even though he was bleeding from his stomach, he still pulled her off the ground with terrible strength. Hands, callused and rough from years of manual labor, ripped at Moira's throat and shoved Dani into the trunk of a tree. Moira punched and kicked, but the weight of his body pressed against her as they tumbled to the ground. He leaned in, straddling her, and pressed his face down toward hers, thumbs pressing against her windpipe. She wriggled her bleeding hand free and shoved her finger into his wound, squelching past muscle and sinew until she hit something solid.

Miller screamed and collapsed to the side.

Behind them, the figure of a woman pulled herself clear of the Pit. Once-rotten flesh glowed pinkish in the firelight as she rose unsteadily to her feet. The formless mass of the Beast squirmed behind her as it struggled to free itself from the grip of a Veronica-shaped tangle of branches anchoring itself to the burning tree.

An evil smile cut across the woman's face.

Moira crawled and kicked herself backwards and away toward Dani.

Wherever she stepped, the earth blackened and shriveled. Bony fingers, their flesh sunken and pulled away from claw-like nails, reached outward. Vines burst from the ground and roped around Miller's arms and legs. Pointed ends pierced the flesh in his legs and wriggled into and out of the muscle and like a threaded needle sewing his shrieking body to the forest floor.

He screamed for Reverend Hopkins to save him, to pull him free, but Hopkins, terrified, fled from the Pit and into the woods with the other members of his twisted congregation.

The woman lifted a single finger, and Miller struggled and choked and pawed at his throat as an invisible force lifted and jerked him painfully against his bonds. Imploring words came out in garbled noise. Vines woven within his tissue pulled backward on his arms and head. The woman opened her mouth, tilted her head, and pulled Miller toward her into a horrifying kiss. His body stiffened and trembled. Skin tightened and crackled like an old paper bag until his flesh sunk inward and his skin hugged his skeleton.

From the screaming, Moira knew he was alive and aware for every long second of it.

The woman cast aside Miller's shriveled corpse with a flick of her wrist. Her body filled and expanded with stolen life. New muscles and skin bubbled and wriggled over old bone and tendon. Wild, black hair whipped in the growing wind. She inhaled loudly, tilted her head to the sky, and let out a shrill scream like metallic thunder brought to earth.

The remaining onlookers either fell to their knees or scattered in terror. Fire reached up from within the Pit and lashed itself to dry trees and bushes, igniting the forest with a great *whoosh* of flame. Moira clasped her hands to her ears and screamed with her, afraid her soul would shatter like glass.

When it was over, the woman turned her attention to Moira.

Once colorless eyes filled with golden brown irises that regarded her with cold indifference. Wildflowers yawned open along the woman's cheeks in a sinister and vibrant smile, sending a wave of terror spiking through Moira's bowels. Even though the woman looked aged, less soft and innocent in the fire's glow, hers was still the same visage Moira recognized from her pictures and from a dream. The figure standing before her was Celeste Martin.

The woman raised her hand to Dani, who had crawled over and jerked her keys from Miller's pocket.

A surge of adrenaline shoved Moira to her feet, screaming, fists balled and ready to strike.

The woman turned back to her. An icy hand squeezed around Moira's throat, effortlessly lifting her off her feet.

"No," a tiny voice pleaded from the din of the Beast's screams and the terrified howls of paralyzed onlookers. "You promised…" Jenny Lake dragged herself out of the bushes by one elbow, her midsection soaked in blood, viscera and bile dribbling from her lips. "You promised."

The woman lowered her arm. Moira fell to the ground.

"You promised," Jenny begged. She reached out. "Wanna go home… take me home… Promised."

The woman knelt beside her, nodded, caressed Jenny's face once, and said, "Shhh." Like a mother about to lift her newborn, she cradled Jenny's head, pulled back a patch of rotted fabric and, bearing a half-rotted breast, popped a perfect, swollen, pink nipple into Jenny's mouth. She held it there for a moment, a shadow of bliss passing across her mangled face.

Jenny garbled and choked. White and red sputtered from the corners of her mouth until her struggles ceased and she went limp.

With a loud, wet crunch and the zip of slowly tearing leather, Jenny's body split open and released a bloody mass like a pea pulled from its pod. The woman stood up straight, pulling a newborn baby with Jenny's dirty blond hair out of Jenny's bloody corpse. The baby settled into the crook of the woman's elbow and suckled on a plump breast.

Moira stared. It was hypnotic, the sight of new life being plucked from death. It was amazing and terrifying and beautiful, at once. So much so that, without thinking, she took a step closer instead of running away.

The woman turned, her face a snarl of madness and rage.

Moira was paralyzed, her body made rigid by whatever power the woman wielded. There was no escaping. She could only hope Dani ran away. Dashed out of the woods, into her car, and was speeding back home to her family where she could be alive and happy.

Slowly, the woman's power lifted her until she hovered, locked in the sky, shivering and waiting for the inevitable end. Visions of Danielle's and her grandmother's faces were clenched in her brain. If she was going to die, she would at least die thinking of the people she loved.

The woman, the mummified figure of Celeste Martin, drew closer. With each step, dried earth burned to blackened ash, yet whenever the baby at her breast stopped drinking to take a breath, milk dribbled past its lips and splattered to the ground, creating tiny stalks of green life that stretched upward, newborn arms of plant life reaching for their mother.

Moira shuddered as a taloned hand, skin silky and warm, reached behind her neck. Fresh earth, roses, and rancid meat wafted out of the woman's mouth. Grubs crawled along her tongue and wiggled from black holes in rotting gums. She pulled Moira's mouth closer to hers.

She stopped. Her brows pinched together as if she'd been asked a strange question, and the answer was sitting on Moira's chin. She edged closer, sniffing. With her face pressed against Moira's neck, she inhaled loudly, smelling her, breathing her. She grabbed Moira's headband, pressed it to her mouth, and delighted in the lungful of its scent.

Wolves howled in the distance.

The look she gave Moira was one of sorrow and elation, as if the human trapped within the frightening Celeste Martin shell, fought to break free. Fingers went limp, gentle, and brushed softly against her skin of her cheeks. She cupped Moira's chin and thumbed a delicate tear from under her eye.

"Run away, little bunny," she whispered. She turned to face the Beast as it screamed above the Pit, trapped in the roots and the light of the burning tree.

Moira landed on her feet when the woman released her hold. Without a second thought, she spun, pulled Dani up by her arm, and bolted out of the forest and away from the clacking maws of hungry wolves closing in on their heels.

2

By the time they broke through the tree line and onto the service road, Moira's lungs were on fire and her thighs were warm rubber. Sweat streamed down her face, turning to ice on her skin as the temperature suddenly plummeted and the wind picked up, swirling leaves and loose dirt all around her. Dani panted and shivered next to her.

Screams followed them, but nobody came out of the woods. Ahead, cars crunched rock and spit dirt and mud as panicked men and women sped away.

Thunder rumbled but didn't quiet. The wind stilled. The humidity felt more oppressive, the temperature colder, as if the clouds fell from the sky and landed on their shoulders.

An inhuman scream erupted from within the forest. They jogged away from it, following the path illuminated by the strange orange glow reflecting off gray-green clouds until they heard human noises and saw the taillights of vehicles rumbling away. They moved cautiously toward them.

A single stationary vehicle remained on the side of the road. The license plate read POLICE.

Lake's patrol car. The driver's side door was open. The engine was running, but there was nobody inside. Moira tiptoed along the road to the passenger side, Dani close behind. The door was locked.

Rounding the rear of the car, she heard a quick series of wet, squishing noises and clicks, followed by what sounded like the unfurling of a flag or sheets whipping on a clothesline. Something moaned.

Lake lay on his back, arms and legs splayed in an X, still alive. Vines, roots, and grass wrapped around and through him like bandages pulling tighter and tighter with each struggling movement. Atop his chest, a giant horned owl, feathers coated in blood and chunks of innards, flipped its head back and swallowed Lake's left eye.

Moira vomited acid on the bumper.

The owl's head perked up. Its enormous yellow eyes blinked slowly, waiting.

Dani waited outside the passenger side door while Moira carefully slid along the car to the open door. "Good birdie. Pretty birdie. Please don't eat my eyes."

The owl flapped its wings and gave a high-pitched screech.

Eheeehr! Eheeehr!

Moira squeezed her eyes shut, only allowing herself to squint when her trembling feet bumped into Lake's foot. He made a pitiful noise and begged for help.

Something vicious within her hoped he lived through all the pain.

Another peal of thunder rattled her ribcage. Wind gusted with enough force to make the heavy vehicle sway on its tires. The black clouds above swirled in ominous curlicues and figure-eights. Flames shot upward above the trees as the heart of the forest belched fire into the sky.

"Moira?"

The hair on the back of her neck stood up as panting and sniffing revealed the wolves sneaking up from behind.

Moira lunged for the car door and kicked herself into the seat, unlocking the other for Dani to jump in. She shifted the car into reverse and slammed the door shut, and then she stomped on the accelerator until she saw a gravel road. She hit the brakes, spun the wheel, and sped away.

More than once, the wind threatened to lift the car off the road, yet she kept it on course. Once the dirt switched to a tar road, the car felt steadier, so she drove as fast as her panicked reflexes could handle. Soon, things looked familiar. Adopt-a-road signs and mile markers were ones she had seen before. Only a couple of miles ahead, streetlights blinked behind bowing pines.

Dani pressed her hand into the dashboard, frightened. "We're headed back to Abrams?"

Instead of slowing down, Moira drove faster. "There's one more. Hopkins. He's running to the church. I can feel it. Feel him." She didn't know what she was going to do, but Hopkins couldn't be left unaccounted for. If this storm, the woman, the fire, was a reckoning for the Beast—for all of Abrams for what they allowed to happen to all the nameless dead resting in that hole—she could at least make sure he didn't escape his comeuppance.

Through the wind and the flying branches, Moira found her way to the church easily, as if the storm parted for her. The wind gusted from behind, urging her on until she passed the cornfield and dilapidated barn next to the church. She slowed and screeched into the parking lot.

As soon as they stopped, Dani pulled Moira's hand up to her face, examining it. "Mo? Are you okay?"

Moira looked. Beneath its scab, the slice on her hand was closed. The burns on Dani's neck and wrists had also completely healed. The only marks on her were patches of dirt and twigs caught in her hair.

Moira blinked. She needed to focus. She quickly checked around the car, eventually finding the knife she stole from the hardware store and had intended to use on Hopkins.

"Come on," she said.

They jumped out of the car and sprinted up to the church doors. Dani followed close behind. The doors slowly opened with a high-pitched sucking sound until the wind flung them open with enough force to split the top and middle hinges. They walked inside.

3

Dani wasn't sure what they were doing at the church or why they weren't running away as fast as they could. She followed Moira partly because she was simply afraid to be alone, and partly out of fear that if she looked away, Moira would blow away in the wind and disappear forever. Regardless of what was happening in this town, or how scared it made her, she wasn't about to lose Moira over it.

So, when the skinny man leaped from the shadows and grabbed a fistful of Moira's hair, Dani attacked him with every drop of strength she had left in her.

A quick punch to his Adam's apple backed him off a step. When he dropped Moira's hair, Dani grabbed his hand and threw herself forward, flattening his thumb against his wrist and twisting his arm until he stumbled and fell to the carpet. Once he was on the floor, Dani stepped past his shoulder and violently spun until she heard the wet crack of his elbow leaving its socket.

Moira reached up between the wooden pews, pulling herself unsteadily to her feet.

Distracted, Dani let her grip slip, earning a kick to her stomach that sent her sprawling backward into the font. She caught her breath quickly and braced for another strike, but nothing came. Instead, Hopkins turned his attention to Moira, who held her freshly sliced palm outward. "It's over, Reverend. She can smell me. She knows exactly where I am, and she's coming for you."

"Stupid little bitch!" he snarled. "Do you have any idea what you've done? I am an instrument of the divine!"

"You're a murdering rapist psycho freak!"

He smiled without humor, like a dog baring its teeth. "Everything I've done, I did to protect my home! Only you unfaithful were sacrificed. What I did, I did for my town and my Lord. Call it murder if you will. It's only words. The truly faithful will understand that what I've done was in the service of a power far greater than your small mind could ever imagine."

The air pressure shifted. Dani's ears popped.

Every window exploded inward, spraying shards of glass all over the three of them. Only Hopkins bled from the cuts.

"You're about to meet that power in Hell, Daniel!"

Dani had never seen Moira like this before. Her hair flowed wildly around her head, and her eyes burned with a frightening purpose. She was the same beautiful Moira she'd always known, but there was also something terrifying about her, almost monstrous.

"I am doing God's work!"

Wind from the many shattered windows swirled around the pews, making small tornadoes out of torn hymns and bibles.

"I know everything you did, every child you killed. I know what you did to Jenny Lake and her son. And I'm going to burn this fucking town to the dirt."

"I saved them," Hopkins spat. "'And as for your little ones, who you said would become a prey, and your children, who today have no knowledge of good or evil, they shall go in there.' All children are holy in the eyes of the Lord, and I needed an unholy child to control the Beast. The Abrams Witch is nothing more than the empty shell of a common whore filled with the essence of Satan and his demons. I have been cleansing this land, keeping that bitch simmering in her own filth with the authority of the Most High."

Hopkins stalked toward her; broken arm cradled in his hand. "I am doing God's will." Thick spittle formed at the corners of his mouth. "And I'll be damned if I'll let a child stop me." He rushed at Moira, pushed her aside, and ran out into the vestibule.

Moira let him run past.

A few breaths later, Hopkins returned, stumbling backward.

Following him, two massive wolves stalked into the nave.

"Dani! Quick!" Moira beckoned. Dani rushed over to her.

Hopkins' breathing came in rapid, shallow gasps. Moisture poured down his face. His eyes darted from window to window, seeking escape.

A deep growl rumbled from behind the altar.

Hopkins' head slowly turned, and his body went rigid with fear.

The growl grew into a dangerous snarling, like the crunching of glass and brittle steel given life. In the center of the aisle between Hopkins and the altar stood a wolf the size of a small pony, its ears pointed upward, tail swaying in the wind. Hypnotic yellow eyes filled with intelligence and murderous intent locked them all in place.

Dani didn't see the pearly fangs, or the pink tongue slathered with pooling saliva. Her focus lay solely on the heart-shaped patch of brown fur over its left eye.

Moira choked, "Gogo."

The snapping of the wolf's massive teeth was louder than the slamming of doors and the scraping of wood being dragged across the parking lot in the wind.

Hopkins' voice tightened into a high-pitched squeak. "G-Gloria?"

She pounced. Trap-like jaws clamped down on his biceps with a wet crunch. Hopkins shrieked and fell under the snarling mass of fur and muscle that bit down and whipped its head back and forth, tearing through the clothing and flesh of his midsection.

Shadows on the walls glowed with red and yellow eyes that materialized into a half dozen more wolves, all bearing down on Reverend Hopkins, ripping at his clothing and flesh as he writhed helplessly on the floor.

"Come on!" Moira screamed. Dani found herself half-running, half-carried away from the frightened, gurgling wails of a man being shredded by dozens of angry fangs.

4

Outside, disaster reigned.

Trees tilted sideways, exposing huge mounds of earth and roots to the world. Shingles blown off roofs tumbled along the road. Chunks of vinyl siding and lawn debris flitted upward and away. People rushed out of their homes and drove away, only to have their cars flipped into ditches or pushed into light poles by the fierce winds. Light bathed all of Abrams in an eerie, fluttering orange glow coming from behind.

Dani turned and gasped.

Dominating the horizon was a vortex of cloud and flame—a tornado set ablaze—bearing down on them, tearing apart every building and uprooting every tree in its path, spitting arcs of red lightning at the ground, igniting patches of fire that raged through the dried fields.

They ran toward the patrol car, but Moira stopped short and yelled in the direction of a tall woman, her black hair whipping and spinning around in the wind, her dress plastered against her thin figure, walking toward the church.

"Heather!" Moira yelled and rushed over. "What are you doing?"

"This is just like my dreams." Heather's eyes were glazed and watery, and she stared at the flaming vortex, eyes distant and head cocked with curiosity. Moira pulled on her arm and tried to drag her into the car, but she refused to move.

Heather blinked, and a semblance of clarity returned to her face. "Do you hear that?" she asked. "Crying? You hear her crying, too? Don't you?"

Another vehicle sped into the parking lot and stopped alongside them. Brian Hopkins jumped out and pushed Heather out of the way to face Moira. "Is this you? Did you do this?" He gaped as the roof of the church was hauled high into the air and thrown into the spreading inferno on the horizon. "You've killed us all. Why couldn't you just die?" He balled his fists and growled, "Don't you understand that none of us can leave?" He lunged.

Before his fingers clamped around Moira's throat, Dani tripped Brian and whipped him down to the pavement with a loud smack. She twisted his arm at a painful angle. "Hands off, shitbrick!"

Moira took off after Heather, who continued ambling toward the church, eyes transfixed, oblivious to the carnage being unleashed. "Heather, we have to—"

"There!" Heather pointed at a dark animal trotting toward them.

The giant wolf with the heart-shaped fur plodded over. It licked Heather's hands and face when she knelt in front of it. "Gogo? Oh, my god and all the saints, it's you. My baby! My baby! My little Gloria."

Brian wrestled himself away from Dani, rushed past Moira, and pulled Heather away. "Have you lost your mind? That thing is not Gloria!"

"It is!" she screamed. "Brian, it's our Gogo. Look! Here! Smell me. Smell!" She shoved her hands in his face, then breathed in herself when he slapped them away. "I smell like her crib, her baby clothes! Brian, it's Gogo!"

He wasn't looking at her. Instead, he stared at another figure walking toward them. A wild-haired woman in rags carrying a child and dragging a tornado of fire in her wake. Words formed around his mouth, but nothing coherent escaped his terrified face. He sprinted back to his car and sped off, abandoning his wife.

Dani tugged at Moira's shirt as the woman stepped out of the field and into the parking lot.

Moira grabbed Heather by the elbow. "Heather, come with us. Please!"

Heather shook her head. "I'm not leaving my baby again."

The wolf rubbed its face all over Heather's body and leaned into her with its weight.

"She's coming." Dani warned.

Heather looked up at the woman. She slowly stood and started walking toward her. "Celly? Celly!" she yelled. Before Moira could grab her, Heather was running away, nearly losing her footing.

The wolf stood its ground between them and Heather. Its deep growl raised a thick line of hair from its neck to its tail.

They watched as Heather wrapped her arms around the shape of Celeste Martin. Her sobs and words were lost in the wind. The woman returned the embrace and spoke into her ear. Heather fell to her knees, pleading, arms wrapped around the woman's waist like a child begging for forgiveness. The woman lifted Heather gently by her chin and kissed her forehead.

Moira screamed something at her, but Dani couldn't tear her eyes away as Heather's knees buckled and the woman guided her limp body onto the ground as if she had fallen asleep.

The snarling wolf lunged at Moira. She jumped back and guarded her arm.

Dani pulled Moira back to the car and got into the driver's seat. The wolf didn't pursue.

Dani drove through town, dodging other cars, flying boards, disconnected branches, and frightened animals. An electrical pole struck the ground with a blinding white fireball and sent a spray of sparks dancing across the windshield. She jerked against the wheel, taking them down an unfamiliar side street.

"This thing handles like a broken boat."

One left turn and two streets later, a familiar shade of blue poked out from the back side of a building. She yanked the wheel and stomped on the gas.

"What the shit, Dani?"

"I'm not leaving her here!"

Dani ground the undercarriage over a speed bump and entered a fenced-in lot of the police station where her car waited.

Once inside, Moira asked, "You think you can out-drive a tornado?"

Dani buckled in. "Dad didn't buy this for its economy."

The tires squealed, the car bucked, and they shot forward down the street. The sudden force pinned Moira to her seat.

The engine roared as Dani sped through town, past the cafe, around the park's upturned gazebo, until there was nothing between them and anywhere else but an open road.

Moira gripped Dani's arm as soon as they crossed the town limits. "Slow down. Slow down!"

Dani did. "I'm slowing! I'm slowing! What's wrong?"

"Stop."

"What?"

Blood streamed out of Moira's nose and mouth. "Stop!" She lurched forward.

Dani slammed on the brakes. Moira fell out of the car and dashed toward the Abrams sign. The blood stopped flowing when she crossed back over.

The woman and the tornado followed them at a supernatural pace. The bloody owl flew out of the fire and perched on her shoulder. Two wolves kept pace on either side of her.

A gentle rain started to fall.

"I can't leave," Moira said. She spit out the last of the blood and wiped her face on her sleeve. "If I leave Abrams, I die." Moira thrust her forearm out to Dani. "This is a mark. It means that if I cross Abrams' boundary, I die." She panted. "I thought it was the Beast, but it's her. She won't let me leave."

"Just like that? You just… you just die?" Dani grabbed her arm and inspected the mark. "What do we do? How do we stop it? What do we do!"

Moira put her arms around Danielle and kissed her neck. "Go

home. Okay? Leave me here. Go home. You have to."

When Dani argued, Moira squeezed her tighter. "Who knows what she destroys if she leaves? I don't know what Hopkins had trapped and I don't know what I set free, but if it's anyone's responsibility to stop her, it's mine. Look at me." She put her forehead against Dani's and wiped the tears of fright and confusion from her face. "I love you," she said and kissed Dani with lips salty with blood and tears. "I love you, Danielle. Go home. If I live through this, I will find you. Go." She gave Dani a gentle shove and turned around to face the figure of Celeste Martin.

Dani shook her head. "No. No, Moira. I'm not going. You can't make me leave you."

Moira cupped Dani's jaw in both hands and kissed her deeply, until Dani felt weightless and dizzy. All she ever wanted to do was kiss Moira, to hold her. To share her breath and wake up next to her. Now that she had her, how could she be expected to just let her go?

A chill filled her belly and her blood.

It was okay. Moira loved her. She wouldn't do anything that would make her sad. It was okay to leave and wait for her like she'd always waited. It was okay.

Her mind a haze of trees and wind, Dani floated into her car, sat down, and slowly drove away from Abrams until Moira's features darkened into shadow in the rearview mirror.

A hard gust of wind caused her to swerve. A single-slice pizza box slid off the dashboard and onto the floor.

Something burned in her stomach. Dani slowed down.

What the *hell* was she doing?

She was driving away, abandoning Moira. She was leaving behind her best friend, the woman she'd been secretly, openly, or whateverly in love with for the past four years just because that nut had it in her head she was the only person on the face of the planet who could save the world. Was she about to just leave her like that? Was she about to spend the rest of her life knowing magic was real and that she gave up the chance to live happily ever after in a magical world with Moira after she just finally got to kiss her?

Like the woman at the store said: fat fucking chance.

Dani slammed the brakes, jerked the wheel hard, and punched the gas until the car spun completely around, facing Moira, the woman, the tornado. Through the glow of the flames and the white of her high beams, Dani watched them. The woman had her arms around Moira, mouth close to her ear, whispering, but her stony stare pierced through the windshield and into Dani's.

What the hell was *she* doing? She was driving headlong into a wall of apocalyptic wind to rescue her half-bonkers girlfriend from a supernatural hag who drank people into husks and could whip the fires of Hell into a blazing tornado that just turned an entire town into an inferno. *That's* what the hell she was doing.

Dani floored it and angled the steering wheel until she lined up her front driver side bumper with the woman. If she was careful and the woman didn't move, she'd only miss Moira by an inch. The engine roared, and the wind answered. The car wobbled and slid as if the road were dreaming of becoming ice, but Dani kept it straight, her eyes locked on the woman's bloodshot glare.

The owl spread its wings and screamed while the wolves snarled, their front legs splayed. Moira's hair fluttered around in circles like some invisible hand struggled to wrap it into a braid. The woman simply stared, smiling, as her lips moved quickly against Moira's ear.

Dani tried to push her foot through the floor.

The world blurred and shifted. The winds stopped. Trees, bits of building, and vehicles crumbled to the ground and rolled violently until their momentum ceased and they came to rest in the fields. The vortex of fire dissipated into an orange smear across the horizon that blanketed the land of Abrams in flames and heavy, acrid smoke. The woman, a smirk on her bloodless lips, faded from existence along with her owl and wolves.

Dani held her breath, stomped on the fat pedal, and cranked up on the handbrake. She veered around Moira and screamed as the car rolled, lifted, and threatened to flip onto its side before coming to a rest just a few feet in front of Moira.

They stared at each other. The sudden quiet made their heartbeats rumble like earthquakes in their heads.

Moira blinked as if recovering from a daze. "What are you doing?" she yelled.

"What am *I* doing? Get in the damn car!"

Moira hopped in and gripped the door handle as the tires shrieked and the car raced away from Abrams.

They rushed through the dark at over a hundred miles an hour until the fire in Abrams was just a faint glow on the horizon. Moira took a breath. "We should slow down!"

"You can slow down when it's your turn to drive."

Moira pawed at Dani's hands and arm. "Slow down. We're gone. It's over. Slow down. There you go. She's gone. It's over. Pull over, Dani. Pull over."

Dani eased off the gas pedal. The car came to a stop with a quiet crunch on the side of the road. She unbuckled, twisted in her seat to face Moira, and flicked on the dome light. "What the hell was that back there?" she demanded. "You thought you could just tell me to leave, and I'd leave, you shit!"

Before she could say anything more, Moira was half in her lap, mouth pressed so hard against hers their teeth clacked together and her jaw nearly unhinged. Salt and dirt swirled between their tongues.

She shivered as Moira pulled away, sucking a little on Dani's bottom lip as she did. "It's safe. You saved me. We're safe now. I promise." She gently kissed Dani's lips. "I love you."

Her heart held its breath. "I love you, too." She couldn't help but smile. "Can we go home now? I don't like Abrams."

Moira collapsed back into the passenger seat with a loud sigh. She smiled and grabbed Dani's hand. "Yes! Let's get the hell out of here." Moira buckled up as the car gradually came up to speed, leaving the ruins of Abrams behind.

Before putting the car in gear, Dani asked, "What did she say to you?"

"What?"

"The woman. The Witch? What did she say to you?"

Moira's eyes shifted in and out of focus as she stared through Dani. "She said, 'Don't be afraid of me.'"

"Just that?"

Moira shook her head.

Dani pulled over again. Something was wrong. "What aren't you telling me? Can we agree that this relationship won't be based on secrets? I don't want us to keep secrets. No more going to strange towns alone, no more digging up curses or witches or horrible stories by yourself, and no more keeping it from me when you do. As your girlfriend, I demand we don't keep secrets or lie to each other."

"My girlfriend?"

"Yes. We're a couple now. I am madly in love with you. I never want to lose you, and I'm sorry if I'm a little scared right now and need some kind of closure and understanding about everything." Dani tried to smile, but when she did, a tear squeezed out of her eye. "I've had a weird couple of days."

Moira wiped the tear away. "Okay. Okay. I'll tell you." She unbuckled herself and faced Dani. "Who you saw was the Spirit of the Abrams woods inside what was left of Celeste Martin's body after Celeste agreed to be her vessel. She took Celeste Martin's body and hid it from the Demon until she was strong enough to defeat it. This whole thing was a plan, decades in its unfolding."

"So, that woman back there, Celeste Martin, she was the Abrams Witch?"

"No."

"Decades?" Dani swallowed back a gnawing concern. "But you were a part of it. And the original woman? Karina or Katherine…?"

"Korey." Moira chewed her lip. "She was my great-great-grandmother. Rachel's mother. She was a helper of the Spirit. It taught her things. It's kind of an involved story."

"Your grandma? Do you think Rachel knows?"

Moira shrugged.

"So, your great-great-grandma was the Abrams Witch?"

Moira shook her head.

"Then who was?"

The cinnamon in her eyes sparkled in the electric glow. "That woman, the Spirit, told me something back there. Told me a secret." Moira opened Dani's dashboard and pulled Mick Dagger from its sheath. She sank its tip into the center of her hand, drawing a pebble of blood and closing it in her fist. "Please," Moira said, her eyes pleading and her lips trembling. "Don't be afraid of me."

She opened her hand. Instead of a smear of blood tracing the lines of her palm, a bright orange and yellow marigold bloomed like a little sun.

The lights on the dashboard flickered, and the engine coughed. Dani's phone beeped with a text message. The screen showed a number she didn't recognize, followed by a brief message.

Please bring my granddaughter home

Dani forgot how to breathe. Between wanting to kiss away the confusion and worry in Moira's eyes and remembering what she said about the beginning of their relationship, Dani struggled to get the words out in one breath. "I'm not afraid. I can be brave."

Moira nodded. "I know."

Dani swallowed the lump in her throat, put the car in drive, and with Moira's hand in hers, drove down a dark highway bathed in the glow of the rising Flower Moon.

About the Author

J.E. Erickson fell in love with horror and fantasy at an early age. The first story he wrote was at age 11 and was about a child walking home from school to discover his own gravestone. He still thinks about it when referring to himself in third person.

He currently writes horror and fantasy stories, and lives in an old house in the Midwestern United States with a nerdy soap maker, two spoiled dogs, and a (potentially) possessed vegetable garden.

You can visit him at jeericksonwriting.com or on Twitter @maladjustined

Printed in the USA
CPSIA information can be obtained
at www.ICGtesting.com
LVHW010009110923
757792LV00002B/230